FLEETIE'S CROSSING

FLEETIE'S CROSSING

K. Bruce Florence

8/29/17

K. BRUCE FLORENCE

LIBRARY OF CONGRESS CONTROL NUMBER:		2017910240
ISBN:	HARDCOVER	978-1-5434-3368-5
	SOFTCOVER	978-1-5434-3367-8
	EBOOK	978-1-5434-3366-1

To order additional copies of this book, contact:
Xlibris
1-888-795-4274
www.Xlibris.com
Orders@Xlibris.com
760989

CONTENTS

Change is a measure of time, and in the autumn,
Time seems speeded up. What was is not and
Never again will be, what is, is change.

— Edwin Teale

To George Ella Lyon,

Each hint of an early morning mist, an errant
feather, and the rock-ribbed determination
of her mountain people has given her the gift
of words she so generously shares with me.

Acknowledgments

Encouragers, family, and colleagues who cared and believed I could write this story include Laura Todd Simpson, Rachel Lane Poe, Virgil Florence, Pam Duncan, Gurney Norman, Linda DeRosier, Debbie Cooper, Ann Pancake, Ruth Bailey, granddaughter, Grace, and Bud Blanton—artist, manuscript editor, and consultant—without whose help and patience, this story would have been forever burdened with too many words and too little life.

Author's Note

This is a work of fiction. While there are events in the novel that describe some parts of life in that time period as it might have been lived in the eastern coal fields of Kentucky, these stories are fictional accounts. No comparisons should be drawn with anyone now or in the past. All the characters spring from the imagination of the author.

Part 1

ALLEGRO

Prologue

BECOMING AWARE

Granddaddy thumbed his nose at anybody in the family who thought I had to behave to suit them. He taught me to drink coffee, cuss without sounding dumb, drink a tonic made with good whiskey for a deep cough, and leave my shoes in the crotch of a big tree on a hot day when dust running through your toes had its own special comfort.

But today, he was gone—and not just on a fishing trip to a good trout stream. He was never coming back. Sitting here on Mummy's Rock on his mountain, I tried hard to make some sense out of the hurt kicking itself through me. He loved me and gave me the space I needed to learn all about myself. With Pappy gone forever, I was left with a brand new way of being alone.

When he gave me his huge bear hug, I could rest my head on his wide, solid chest and know nothing could reach me there. As a baby, I was prone to screaming colic fits. He was the only one who could pick me up and soothe away the bubbles. I would fall asleep in his arms, and if needed, he would hold me for hours. Mother plied him with every delicious dish she could concoct to entice him to come often and stay long. Without him, she might have been sorely tempted to smother me in my crib. The tales of what a miserable baby I had been were legend in our family history. I wasn't much better as a toddler, and when I was five, everything and everybody but Pappy made me mad. I stormed and stomped and developed a rotten reputation for being impossible. He brought me around because he refused to be intimated by a little kid's bad humor, and finally, I realized that the defenses I had put up against the world were not that important after all.

Just thinking these words started my sobs all over again. They seemed to be coming from somewhere not even connected to me, and no matter how much I cried, there was no relief from this black hole carved into my life. With nothing but my own misery shrieking in my ears, I didn't hear Daddy making his way up the mountain path carved by generations of skittering critters. To everybody else, he was Ed Ramsey—mountain boy, lawyer, and Pap Ramsey's baby boy. To me, he was the closest thing I had ever thought of as my hero. Pappy was my buddy, and Daddy was the man who got things done and put up with no nonsense. He was a tall, strong man with a shock of curly blond hair that probably, by nature, made him look a lot more approachable than he really was.

He startled me, even using his best whisper. "Rachel, your mother sent me to find you."

I couldn't answer, and he walked toward me and passed through the broken-down fence just on the other side of a patch of scattered boulders. In some ancient time, those boulders might have broken off Mummy's Rock when all of them were thrown here by the tremendous force that formed the mountain, scratched out the river, and blew the valley flat. He hoisted himself up the side of the rock and sat down beside me. He didn't say a word at first, just put his arm around my shoulders and held on. He didn't really pull me close, just rested his arm there in case I didn't know that someone else also knew how awful this was.

"I brought you a jar of water, Rach. Look here what else I stuck in my pocket."

I managed to squeak out, "What, Daddy?"

"One of Pappy's bandanas. Let's pour some of the water on it and wipe your pretty face."

He wet the red handkerchief and handed me the open jar to hold. He pushed back my long braids and put the cool cloth first on my forehead and then on each cheek. He was as gentle as Mother might have been with my baby brother, Logan.

"You've got to stop crying. It only helps a little at first, and then it begins to make you feel even worse."

I kept sniffling, but this time, I was making an effort to stop the tears. "What are they all doing down there, Daddy?"

"About to push me over the edge. If one more person asks me what I am going to do without Pappy, I might hit them."

In spite of my misery, I smiled at him. The idea of him hitting one of the relatives or neighbors struck me funny.

"I have no idea what I am going to do without him, and being reminded every two minutes doesn't make the answer come any faster either. And, little girl, everyone keeps asking where you got off to, and I'm running out of answers."

"You could tell them to mind their own business."

Daddy chuckled. "Oh well, honey, it's just something to say. All our folks are pretty hurt about Pappy too. Aunt Sook has cooked dinner for all of us, and she could use your help to get it on the table. Come on now. Will you go with me?"

I struggled to choke down rolling sobs without making much headway. He pulled me up like a rag doll and wrapped his arms around me and squeezed so tight, I could barely breathe. But it worked, and slowly, I gained control as the sobs subsided to snubs and gulps. Around here, when somebody died, everybody hugged one another. Somehow, it made it hurt a little less. So I guess Daddy just held on because he didn't know what else to do with a hysterical fourteen-year-old. It took a little while for me to appreciate that Daddy was having his own sorrow to deal with, and yet here he was on the mountain with his arms around me. Right at that moment, he was probably hoping that my crying wouldn't make his eyes spill tears too, but some of my pain did begin to melt away.

"Feeling better? Want a drink?"

I shook my head.

"You know, Rachel, Pappy Ramsey is not all the way gone."

"He is all the way gone, Daddy, and the world is empty." My voice broke, and he pulled me closer.

"Can you remember him laughing at you when you fell in the creek going after that big bass?"

"He had to build a fire to dry me off."

"Sweetheart, anytime you can remember him doing something like that, he is somewhere around. You will feel him walking along the creek, sitting by the fire, or heading up the mountain. Anybody as much a part of this place as old Pappy can't be all that gone."

"But I can't talk to him or see him, and he can't tell me what to do when I need to know."

"Don't push against what will help, Rachel. You just have to settle for what you can get. He is around and will always be, but you have to open up to see it. Don't fight it off because you are so mad, you won't take what's there."

I was beginning to feel rankled and shot back at him. "How do you know?" Pappy was gone and not coming back, and now Daddy seemed to know stuff about him that I should know and didn't.

"Storm Cloud, if you would listen instead of all the time stomping around, bossing people, you could feel what this mountain has to say. When my Papaw died, Granny told me all this, and she was right. Don't be so stubborn. You can't be helped."

I stood perfectly still, torn between wanting to stay on the mountain, away from the sadness down below, and doing what Daddy asked.

"You ready now to go back down? The men are already in the barn, planing the boards for Pappy's casket. It won't be long before you and the other women will line it good and soft for his skinny bones."

I still didn't move, and he took my hand in his and leaned forward to jump down off the rock. I jumped with him. Still holding hands, we started down the mountain path but not before I turned around to take another long look at Mummy's Rock. It was where I had always brought my frustrations and loneliness. The water jar was still sitting on top of the boulder, and I reached for it, but my arm wasn't quite long enough. Daddy lifted his arm over mine and picked up the jar. He took a long drink and offered it to me. This time, I did take a drink and found out how thirsty I was. As I was gulping down the water, it occurred to me that today, the rock gave something back; Pappy's spirit was still here on the mountain, and if I but will, I could hear him and feel him near.

I turned and walked with Daddy past the boulders. He took my hand and sort of acted like it was because the path was rough, but of course, I had skipped up and down this hill for so long, every rock and dip was permanently etched in my brain. He knew I didn't need help, and I knew I didn't, but his hand was strong and warm, and I felt safer with my hand in his.

Map of Ross's Point

Chapter 1

THE POINT

Appalachia makes up a vast slice of the American continent, reaching from Georgia to Maine, but the part of it I knew the most about was a tiny Eastern Kentucky valley surrounded, fort-like, by imposing tree-covered mountains, a place where the sun rose late and set early and the blue sky and white clouds hovered like a watchful mother.

Above my valley, a point of land stood high over the Cumberland River, and anyone standing on that point was offered a sweeping vista of the river bend, a wide valley floor, and beyond the valley, the ever-present, brooding mountains that dared us to leave or others to enter the valley.

The point was a perfect lookout for river traffic, and the number of arrowheads and pottery shards found there told a story of ancient eyes on guard against bears, mountain lions, and marauding young Indian bucks paddling the enemy canoes that could slip down the river just below them.

A white settler, Alexander Ross, traveling with his and three other families from Virginia, looked for a safe place to build cabins, staked off the point, and gave it his family name, Ross's Point. After camping there for a few weeks, the party, especially the women and girls, realized that the lack of water on the point and the difficulty of digging a well by hand in the rocky mountain soil would cause more hardship in a land already harsh enough. Quick access to water was needed for both the humans and their animals. So Ross took his family and the others to the green valley below. They built sturdy cabins on a gentle rise near one of the clear streams that formed the headwaters of the Cumberland River. He still defended the point and would not sell or allow anyone to squat there. Eventually, the entire valley took up the name, and the tiny settlement became known as Ross's Point.

Years later, after the development of the coal fields, there were those who had other names for the area. Poor Fork was one, named because very early, it was thought there was no coal under these particular mountains. The coal was there, but the name stuck, and it was convincing enough to discourage early attempts to start a mining operation. Back then, the thick seams of coal in that section of Southeastern Kentucky were so plentiful that no one needed to take a chance on a valley known universally as the Poor Fork. So we became Ross's Point up Poor Fork. Daddy called our mountain place Steep Acres. I never thought much about the name Poor Fork. The fact that Daddy's land included the original Ross's Point also failed to make much of an impression on me.

Besides, the point itself was long ago blasted away to provide a nice straight stretch for the railroad to chug through our valley. Gone was the overlook, and left in its place was a raw cliff of crumbling orange dirt that was so poor, it would not grow weeds or vines. But gone or not, we still called the top of that cliff the Point, and what was left still provided a good overlook to the valley and the river.

During this time, not too long after World War II, mine wars in Eastern Kentucky were raging between owners and union organizers. The bitter conflict pitted friends, neighbors, family, and strangers against one another in deadly skirmishes along the creeks and ridges of all of George's County. It raged even into Poor Fork and Ross's Point. There were no mines, but there were miners who refused to move into the coal camps and instead kept their small homesteads. The mining jobs and steady pay were too tempting to resist, but the land was too precious, too much their inheritance and heritage, to sacrifice for the hardscrabble existence in the camps, and so they held fast.

Burl Sargeant owned one of these homesteads, and when I could escape my duties at home, this was where I spent most of my time. Leatha Sargeant, daughter of a miner, and me, Rachel Grace Ramsey, daughter of a mountain-born lawyer, were inseparable. On the morning of the trouble, we were at Leatha's kitchen sink, washing dishes after the six of us had gobbled down our breakfast of gravy and biscuits. All four of Fleetie Sargeant's kids had chores to tend to. No child older than four was given a free pass. Everyone worked, and surprisingly, there was very little complaining. At my house, perched high near the point, right above the Sargeant house, my sister and I often pushed back against work orders, but the Sargeant kids never did.

Even if they didn't want to mind Fleetie, the kids were not dummies. They could tell there was trouble brewing around them, not a little trouble but the kind that had grown-ups talking loud in the night after the kids were supposed to be asleep. Mothers and aunts were apt to break into tears after a neighbor brought news of more shooting and blasting. It was time for the kids to stay out of sight and hearing as much as possible. You never knew when out of the blue, you might get yelled at just for being near when some adult wanted privacy.

The whole county was in the turmoil of a general miners' strike. There had been shootings, ambushes, explosions, and cold-blooded murders brought about by the conflict between miners and the owners and operators. The miners wanted to join a union for better pay and working conditions, and the owners and operators wanted to keep union interference out of the coal fields. The strike trouble had all of us plenty scared. It wasn't a good time for any of us to be kicking up a fuss about anything. This was real and real scary. On one side, the scabs and goons hired by the mine owners were pretty quick with their pistols, and on the other, the miners had lots of dynamite, and they did not hesitate to blow up the tipples and bridges used to move coal to the railroad gondolas. Both sides were always spoiling for a fight, and many men died or were so badly injured, they would never work again. The threat of death and knowing what grown men could do to one another brought us up short. We all knew it was time to behave and stay out of sight as much as we could.

Burl Sargeant had been walking the picket line all night, and before he got home, Leatha and I were planning to be long gone. After his shift, he was always gruff, and our getting in his way usually meant a head-knocking or worse, but our timing was off that morning, and just as we finished with the last of the cleanup, Burl rolled out of his derelict truck, took one leap up the back steps, slammed the screen door, jerked his rifle off the kitchen wall, and yelled for Fleetie.

I scrambled under the table with Leatha right behind me, and we watched him balance the rifle on the bend of his crippled left arm. He broke open the barrel, checked the magazine, and yelled again for Fleetie. Then as he turned to leave, he ran smack into all five feet of her blocking the door. You might think that his six-foot frame, broad shoulders, and muscled arms could wipe up the floor with her, but not today. Most of the time, Fleetie could handle him pretty well, except when he was drinking. Today, she was worried about protecting her kids and stood up to his bluster.

"Where you going with that rifle, Burl? If you're headed out to join them marchers, you can't be taking no gun. We've got us a houseful of young'uns, and you can't do them no good with a bullet hole in your head."

He jerked around to go out the front door, but Fleetie grabbed his arm and pushed him hard against the door, facing him. "I'm telling you, Burl, leave that rifle here. You can't be caught carrying no gun."

He yanked his arm loose, and as he did so, the rifle slipped and hit her hard on her mouth, smashing her lip.

"Damn it, Fleet. You're not making no fool out of me. Them boys out there in that truck is going to fight to keep our jobs, and by god, no damn woman is 'bout to stop me. Get out of my way. I mean it, Fleet. You're fixin' to make me mad."

As Burl stormed out the screen door, she clamped her hand to her mouth to stop the blood before it dropped on her clean dress. Leatha and the other kids always cried at the sight of blood. They acted like they hated blood more than the injury.

I could see Fleetie's mouth was beginning to swell. I scurried from under the table and grabbed a soft washcloth off the rack and held it under the cold water in the sink. As I handed the wet cloth to her, the three of us stood behind the screen door to watch. Burl pulled away with seven men loaded in his truck. They were all hell-bent on joining the union march against the operators' scabs and goons. The scabs were men who would walk through the picket line for a job in spite of the sacrifice of friends and neighbors to chance the miserable work conditions and lousy pay. The goons, on the other hand, were trucked in from who-knows-where to serve as enforcers. Both sets of men were hated by the miners, but the goons would kill at the blink of an eye, and that terrified the miners' wives and children.

Fleetie shook her head. "", they act like little kids out raising a Halloween ruckus. You'd think they never heard tell about how quick them goons are with their rifles,

We watched as the truck tires threw up a spin of sand and gravel as a choking dust cloud billowed behind the truck. Almost before the dust settled behind the overloaded truck, Fleetie gathered up the kids and started herding them toward the river crossing. About five miles north of the valley, a small mine that was worked by men who were not yet union members was the temporary headquarters for the owner and operators and their hired henchmen. If they used the same location too many times, it would be blown up. The rumors had it that the union organizers and miners were planning to march to the mine and "show them goddamn union busters." Showing them would mean using the shotguns and rifles they all mostly carried on their shoulders. Bloody battles during coal strikes were pretty common, and if the march really happened, it would be headed straight for Ross's Point with Coburn's store sitting in the middle of the skirmish.

Fleetie didn't have time to wait for me to go home and get permission to go with them, and without Mother's okay, I knew

Fleetie's answer, even if I begged to go. She would never go along with anything that Mother did not first approve.

I watched them as they hurried down to the riverbank. By crossing the river, she could cut off the two miles extra it would take to go along the track to the road and double back to the store. She'd get to the settlement that much sooner to wait out the march with the rest of the wives and children. Leatha waved to me, and I wanted to cry, knowing that whatever happened, it would have been better if we had stayed together. Ever since we were toddlers, the world always seemed a safer place when we stuck together. If she thought it, I could answer. If I wanted it, she would find it. We quarreled often with our sisters but never with each other.

The fishing boat was not big enough for all of them. I watched as Nessa, Dorotha, and Leatha took off their shoes, tied the strings together, hung them around their necks, stepped into the cold water, and waded across the shallow river. Fleetie settled Emma and Rebecca into the boat, untied the mooring rope, and began poling across the shallow water. Usually, this trip was as much fun as swimming. We'd skip rocks, splash one another, and race to see who could get across first. But today, even the youngest kids were silent. They watched Fleetie's every move as any hint of fun floated down the cold stream.

Just as soon as the boat shuffled upon the narrow bank at the far side, I could hear Fleetie say, "Hurry up, kids. Get your shoes back on. We have to get on up the road to Susanny's. Them men'll be tromping through here and run over ever'body in their path. Quick now."

Susanny was Fleetie's favorite aunt, and she lived in the middle of the settlement and not far from Coburn's store. Her porch would be filled with the women and little children, while nearby, the old men and young boys would gather on Coburn's porch to watch.

Fleetie carried Rebecca and pulled herself and the other kids up the steep path from the river. The older kids were waiting for her at the top of the bank. They crossed Lloyd Wallace's field that lay along the river's edge and hurried to the paved road and walked a good quarter mile toward the settlement before I lost sight of them.

I turned from the river and left the Sargeants' yard. All our foot-tromping during the cold winter had left the yard as bare as a barn floor. After Burl's getaway, the yard gate was still hanging open. You would think with Emma and Rebecca so little and as close to the road as they lived, he might stop to shut the gate. But no, not Mr. Meany Burl. That piece of carelessness was just one more in my long list of reasons why he made my blood boil.

As I plodded up the long hill, the railroad crossing well behind me, I spotted my little brother, James Logan. He stood looking past me, and when I turned, I saw a line of men marching down the road that ran parallel to the river and the railroad. Talk of the strike and picket lines had been on the tongue of every adult in the valley for weeks. Logan had heard much of the same talk as I had, and even though he didn't know what picketers were, he knew the angry-looking bunch of men walking along the road looked out of place.

"The picnickers are coming, the picnickers are coming." Logan's short legs pounded down the driveway that girdled our twenty-acre hillside farm. He got to me just as I curved into the yard. He hurled himself against me and, using my bones and flesh as ladder rungs, scrambled up and wrapped himself around my neck. "Picnickers! Picnickers! Hide, Rach, hide. They get us."

"They are picketers, Logie, not picnickers." I tried to break his strangle hold.

"They're coming. I see them." He slid down my side and grabbed my leg and then began pulling my hand as if to retrace my steps down the driveway. "Look with me."

"No, Logie, let's go to the point." I swooped him up in my arms and ran across the field to the persimmon tree that grew just above the cliff where the point once stood.

The point, a sheared-off nose of land cut fifty yards from our house, jutted out above the railroad. From there, we could see the entire settlement of Ross's Point. We watched as the miners' picket line formed itself three abreast on our far left and marched from the Gaton Gap and down the narrow valley. As the picketers moved south, a gathering of thugs worked around Tunnel Hill and marched north toward the picketers. A gradual rise in the middle of the valley blocked one group from seeing the other.

We were standing where we could see both lines as they moved closer and closer to each other. From the kitchen window, Mother spotted us staring at something beyond her view. She yelled, and I could almost feel her racing around the house and across the yard, coming to us on the point.

At breakfast that morning, all the conversation was about the strike, and Daddy left us early to talk to Mr. Ben across the valley. Ben was almost as old as the rocks on the mountain and kept his thumb on the pulse of the entire valley.

As Daddy was about to leave the house, my sister Jane threw a tantrum to go with him. It figured. We didn't call her Bug for nothing, pet that she was. Daddy gave in after about two seconds. It occurred to me that I should have stuffed her mouth with a sock—as if that would have made any difference. Her blond hair, blue eyes, and pretty little face could win any argument. I gritted my teeth as I watched them take off together.

The miners, many of them neighbors and friends, had been getting more desperate as winter wore old. On the other hand, mine bosses, determined to get the mines open, pushed the goons and scabs.

Now Daddy and Jane's path was headed right into the middle of the battle. Blocked by a row of pine trees on a rise of land, Daddy couldn't see the angry two-headed parade coming toward them, both sides ready to explode with the hatred of months of anger and frustration built up between them.

Logan yanked my shirt. "Look, Daddy and Bug."

As Mother came nearer the point, she saw them too, Daddy walking across the valley with my baby sister. Her hand was swallowed in his, and her blond curls had to be flying under the green felt bonnet, which I could see bobbing along beside Daddy.

I heard Mother whisper, "Oh my lord, no!"

She tore down the rocky path from the point to the valley. Loose rock rolled beneath her feet, and she seemed to defy gravity as she flew, barely touching the ground. Logan and I waved and screamed, but our warnings were lost in the wind circling past us. Maybe it was because we wanted it so, maybe one of our piercing yells found its mark, or perhaps it was luck, but something stopped Daddy.

He swept Janey into his arms and ran up the rise where he saw the two dangerous columns advance, ready to engulf the two of them. Way too late for them to run for the safety of the mountain, he perched Bug on his shoulder and began a slow, deliberate walk directly into the path of the two sides of men as they moved ever closer to each other. I could almost hear him humming his steadying tune, "John Peel." He even turned and waved at us high up on the point as the two angry armies came near enough to strike blows.

Mother's frantic run took her behind a long row of pines, and she would have lost sight of Daddy and Jane. Hidden as she was, she couldn't see that Daddy had deliberately taken himself and her baby girl into more danger than her heart could stand.

Both "picnickers" and the sullen-faced scabs slowed then stopped and stared at Daddy, who was standing in their path. Daddy turned and spoke first to Burl and his brother. The two studied the ground and lowered their rifles. Then he turned to the other group and singled out that sorry Jimmy Bascam and Larry Hensley. Those two were always looking for one fight or another. This time, they were lined up with the operators against the union. They loved to fight, and neither one cared who they worked for just so long as there were money, whiskey, knuckles, and blood.

We could make out a word or two of what Daddy was saying to them, but I didn't have to hear it then. He preached the same sermon at me every time he got really worried about the miners. He would urge them to put away the guns before there was bloodshed and warn that if there was a killing, the governor would call in the troopers, and nobody would win. I figured he would add for good measure the warning that a man oughta think about what would happen if there was no contract, no coal, nothing.

Daddy held great store with thinking. He started lots of sentences with "A man oughta . . ." It was his way of telling people to stop and think before they went off like a bottle rocket and got themselves and others in big trouble.

A hateful moan rose from the strikers, and I could see a ripple of anger skip through the cluster of scabs and hired guns. The two crowds pressed closer, watching to see who would be the first to attack a man with a child perched on his shoulder. With all the anger and frustration goading them, there was no one willing to play coward and turn from the fight. My heart beat so hard, it caused a roar in my ears.

I held on to the hope that it must be hard to make a move against a man who was one of them. At one time or another, many of those men had gone to Daddy's office for advice, wills, or settlements. He hunted, fished, and got drunk with them. He played the fool for their kids. The men knew Daddy was honest, a quality pretty scarce among the big wheels in the county, and they trusted him whether it was in a poker game or the courtroom.

Daddy waited and watched both sides, but as far as I could tell, no one gave an inch. The men showed no sign of stopping this fight. He moved slowly and lifted Jane from his shoulder. Holding her high, he pointed to Mother, who now stood just inside the ring of miners who were crowding close.

My knees trembled when I saw Mother move through the cluster of miners. She looked so tiny and defenseless. Even little Logan knew she was in danger. He jumped into my arms and threw his face into my neck.

"Don't worry, Logie. Mommy will be fine." I hoped with all my heart I wasn't lying. It was one thing for Daddy to be facing a mob, but Mother was not strong or tough or even very well liked. Too many people thought she was stuck-up, and no one could deny that she was not a mountain girl.

I could see her as she began to speak to the men as she walked by. Many of them were our neighbors, husbands, and brothers of women she knew well. Daddy stooped down and placed Janey's feet on the ground. He whispered to her as he set her on a path through the miners. She turned and waved bye-bye, and with her joy at seeing

Mother, she plunged into the middle of the crowd. The knot of miners split apart as she bobbed her green bonnet and golden curls through them.

Daddy turned and strode into the huddle of scabs nodding and shook their hands and called each one by name. The wind was picking up, and I could no longer hear him, but I knew Daddy would ask about their mothers and grandmothers, their dogs, their children. Every man was forced to talk to him. He skipped no one. Whether they liked him or not, people found Daddy an impossible man to ignore. The crowd began to separate, and the men broke off into smaller groups. Even way up here, it seemed some of the anger had cooled. Fists dropped, and rifles came off shoulders to lean against legs. The loud shouts stopped, and in their place was a soft murmur.

On the other side, the miners focused on my briggedy sister and my terrified mother as they made their way through the men. Mother's courage might have deserted her, but her good manners and instinct held firm and forced her to ask the men about their wives and children. I could see her holding Jane's hand, moving rock steady through the quarrelsome men. She would be asking about their children by name, forcing each one to look at her and acknowledge the common ground they shared. Slowly, the boiling anger cooled for them too, and they began to move back down the path that had led them here, spoiling for a killing. Daddy moved closer to where Mother was standing, but she gave Daddy "the look." Poor Daddy. It was going to be leftovers and slammed doors for a good spell. She picked up Janey and, without a word or a smile, traced her steps back through the scattering miners. Relief shot through me. She might be mad at Daddy, but she was on her way home.

"Look, Logie, here comes Mommy. I bet she wants to see you."

A little more liquor, a few rifle shots, and four or five hours later in the day, and stopping the fight would have been impossible. Daddy must have sensed the men were farther down a dangerous path than any of them wanted to risk. I never could figure out how he did it, but he could always understand both sides of an argument and figure out a way to shut it down. Pappy always said, "Ed's staring brown eyes can see right through the righteous and the unrighteous."

Maybe he was just lucky because you could count on it that both sides would be at it again. The strike had already brought gunfire echoing in our troubled valley. Mothers cried as good men and bad died for little more than a day's pay. But today, Mother, Daddy, and my baby sister had tricked Logan's picnickers into a short peace.

Chapter 2

THE VISIT

Black winter had sunk its roots into the mountains surrounding us. An unusual cold-weather drought just plain refused to give way to spring. With no early spring rains to nudge the weather on, we stayed trapped in the long ugly season. The valley hunkered down to wait it out.

The Ross's Point march had pressed the union negotiators' and operators' lawyers into new talks, filling the court café and various warm offices, but clouds of smoke from the rusted metal barrels still hung over the weary picketers standing as sentinels at the gap. The cold worked through freezing gaps in every layer of flannel and shrunken wool the women could scrape up for the men to wear. The meager fires gave off more smoke than heat and more gas than spark.

In spite of their desperate hardships and what seemed like no hope, the striking miners stayed on the line. I hated to look at them. It felt rude, like I was seeing them cry when they would be ashamed of their tears. Of course, they didn't cry, and there was even harsh laughter and roughhousing, mainly, I guessed, to keep their spirits up.

I had spent the night with Leatha, and when I was standing by the front door, trying to talk myself into going home, Fleetie reached behind me and picked up her granny's ancient shawl and wrapped it around herself against the biting cold. Once, the shawl was probably deep black with bright pink trim, but the years had left it more gray than black, and the pink so faded, it was almost white.

"Dork, Nessa, you watch the little'uns. I'm walking up to Mrs. Hill's." She wrapped herself in the knitted shawl against the raw cold. Leatha grabbed her daddy's mackinaw, and we took out across the porch, giggling like we had pulled off something feisty. We crossed the dirt road and raced up the steep bank leading to the railroad crossing. We both stopped to throw pebbles in the creek that flowed by the road while we waited for Fleetie to catch up.

Leatha's aunt Geneva was already just a few weeks away from delivering another baby to join the toddler twins now crowding her lap. The custom was to provide for necessities and extras by giving the new mother a shower. A few days earlier, Fleetie sent out the word and invited a houseful of cousins and aunts to the party. Everybody in the valley loved Gen with her huge blue eyes and hair as black as a miner's eyebrow. She wasn't as big as a cricket, and when she was pregnant, which now seemed like most of the time, it was hard to tell where the baby stopped and Gen started. Her voice was as soft as a mourning dove and almost as melancholy, but her children were a perfect delight, and she made us feel that her babies belonged to everybody.

On the walk up the hill, Fleetie ordered us ahead of her. "I can't think one clear thought with all your jabbering," she said. "Get on up the hill and give my ears a rest."

As she fell silent, Leatha and I ran ahead and left her with her head down, a deep frown dividing her brow. Most of the women in the valley wore the same half-sad, half-scared look. At the top of the hill, she walked around the house and, just below the kitchen windows, stopped and took a long look down the valley. Standing there, you could see the curving river, the county road, and the small village across the way. This was her view when she was a child. Her aunt Myrtle and her uncle John once lived in the house. She stood there for a minute to catch her breath, while both of us waited with her. She finally turned and walked the flagstone path to the back door and knocked. I stepped ahead of her and pushed open the back door. Mother had seen us and was waiting just inside.

Before I could say a word, Fleetie blurted out, "Kathleen, would you mind to come to Geneva's baby shower?"

There was a broad and obvious gap between Fleetie's mountain raising and my somewhat refined mother. She always said she didn't fit at Fleetie's gatherings, and I saw her force a smile to hide her dread of another miserable afternoon. The women were unfailingly polite, but Mother's attendance would dampen the laughter and fun of the party. They all acted too conscious of faded dresses, run-over shoes, and work-roughened hands. Not a single one of them would have said that Mother ruined the party, but they did think she was "quair." She didn't put on airs, she wasn't fancy, and she was soft and gentle, but she was different. They knew it and let themselves feel judged.

"Oh, Fleetie, I don't know. When is it? I may have to help Ed at the office."

"Saturday afternoon at two o'clock. We would be purely pleased for you to be there."

You could tell it took real effort for Fleetie. She tried hard to say the right words now that she had gotten the nerve to ask. The air was sticky with her effort. I stood there with my fingers crossed behind my back, knowing how a turndown would shame Fleetie. I could just hear Burl's mean laugh taunting her foolishness. He never had a care for Fleetie's feelings—wouldn't ever either, I could tell.

"When is Geneva's baby due, Fleetie? Seems like she just had the twins last month."

She was stalling. Mother had told me that with Fred on strike and Geneva ready to deliver her third child in sixteen months, their situation was desperate. How the neighbor women were going to scrape out gifts from their meager reserve was a mystery. Given half a chance, Mother would have carried in armloads of things we had outgrown. But as little as she knew about how to make friends with the women in the settlement, she did know that playing Lady Bountiful would ruin it forever. After you earned their loyalty, mountain people took it with them to the grave, but on the other hand, they would refuse to forgive with the same passion. Forgiveness might take as long as fifty years; a quarrel can last that long or even longer. Moonshining and murder in a righteous cause were lesser offenses, but lying and puffed-up pride would bring the wrath down.

It was beginning to look like it was going to be years before Mother would ever understand the innate dignity of the women in the valley. As she told it, her Bluegrass people used wealth and land to size up one's place in the social scheme of things. With little material wealth to measure, mountain kin settled on other standards. A big garden, early rising, a clean swept yard, good manners, a soft voice, clear moonshine, a good aim, and well-trained hounds were traits found in the respectable members of the clan. Could you kill a snake? Were you honest with your neighbor? Did you take care of your own? Or were you prissy, a put-on, a drunk? Were your kids' clothes dirty, your sugar jar empty, and your fence so poor, it wouldn't hold your milk cow? This was how judging went in the mountains, not much like counting out stacks of dollar bills.

"Them twins is just over a year old. She is gonna have a mess of babies in that house in a week or two. I worry about her some. She's not strong like she oughta be with all she has on her. She makes me uneasy."

"Less than a month? Poor child. I suppose Fred gives her a lot of help?"

Fleetie clamped her hand over her mouth and smothered a laugh. Fred Clement had never known a minute of woman's work and never would. Mother didn't seem to reckon on how it was.

"Fred's never been much of a hand around the house. Mammy spoiled him pretty good. But all us is trying to help out 'fore it gets here. Burl don't know it, but I'm seeing to it that he's puttin' her up a new clothesline. Susanny has went and got a new zanc tub. Dolly has found rubber pants over at Middlesboro. Did you ever? You don't have to bring something new. Just any old thing you might have left from your own babies would do. Do you think you might come?"

Mother gave up. She must have sensed the urgency, even though you could not hear it from our matter-of-fact salt-of-the-earth neighbor. "Thank you for inviting me. I'll be pleased to come. What can I do to help you?"

I uncrossed my fingers.

Fleetie blushed red. "Oh, that's all right. I'll put the young'uns to the mopping and cleaning. It's nothin' they can't knock off real quick."

Mother had run smack into the wall again. The day had not yet come when these two women could sweep each other's floors. Their friendship was tied up with competing rules of what was proper and seemly to say or do. It was not an easy foundation for a relationship, but somehow, the two women managed to cross enough of the gap to care for each other. Kids covered some of the barriers, but even there, you couldn't help but see the differences. The Sargeant children could never come up the hill unless invited. Never go into the house. Never ask for a Band-Aid or accept lemonade and cookies. Never leave a mess in the yard. Never call her Kathleen—especially strange to Mother since they all used Daddy's first name.

"Where are my manners? Please come in, Fleetie. I want to show you the matching dresses I am sewing for the girls."

Fleetie hesitated as usual when she was on our doorstep. Some paths just naturally seemed to stop at the door, and others led right to the kitchen table. Fleetie always stopped at the porch. She hesitated for a minute as she pulled her gray shawl closer around her and turned to leave.

Mother seized on the tiny pause. "Could you help me just a minute? I need another pair of eyes to help me decide how deep to take the smocking. I usually get it too shallow. Just one look?"

"Yes, I will be glad to look at the smocking. It is easy to misjudge. Once, I was smocking and got sleepy and forgot how far down I had gone and about near smocked the whole front of the apron. It turned out pretty, but law, that was a lot of work. I could have done two aprons for it. Pretty soon, I'd better get on back down the hill. I hate to leave the young'uns in the house when the stove is hot, but I reckon I can step in just a minute."

25

Fleetie wiped her feet about twice as long as needed before she stepped into the house that seemed such a marvel to her. Leatha had told me that her mother said if times turn good, this house was exactly what she wanted her own house to be. It was simple enough, but everything in it seemed just right—soft rugs, puffy white curtains, crisp slip covers, and little pretties sitting comfortably at home on tables, shelves, and bookcases. She told Leatha that the place always took her by surprise. It had been not much more than a shotgun when her uncle lived in it with two porches, a stove in the front room, rough-hewn wood floors, a pump in the kitchen, and solid shutters at the windows that let in precious little light.

Mother had the soft dimity dress spread out on the kitchen table. The smocking was well on its way, and for a moment, Fleetie let her hands run through the soft buttercup folds spilling across the table, looking for all the world like billowing silk.

"Law' me, Kathleen, look at that. You couldn't be laid out in nothin' finer," she said.

"My aunt in Lexington sent me the cloth for Easter outfits. It's a simple pattern. That's why I wanted to do the smocking. It adds a little frill for trim. There is a lot of the material left. What do you think if I made the baby a dress and matching quilt?"

Fleetie paused a long time. "Geneva would just downright cry, but Saturday is right on us. You might not have time to do a quilt."

Mother fell silent. "What if I tied it instead? I could tie it with tiny yellow bows instead of heavy string or yarn."

"I never seed that done. Would it hold good?"

"No, it wouldn't hold for much washing. It would just be a quilt for church or a party."

Fleetie stared at Mother. I wondered how Mother thought Geneva would ever walk the two miles to church, carrying her new baby wrapped in a fancy quilt and pulling the twins along with her. Fleetie probably wanted to ask Mother to give Gen some hand-me-down receiving blankets instead, but asking anything came hard for Fleetie. Anybody would know that Geneva would love the dress and quilt a lot more than a plain old tub or clothesline.

26

Fleetie laughed a nervous laugh I had never heard before. "She'll be proud. Probably won't ever let the baby use it though. Geneva is one to save back."

"Saving back is not all bad. You never know when there will be a call for something special, and having a little extra hidden away can come in handy," said Mother.

Fleetie took a long measuring look at the smocking and added, "I 'spect about three more rows would be just about right, don't you?"

"Oh good, I don't mind smocking, but it is slow work. I have about worn out my thimble. Would you sit down and have a cup of tea? The girls can have some ginger ale and cookies. It'll give us a little lift before we have to get supper on the table."

It was one thing to help measure smocking length, but passing time over a cup of tea was different. Fleetie was a proud woman, and she was careful not to step beyond the rigid, unspoken customs. She had stepped through Mother's door unbidden. To stay beyond just a scant few minutes to carry out the necessary errand was simply not done.

"I better get on back. Thank you kindly. We'll be seein' you come Saturday. Come on, Leath. Tell Mrs. Ramsey you had a nice time."

Leatha squeezed my hand. I knew she wanted to sit down and have a drink and cookies, but Fleetie's fear that she had already overstayed took them out the door. She gave a quick wave and hurried around the house and down the long dirt road.

Mother stood in her front window and watched Fleetie until her white bonnet disappeared down the grade. She said, "I'll have to remember that if I mention tea, she's gone! Next time, I'll pour the cups first without asking."

I helped Mother fold the dress and fabric and put them away. "I'll finish Janey's dress later. I better start on the baby dress right now if I am going to get it and a quilt finished in time. You know, it's been more than three years now since I did Logan's layette. It's going to feel good to have baby stitching to do again."

"Why is it better than making dresses for me now that I'm bigger?" A twinge of jealousy wormed itself to the back of my mind.

"A new baby brings so much promise. Will it have blue or brown eyes? Will it be happy and curious, active or colicky, maybe have curly hair or straight? Just a world of things to think about with every stitch."

"It doesn't look like much fun. I'd rather climb a tree after apples or mistletoe," I said.

"Grown-ups play different as we get older. Someday not too far away, you'll see." *Someday* was her favorite word for me.

Chapter 3

THE PARTY

On Saturday afternoon, as Mother and I walked down the dirt driveway, the sky seemed heavier than usual. From high on our hill, we could see the guests coming to the party by four different paths. Mary Middleton walked down the creek bed on our side of the mountain. The cousins from Tunnel Hill were walking on the county road. The valley women were on the railroad tracks, and there was even a tiny rowboat carrying Susanna and Dolly across the drought-stricken river. They landed on the bank right behind the Sargeant house. None of us paid any attention to the threat of rain.

Any kind of get-together or party was a rare treat in the midst of the strike fury and tension. The men walked the picket line and vented their frustration with threats, fights, and curses. But the women, for the sake of the kids, did their best to hide their fear. The kids knew better, but their mothers still worked to keep up what passed for normal.

The march a few days back frightened everybody in the valley. Daddy somehow managed to keep the killing at bay that time, but we all knew the danger was not over. It would only be a matter of time before the fear and anger would boil over again. The weight of what the next battle could bring hung over the valley.

It seemed that all of us managed to arrive at almost the same time. When Mother and I stepped inside the front door, everyone was talking and answering at the same time. Laughter and teasing filled the room, and we greeted one another like long-lost kin.

Geneva took the presents with a wide smile. "Oh, Kathleen, you didn't have to bring nothing, but thank you kindly."

Mother probably fretted too much about ruining the party because all the women were enjoying themselves, and while no one talked directly to her, they all talked plenty loud to one another.

Leatha and I sat on the floor in front of the sofa to save room for the overflow of company. It positioned us right where we could take in all the gossip and fun. Fleetie acted as nervous as a trapped cricket and rushed out with her box of games just as everyone was finding a seat. The first game required that we unscramble words directly connected to new babies. There were giggles over the easy ones like *nettibass* for *bassinet* and groans over *alumrof* for *formula*. The list was long, and we soon began to peek at one another's papers. Mother was a great source for answers. I was the only one in the room who knew she was at her happiest when she was in her world of words. So it was just natural that the answers to the games would fly from her tongue and pen. I could tell she didn't even try to cover her paper, and she puzzled the words aloud, so more than a few of her answers slipped out. She was so generous, even Leatha and I got most of them untangled. There were lots of ties. The prize, a pint of Fleetie's coveted pickle relish, was won by guessing a number. Fleetie's sister Hattie picked fifty-eight, their mother's age, and won the prize.

Hattie was the exact opposite of Fleetie. Her hair was as straight as Fleetie's was curly, with Fleetie short and Hattie tall. The only way you could tell they were sisters was by the dip of their brown eyes. It made them look sadder than they ever told.

Fleetie was so pleased with how the first game worked out, she would give us no rest. She had us forming little words out of longer words, rhyming funny rhymes, and making lists of baby names and relatives now long dead. As soon as one game was over, she pushed us to start another.

Finally, Geneva rebelled. "Fleetie, I'm plum tuckered with games, and so is everyone else."

"You know better." Fleetie laughed and picked up her old bassinet now filled with bright packages. "If you won't play, then you can get to work and open all these pretty presents!"

Leatha and I moved so we could squeeze close to Gen. As each present was opened, almost the same words rolled out. "That's so pretty. I remember when Tressie wore that for her first Christmas. You will get a lot of good out of that. Diapers—can't have too many of those." Each gift brought on a chorus of expected polite and correct comments.

As the pile got smaller, the noise level got louder, and Geneva reached for the last gift, Mother's large yellow package. Gen slipped off the wide ribbon and tried hard not to tear the shiny wrapping paper. Since we were in on the surprise, Fleetie, Leatha, and I hung even closer to Gen. I almost held my breath. Sure enough, when the top came off the box, Geneva caught her breath, and tears filled her eyes.

She lifted the tiny baby gown trimmed with delicate cut lace, embroidery, and almost invisible smocking stitches. The room was quiet as Geneva unfolded the shimmering quilt. A wide satin ribbon framed the coverlet, and each square was tied with a tiny yellow bow with an embroidered bloom in the center of each knot. The care and workmanship that had been poured into the gift silenced everyone in the room, including Fleetie. I swear I could hear the clock in the bedroom ticking. No one stirred or even looked up.

Mother had done it again. To be as smart as she was, it was a pity she didn't seem to use good common sense sometimes. The quality and beauty of the gift put all the rest of the presents to shame. The aunts and cousins had given the best they could share, and the condemning silence in the room made my ears throb.

Geneva finally and blessedly broke it. "Kathleen, this is the prettiest baby gown I ever saw. You make the littlest stitches there ever was. I love it. I never saw a quilt tied with ribbons. It is just beautiful."

"Thank you, Geneva. I had the material left over from some sewing I was doing for the girls."

The uneasy silence lengthened. Oh lordy, my poor mother! Not only was the gift more expensive both in labor and cost than all the others, but she also put it down as being made from scraps from her kid's clothes. Why didn't she know better than to show up the others by overdoing?

Mother didn't seem to have any notion about how important it was to avoid "the slightest hint of putting on." It just came natural to us kids. If you were called a "put-on," no one would be caught dead talking to you. It was a lesson ingrained from birth. Mountain-borns never make such a mistake.

Fleetie flushed red and whispered to Mother, "Would you like to help me fix the plates?"

Mother practically jumped off the horsehair sofa in her rush to escape the room. I moved to the kitchen too. It was too hard to stay in living room right then. With both of us gone, the rest of the women would finally begin to talk again.

Fleetie and Mother were almost silent while they placed banana-and-peanut-butter sandwiches on plates, added candy corn, and poured Kool-Aid. When there were words, little was said other than what was necessary for directions. Mother kept her head down and bit her lower lip. She knew things had gone wrong again, but as usual, she was at a loss to know what or why. Over and over in her years living in Ross's Point, I had seen her try to be one of the bunch, but her efforts to make real friends with neighbors in the valley always blew up, just like this one.

For starters, marrying Daddy, a favorite of theirs, made everybody judge her hard. Fair or not, her every move was watched, discussed, and analyzed. They talked nice about her beautiful skin, deep blue eyes, trim figure, and soft laugh, but they could not forgive her "airs."

Fleetie finally spoke up. "Kathleen, you have the best heart I 'bout ever knowed. Geneva will always cherish that baby gown and quilt. Thank you. You are so good."

Mother bit her lip, probably struggling to understand what had happened. "I love to sew baby things, and since I had the material, I thought . . . Shouldn't I have sewed for her baby?"

"We can be funny about things sometimes, Kathleen. Don't you try to change nothing. Someday, they will all know better how to take you. Ed is right smart. He knowed a good thing when he found you. Before long, you will get the hang of our quare ways. We aren't none of us too far off from the other."

I looked at Fleetie's soft brown eyes. You could just about fall into them as they swept you up. It looked to me that both of them were about to break into tears just as we heard raindrops sprinkle the window. We didn't know it right that minute, but the winter drought was over.

Chapter 4

AND THE RAINS CAME

Only the first drops were light. The storm, pushed by a rising wind and joined by rumbling thunder and flashes of lightning, soon caught up with itself. The rain pelted all of us as we hurried our goodbyes and rushed away. Leatha and I ran out the back door and down to the riverbank to watch Dolly, her mother, Susanna, and Dovie Rose pole the boat back across the river. Dolly asked Dovie earlier to help her get the boat across the river. She knew the river would be up. Waters in these mountains didn't waste any time rising.

We were all getting drenched, and rain began to fill the bottom of Burl's little rowboat. Poling over had not required more than an occasional prod to avoid the larger river stones. But now, with the current much faster and the water rising fast, they had to work hard to keep the boat steady and move across as they struggled to get it to the far bank. Cold chills raced up my spine as I watched the river surge in its shallow bed. It forced the water over the gunnels and into the boat. The rain must have started upstream somewhere over Black Mountain. No telling how long it rained up there before it got to us.

Dolly and Dovie Rose, both young and strong, were fighting to keep on course. They pushed their long poles hard into the soft creek bottom or wedged them against the largest stones to maintain the crossways movement against the current. I held my breath each time a pole was pulled away from its anchor hold because the other pole had to be shoved in place right then, or the little boat would take off down the creek and away from the mooring post on the far bank.

Fleetie came out the door looking for us and stood stock still as we watched from the bank. I could see her body strain with each lift of the pole. Susanna had moved to place all her weight—and she wasn't little—right in the middle of the boat. There she sat, the rising water sloshing around her ample ankles, arms welded to the gunnels, rocking gently forward with each push against the poles as if she too could help propel the boat to the far bank. In spite of the rain, the water carried their voices back to us through that peculiar silence that a flood brings with it.

"Mama, sing 'Rock of Ages'!" yelled Dolly. "We're just about there. It'll help us get the poles up and down."

"Sing? '. You're pure soft in the head," said Susanna. "I can't hardly breathe. If I go to singin', I'll purely drown, and then where'll you be then? I'm the only thing keeping this old boat steady now."

In spite of the rain or perhaps because of it, all three laughed at the idea of Susanna drowning on her own song. "Henry will be all over us for being on this river in this storm. Just you wait," said Susanna.

"I'd like to see how he would get across if he was here."

"You know Daddy, Dovie. He'll probably tell us we should've walked under the boat and waded across," said Dolly as she fought to give the pole one last hard push. She was rewarded as the boat shuffled up to rest on the narrowing bank. They were now beyond earshot.

Dovie scrambled up and out of the water onto solid ground with the mooring line in her hand. As she wrapped it around the post that now seemed to be sinking in the rising water, Dolly helped Susanna step out and climb the sloping bank. Dovie Rose turned to wave at all of us, standing in the rain across the rising river.

Susanna scowled, slipping and struggling for secure footing on the slick grass. I had just begun to breathe easy again as we watched them disappear into the strand of pines just beyond the riverbank.

Mother walked around the corner of the house and found us watching the little party struggle away from the sheer bank.

"I'm telling you, that Dolly is strong as an ox," said Fleetie. "You'd never think it, as poor as she is. She never eats nothing."

"She's wiry. She must get her strength from hard work," said Mother. She gave Fleetie a quick hug. "Thank you for inviting me. Please come see me soon."

I grabbed Mother's hand, and we held on to each other as we hurried through the gate. We ran across the county road and up the steep railroad crossing and to begin the long drag up the mountain to our house. Mother's coat was soon soaked, and water dripped from the brim of her hat. We were both drenched. I shivered and pulled at Mother's hand as we moved even faster to shorten the time it would take us to get to the house.

I looked back down the stretch of railroad running parallel to the road and saw four of the women covering the railbed as fast as they could negotiate the cross-ties. Mother saw them too.

"It is such a long way for them to go in this rain. Wonder why they won't wait for just a little while. They're going to catch their death."

I knew that none of the women could wait it out this close to suppertime. There was work to be done, men and children to see to, cows to milk, stock to feed, and water to carry. Each day divided itself into divisions of heavy labor. Nothing could be neglected for long. It was not that Mother was lazy or spoiled, but bless her Central Kentucky heart, she just didn't get it. Lives around here were hard, and rain was just one more irritation in a life full of them.

Chapter 5

FLASH FLOOD

Rain pounded the valley that afternoon and showed no sign of letting up as evening came on. It kept sluicing and pouring right into the dark of night. I stood at the living room window and stared at what was usually a wide view of the valley that flickered with house lights, but tonight, it was futile trying to see through the torrents. In a few minutes, I did spot the lights of Daddy's car. As the front beams jerked, they drew jagged pinnacles against the darkness as the car hit gulley after gulley. I knew the tires would be spinning a hail of water, mud, rocks, and gravel. Whenever there was rain like this, Daddy had to fight the wheel over the ruts cut by the cascading water speeding down our hillside road.

I always loved watching the freshets that would form and break free after the heaviest rains. They could cut deep into the light soil in no time. These new streams made their own temporary creek beds with a thick arm of water that raced down the mountain. Of course, the freshet streams never lasted more than a day or so, and in their wake, they left eroded ditches that made even more deep gullies in the roads and driveways. I didn't dare say how much I liked seeing the temporary creeks, or in the next dry spell, Mother would have me hauling rocks and gravel to repair the damage. Since I was so fascinated by the bubbling streams and the erosion, she reacted as if she thought that I was somehow responsible for the ditches and erosion. It was a good lesson for me about keeping my mouth shut. Pappy never exacted the same toll on my curiosity. He just rolled along with me and let me discover consequences on my own. How I missed him.

Daddy pulled the car around to the side of the house and parked in the turnaround. He missed Pappy too, but being man-like, he wouldn't talk about it. He ran from the car as I held the screen door open. He seemed to be flying through the air over the deep puddle swelling at the base of the porch steps. His feet slammed onto the porch, and he all but threw his briefcase and a sack of groceries at me while he grabbed my shoulders to keep from landing flat on his bottom. Both of us exploded into laughter.

As soon as the both of us could catch a decent breath, he shouted, "Let's eat!" The sky could be crashing around his ankles, and still, the first words out of his mouth after work were always the same. I knew, with that phrase, he really meant we were all safe, he was home, and the night was good.

Mother stayed at the sink, and Daddy stood close behind her, waiting for her to turn around. She had been silent ever since we got back from the baby shower, and all he got was her back. I had been here before, more times than I wanted to remember. Next, Daddy would say something to her, and Mother would throw back some sarcastic remark, and before I could skedaddle out of the way, the room would go cold and angry. A hard knot grabbed my throat, and anger hung right behind my ears. It wasn't Daddy's fault that Mother had prissed herself down to Fleetie's with a present that made her look like some high and mighty do-gooder. I had heard it before. She would twist it around and somehow make him responsible for what the women at the shower had said or done. "His people!" She had spit that accusation out more than once. Tonight, it was one more time than I never wanted to hear it again. No telling what Mother would think up this time to yell at Daddy.

I jumped in. "How high is the river? Did you have trouble getting through?"

"It's lapping over the county road. If it keeps this up much longer, there'll be a tide before morning."

I was grateful when Jane ran into the kitchen to collect the funny paper from Daddy's *Courier*, her nightly ritual. She was too little to read, so she reported on what the pictures told her. She could be laugh-out-loud funny. A car wreck picture was the "ninny-bye went boom," and one time, when a bridge was demolished, she commented, "They need Burl's boat."

"Help me, Janey," I said. "Let's put dinner on the table. Can you be a big girl and pour the milk?" I knew she would like that job because she was never allowed to touch the pitcher. I got lucky. Mother ignored all of us as if we were invisible.

Daddy moved to his place at the head of the table and reached to help Jane steady the pitcher. She bit her bottom lip as she strained to hold the heavy milk jug and pour at the same time. I dreaded the mess that was bound to hit the floor. I couldn't watch. Instead, I grabbed a hot pad to lift the cornbread skillet out of the oven.

The rolling heat hit my face as I pulled the pan from the hot stove. With one hand, I slapped the oven door shut, and with the other, I flipped the pone over the plate and gave it one sharp rap on the cabinet. No matter how many times I slapped that skillet, I was always afraid the pone would fall apart, fly through the air, and land no-telling-where. It never did, but I kept up the worrying. I forked up the pork chops and stirred the fried apples.

Daddy started teasing. "Now, Rach! Are you sure you trust me not to eat half of these?" His love of pork chops was a family joke.

"Better not! We will eat all the apples if you do."

"Wicked girls. Logan and I are going to have to beat you with a heavy stick."

Janey got so tickled at Daddy, she had to run to the bathroom, and then all of us were laughing. Even Baby Logan, perched on Daddy's knee with his spoon clutched in his hand, broke into giggles too. Well, almost all of us. Mother still looked like the thunderclouds had settled on her shoulder.

The pork chop skillet was still hot, and I sprinkled some flour and salt in it and stirred fast before I poured the milk over it. The lumps came anyway, but Mother kept ignoring me. After it came to a good boil, I poured the gravy into the green gravy boat that had belonged to Grandmother and dished the fried apples into the blue fruit bowl, finally getting the rest of our dinner on the table.

"Janey, look at you," I said. "You did not spill a drop. How big you are!"

She strutted around the kitchen table, proud as a banty rooster. Mother lifted Logan into his high chair and Daddy gave Janey a boost onto the tall stool. Maybe the pending storm in the kitchen was over, but I didn't congratulate myself yet. With those two, you never knew. They were just as likely to yell the roof loose as they were to stand wrapped in each other's arms for what would seem like forever. Who could figure them out? Not me.

Toward the end of supper, the steady rain broke into a thunderous downpour so loud I stopped eating and looked at Daddy. The worry crease always resting between his eyes deepened, and I could almost feel his dread of the danger a rain like this was apt to cause everyone downstream. Living up this holler all my life had taught me about the destruction a flash flood can bring down and quick too. Every tiny stream flowing from the top of our mountain would get a hurry on and join the bigger creeks, and together, they grew and chased one another in a mad race for the river. Your smokehouse can be flung down the mountain before you can get the hams out. The flood comes so fast, it roars and crashes down on everything below before you can pull on your hip boots.

During the evening, Daddy and I tramped again and again to the brow of the hill, straining to see through the dark as we tried to catch a glimpse of the river level. The flashes of lightning helped and showed us that the river was racing toward flood stage.

"Damn, Rach, right there is why we live so high on this hill." I wondered if he meant to whisper. "I know it makes it hard when the road washes out, but it beats what is coming at Fleetie and Burl. When I was a little boy, I made up my mind the last time I saw Mam and Pap flooded out that I'd never live where a creek could reach me. Remember, it's much better to be on high ground. It's hard to watch the destruction, but it beats being wiped out and mucking all that filth out of your house. It never feels quite right again."

I loved it when Daddy told me about his life before I was born. It made me feel solid, like nothing could dislodge me. He had lived through a bunch of bad stuff, and here he was, strong, a grown-up with his own family and home place. It made me sure that if he could make it, so could I. And if a flood couldn't get me, neither could snakes or typhoid fever or things that lurked around in the dark, just looking for someone to grab. It was the safest feeling I would ever have.

When we got back to the house the last time, Mother had already put Logan to bed. We were still stomping and shaking the rain off when we heard a wild pounding at the front door. Few people ever came to the front. As much as Mother fussed, most of our visitors made their way to the back door. Daddy beat me to the door, and there stood Nessa, Fleetie and Burl's eldest daughter.

"Ed! Ed! Can Mrs. Ramsey come?" Nessa was a beautiful girl, hair as black as pokeberry ink with her snow-white complexion and gentian-blue eyes. Daddy once called her a root out of dry ground.

Daddy said, "What's wrong, Nessa? Is someone hurt?"

"Hit's Geneva. Oh lordy, hit's Geneva. Hit's her time. Oh, can Miz Ramsey come? Mommy said to say please. She said for me to tell her that she can't handle her alone. Gen's having a bad, bad time birthing this baby!"

Before Daddy had time to reply to Nessa, Mother was at it, barking orders. I learned when I was about three to jump when she was dishing out work in that tone of voice.

"Ed, pull the car around. Nessa, I need for you to stay here with Logan and Jane. I'm going to take Rachel with me to fetch and carry and keep Leatha company."

Well, hallelujah! For once, something was going my way. Whatever was going to happen with the flood and the birthing, I was going to be right there to see it.

Mother was pulling on her coat. "Logan and Janey will be tickled to death you're here. Tell them some of your Granny Clement's stories. Put your wet coat on the hook by the stove to dry. You will find some pork chops and gravy with apples on the back of the stove and fresh pie in the oven. I bet you haven't had a bite of supper."

Nessa forgot the rules and shook her head. "Pie sounds really good, Mrs. Hill. Nobody has a thought for eatin' with Gen so bad . . .," she trailed off.

I could see fear flashing in Nessa's dark eyes. Mother must have seen it too because she stopped rushing around and barking out orders and put her arms around Nessa. She spoke softly to her and put on one of her sweet smiles. "Don't you worry now. Gen will get along fine. This baby business sounds worse than it is. Some babies just take their time getting here. They can be awfully slow. I promise Ed will come back up real quick and tell you what's happening. You know they don't let the men hang around very long when babies are on the way."

Nessa smiled in spite of trying hard not to. "When Geneva starts moaning and crying out, Fred and Daddy both run out the back door right into the rain. You can hear her all over the house, and it's pretty pitiful. Men just ought to try to have a baby."

"Now, Nessa," said Daddy. "Don't pick on us just because we men are worthless, good for nothing, and lazy to boot."

Nessa laughed. She must have forgotten for just an instant the trouble at the foot of the hill. But Mother, ever the boss, broke in. "Ed, go on and get the car before the road washes all the way to the river."

He must have decided to let her have her way this time because he threw on his jacket and plunged into the driving rain. He ran to the turnaround, and we could hear the old starter grinding all the way inside the house, but the spark finally did catch, and the car shuddered awake.

Mother piled sheets and towels in my arms and picked up her sewing scissors and Daddy's bottle of whiskey. She pushed it between the towels I was carrying and then took them back into her arms. I guess she didn't trust me to carry the whiskey. Instead, she handed me the sheets and scissors. We ran down the front steps in the pouring rain. By the time I closed the car door, my feet were making squishing noises in my shoes, and water dripped off my nose, but the sheets were reasonably dry. I had held them close to me and bent over as I ran.

"Katie, the river gets into that house every time we get this much rain. It'll be dangerous for Geneva to have that baby down there. We need to get her up the hill, or the river might roll right into the cradle."

"You tell Burl and Fred, and I'll work on Fleetie. Maybe you can talk them into taking her to town to the hospital. If you go up the county road and cross over to the highway, the water won't stop you. I've heard Burl say it would take a hundred-year flood to cover the county road going north."

Daddy drove down the hill, doing his best to avoid the new trenches being cut across and down our dirt driveway. He bumped over the crossing and stopped right in front of the Sargeants' gate. Mother and I moved out of the car as fast as we could and headed for the front porch. I could see over my shoulder that Daddy was driving back over the tracks to park the car on the rise in front of the Willis place. The water never got that high. Old Man Willis knew what he was doing when he chose that rise for his home place.

As we shook the water off us before we went in the door, I could hear the scary sweep of the river just in the back of the house. Big water moved deep and fast, and instead of lots of splashing noises like a waterfall would make, it gave off something like a muffled roar—not terribly loud but a rumble that shook the inside of you. That sound might not be loud, but it was a sure warning to those who lived on the river.

Mother took a deep breath before knocking. Fleetie would expect Mother to know what to do to help with the birthing, but from the way Mother was gripping my arm in a death clutch, I was pretty sure she didn't feel all that sure of herself. She had always been just a helper, not the official midwife. No one had ever expected her to answer questions or make decisions if things got tricky. And from the sound of the river, whatever had to be done better be done pretty quick, or the water rising higher and higher up the back steps might swamp all of us.

"Mother, are you okay? Do you know how you can help Gen?"

Before Mother could answer, Fleetie opened the door. Her face was almost as pale as Nessa's. I could see through to the kitchen where Fred and Burl looked like they were glued to the back wall. All four kids were sitting in the front room, as silent as stones.

Mother and I followed Fleetie into the bedroom. She had draped white sheets on the bed and over the bureau on the side wall. Geneva was lying on the narrow bed, her face and arms wet with sweat and her fists clasped so hard that they didn't look like hands, more like two clubs. Ridges, never there before, traced paths down her cheeks. With each breath, she let out a soft moan. Her brown curly hair was soaking wet and plastered to her head. She didn't see us, or if she did, it didn't register with her. The pain seemed to have captured her and taken her somewhere far away.

All the talk I had heard about having babies was nothing like the misery I could see and feel in this room. I made up my mind right then that all the baby-having was going to have to be done by someone else in this world besides me. Leatha stepped in the room and gave me a long look. Things in this room were scary. It was one of those times when you were faced with being your mother's big girl, and all at once, you felt small and helpless. Leatha and I would just as soon run into the next room and stay with the little kids, but we were fourteen and so expected to stay and help. We depended on each other as we took the orders and did what was needed.

"It won't come, Kathleen," whispered Fleetie. "I ain't never helped with birthin' trouble like this. Them twins just popped out easy as you please, but this one won't budge."

"Is it breech?"

"Don't seem to be, but I can't see its little head. It's before her time. It's too far up to deliver yet. She still needs to do some real hard work, but she's weak-like. There's no strength in the pains."

"Fleetie, can't we take her to town to the hospital?"

Fleetie's eyes went wide. Mother should have known that if that was the only way Gen could have this baby, then hope had deserted the doorstep. The small private hospital would not take Fred and his pregnant wife without payment up front. The striking men could not have dug up ten dollars between them, much less the fifty the hospital would demand. Besides that, the hospital was owned by rich men who also owned the mines. Miners' families were not welcome at any time, money or not. Doctors knew this and practiced in spite of it. Dr. Parks outfitted his large clinic with extra beds just so he could help some of those who would not be admitted no matter what the condition of the patient might be.

"Kathleen, we can't go there. The hospital won't take strikers. Can you help her?"

"I don't know, Fleetie. I'll do anything I can, but this is dangerous. You and I don't know how to turn a breech. We could hurt her really bad. And this may not even be breech. We can catch a baby when nature is working, but there is no telling what may be working against her."

Fleetie caught her breath. "We're all she's got. They's nobody else."

Mother went as pale as the rest of them, looked beyond the suffering Geneva, and fell silent as sleep. I figured she was thinking hard to pull up every scrap of knowledge she had ever heard or witnessed about stubborn deliveries. Mother was a thinker. I had seen her think our way through lots of trouble, but it took her a few minutes to do it. She stood there motionless for what seemed like forever. Fleetie stood still like me. We were afraid to move as we waited for an answer. Finally, Mother spoke, and the tension broke.

"Fleetie, I don't know if I know enough, but I remember some things that may help. We'll try it. Anything is better than letting Geneva suffer like this. Help me, and we'll get things going."

Fleetie smiled for the first time and wrapped her arm around me and Leatha. "Just tell us what to do."

Mother walked to the door. I wanted to laugh but didn't dare. The captain was back in charge, and she was getting ready to snap out orders. I got ready to jump.

"Dorotha, come here. I need for you to run out to the car and tell Ed to drive to town and get Dr. Parks. Tell him I said to bring him here if he has to throw him in the trunk. Say it just like I said it. I mean it! Tell him I said to hurry fast and don't use the county road. He will want to try to save time, but the water will be over the road someplace near Gaton, more than likely. Move, Dork, hurry. Do it right now!"

Dorotha, the second-eldest Sargeant daughter, had something of the look of a kid who had been assembled with spare parts. Her white-blond hair and black eyes didn't seem a good fit. Her legs were long and slender, but her knees and elbows were too big and made her look as awkward as she was. She had a tiny waist and shoulders so broad, they looked more like a boy's than hers.

As a twelve-year-old, she was as strong as Fleetie, but she was full of the dickens. She was Fleetie and Burl's odd child out, kin to none of the clan in temper or looks. She was funny most of the time, but she could turn on a dime and drive us all silly with her bossy demands. All of us who knew her wavered between laughing or secretly wishing to take after her with a long stick. Susanna, Fleetie's aunt, swore she had been switched at birth by gypsies.

Mother's order filled Dorotha with self-importance. She tore out of the house without even a scarf to turn the rain. Like all Fleetie's children, she loved Daddy. Now she had a good excuse to climb up into his car and hear his teasing directed just to her.

Mother moved to Geneva's side and crouched beside the bed. "Geneva, honey, we have got to get you out of this bed. You are going to have to walk around the room. The baby is way high, and we have to help him move down some. Will you let us get you up?"

Geneva nodded through her fog of fear and pain and tried to sit up. Mother and Fleetie grabbed hands around Geneva's back and cradled her onto the side of the bed. Geneva's legs trembled as she stood and began taking unsure steps. Fleetie and Mother supported her, praised each step, and helped her establish a rhythm of step, step, step, breath, step, step, step, breath. As each new contraction grew, it brought a grinding moan rumbling from deep inside her. Instead of crying out, she doubled over, rocked back and forth, and fought the pain with a low agonizing bellow. As her body struggled, they rubbed her back and murmured the same soft sounds they used with fretful babies.

As each pain subsided, the two women walked Gen in a circle around the room.

Dorotha, acting briggedy as usual, pranced herself into the bedroom to report that Daddy was on his way to town.

Mother looked up and spoke before Fleetie could snap. "Thank you for helping. We are proud of you."

She sailed out of the room to brag to the other children. They were not playing her game that evening, and they ignored her as much as anyone could ignore a buzz saw swinging around the room in bigger and bigger circles. That girl was a sight with her constant jabbering and pestering. I slipped back into the bedroom, and Leatha and I sat on the floor beside the door and watched as silent as a summer schoolhouse.

After two hours of walking, Geneva began to beg, "Oh lordy, Fleet. Let me rest. I can't stand it no more. Please, please. God, oh please, take me. I can't bear this."

I couldn't listen anymore. "Mother, this is awful. Why can't she lie down? Please let her just lie down."

I had little hope that she would listen to me, but I couldn't stand to hear this much pain either. But I pretty well knew that Fleetie and Mother were too afraid for Geneva to pay attention to any begging, Geneva's or mine. The deep moans ringing through the house left Fred alternately frantic then weak with frustration at being able to do nothing to stop his wife's misery. I had seen the birth of kittens, pups, and calves, but those natural births bore no resemblance to the sounds of fear and pain punishing my ears and twisting my stomach.

I could tell Geneva was aware of nothing now but the black pain that filled all her world. She couldn't see us or hear us. It seemed there was nothing left for her but agony. The pain-induced panic took over her sunny personality. Fleetie and Mother were losing her, not so much to the hard work of birthing but to the monster of fear that had now trapped her reason.

"Fleetie, she is making my veins ache. This girl is never going to deliver this baby unless we calm her down enough to reason with her. Girls, Fleetie needs a break. You two keep Geneva walking, while I go tell Fred and Burl they are going to have to help us!"

Leatha elbowed me and rolled her eyes. "Ms. Ramsey don't know trouble till she tries to get ole Burl working for her."

I figured Mother must have been about as desperate as she could ever be. She didn't like Burl any better than I did, and now here she was, about to get him to help birth a baby.

Mother hurried out of the bedroom and threw open the kitchen door with me close on her heels. "Burl, you and Fred get the double tub and fill it with hot bathwater from the stove tank. Fill it full. Boil extra water right now. You have to get this kitchen hot, and you have to keep warm water coming when we need it. And get me your bottle of whiskey. I know you have some buried somewhere around here. Just get it and do it quick. I brought Ed's bottle with me, but we may need both of them."

She turned on her heel and about knocked me over. Fred and Burl just stood there, looking as silly as usual.

"Burl," said Fred. "I reckon we better do what she says. Ain't nobody else trying to help Gen. Where's the damn tub and that liquor?"

"That is the blamed bossiest one woman I 'bout ever run into."

"You're just too goddamn stubborn to take orders from God or anybody. Move it, Burl. My woman's bad off. She needs help, and it'll shore help me to do something besides listen to her moan and you mouth off."

"Fleetie, do you have any cure herbs stored here in the house?" Mother said. "We need basil, cinnamon, chamomile, mint, and rosemary."

48

Fleetie looked puzzled. "I've got chamomile and a mix of yarbs that cooks up to a nerve tonic. Do you reckon they'll help any? She's pretty bad off, and they's right tame."

"We're going to try it, and I'm going to make a strong tea to put in the water," she said.

"In the water? What good will they do in the water? I ain't never heard of such."

It even sounded strange to me, and I'd never even seen a baby birthing. I could tell Fleetie wondered if Mother was all there, but she must have been so frantic to help Geneva that she didn't argue. She went to the back-porch cabinet and dug out two gallon jars of mixed herbs and took them to the kitchen.

Burl gave Fleetie the big eye, but she never gave him a glance. There was no time to listen or to fight her way clear of him right now. He hated orders of any kind, and female orders triggered his temper quicker than anything else. He was already mad at Mother, so poor Fleetie was high on his list right then. But Fred banged on the back door, and Burl had to stop his deviling and help him carry the tub to the middle of the kitchen.

The fire was roaring in the cook stove, and water was set to steam on every cap. Fleetie went back to the porch to grab towels for the bottom of the tub. As she reached above to grab them off the porch line, she whispered to Leatha, "Oh lordy, young'uns, help me look out the back door. Where's that river up to by now?"

Leatha and I stood at the screen door and strained our eyes into the falling rain. It was like trying to look through black lace. You first think you could see something, and then you couldn't make out what it was if it was anything. It sent a trickle of fear working down my neck.

Fleetie whispered, "You hear that?"

I turned my head to catch the sound, and there it was, the heavy rush of a water-borne wind rising to follow the hungry, swollen river. We could hear the throbbing urgency of the water as it rolled deep in its bed and drummed low from the top of the banks.

Leatha cried, "It's a-coming in, Mommy, it's a-coming!"

Fleetie knew from her hateful experiences with the river that time was short. She had seen it happen before. The water would come crawling up the back steps and sweep its greedy fingers around everything in the house. A plague of snakes, frogs, and muskrats would follow, and the house would be left in a ruin of mud, slime, and muck.

Fleetie had watched five floods drive them from their home. She could measure by the sound and length of the rain when it was going to deliver a ravenous high tide. She had long ago struck a bargain with the river gods. She surrendered a ransom of furniture, clothes, and dishes and denied them her children. The fear of losing a child to the whorls and the undertow always drove her over the railroad crossing and up the mountain well before the crest could snatch away a baby child. On those drenching treks, she counted each of her kids over and over.

Tonight, it was no secret that time was up. We had to get out of the doomed house. I knew Fleetie would send the kids up the mountain to Hobe and Mary's. None of her children, except Dorotha, could stand to go near that place if Hobe was home. He was sour and too quick with his belt or cane. I knew the last place she would let them go was to our house. By the time we got there, all of us would be muddy and bedraggled, and she couldn't stand the thought of all that dirt in Mother's white kitchen. That thing that set Mother apart might have been narrowed with all that was happening around us right then, but even then, it was not enough for Fleetie to ask such a favor of Mother.

Flying back into the house, Fleetie yelled, "Hurry, young'uns! The water's already up to the smokehouse. It'll be in here quick. You all get moving up to Hobe's. It won't suit him none, but Mary will beg him off, and I'll let you all go over to Susanny's tomorrow."

The night's turmoil of storm, rising water, and Geneva's cries had done its work. The children, nearly numb with fear, made no protest and grabbed up a doll or blanket or whatever they could carry and scurried to the porch. I picked up a pile of the sheets we brought too, and we waited on the porch, while the grown-ups sorted it all out.

"Damn, Fleet, what about Geneva? She can't get up that hill to Hobe's in her shape," said Fred.

"Fred, pick her up and pack her up to the Willises. Don't tell me about your bad back. You'll carry her, or both of them is gonna die! Hear me now? Do what I say," said Fleetie. She sounded just like a big sister making the baby boy mind.

Fred, in a daze of panic, fell right into the old pattern of following her orders.

Mother gathered the children on the porch. The small yard around the house was working alive with the rush of water. Water was also sweeping down the road just outside the yard gate. Everywhere around us, the water was at least three inches deep. We would have to wade through the yard, across the road, and up to the railroad crossing. Just across the track was the steep path that ran beside Hobe's branch, now grown into a white water monster too big to mess with.

"Children, listen to me," Mother said. "I don't want you to go to Hobe's. He could go off and flog the whole bunch of you. Go on up to my house. I know it is a longer way in this rain, but Nessa's there. That way, you can all be together. Hear me now? I will make it all right with Fleetie."

Leatha nodded and nudged me. "Mommy's going to have a fit."

Six-year-old Rebecca tried to hide behind Leatha. Five-year-old Emma's usual grin melted into tears that ran down her chubby cheeks. The kids knew they were never to go to Mrs. Ramsey's unless Mommy said. But on this night, when everything was strange, they obeyed any adult willing to speak to them.

Leatha and I stepped off the front step into the rising flood. The chance for us to spend the night talking until we were purely tired of it was enough to keep our feet moving in the rain-sluiced dark. We picked up the baby twins. Their toddler feet and little fat legs struggled to keep them upright. We were soon waterlogged as we sloshed toward the crossing. The dirt road was a mudslick, and I fought for balance until I made enough progress to pull the twin and me free of the water, and we moved to the top of the crossing.

In the heavy, wet dark, instinct and memory served as our missing flashlight.

Dorotha began quarreling before we covered the few feet up the hill to the old mulberry tree. "Mommy's gonna whip us good for going up to Mrs. Ramsey's."

"Hush, Dork," said Leatha. "You want to go and set Hobe off? Sometimes, Mary and Ginny can't keep him from beatin' them. How's they gonna keep him off us?"

"Hobe's not that bad. Our whole house will be under before morning. He won't say nuthin'. He'd be 'shamed to. He only gets off when he's been drinkin' that ole moonshine."

"Well, if you're so sweet on him, you go right on up that branch and take your chances. He chased me and Rachel last week when we were just making a playhouse for the little kids by the culvert. We weren't even up on his bank. Go on, I dare you. You gonna pass up a dare?"

That was all it took. Dorotha stomped off, letting the dark and the rain swallow any sight of her.

Rebecca, Fleetie's fourth child, screamed after her, went to her knees, and refused to move. Water dripped off her hair, and her knees were covered with the thick mud on the road.

Leatha took charge. "Rebecca, get up! We're goin' up this hill right now. We don't need Dorotha. She'll just worry us to pieces. Hobe favors her over all us anyway. He won't take after her the way he does you and me. Come on. We'll just let her take her chances."

Little Emma wrapped her arms around Rebecca's head and, with sobbing gulps, pulled at her until Rebecca gave in and stood up. By now, both girls were sobbing.

"Meany Leatha!" Rebecca screamed. "Stop bossin' me. I'm telling Mommy you are the meanest girl she's got. She's gonna whup you good."

"She can't whup me 'cause I'm here and she's down there! I'm going up this hill and leavin' both of you standing. If you don't want to be out here alone, you better stop that blubbering and come on."

Still snuffling and wiping tears, the two held on to each other and fell in just behind Leatha. The dark and the rain lost the fight for them.

Standing in the dark just beyond sight, I spotted Dorotha as she listened to her sisters quarrel. She grinned and started for the fork and the steep branch that led to Mary and Hobe's. Hobe's cliff house was a fearsome place full of dread for all the kids up this holler. Hobe would just as soon knock you down as say howdy, and no one in his path was safe if he was drinking or just having a bad turn. Dorotha, for all her flighty, nervous nature, did not have a scared bone in her long lanky body when it came to doing what she wanted to do. She was only scared of those things that other people brought down on her head, like school, reading, and sitting still in church.

Alone now, I could see her climb the narrow path beside the raging branch. The pounding branch waters skirted over the path that wound around the hill to Hobe's place. Dorotha was soon out of sight.

I hurried to catch up with Leatha. "You go on up to the house. I'm going back to help Mother until Daddy gets back with Dr. Parks. There's hot food on the stove. I won't be too long."

"It's dark. Don't fall and get swept plumb down the river. Ed'll skin all of us if you turn up like some drowned rat hanging off a sycamore."

"I love you too. You're liable to fall off the mountain and get eaten by a panther."

"Make Burl's day. One less of us to feed, I reckon. See you after a while."

Chapter 6

CHASING HIGHER GROUND

As I made my way back down the hill, I had time to think up a good reason for why I didn't go home with the rest of them. But the real truth was that I knew Leatha and Nessa could take care of a dozen kids, and whether Mother would admit it or not, I could see she was pretty shaky.

When I got to Fleetie's porch, Mother was standing right there, looking for us through the rain. She pounced quick as a cat. "What are you doing back here? I thought I had you safely out of this mess."

"I decided to wait for Daddy with you. You might need me."

"I needed you more to mind me and get on home." She wasn't even looking at me. Her heart wasn't in giving me down the road, and her words melted into the rush of rain and black night.

Fleetie pushed open the screen door. "What about the tub and the herbs? Want us to pack them on up to Helen's?"

"Yes, she still needs them, and Helen's tub is probably rusty. Fleetie, her whole place will be filthy. Don't you think Fred could carry Geneva to my house?"

"Fred's back is so bad from that slate fall, he'll do well to get her up the crossing to Helen's. Burl and me'll carry a load of clean sheets and quilts in the tub."

"Fleetie, what about your things? Your papers, your clothes, the children's pictures—can't we save some of them?"

"Law' me, Kathleen. We are flooded out so much, I put the keeping stuff in the attic. It's never got in the attic. We'll be all right. Someday, I hope to never have to run from a flood again, but that's not today. Would you put this quilt around Gen while I finish putting these things up?"

She stretched to place articles on the ledge that ran completely around the front room, solving the mystery of why each of Fleetie's rooms had such a peculiar high shelf just inches from the ceiling— flood insurance!

I took the blanket from Mother, and she began putting things up too. Mother was taller than Fleetie, and the work went quicker. I took the quilt from Mother's hands and wrapped it as snug as I could around Geneva. Poor little thing. She made me want to cry. There was no way she could escape what was happening to her besides death. How desperate is that?

I swear I thought she read my mind because the next thing I knew, she said, "Miz Ramsey, am I going to die? Is this baby going to purely kill me this time?"

"No, honey, but we've got to move. The water is coming up fast. You're not going to die. You're going to have this baby soon as we get you up out of this water."

"Be good now," said Fleetie as she put up the last of the small things she wanted to save.

Fred swept Geneva up in his arms, and his knees almost buckled under the quick weight. I pushed the screen door open as wide as it would go, and he stepped out to the porch with her. The rain pelted them, but his feet stayed steady with her balanced on his broad chest. Sweat mixed with the rain that trickled down his face and neck. Even though they were just in front of me, the black night almost swallowed them as he slogged through the water to the steep crossing and safer ground.

Fleetie and Burl hoisted the loaded tub to their shoulders. Mother and I followed behind with more supplies, and we all followed the rest as they sloshed through what looked by now like at least four inches of water that swamped the yard, crossed the gravel road, and commenced to climb up the steep crossing.

Halfway up the crossing bank, Burl yelled, "Fleet, the grade's too steep. This damn tub is about to slide into the water!"

"Put it down. I'll pull it up over the crossing."

The tub came down, and all four of us pushed and pulled it over the crossing. At the top, Burl and Fleetie picked it up by the thick handles and hurried across the fifty yards to the steps leading to the Willises' front porch.

We could see George looking out the front window. He was probably trying to see the high water and the swollen branch running by the side of his house. He surely wasn't expecting to see us tramping up his steps, but you'd never know it because his voice thundered across the porch. "Hold on, Fred. I'll get the door."

Fred's face was twisted in pain, and I could see his arms trembling, even wrapped hard around Geneva. George threw open the door, and before he could say howdy, Fred carried Geneva into the dim front room and lowered her to a high-backed chair.

"Helen, get up and come here," George bellowed. He didn't wait around on ceremony. His usual mild manner and low voice were gone as he sized up how desperate we all looked.

Helen must have heard the demanding tone in his voice because she jumped to the door with sleepy eyes and a confused look on her face. Right behind me, Fleetie, Mother, and Burl stepped through the front door, carrying the muddy tub, all of us dripping small rivers on the floor.

Mother and I followed Fleetie to the kitchen, where we studied the condition of the stove and sink. It was worse than I thought it would be. Fleetie came up here once in a while, so she must have known about the mess greeting us. Years of grime had almost glued the stove caps down, but Fleetie wrestled open the coal hole on the side of the ancient range, poked the embers, and threw in lumps of coal from the bucket beside the stove.

Mother checked the water reservoir. Both women just went on like they had walked into their own clean kitchens. It occurred to me that maybe Mother had two sides to her too. If she didn't, she was sure putting on a brave front. That kitchen was a brand new experience for me. That people actually lived in this much dirt seemed like something made up, maybe a nightmare. I tried not to touch anything.

Fleetie spoke to Helen in a soft voice, almost like she was talking to a baby. "Helen, we've got us a mess here. Geneva's bad off, and the river's runnin' in the doors by now. We've got to get hot water in this here tub quick. Geneva has about done all she can do, and Ed and Dr. Parks must be behind high water. If these two are going to make it, we are going to have to help her have this baby. Kathleen knows what to do."

Helen nodded, mute as a monk, and backed her way to the stove. Not until that moment did Helen realize that Mother was standing in her house. All their encounters had been in the open, far away from her dirty stove and grimy floor. Her face flushed red, and I could almost feel the humiliation crawling up her back and settling in her craw.

"Law' me, Fleetie, I hain't been well, and thangs is a mess. We can't birth no baby in here. This ain't no proper place for Mizrez Ramsey."

There it was again. Even as desperate as we had to look, here was Helen worrying about my highfalutin mama standing judgment on her pitiful house. Poor Mother. She would probably never live long enough to be considered a normal, sweet, good woman willing to come out in the dark and rain to deliver a baby. It was enough to make me stomping mad. I could have flung a fit too, but right then, no one would have noticed. Why waste it?

Fleetie ignored her whining. "We've got to get the tub full of warm water. There's a little warm water in the tank. Fill up your kettles and these two we brought up from the house. I'll poke up the fire. We're going to need the coal bucket filled too." Fleetie set a small pan of water on the front cap and threw in more dried herbs to steep. "I'll go get some coal."

Mother broke in. "Fleetie, stay here Rachel will get it."

Fleetie handed me the empty coal bucket. "The coal pile's out back at the corner of the house. Mind the barb wire. It's fell down along the side of the pile. Go ask Fred or Burl, and they'll help you carry it."

Fred heard her and grabbed the bucket from me. I guess he was grateful for something to do. Fleetie knelt by Geneva and helped Mother rub Geneva's back, arms, and legs, trying to keep a chill from setting in. The last thing she needed was to start shivering.

"Burl," said Mother, "where's that bottle of whiskey?"

"Sittin' on the front porch where I dropped it before we come in. Why?"

"Go get it. I want to give Geneva a dose of it before the next pains start."

Burl followed Fred out the door.

Geneva shook her head. "Fleetie, I can't stand the smell of liquor. Just let me die. I can't stand no more. I can't stand no more . . ."

My stomach twisted. She sounded so helpless.

Burl walked back in the kitchen, the offending bottle under his arm. He would never live long enough to think of whiskey as anything but contraband. Fred put the coal bucket down by the stove.

George followed him in. "Fred, help me, and we'll pack my old army cot down from the attic. We can set it here for Geneva. It'll be covered with dust and soot, but I'll get Helen to clean it up."

Fred followed George up the back stairs.

"Kathleen," Fleetie said, "can you get her to take this? She's not going to let me get it down her. I can't hardly blame her. Whiskey burns like fire and tastes worse."

Mother took the bottle and poured the glass half full. She made her voice low and harsh. It was her "gonna get a-switchin'" voice. "Geneva, this will help you relax. You have to get it down, and you have to keep it down, hear me? It will take some of the pain away. When you aren't hurting so bad, you can work with us to get this baby born."

Geneva shook her head.

"Do you want to die and kill your baby and go straight to hell? We're not listening to any more silliness. Drink this, and drink it now."

Fleetie shot me a startled look hot enough to burn my skin. She didn't know Mother could blow off like that. I shrugged. I had heard it lots of times. Mother had a temper and resembled Mammy Yokum when she got riled. Soft giggling came from the Willis children huddled at the top of the ladder leading to the sleeping loft. Grown-ups yelling in the middle of the night in their kitchen was better than a Saturday movie.

Startled, Geneva gave up and choked down the liquor. It took her breath, and she erupted into coughing spasms, and tears ran down her cheeks. Gasping and sputtering, she moaned, "Why would anybody drink that filthy stuff if they didn't have to?"

Fleetie took her hand. "To prove they're strong. Men are plain simple, Gen. Strong drink and a strong back. It's pretty much the same with them. And here you are, about to bring another one into the world that could very well be a boy."

"I'll teach it better if it is," whispered Geneva.

"Baby boys start out the sweetest of all, Geneva. It's the world that gets in their heads and messes them up," said Mother.

Geneva smiled a crooked smile at her, the whiskey already working.

Fleetie slowly poured the hot steeped-herb water into the cooling tub of water. The woodsy scent filled the kitchen. Mother spread two clean sheets wide around the tub to protect Geneva from the filthy floor. Mother tested the water, and Fleetie slipped off her robe, and the two of them held Gen as she stepped into the double tub and eased into the water. As she slipped deep into the warm water, another round of pain began to gather strength, but this time, she had something to help the struggle.

Fleetie held her hands, and Geneva, following primal instinct, began to breath hard and fast. The increased oxygen, liquor, warm water, and herbs combined to give Geneva her first respite in hours, even in the middle of a labor pain. Mother winced as Geneva writhed in pain, but we could all see that Geneva was more in control. She could now focus on Fleetie and Mother as they sat on the floor beside her, holding her hands, rubbing her shoulders, encouraging her to breathe deep and relax.

The change was subtle and hard to tell, but if you looked close, you could see Geneva was making the first progress in hours. She had lost the crazed fear flashing in her eyes. In its place, there was something like a clinched-jaw determination to get this job done and over with.

"That's the way, Geneva, you're doing a good job. It won't be long now. Ed will be here soon with Dr. Parks. He will be surprised to see how well you are getting along. He'll give us a lecture about setting off a false alarm."

From between clenched teeth, Geneva whispered, "Kathleen, this is so much worse than the twins. How could it be worse than the twins? Is something wrong with the baby? Oh lordy! Don't let me and my baby die."

"Gen, stop this carryin' on," Fleetie said. "We're not doin' any dying around here. You are just having a baby. Babies come hard. We always forget how hard it is. Them twins didn't come free, remember? Listen now."

"She's right, Geneva. If you will work with us and don't take on, we will get this baby here, I promise," said Mother.

Geneva nodded, and as the relaxation deepened, her breathing settled into a steady rhythm, further loosening her cramped muscles. There was no relaxing the worry lines in the other two women's faces. No matter what they said, there was a limit to how much longer Geneva could keep this up.

Standing at the stove, brewing more herbal tea, I heard Mother whisper to Fleetie, "Where could Ed be? Something must have happened. He wouldn't be this long if he had walked the whole six miles."

Fleetie shook her head and closed her eyes. The adrenaline rush of fear that pushed all of us as we ran from the flood had long since fled. In its place was a worm of fear gnawing away at our nerves.

Mother leaned over and whispered, "What is it, Fleetie? Why did you shake your head?"

"Bad thoughts about losing her. She seems more like my girl than a sister-in-law. I can't stand the thought of those twins and this one too not having her. Ain't nobody in the whole valley that's not just crazy about her and them twins. I feel plumb useless."

"We're just tired and scared, Fleetie. They're bound to come soon. We can hold on. She's depending on you. I'm stubborn as a mule, but I've never known a woman as strong as you."

"Strong is just doing, Kathleen, and mostly, that's all the choice there is. Stubborn is probably a heap better."

It must have struck them funny because both women laughed. I rolled my eyes and shrugged my shoulders at the Willis kids. We didn't see anything funny in that dingy kitchen with steam thick enough to pull the curl out of a sheep pelt and the rain pounding the roof like a band of imps from perdition.

Chapter 7

Barn Lost

Burl threw open the front door. "Goddamn it, Fleet. Hit's our barn coming right down the goddamned river. Fleet, look!"

I stepped out of the kitchen and walked behind Fleetie as she hurried to the front porch. Burl's night vision, honed through years of hunting and trapping, could make out the outline of a building moving down the swollen river. His voice dropped as the black outline of a building bobbing up and down in the racing water moved past us. "Hit's our barn, our barn."

Because of the shock at losing his barn, Burl had not spotted a small light moving down the tracks toward them. It was just a pinpoint, but I could tell by the way it moved that it was a flashlight or lantern. The light jumped from right to left, seeking a path along the tracks.

Ignoring Burl, Fleetie and I raced down the steps to the crossing. We stepped over the rail to the crossties. No one else would be crazy enough to be out walking in this storm. It had to be Daddy.

"Oh, Lord, please let the doctor be with him," I prayed as I walked toward the light and shuffled my feet to feel for ties. Crossties were always too close for one step, too long for two. Daddy said railroad tracks were designed to keep people away, not provide a path for hikers and hobos.

I yelled toward the light, "Daddy, is that you?"

"It's me and Dr. Parks."

Burl had followed close behind us, and he shouted, "Ed, my barn is going down the river! I ain't never seed it this bad. What put you on the tracks?"

I ignored the awkward railroad ties and ran toward Daddy's light as the two men moved close enough for us to see them.

Fleetie called, "Ed, oh, Ed, hurry! Geneva's really bad. Don't pay Burl no mind. Gen is lying up there, tryin' to have this baby, and all's on his mind is the barn's gone floatin' down the Cumberland."

Soaked through and looking cold enough to freeze a fire, Daddy still couldn't keep from laughing. A pouring-down rain, a baby on the way, Geneva suffering, and now a flash flood that threatened to sweep half the valley away, and these two were standing in the middle of it, yammering at each other.

Dr. Park's stern voice stopped all of us. "Where is Geneva? Let's get in out of this damned rain."

"When the river come up, we brought her up here to Helen's," said Fleetie. "We left the tracks and moved up the path to the front steps. Doctor, watch them front steps. They might be awful slick."

Because of the dark, Fleetie had not realized that the rain sluicing down from the leaky gutters had washed off the steps and swept away the accumulated dirt that Helen never bothered to sweep. The two men hurried up the steps with the three of us trailing. Daddy pushed open the front door, and he and Dr. Parks stepped across the living room and swung open the kitchen door, where Mother was kneeling beside Geneva.

The men, with their soaking wet clothes and standing in the heat of the kitchen, were enveloped in angelic halos by the dim back light of the parlor. Mother caught her breath. No one was expecting angels, but for just a second, that's who it looked like were standing there, crowding the room with their presence.

Mother caught her breath and ran to grab Daddy, wet as he was. "We have been worried to death about you," she whispered.

Through the fog of her pain and misery, Geneva must have noticed the same blurred images. "Oh my god, I have died. My babies, my babies . . ."

We all broke into a nervous laughter and tried to hide it except for Dr. Parks. He laughed and slapped his knee like it was the funniest thing he had heard all day.

Fleetie, sitting on the floor beside the tub, put her arms around Geneva and held her tight. "Geneva, honey, you aren't dead. Shush now. Listen to me. It's Ed and Dr. Parks. Dr. Parks is here. Everything is going to be fine. Shhh, hush now, it's all right. It won't be much longer now." She soothed and rocked Geneva as gently as if she was the new baby.

"What the hell, Kathleen? Are you trying to cook the poor girl?" said Dr. Parks. I flinched at his gruff quarreling at my mother. "Let's get her out of that water so I can examine her, for god's sake. I've seen it all now."

She ignored him and moved quickly to help Fleetie lift Geneva out of the water. Daddy took off for the front room. Since I was trying to be invisible, I kept my mouth shut. I wanted to tell Dr. Parks how the warm water had eased Geneva during the worst of the labor, but I knew better. Dr. Parks was almost godlike to all of us in the valley. No one told Dr. Parks anything. We only listened, grateful that he was helping us.

Mother also kept silent. While she was not as much in awe of him as most were, she had been telling us about the effort it had taken for him to travel through the flood. She was right. Who knew what it took for those two to get here? At the very least, they had walked two miles from the bend in the road at the point. They had probably been forced to wade through the flood waters more than once to reach us.

The women helped settle Geneva on the army cot that George and Fred had resurrected from the attic. When they brought it down, Fleetie had been careful to use her quilts to cover it with several layers. Dr. Parks scrubbed his hands as Geneva began to moan from another wave of pain. Her clenched fists pushed against the sides of the small cot with enough pressure to bend the rails. Her back curved with the pain of the contraction, and with her head thrown back you could see her neck threaded with roping veins and sinew.

Mother took Geneva's hands off the side rails and held them fast. "Rachel, rub her feet. Look how they have cramped."

My head was spinning, and every part of me hurt for her. Her feet were as hard as stone—the cramping had a big head start on me. If my feet were cramped up like that, I would have panicked and screamed, but maybe everything hurt her so much, she didn't know one pain from the other.

Mother whispered, "You never forget, do you, Fleetie? She has to feel like her whole world has her trapped under a rock as big as the Pine Mountain overhang."

"I remember with Dorotha, I was sure the pain would never stop again. She was the worst, but none of them was easy."

Listening to them made me shiver as I made a silent vow to leave baby-having to other people. Why go through all that? There were lots of babies around that no one wanted. Better to love the little orphans instead of going through all this grief and misery.

As Geneva's wave of pain began to subside, Dr. Parks listened and poked and listened some more.

Mother checked Gen's feet and patted my arm. "You've made her feel better, Rach. Let's slip out a minute and talk to Daddy. Fleetie will be here to help Dr. Parks."

We stepped out of the kitchen into the living room. I put my arms around Daddy and closed my eyes. He was an island of comfort in this flooded world full of pain and danger.

He gave me a long hug and talked over my head to Mother. "Katie Bell, the water came up so fast, I was afraid you all wouldn't hear it until it was running in the back door," Daddy whispered. "What about Jane and Logan? Are they alone?"

"No, Nessa and the other children are up there with them. When we saw how fast the water was coming, I just knew the car had been swept off the road. You went the short way. I saw you. It is a wonder you haven't left me a widow and your children orphans."

Daddy frowned and clenched his teeth, rippling his jaw muscles. "Don't start on me, Kathleen. Dr. Parks was in Evarts. There was a slate fall, and two scabs were killed, and three other men were crushed bad. Parks didn't wait for the ambulance. He brought them to town in the company dead wagon, and we left Doc Begley working on them. We're lucky Parks would come at all. Neither doctor has been home in two days. How bad is Geneva?"

"As far as I can tell, she is no nearer delivering now than when you left. I hope Dr. Parks brought a miracle with him. She has relaxed some, and she is determined to get this job done, but her strength is gone. There is so little she can do to help herself now."

Fleetie pushed open the kitchen door. "Kathleen, can you come back? He is goin' to have to take the baby." Fleetie disappeared back into the kitchen, and Mother almost staggered. She looked like her knees had turned to rubber.

Daddy grabbed her and wrapped his arm around her shoulders to steady her. He pulled her near. "Hold on, Katie-girl. You are hard as flint. Don't give in now."

She squeezed his hand, pulled away, and slipped through the door.

Daddy looked me straight in the eye. "Watch out for her. She's not really very tough, but you are tough enough for both of you. Hear me?"

Tears jumped into my eyes, but all I could do was nod at him and stand as tall as my five feet and one inch would stretch. Daddy didn't ask much of me, but when he did, I knew it was something so important that I would do anything he asked. His lessons went deep and stayed as long as there was a me to give them a home. I didn't know I was tough, and right then, I didn't feel much like it either. But he said it, and there was nothing left for me to do but put it on and push forward—scared or not, and I was, but in fact, I was not as shaky as before. His words must have worked.

Daddy turned to the three men sitting helpless around the living room. "Boys, we need to find two sawhorses. That cot is way too low. We've got to set her higher so Dr. Parks can see what he is doing."

The men flew out the front door and returned with the water-soaked sawhorses, Daddy and George carried them to the kitchen. Under the cover of the commotion, I slipped back in the kitchen and slid down beside the box of firewood. The men positioned the sawhorses directly under the light in the middle of the room. Daddy, Fred, and Burl lifted the cot with Geneva on it and lowered it on the supports.

Dr. Parks scrubbed and gloved his hands. He gave Mother and Fleetie gloves and gave them the rundown on what he expected them to do.

"No doctor in his right mind would perform a section here in this kitchen, but I've no choice. We'll just have to use what we've got. You two are strong and young. You can help me do this. The dangerous part of all this is keeping Geneva sedated enough so I can operate and get that baby out without letting her respiration and heart rate get out of control."

"What can we do if there are more problems than we know?" said Mother.

"Don't dwell on it. Just do what I say. I'm just guessing here, girls, but we've got no choice. I've measured her and guessed her weight and mixed the sedation." He picked up a short brown bottle and leaned toward Mother. "Kathleen, I want you to pour this drop by drop onto the cone. Hold it steady over her mouth and nose." He pulled his stethoscope off his neck. "Use my stethoscope, and keep your ear out for sudden changes in her heart rate. It will increase some as we go, but unless it races away on us, we'll be okay."

Fleetie's job was to take care of the baby while he did the suturing. The room was as hot as a brooder house. Fleetie had been throwing coal on the fire since we walked in the door. She was convinced that Geneva had relaxed because of the heat. Preparing to sponge off the baby, she lined Helen's battered dishpan with a scalded towel and filled it with warm water. A small stack of tiny undershirts, diapers, cord wrappers, and gowns appeared from the middle of Fleetie's almost endless stack of quilts. She laid two receiving blankets,

Dovie's shower present, over her shoulder, one for cleanliness, the other for swaddling.

While the women were busy, Dr. Parks stepped out of the room to see Fred. Since he left the door ajar, I could see the three men squatted around the wall of the tiny living room. They jumped to their feet.

"Fred, I've got to take the baby, and it won't be the easiest delivery I ever done. Hold on the best you can. Ed, see if you can't find some kind of rotgut around here. He needs to swill about half a pint."

Fred's voice broke, and you could see fear in his eyes and on his flushed face. "Doc, is she going to die?"

"Hell, Fred. If I thought she was going to die, I wouldn't have taken out in all this water and black night. Of course, she is not going to die, and neither is your baby." That was probably as long a speech as he would make all night, and it was hard to tell if it was as much for Fred than it was for all of us, him included.

As Dr. Parks stepped back into his makeshift surgery, Daddy reached out to grab Fred by the shoulder. But just at that moment, Fred exploded. He took a wild swing and slammed Daddy's chin with a ripping uppercut.

Burl jumped up and grabbed Fred with a vise grip out of proportion with his skinny, wiry frame. "Boy, hang on there. Ain't no use fightin' us. We can't do nothin'."

Fred was the easygoing member of the family without a mean bone in his body, but just for that moment, the fear took over, and it looked like it delivered Fred a white-hot anger that left him ready to take on the lot of us.

"Nobody can do nothing to get us back to work. Nobody can do nuthin' to stop this goddamn rain. Gen is about to die, and nobody can do nothin' to help her. Don't be patting me on the back like some child. I am damn sick and tired of nothing."

Blood trickled down Daddy's chin and on his neck, growing a stain on the front of his white shirt.

Burl pushed Fred toward the door. "Let's me and you get out of here. George has got some 'shine laid back up on the flat. We'll git. George can help if they's need."

"Shore, boys. It's right there. You can't miss it," George said. He grinned to himself, and I figured he liked the idea of Fred and Burl floundering around in the stubbled cornfield, looking for his stash. Old George might be grinning, but I knew Burl was too smart not to know they were on a fool's journey. Fred was in bad shape, and a good soaking in the driving rain might clear his brain. Fred tore out the door, running for some relief from the misery inside the house.

With the excitement dying down in the front room, I stepped to close the kitchen door. "Daddy, your chin is all bloody. I'll get you a wet rag from the kitchen."

"Thanks, Rach, but we better stay out of there. They've got their hands full. I'm going outside and checking on the river anyway. It'll wash off soon enough."

As soon as he stepped on the porch, I slipped back in the kitchen and pulled the door shut and slid back down beside the wood bin.

Chapter 8

SNATCHED BACK

I was sitting behind Dr. Parks when he picked up the scalpel. I was afraid for Geneva, but I couldn't help watching. It took almost no time. I could see his hands work the shiny little body out of the incision. He moved fast, and there it was, a baby boy, but he was so still, I was sure he had been stillborn. His slick little arms and legs weren't moving, and when Dr. Parks put his finger into the tiny mouth to clear out the gunk and gave him a little shake, there was no response. He shook his head and placed the baby in Fleetie's draped arms.

"I was afraid we'd lose him. Do what you can. I've got to suture and get her off sedation. Kathleen, no more drops. Just hold the cone on her face for another five minutes while I finish up."

Fleetie checked the baby's mouth and throat and slipped him into the small tub. The cooling water sent a shock through him, and his body reacted in a jerk. Seeing his reaction, Fleetie got a firm grip on his tiny ankles and, placing her hand on his back, began to swing him in a wide, high arc three times, and then she returned him to the cold water. She dug her thumbnails into both his heels and pulled him out of the water again.

"Rachel, come over here and help me dry him off. I have to get him warmed up right now."

Dr. Parks stepped away from Geneva's cot and took him so he could listen for heart sounds. "Goddammit, Fleetie, we have a heartbeat. Whatever magic you're conjuring, keep it up. While you're at it, rub his arms and legs, back and neck. Let's get that blood pumping. Lucky night. We might save both of them if Kathleen doesn't drown Geneva with chloroform."

"More likely, she'd be bent double from all those crooked stitches." She grinned at him and handed him a large neatly folded dressing for the incision.

He placed the bandage on the incision and then used more gauze to wrap around her back and across the black stitches to secure the dressing. When the bandage was secure, he checked her heart rate and then lifted the cone from her face as he moved away from the table.

"Kathleen, try to get her to talk. We need to make sure she is coming back to us." He walked four steps across the room where Fleetie was working with the baby. He checked the baby's heart and reflexes before he said, "Keep rubbing, Fleetie. We need to hear that baby give us some good loud cries."

Fleetie kept massaging and turning the tiny body. The deep purple of his skin was beginning to fade. He wasn't showing a healthy red yet, but his arms and legs were squirming under her strong hands.

All at once, there was a soft whimper followed by a hiccup and a bit louder cooing. Each sound built on the other until there was sustained, audible cry. Not a strong one, but a cry. Instinct driving her, Fleetie picked up a blanket and began fanning him. The cold air stimulated him to a more regular fit of crying.

I said, "He looks so pitiful, Fleetie. Let's dress him in his diaper, gown, and belly band and wrap him in a soft blanket."

"I want to keep him crying." But as she said that, she reached for one of the diapers and belly bands lying beside the little tub. "Every time I let him get comfortable, he wants to go to sleep." Her quick hands fixed the band and pinned his diaper as smoothly as one might expect from a mother with five babies of her own. "This little'un is going to have a time catching up. Kathleen, is Geneva about awake yet?"

Mother nodded.

"Too bad we can't let her sleep. She has to be plumb wore out."

With the baby in the crook of her arm, Fleetie reached down and smoothed Geneva's matted hair. "Lookie here, Gen, it's over. You have your little boy. He's so pretty and cryin' up a storm. Can you hear him? How about you having a big boy? Fred's gonna get the big head. Dr. Parks will go get him soon as you are good and awake."

I could see Geneva was struggling to open her eyes. "Can I hold him?" she whispered. "Is he all right?"

"He's doing just fine. He's got all his fingers and toes, and it looks like he might have blue eyes like Fred." Fleetie stepped to her side, and Geneva's arms immediately wrapped around the tiny baby.

I patted her arm and whispered to Geneva, "We don't even have a gown and blanket around him yet. I'll take him in a minute and dress him for you."

Geneva smiled. "A boy. The twins will spoil a brother."

She immediately drifted back to sleep, and I picked him up and gave him to Mother, who was standing with his gown and blanket. Because we all had fought so hard to save him, holding that tiny bundle made all of us want to fight the world for him. Just a few minutes ago, I had been pretty impatient with him for being so slow getting here, and now I would have fought a panther to keep him safe.

Dr. Parks loaded his bag and issued orders that he knew would be carried out no matter how difficult they might be—cod liver oil, clean dressings, plenty of liquids for Geneva, sterile sugar water for the baby, and his first breastfeeding in the morning. They were to get to town for a follow-up in a week. Turning from his packing, he took his bag and pushed open the door and stepped into the living room, where the men were waiting.

"Ed, what are the chances of our getting back to the car so I can get to town?"

"If we stay on the tracks, we'll get back to the car all right. Railroad people are too smart to put rails below flood level. Katie,

I'll be back by early morning. You all sit tight. The water won't get this high."

Dr. Parks stopped and stared at Daddy. "How'd you get your chin split? Let me look at that."

"It's stopped bleeding. It's nothing. We better get going."

"Don't tell me it's stopped bleeding. It's still dripping on your shirt. That needs a stitch or two. What have you been doing? Wrestling a bear? Goddamn, if it's not one mess, it's another out here. Sit down and let me see what it looks like. You could get lockjaw, typhoid, and tetanus all in one stroke if you aren't careful." He opened his bag and took out his flashlight and gave Daddy's chin a long look. "You're a bleeder. It'll heal up without the embroidery, but you'll have a little souvenir of the fight every time you look in the mirror."

"And not a drop of whiskey to blame," said Daddy.

Parks rummaged in his bag and found gauze, tape, and a bottle of iodine. It made my eyes burn just looking at it, but Daddy didn't flinch. Guess his chin was numb after Fred socked it so hard.

I followed as they walked out the door. The rain had slacked off to a fine mist. Across the way, Fleetie's house stood engulfed by the spring tide. In spite of high water and swirling debris, a naked light bulb, hanging in the front room, cast a yellow light through the broken windows. The glare shimmered through the window and in the black of early morning. It caught the swirl of water and danced circles around the marooned house.

"I wish you'd look. I've seen it all. How the hell is that light still burning?" said Dr. Parks.

"Heavy-duty wire filched from the mines," said Daddy.

If there was no more rain during the night, by morning, the swollen streams coming down the mountains would return to their banks, and in twenty-four hours, the river would begin to ebb. After daylight, more and more damage and misery would reveal itself throughout the whole valley.

Mother came up behind us and gave both men a strong hug, and we watched them walk down to the tracks and soon out of sight.

Standing alone in the wet darkness, we could hear the soughing sound of the swollen river.

"Rachie, just think, all this is in the power of a rain drop. The same drop that feeds us and cleans us can turn around and sweep away and destroy all we have. And right through it all, a tiny bulb fed by a thin wire managed to stay high enough not to be swamped. Remember this when you feel too small to defeat big stuff. That little bulb and that thin wire beat the odds, and you can too."

That was one of the few times that I knew Mother realized how much I missed Pappy. What she said to me then was the kind of thing he would say to me, and that was the first time I knew she was aware of how he used examples to teach me about the world.

"You could write that up in one of your poems. Too bad we can't call the baby Stormy. It sort of fits his story," I said.

"Maybe so, but he is destined to be Fred Jr. Not quite so dramatic."

"I'm gonna call him Stormy anyway."

"You do that, and someday, he'll chunk you in the back of the head with a rock for making him sound silly," she said as she walked back in the house.

Chapter 9

Deep Water

Helen felt dismissed from her own kitchen. Fleetie, Geneva, and the baby crowded the room that was small to start with, and then the doctor moved in, and the men came in and out, setting up the cot and bringing more coal for the stove. Helen perched herself at the top of the attic steps and watched the procession with a scowl on her face.

The Willis place was the filthiest house in the valley. Up our holler, Helen was the only slattern of a wife and mother. All her neighbors took pride in white laundry, scrubbed floors, and swept yards filled with clean, well-behaved children. But Helen would have none of it. Her children were always dirty, hungry, and mostly left to care for themselves. Their behavior was a disgrace. They would beg from all the neighbors, and since that mostly didn't work, they would steal. They had to learn early how to live by their wits, even daring to steal potatoes right out of the ground. Apples hanging on a neighbor's tree were a sure target for their grimy little hands.

Every July, Leatha and I battled them over the fruit from our old mulberry tree growing on our driveway. They had long since claimed it as their own, even though it was well past the property line. That the tree and its sweet fruit belonged to someone else did nothing to prevent the warfare they put up if they caught any of us under its branches.

The once-substantial Willis home place was mostly in shambles, caused as much by Helen's shiftlessness as by their poverty. There was never enough of anything after George's spine and ribs were crushed in the mines. His accident also seemed to give Helen the excuse she wanted to abandon her responsibilities to the family. George did the best he could, but he could no longer hold up to the punishing labor needed to dig coal.

He was a decent carpenter and did his best to pick up day work at the mines and in town, but there was little demand. Woodcraft was a part of every family's heritage in our part of the world. Most men, by nature, training, and necessity, built their own cabinets, tables, chairs, and often their entire house. It was the rare household that needed George's help.

The impoverished Willis family subsisted on what they could grow, forage, and scavenge. Living off the land required constant work, the solid leadership of a strong woman, and several children for labor. There were plenty of children. Helen and George had six, but she let the children fend for themselves. She made only a minimum effort to fill the canning shelves in their dry cellar. She complained about the garden work and generally neglected it. She would rather try to bewitch a fresh cow than milk it. Plenty of us had seen her standing in front of the milk cow, almost head to head, as she talked to the cow as if both could understand each other. Often she would give up milking her altogether and just walk away. Maybe that was how they did it over across the mountain where she hails, but around here, we took charge of the cow and let her know who was boss. That was how you filled a milk bucket, not standing in the pasture, passing the time of day with good old Betsy.

George lived his days in pain, and the only painkiller available to him was moonshine, cheap but dangerous. I once heard Daddy tell that George dreaded the sickening feeling the liquor left in his empty stomach and that he hated the loss of control, slurred speech, staggering steps, and fuzzy memory. When the pain got so bad that he had to resort to the mason jar of 'shine, he took himself out of sight far up the holler to Shelter Rock. He didn't come back until he slept away the worst effects of the rotgut.

Their one blessing was that the house was on the high side of the railroad crossing, elevated enough to avoid the flash floods that lashed the low-lying houses and fields. That was just about the extent of their good fortune. If their household goods were to go down the creek, there would be nothing left for their survival.

As she sat there at the top of the steps, Helen's face resembled an angry mask. Her main duty in her own home seemed to be to keep her own children out of the way. Seeing me coming and going in her house must have irritated her even more. I watched her move farther into the sleeping attic and walk to Lucy Nell's sleeping cot. Lucy was her oldest daughter and the one who carried most of the burden of watching the rest of the kids.

"Lucy Nell," Helen said, "you keep these young'uns up here. I'm going to see what's goin' on with the flood."

Lucy Nell whimpered, "Don't go, Mommy. That river is too high to mess with."

Ignoring her, Helen flounced down the steps and ran smack into George, who heard her footsteps creak the risers.

"I'm goin' out to see what the water's doing," she said. "I bet the road is gone."

George sighed, grabbed his hat, and went with her through the door into the driving rain. I went outside to watch them from the porch.

"You can't see a whole lot out here, Helen," he said. But I expected he was just as glad to have something to do. Chasing Helen was better than sitting there and listening to the moans and muffled orders coming from his kitchen.

Helen gasped and stopped him. "Look, George! Can you see them cows? What are they standing on? How can they be out there in the middle of the river? They's not no island out there." The dim outline of an animal against the stormy sky standing on water almost in the middle of the swirling river seemed an impossible sight.

"They've got caught on something out there. That big poplar is down, I bet, and them cows is caught up in those big branches. It must be damming up the water on yon' side of the bank," said George. "It probably won't hold 'em long. I can see four or five head out there."

"Pore ole things. It'd be pitiful to know how scared they have to be," said Helen.

George snapped, "Scared critters, lord! We could all be drowned by morning, and you're mooning about cows. I swear, you beat all I ever seed in my life."

Helen ignored him as usual. "Fred and Burl's gone up the hill drinking, and all them cows carrying calves is going to drown, practically in Burl's backyard. That'll set 'em back some, I'd say."

George's lips had compressed into a thin slash across his face. Before he got hurt, he and the other men could have pulled the cattle out and saved some of them. But now all he could do was stand by, helpless as the doomed animals struggled in the flood waters.

"I'm going back in the house," Helen said. "It don't do no good to stand here and watch them die. I can't stand it. Move over and let me by, Rachel." She pushed by me as if I was one of her own neglected brood.

"Don't pay her no mind," said George. "'Times I think she's about half daft, and on the other hand, I know it." He slapped his knee at his own little joke as he walked down the steps and into the darkness toward the river.

Chapter 10

Morning Misery

Along about daylight, George pushed open the front door, and his movement and the rush of cold air woke me up. I was stiff from my night on the floor, but I shook it off and pulled myself up and followed him. As far as I knew, Daddy was not back from town, and it was way past time for him to be here. George stood on the porch and shook his head at all the damage from the overnight flood.

I said, "Did Daddy come in while I was asleep?"

"Nope, little lady, but if you look down the track, you can see his car coming up the road. Looks like the water has gone down enough to let him by."

We stood there and watched the car pull over the crossing. He pulled in front of the Willis house, and I ran down the step to meet him.

George was right behind me. He said, "Get Doc back to town, did ya? What's it look like downstream?"

"Pretty bad. It was worse a few years back, but there's a mess everywhere you look. The boys have all left the picket line and, I guess, are trying to round up livestock and muck out their houses. Anybody get any sleep in there?"

"The kids is 'bout all. Fleetie and Helen is making breakfast. Come get some coffee. You must be plumb wore out."

"We're gonna need a big pot before we get that mess across the road cleaned up. Burl seen his barn tipped on its side yet?"

"He's inside, on the floor. I figured might as well let him sleep. With what he's got facing him when he wakes up, he can see it soon enough."

The three of us stood and looked through the hazy dawn at Burl and Fleetie's place. All the small riverside farm looked like the pictures of WWII battlegrounds I had seen in *Life* magazine. The river was still running five feet high through the east windows and out the west. The barn had been swept fifty yards down the riverbank and was leaning against a giant sycamore tree. When the water receded, the barn was going to be pitched at least thirty degrees off level with the front doors now facing upstream. Two of his cows, both nearly ready to calve, had either been swept or had swum to the far bank and were now stranded in a cornfield below George Saylor's place. By some miracle, the toolshed stood its ground, but the smokehouse and outhouse had tipped all the way over. The old cabin at the east corner of Burl's land stood, but water was running through the logs.

"Lordy, lordy, George. It's going to take all hands and the cook to put that place back, and then what do they have? A cabin and a shotgun just waitin' there for it to happen again."

"Low ground crops good."

"Hell, George, you can crop the land without living on the riverbank and taking the chance of being swept into Bell County every spring."

The fear of being flooded out never bothered George. His location, well above most danger, had insulated him against the misery of a water-ruined house. Daddy, on the other hand, would start to dread flood season almost as soon as Christmas passed. The pervading smell, unlike any other torturous scent you might have to endure, could be triggered in him by any moderately heavy rain. He told us often, "No matter where I traveled, even across the ocean during the war, the memory of the smell of a flood never left me." He made it plain how it bothered him that he, Burl, and the others would restore the house and the barns and they once again would be right back in the path of the next swallowing tide. The two men dropped the subject.

"Daddy, let's go in, and you can see the baby. He is so pretty. You won't believe it."

"You bet we will, but you know, Rachel, I don't know as I ever saw a ugly baby in my whole life."

As we stepped inside, all you could see were sleeping bodies strewn about the living room. They looked as if they had been bewitched where they lay. Even Mother was curled up in the horsehair armchair.

Daddy leaned over her and whispered, "Rooster's up, sleepyhead!"

Mother never woke willingly. Each morning would find her hungry for more sleep. This morning, with not even one restful hour to count as hers, her mood was light as Christmas. "Oh, Ed, the baby has taken some sugar water. The little fellow is putting up a good fight. Come in the kitchen and see him."

I went ahead of them and pushed open the door. Daddy pulled Mother up out of the chair, and they stepped in behind me.

Helen was at the stove, scraping blackened grease off the grimy top, while Fleetie held the tiny baby and rocked him in a straight-backed chair. The chair's rock and bump looked too noisy and jolting for sleep, but somehow, mountain babies loved it.

"'Bout ready to get on up the hill, Katie? We need to head up before Burl has to face the carnage across the road. It'll be harder with all of us gawking at his misery."

"You go on with Ed," Fleetie said. "Them kids will be hungry as bears. Soon as they's awake, Nessa can take them over to Susanny's. This baby and us is going to be fine!"

Daddy had a way of knowing what the other fellow was suffering. It was a big reason so many people, including me, thought he hung the moon by himself. Whatever it looked like across the tracks, Daddy figured Burl would face it better if Mother wasn't there. He was a troubling and troubled man, and as much as Fleetie would suffer from the flood, Burl would hate it even more. He would feel mocked by the very land he built on and the very stream he crossed and fished and dammed. Fleetie would take up for Burl and his foolishness. I had heard her tell her girls, "Hit's a whole lot harder to be a man. Be good to him."

Chapter 11

THE AFTERMATH

Mother, Daddy, and I slipped out the Willises' front door and headed home. I hurried on ahead of them so I could see the damage from the top of the hill, where I had a long view all the way up and down the valley. At the brow of the hill, I stopped where the hillside cut flattened out and the road went level. There below me was the whole flood tide sweeping its way to the Mississippi.

Most of the time, this headwater of the Cumberland River was little more than a meandering stream, but now it was ravenous as it swamped all the low valley. The yards of the Ross's Point community had gone missing, and the water ran straight through the front doors and out the back. Some of the lucky houses were set farther away from the river, and for these, the water climbed up the steps but seemed to stop just as it nudged the front door.

Overnight, hundred-foot poplars and sycamores seemed to be shoulder deep in the racing river. The branches, caught by the tidal wind, rose and fell and rose again above the swollen river. The lower branches were draped with debris that left them looking like they were covered with rags and tatters. I shivered at the scavenger birds as they teetered on the black water-slick limbs. The birds flew from tree to tree and cut deep outlines against the gray sky, and below them passed a veritable parade of flood-captured discards. The current had to be much stronger than it appeared because all manner of possessions bobbed and swirled past right below them.

Even cars, stoves, roof trees, baby dolls, empty bottles, spinning tires, chairs, couches, cots, stoves, oil drums, and small, nearly intact buildings rode the waves in a rampage down the valley.

As I was standing there, it struck me that all these things had been snatched from people's houses, people with kids and old people who, like the Sargeants, had little enough to begin with and now had even less. I wanted to feel lucky because my clothes were safe, my bed dry, and the smokehouse still in place, but no good feelings would come. Instead, I felt only an ache. I hurt inside for all those people who, like our neighbors, faced another uphill struggle. For some, their lives would never be the same.

Across the valley, I heard the cry of a bird dog. It echoed through the unnatural hush and rose from the muffled moan of the flood tide. I could only guess what misery he was reporting with his deep baying. For an animal who lived by what his nose told him, the watery world around him today must have had him bewildered and maybe even lost.

The water's relative quiet almost hurt my ears. It would have been more tolerable if all this destruction had come with explosions and crashing. But no, the flood somehow seemed more ominous because of the sweeping quiet of the swollen river. I fear snakes more than attacking dogs. It's the snakes' slinking silence that gets me. Today, I felt the same snake dread with the silent waters tearing at my valley all around me.

Mother and Daddy reached the top of the hill behind me. Mother looked out over the valley, and tears trickled down her face. She had shown almost no emotion through the long night. But the sight of the havoc below us had released all the tension and fear of the long hard night.

Daddy wrapped his arms around Mother and let her cry it out. No words, no platitudes, no whispers of consolation. If needed, he could talk a whip-poor-will out of its song, but today, he just held her, while the tears did their work. He was a man, and he felt compelled to protect his delicate creatures, two daughters, a baby son, and his wife. We let him. His protection gave us a comfortable place to live.

I was perfectly willing to let Daddy take charge, so I turned and looked back down the valley, and I couldn't believe my eyes. "Daddy, look, coming down the railroad."

Daddy looked too and whispered to Mother, "Katie, look! I stopped over at the settlement on my way to town and told Coburn how bad it was over here. Looks like he got the word out in a hurry."

Along the railbed below us, a dozen men and women with tools or bundles had walked around the river bend. It was at least two miles before they could reach the railroad right of way. But there they were, almost to Burl's crossing.

"They're headed for Burl's to help. I'll go back down the hill directly and get the car to make a run to town for groceries. Flood work will have everybody starving before long."

"Would you stop by and see if Aunt Roberta will come out today?" said Mother. "She can stay with the children so I can help with the cleanup."

"Katie, don't you go down there and slog through that flood filth. You'll help just as much if you stay up here and keep the washer running all day. Every stitch they own will be soaked with mud. The kids can use their wagons to pack the dirty clothes up the hill and help hang out the laundry."

"I'd like to help keep the misery from the little ones."

"It's their misery, Katie. They survive by learning how to work hard and by learning it early. Don't get into it. It's the way it is, the way it has to be. Leave it alone."

Mother froze where she stood, and Daddy and I braced for the argument that usually followed his "living in the mountains" lectures. But Mother looked past both of us. Something had alerted her. Not a movement, not exactly a sound, but something. That's the thing about Mother—she just knew things. It was a part of her, like having ten fingers and brown hair.

"Ed, something is . . ."

"What? Katie, where are—"

In a jerk, she stepped from the edge of the road, took one long stride across the road, and scrambled up the bank of the steep cut that ran along the fence line. She ran past a large boulder at the end of our small orchard and then slipped out of sight. Daddy followed her up the cut. His feet threw rock and gravel as the retaining bank began to collapse with his weight. I had to scramble up behind him with the dirt, mud, gravel, and rocks cascading around me in a small avalanche. He grabbed me and the trailing branch of a small persimmon tree and flung himself over the edge of the retaining wall. I held on for dear life as the dirt under my feet kept sliding away.

"Damn it, woman!" he called to Mother. "Slow down, you can about near fly." He gave me one more hard jerk over the wall and pulled me around the moss-covered boulder.

Just ahead, Mother was on her knees, resting beside the bunched-up figure of Dorotha. She must have curled herself under the rock overhang that jutted from under the roots of an ancient apple tree and fallen asleep.

"Dorotha!" he whispered. "What the hell . . .?"

Mother slipped an arm around as much of her as she could reach and patted her face. She whispered, "Wake up, honey, let's go to the house with Ed and get something to eat."

Dorotha jerked awake and flailed her legs and arms about as if she was going to take off running down the hill, but then she realized who we were and stopped struggling to get away. Mother helped pull her to her feet. She teetered a little before she got her feet under her.

Daddy broke in. "What are you doing out here? Why aren't you in the house with the other kids? What the devil is going on? Kathleen, I thought you had all the kids in the house with Nessa."

"Ed, it ain't Miz Hill. I went to Hobe's, but I . . ." Dorotha's voice trailed off.

"Ed, for pity's sake, you can cross-examine her after she has some warm food and dry clothes. She just wanted to come on over from Hobe's. Nobody in their right mind wants to stay up there. She cut across the hill instead of going back down the road. Isn't that what happened, sweetheart? You got lost in the dark in all that rain?"

Dorotha nodded. It was pretty thin stuff. Her being lost anywhere up this holler was not likely, and Daddy had to know it, but the story did stop him from yelling loud enough to raise the dead. To be as smart as I knew he was, I thought it was peculiar that his first inclination with something that flustered him with kids was to yell. Mother took Dorotha's hand, and I saw scratches scraped deep in it and her arm.I took her other hand, and we walked with her as we turned to walk through the orchard and across the side yard of the house and onto the back porch.

I caught the look that Mother threw Daddy. She probably thought I wouldn't notice. Parents! They hadn't caught on yet. I noticed everything around me that held even the mildest promise of excitement. Living life on a mountain had given me more than a touch of curiosity and sense enough to sit back and watch. What I didn't find out by just observing, I would fill in by using my imagination to create a likely story. Whatever had happened to Dorotha could turn out to be quite a story, one that Mother might not guess at. Hobe was mean and unpredictable. No telling what had happened to Dorotha.

Dorotha and I were slipping our feet out of muddy shoes when Aunt Roberta opened the kitchen door, every inch of her considerable height towering over us in what looked to me like alarm and irritation all mixed up.

"Roberta, how did you get here?" asked Mother.

As usual, Roberta gave no explanation. That was Roberta. She never offered to explain or ask or tell. I didn't think anything of it. Kids had it straight. We just knew that adults did not have to justify. It was as simple as milk and cookies or Kool-Aid on a hot day.

"Mercy! Look at you all, creeping up on this clean porch! Looks like you all need some warm food and a hot bath. There's fresh coffee on the stove. Let me see to this child."

Roberta and Mother exchanged a long look over Dorotha's tangled head. There it was again. I guess they thought I was totally blind to long looks and pauses. We followed Aunt Roberta and Dorotha across the kitchen to the tiny warm bathroom.

Whatever may have happened at Hobe's that night was not going to become a part of the flood's gossip. Aunt Roberta and Mother formed an alliance of silence that not even helpless Dorotha dared test with the truth. Daddy seemed convinced that Hobe had driven her out into the spring storm. I really wanted to know what damage Hobe inflicted on her to make her desperate enough to run into the black night and driving rain. But I was going to have to wait. Right now, the secret was buried in the bathroom with two mighty lionesses protecting a helpless cub.

"I'm really hungry," I announced to nobody. I could have peed on the floor, and no one would have even noticed. But I didn't. I could fix my own breakfast, and right then, it looked like if I wanted to eat, I was it.

Chapter 12

THE DUST FLIES

I grabbed some cornbread out of the warmer, poured cold buttermilk into a pint jar, capped it, and went out the screen door, planning to make my way back down the hill. I was careful not to announce where I was going. If Aunt Roberta saw me, she might decide I was too dirty to live and throw a monkey wrench in my plans.

Leatha was right outside the door, sitting on the porch, looking about as lost as Dorotha.

"Hi, Leathie. Want some cornbread?"

She shook her head without looking at me. "I want to see the baby."

"That's where I'm headed. When I came up the hill, I saw a big bunch coming over from the settlement. I bet they're already taking turns holding him."

It only took one nod before we took a long stride off the porch. We ran through the orchard that spread itself up the hill from the road cut. It made good cover from the house windows. Aunt Roberta had eyes everywhere, so it wasn't the best protection, but we made it to the top of the hill without being stopped, and we ran all the way down the hill.

Just as we got to the creek, a small army of cousins, other kin, and friends stepped off the tracks and walked through the Willis yard and up the rickety steps.

George swung open the door. "Come on in, boys. Looks like we've got a mess, ain't we?"

This was the first time I had ever seen some of these men and women near his place. Helen's sorry, wild wandering and the kids' thieving isolated them from neighbor and kin. It was pretty clear the Clement baby, swaddled in the Willis kitchen, and the flood destruction across the road had drawn them to the Willis doorstep. Since Helen had turned so peculiar and George's mining accident had crippled and slowed him down, he had been deprived of the pleasure of good visits and local gossip. He didn't even try to hide his excitement.

The men were discussing the damage spread throughout the valley and Burl's place in particular. The women, who knew the damage meant nothing so much as more hard work for them, ignored the men and slipped inside the house to see the baby. Susanna and the rest stopped dead still at the kitchen door, barely willing to breathe as Fleetie rose and carried the baby to them.

"Here he is, the image of Geneva. Isn't he pretty?"

He was too. Most babies were fairly sad little creatures with red faces and funny-shaped heads, but this one was fair and delicate. As pretty as he was, he gave you the feeling that he was not tied to us good and hard. It was a look the women all knew and dreaded. Not a family in the valley had been spared the grief of losing an infant child despite their desperate will to save each one. I got some of the same sick feeling looking at him. Somehow, I just knew he was in for a struggle he might not win. He seemed so very fragile. There was nothing robust or noisy about him. Newborns should be able to raise a ruckus when they want to. It protected them and warned everyone to pay attention to their needs. This baby was so quiet, it scared me.

"Fleetie, what did the doctor say about moving Geneva? Can we take her in Ed's car to my house?" asked Susanna.

"Dr. Parks said not to move her until he got back around to check on them both. She had a right bad time. I guess we're here for a while anyway," said Fleetie. She dropped her head, and I could almost feel her wishing she could just walk her two patients right out the door.

Susanna spoke. "We talked about it when we were walking over, and that's about what we figured. Parks don't like a lot of sashaying around when you're down. Dr. Begley's not a whole lot better. We all made it up that we could give Helen a hand with all this company."

Leatha poked me in the ribs, and I grinned. We knew all the polite talk really meant Helen's house was in for the cleaning of its life. They were not about to let one of their babies die because of Helen's dirty house. They must have decided on the walk across the valley to scrub, dust, mop, and scour until the place was, at the very least, half decent again. So to make it all right, they were going to pretend to one another and to Helen that they were helping her.

They told Helen it was so good of her to open her house during the flood, to give her ground enough to save her dignity, but dignity or not they were going to clean the house. No one was about to stop the plan and especially not the outnumbered Helen. Not only was she from across the mountain, but she also had not a single relative in a twenty-mile stretch to stand up for her.

I figured Helen knew this. She also knew well enough not to cross any of them. There had never been a time in her marriage when any of them had accepted her. She was from the first about three steps behind the pack. They had all commented at one time or another that Helen was a Webb and that "all them Webbs was strange by nature." The Webbs lived across the mountain in Leslie County. They 'stilled good moonshine, but customers were hard won. A man never knew whether he might have to face more lead than liquor going up the holler to their place.

George Willis was one of the rare people who had faced them down at their game of bluff and black powder. He had seen Helen downtown in Hyden and was fascinated by her from the first. I guess he didn't care if she was a Webb or not. He moved on his intention, and he did not intend to be driven away.

Like most bullies, the Webbs had more bluster than fight, and George and Helen were soon left alone to their courting. George's family, on the other hand, took an immediate and permanent dislike to the peculiar girl with her head in the clouds and her shoes tied over her shoulder. They took great pride in their fine two-story house perched high above the meandering Poor Fork branch of the Cumberland River. They owned and farmed wide fields in the narrow valley, where such land was scarce. George was brought up better. Why he ever fancied such a worthless girl was more irritation than mystery. His kin all admitted that Helen was a pretty little thing, but they predicted a poor end.

It was clear to both Leatha and me that before the day was over, the women intended to remove years of neglect and dirt. And since we were determined to hang around, we soon found ourselves right in the middle of it. The women about ran our legs off. I liked it, being such a good cause and all, and besides, I wanted to see the house fixed up. I loved to take something old and battered and make it look new again. Something about restoring things gave me the same good feeling as reading a really long hard book. With this many of us working, I didn't think there would be anything that wouldn't shine, gleam, or sparkle.

Later in the day, we even corralled the children and, in spite of their protests, dunked them in the double-zinc tub sitting on the back porch. The water was warm and sudsy, and after a little while, the children seemed to like it so much, they didn't want to get out. After the bath, Leatha and I braided the girls' hair and dressed them in spotless if slightly damp overalls. There was no way we could get the clothes completely dry with all the dampness surrounding us.

Susanna divided up the labor—Mary's group organized washing the curtains and throw rugs, Naomi and her daughters attacked all the scrubbing work, and Dolly's trio was assigned to the kitchen. Leatha and I followed Dolly. Once the women commenced their work, no corner, no child, and no man was safe.

George built a wash fire in the backyard, and Helen's ancient cast-iron kettle was filled with lye soap and buckets of water. The cauldron served to boil clean every garment and piece of fabric wrested from its usual place in the house. The heat that rose up from the big fire also helped dry the things hanging on the line just a little ways up the grade. Susanna appointed "pot watchers" who stirred and pummeled in turn. Even Leatha and I got to do some of that.

Naomi parceled out scrubbing rags, pieces of coarse steel wool, and scrub brushes. She was the cleaning superintendent for every window, wall, and ceiling. The women competed with one another to make sure each area received the same antiseptic treatment.

In the kitchen, we scraped and blacked the coal-burning cook stove. The grimy sink, encrusted with rust and hard water residue, stubbornly resisted Dolly and Nona until George mixed a smelly combination of acids in a small bucket and doused it thoroughly. He warned Dolly not to touch the liquid, so she wrapped her hands in heavy rags and scraped and polished until the formerly disreputable-looking sink was restored to a nearly spotless white.

The linoleum floor had long since lost any look of pattern or color under the layers of ground in dirt and grease. Here right before me was a possibility of pulling something back from oblivion. If that floor could be resurrected, it would be a near miracle. I volunteered and dragged Leatha and her two cousins, Nona and Peachy, with me. We dipped buckets of lye water from the washing cauldron and scrubbed the old rug with wire brushes. The lye water helped loosen the filth, and slowly, the dirt layers began to give way to the elbow grease. After a while, the squares and whorls of the once colorful brick-patterned linoleum began to surface. The harder we worked, the better it looked.

"It's almost pretty, Rachel," said Leatha. "Maybe it was worth scrubbing this hard." But with that, she threw her wire brush at me.

I was ready to go after her with a soaking sponge, but Susanny walked into the kitchen. "Lordy, look at that floor, would you? Come here, everybody. You won't believe what Leatha and them girls have done to this old floor."

With that, Leatha was one big grin like the whole project was her idea. That's the way it goes sometimes. You just have to strap it on and head on out.

The oak floors in each room were also scrubbed with a lye-and-soap mixture, rinsed twice, and then waxed with Johnson's paste. Then the fun started for the little kids. After the paste wax set for a little while, they were given large dry rags and were told they could slide and scoot on the floor using the rags as their sleds as much as they wanted. Their shrieks and giggles filled the house, while Mary's team was ironing. The old curtains, dispirited gray shrouds, were boiled, stirred, bleached, starched, and now werebeing ironed. The women had uncovered ruffles and folds long hidden in the dust and grime.

Fleetie had earlier set a pot of soup beans to simmer on the back of the clean stove. Leatha and I ran down two bedraggled chickens lost from their flooded roost. It took some doing, but we managed to corner the doomed birds. Susanna wrung their necks and cleaned and tucked them into a scoured roaster found in the depth of Helen's neglected oven. Dolly stirred up cornbread batter and set it aside, ready to pour into a smoky skillet for dinner. Each woman had a turn rocking the baby, moved now to the living room with his mother.

By the time we stopped at noon to eat dinner nothing in the house was undisturbed. The Willis children, after making the floor shine, had mostly scattered far from the house. During the afternoon, all the windows, sills, and sashes were finished, and the last of the clothes were gathered off the line, folded, and stacked on the steps leading to the sleeping loft. As the day wore down, the women prepared to leave a house that looked much more like it had when the old Willises lived there. The long shadows creeping down the mountain warned everyone of the work waiting for them at home.

"Lordy, I hate to leave you here, Fleetie," said Susanna.

I could feel the unspoken fear hanging in the air. If they left, no one would be there to push away the worry lurking over the fragile baby and his mother. All of us up and down the valley and into the hollers always felt safer with our kin around.

George urged each one to stay and have supper.

"Helen will drive us out with a shovel if we don't go on and git," said Dolly.

George could figure that this rare gathering had little chance of being repeated. We all hated to see the day end for our own reasons, but George seemed to hate it most. All the work had uncovered forgotten traces of his old home place. As long as Geneva could not be moved, he would be able to enjoy the cleanliness and order the women had restored to his home. It would be a brief time for him. Soon as everyone disappeared, we knew Helen would go back to her old ways.

"Leatha, go up the hill and get the young'uns," said Susanna. "We're goin' to the settlement. Gather them up so we can git. We've got to milk and get supper for Henry and the boys." Henry, her husband, and Hulan and Guy, her two grown sons, had left the house well before dawn, driving the county bulldozer to remove fallen trees and cut through mudslides on the roads. "Hurry up now."

It didn't take long for us to find them. They were sitting at the top of the hill, watching the excitement going on. Fleetie was right behind us, demanding that each of them behave and help Susanny and stay out of Henry's way. She never asked anyone to step in for her, but this time, she was helpless. She did not have a dry house, a bed, or a table to use to care for her own. I saw her shoulders slump as she watched each of the little girls trail down the long driveway to begin the long walk to Susanny's. She wrapped her arms around herself as if she was holding herself from running after them.

Dolly tried to comfort her, and she chided herself, "No use gettin' them girls stirred up. Better they go on happy." It was not her way to hold them close and refuse to let them out of her sight. "What was was," Mammy had always told her. "Nothing to be done about it."

Standing on the driveway, we could see the men across the road working to set up one of the outbuildings. The force of the water had left the sheds and lean-tos lying on their side or caught at a crazy angle against a big tree. The ravaged wreckage of broken fences, shattered windows, and debris decorating every tree branch didn't look that much improved. I had wondered for a long time why it was women could just go on and start working, but men had to stand around and spend time trying to figure out the best way. Seemed to me the best way was just to go ahead and tackle the mess. I bet if they had said, "I allow a man ought to . . ." once, they had said it a good dozen times. Daddy too. I decided it must be a man thing.

For all its fury the night before, the water had nearly dropped below the floor of the house. By morning, the house would be empty of flood water, and the work inside the house could begin in earnest. Another long day tomorrow stretched out in front of everyone willing to help.

Leatha and I immediately began begging to be allowed to spend another night together.

"Don't you two start nagging at me. You all are not spending one more night under Kathleen's feet. She hasn't taken the Sargeants to raise," said Fleetie.

We were still mumbling our disappointment when Daddy drove up in his old car and insisted on taking all the women home. There was no way to fit everyone in the Plymouth, and Dorotha and Leatha were left out of the car ride. I started begging again, and this time, Fleetie had to give in. The two girls would spend another night on this side of the river. It was going to take more maneuvering for them to be allowed to sleep at our house, but now there was a glimmer of hope. There was no place for them to sleep at the Willis house except on the floor, and even in all its clean glory, that would be pretty miserable.

The loaded Plymouth bumped over the steep crossing as Mother and Aunt Roberta appeared over the rise of the long driveway. Their arms were loaded with clean laundry.

Fleetie yelled at us, "Hurry, young'uns! Get up there and pack that load of clothes down here."

Along with clean sheets, quilts, clothes, and diapers, they were pulling the wagons loaded with covered dishes of vegetables and dessert. As soon as they got down the hill, Mother said, "Fleetie, since Geneva can't come up the hill—and I know you don't want to leave her and the baby—I brought some supper down. I thought we could all eat together tonight."

As soon as she stepped into the Willis yard, I began imploring for the necessary permission. "Mother, if Leatha and Dorotha stay at our house, we can all help with the washing and carrying. We need them, don't we?"

Aunt Roberta put her finger to her mouth and winked a warning. My furious begging and Fleetie's chagrin at the outpouring of clean laundry and supper bowls almost guaranteed the answer would be no. Fleetie would give away her most precious possession if she thought someone needed it, but when it came to accepting a kindness for herself, she just froze. By accepting, she felt shamed. People might think that she and Burl could not provide for themselves and their children. Standing there with her house in shambles and her family scattered, it was easy to see she was nearly frantic with helplessness.

Mother, in spite of her lack of clan savvy, knew this time, she had to give Fleetie the upper hand. She put her arms around Leatha and Dorotha. "Please, Fleetie, could you lend me these two to help? They're so good with the washing, and there's another big pile to feed through the wringer and hang yet. I promise to send them to bed early."

"Are you sure, Kathleen? Those two can be a caution if you don't watch."

Aunt Roberta added, "Mrs. Sargeant, they will be a big help if you can spare them."

Saying no to Roberta was not easy. Her bearing at five-foot-ten alone created a presence that could intimidate strong men, and Fleetie's tiny five-foot frame was no match for her. Afterward, Fleetie would probably quarrel with herself over letting the girls go, but right at that minute, she could not find the words to refuse this tall, commanding woman with her quiet words. Aunt Roberta was a lot like Daddy, and folks mostly did what she suggested. Fleetie had been flummoxed, and I doubt she was fooled. No one but Burl could get one over on Fleetie. I guess being extra small also made her extra feisty.

Chapter 13

THE AIR DUCTS

After the laundry was wrung out and the last line filled with the damp clothes, I tapped Leatha on the shoulder and nodded toward the cellar, our hiding place. Just as we lifted the cellar door, Janey started begging to go with us, and I let her trail along to buy some peace. If we ran away from her, she would scream to high heaven and bring Roberta and Mother both down on our heads. Better to put up with Ms. Question Box than to be given another big pile of work to do, Mother's favorite way of keeping the peace.

Leatha promised to French-braid my hair, and I was going to put hers up in my brush rollers. Yesterday, Mother gave us a brand new bottle of nail polish and warned us not to use it on our fingernails— toes only. She assured us fingernail polish was tacky unless you were at least eighteen. I wondered what it was that made fingernails at eighteen not tacky. Probably nothing. Most of the time, adults had a contrary opinion of almost everything kids like to do. It was irritating but predictable.

As we brushed our hair, we could hear Roberta and Mother's muffled voices through the air ducts. I followed the sound of their voices and went deeper into the furnace room, and I could hear every word they were saying.

"If that man hurt her, we have to make sure she is okay," said Aunt Roberta.

"We don't know what happened, Roberta. Maybe Dorotha was just mad at herself for not following the other children up here. I can't bring myself to think that Hobe would lay hands on Burl's child. The whole valley knows that Hobe abuses Mary and the children, but he has to know that if he touched that child, Burl and his kin would never let it rest. Barns could burn, gardens could get trampled, and apple trees could be found girdled. Mountain justice won't let a man who would do this off easy. It's the knowing revenge is coming that keeps much of the trouble down."

I could tell from the conversation that Roberta wasn't buying the idea that Hobe was too afraid to hurt Dorotha.

"Kathleen, it's quite possible that Dorotha was raped, and if that happened, she needs an adult to step in right now before the night terrors set in to devil her. If this is left alone to fester and corrupt, she could be hurt for life. We don't want her to be deviled with night terrors, depression, and festering angers that could haunt her. If Dorotha was just mad, she could have taken the path. Those scratches are deep. She was scared and running from something. We better be finding out what."

Their voices trailed off as they walked to the back of the house.

Before supper, Roberta walked to the bathroom door, saying she was checking to see if we were washing our hands.

"Aunt Roberta, we are old enough to get our hands clean." I was tuning up to protest loud and long, but as we walked out of the bathroom, she stepped in front of Dorotha, and the door was pushed shut to keep us out. I stopped to listen, but the sound was so muffled, I couldn't make out any of the words. Since there was no heating vent leading away from the bathroom, I had no way to listen in. After a few minutes, Leatha and I gave up and went on upstairs, even though my brain was wild with curiosity.

It was nearly an hour before Dorotha climbed up the steep staircase to join us. Her face was streaked with tears. She closed the door behind her and walked to one of the twin beds. She wrapped herself deep in the quilts and fell silent. Leatha and I exchanged looks and then made a big show of ignoring her. But we couldn't stand it long. I tiptoed across the room and pressed my ear to the cold air duct in the floor. It was a perfect sound funnel, and because of it, there were few secrets in our house, and today, it worked again. Mother was talking to Roberta.

"You mean? Why do you think she is lying? Why on earth wouldn't Dorotha let us help her?"

"Because that little one is scared sick of something. Barn burnings and dead cattle come to mind. Even the very young children know what can happen when a family is wronged. The trouble can last for years. Dorotha is more than likely scared of what might happen to her daddy and mother. Mind my words, we have not seen the end of this. There will be more."

Part 2

SCHERZO

Chapter 14

COPPERHEADS AND PICKET FENCES

Early the next morning, Daddy announced there would be no school for Jane and me. The city school had not been flooded, but dry or not, I wasn't going. All hands were needed for cleanup, and we were going to be part of a flood relief platoon. As Daddy told me, this was the perfect opportunity for me to witness firsthand the misery living on a riverbank could bring. Besides that, our neighbors needed us. He insisted that just because we lived high on the mountain didn't mean we had a free pass to excuse ourselves from the needs of our friends and kin. He went on to say that until I actually lived it, smelled it, and had been repulsed and angered by the helplessness of it, I couldn't really understand the devastation that was brought down by high water.

We woke up very early the next morning and rolled out of bed, all four of us—me, Leatha, Dorotha, and Janey. We pulled on our clothes, swallowed down Aunt Roberta's hot breakfast, and tore down the hill to join the neighbors in the big cleanup. As soon as we came to the brow of the hill, our excitement evaporated just about as fast as the creeks had poured down the mountain. Nothing in my life had prepared me for the havoc I saw around and inside the Sargeants' house. Nightmares invaded my sleep and had as long as I could remember, but even my wildest, scariest nightmares hadn't conjured up such destruction and havoc. Nothing was left in its original place.

All the furniture had been swept into a jumbled, mud-encrusted heap stacked high against the west wall of each room. Mottled sun rays from the mud-splattered windows blotted out any trace of reality.

As my eyes adjusted in the low light, loss after loss became evident. The first thing that I spotted was the basket that we had used to hold all the shower presents. Somehow, it survived, but it was now filled with mud, rags, and broken dishes. Tossed against the walls were soaked books, a twisted bedframe, and Fleetie's beautiful braided rugs, now soaked in filth. The sickening smell both burned my nose and then settled deep in my throat as if it was going to take up residence inside me. Daddy had warned me that he had never forgotten the smell of a flood. I hoped he was wrong because the smell seemed to me to be a devil's blend of burned oil, rotted vegetation, and sulfur churned up from deep in some tortured hell. Human waste, animal dung, coal oil, and dead animals also added to the hideous mix. The sickening odor worked its way into the fiber of my clothes and even into my shoe leather.

The men were busy shoveling the dead animals, frogs, snakes, cans, bottles, clothes, books, and trash of every description out the doors and the broken windows. There were several wheelbarrows under the windows and near the doors where all the damaged articles were pitched and would be later dumped onto a growing mountain of debris to be burned near the riverbank. The flood mark in the house was at five feet. A telling ring of mud measured the walls—above the mark, dry, and below the mark, water-soaked and damaged.

The women carried each piece of furniture that could be saved out to the yard, where it was scrubbed and disinfected. The older children gathered up clothing, bedding, and any other flood-dirty fabric found in the house. Burl rigged an electric hookup on the front porch, and the wringer washer ran all day as it wobbled a slow ring on the flood-warped porch. Leatha and I hung and folded load after load of clothing and bedding during what was turning out to be a long, long day. Mother and Roberta brought down our old red wagons and hauled even more clothing up the hill to be washed. Mother asked me to walk up the hill and retrieve the wagons for the next load.

I swear Burl and his brother Junior seemed to take delight in tearing down the warm morning heater and the cook stove. They were like little kids as they piled pieces all over the porch and into the yard. It took them forever to get on with the job. By the time they discussed and cussed each piece, they could have built a pyramid. "Was it broken? Did it need oil? How about scraping rust?" All of us lost patience with the project. It looked like it was going to take forever, but in spite of our doubts, sure enough, before the middle of the afternoon, the stoves were clean and reassembled. Soon, the heat from the two stoves began to dry up the dampness that remained throughout the house.

Earlier that morning, the men also built a coal fire to burn debris, limbs, broken furniture—whatever could not be repaired or cleaned and saved. Beside the bonfire, the old cooking pit fire, covered with a heavy metal grid, held the double tub that bubbled all day as Leatha and I pumped cold water to keep it full and then carried bucket after bucket of hot water to those waiting for it. It started to seem that every time we walked two feet from the well, the cry would go up for more water.

Emma and Rebecca, Fleetie's eight- and nine-year-old cousins, dug out the dishpan and washed and dried dishes, pots, pans, knives, spoons, forks, lamps, and anything else washable. Their stubby fingers would reach into the pile of discards and save pieces that only needed a good washing. As soon as they stacked their clean, wet dishes, Fleetie took a bucket of our boiling water and scalded them. She also scalded anything else that might be lying around and she thought might need a good germ killing.

"Watch out, Leatha, she is going to scald us next, as dirty as we are," I said.

"Maybe the lye soap and hot water would feel good. At least we would smell better," said Leatha.

Fleetie spent the day running from the yard of her own flooded house back to Helen's to check on the baby and Geneva. On one of her trips, she managed to put together a hot lunch of bean soup, cornbread, and a jar of sweet pickles resurrected from where we dared not ask. The lunch was hot and good, but the cold air and the hard work soon made all of us ravenous again for a good supper.

Earlier in the day, Daddy, always using his head, went to the A&P and brought home the biggest roast I had ever seen. On one of my trips up the hill, I could smell it cooking as soon as I stepped into the house. We might have all been too tired to eat, but the signs pointed to the possibility of a full table of good hot, filling food to keep our forks busy.

A weak sun managed to shine all day, and a drying breeze meandered itself down the mountain. As the long afternoon wore on, the house was again nearing normal. The mattresses and pillows were still damp and would be for days, but stacks of newly washed clothing, blankets, sheets, and towels, already dry, were put in the drawers and shelves, ready to use again. The wooden furniture, kitchen chairs, tables, and bedsteads were some dryer and placed back in their old places. The broken windows were covered with plywood, and the windows that had survived were now clear and almost shining. The sink was scrubbed back to white, and the stove was covered in a coat of fresh black. Piece by piece, the Sargeants' flooded household goods were moved back into the house.

Leatha, Dovie Rose, and I kept trying to sneak away to check out our clubhouse hidden in the back of the toolshed. We knew it had to be a mess, and no telling what might have been swept there. Every time we tried to slip away, we were caught, and more work was dumped on us. But just about quitting time, Dovie Rose and I finally slipped away. Leatha was still putting up quilts. Dovie stepped up to the door of the shed and gave it a hard push and quickly stepped inside. Her nerve-rattling scream filled the air and froze every person in the yard.

"Copperhead!" She screamed it over and over. I echoed her shriek.

Riled by the flood and startled by Dovie's sudden step, the snake sank its poison fangs deep into her ankle. No terror equaled snake terror for any of us kids living on Nolan's branch. We thought Dovie Rose would die or go blind or go blind first and then die. Every parent up and down the river brainwashed each one of us against snakes. We lived every day with warnings that snakes lived only to lie in wait and kill one of us.

The adults flew into the lifesaving dance that had been choreographed through a hundred years of indispensable experience about how to rid victims of the snake venom right now pulsing inside Dovie Rose.

Burl killed the snake and hung it high on the fence to ward off more evil. The men held Dovie Rose to the ground as Susanna burned her knife in the fire coals. Fleetie wrapped her apron strings around the leg and twisted the makeshift tourniquet. Aunt Roberta took the knife and, before the children had time to look away, cut a squat X across the bite marks. I saw Dovie's body go stiff as the knife cut her leg. Her eyes opened wide, and her mouth flew open, and she yelled and moaned at the same time. Her eyes rolled back as she fell limp in their arms. Aunt Roberta sucked blood from the cut and spat it on the ground. Blood drops stained her white apron and trickled down her chin, terrifying the little children even more, and they did not move an inch. And even more surprising, they did not cry. Somehow, they seemed to know that no one had time to comfort them anyway.

With most of the fence swept away, Daddy pulled the car right into the yard. Susanna and Dolly wrapped Dovie Rose in one of Fleetie's clean quilts and pulled her into the back seat. As soon as they shut the door, Daddy tore out of the yard and onto the county road. Total silence filled the yard as each pair of eyes followed the car long after it had disappeared down the drying ruts of the dirt road.

With everyone in the yard stricken mute, Mother took charge. She leaned over and gathered every traumatized child in her sight. She went down on her knees, and with her arms wrapped around as many as she could squeeze in, she whispered, "Would you like to go with Aunt Burba and me up the hill to bring down some supper for everybody? We'll take turns pulling everybody in the big red wagon. How about it?"

In spite of the snake bite shock, some of the children began to grin. But even a copperhead was not enough to make them forget that no one went up the road to Mrs. Ramsey's house without permission.

Each child's head hung low. They knew better than to ask to go up the forbidden hill.

Looked like Mother had forgotten her place again, but it didn't slow her down any. "Fleetie, are you about ready to stop for the day? Roberta and I have hot supper nearly ready. I need these children to help me bring it down to Helen's."

Every child in the huddled group began to smile. There it was, the excuse that would let them ride in the red wagon and go up the hill to Ed's house.

"Law' me, Kathleen, it would be a sight if any of us could eat after all this."

Mother wasn't buying it. "Men always eat. It'll perk up the children too," Mother added as she walked across the road to the railroad crossing, herding the children before her. She turned back at the top of the crossing. "I can't believe how much everybody has gotten done. In spite of all that damage from the flood and the never-ending rain and snakes on top of it, the place is actually moving back to normal."

Fleetie sighed. "Can't hardly remember normal. That must have been way back. Lordy, I've got to see about Geneva. I plumb forgot her and the baby with all this."

"Boys, you better keep sharp," said Burl. "Them copperheads always runs in pairs. There's bound to be another'un somewheres nearby."

A shudder rippled through the group.

"Smell for cucumbers," Nessa said. "Copperheads smell like cucumbers."

Mother and Roberta moved out, and they began to pull the wagon up the long hill. Roberta had the children take turns by age—the youngest first and all the others ran alongside. While they were having fun, I could not keep from watching for snakes. I never lifted my eyes from the vine-covered bank as we passed by. In spite of myself, I flinched at every shadowed movement on the steep banks. Down below us at the Sargeants', Burl moved along the fence line to set up a fallen gate. The second copperhead lay low under the pickets, and as Burl tightened the barbed wire, he leaned down for the gate. He spotted the copperhead just as it sprang to strike. It threw itself against the barred gate Burl had grabbed as a shield against the deadly strike.

"Goddamn it. There you are."

Copperheads liked a good fight, and as Burl scrambled backward, it sprang again toward his leg.

"Hellfire. Junior, pitch me the hoe," he yelled as he dodged the third strike. "Damn you! You're gonna die right now."

Catching the hoe, he continued its arc and, with one powerful downward swipe, chopped off the head. The copperhead's mouth was still stretched open, ready to sink its white fangs into Burl. With muscles still reacting, the headless snake continued to move. Burl was as white as the sky, and we saw him lean against the fence post as his knees turned to water.

Dorotha screamed as she pulled away from our little group and tore down the road and across the track. "Did it get you, Daddy?"

Her scream stiffened Burl's pride, and he stopped his shaking. As Dorotha ran toward him, he swept the hoe under the moving carcass and held it up, blocking her. She gasped and fell backward. Her tears flowed down her cheeks, and her slender body shook.

Mother and Roberta, who had gone down also, were right behind her, and as Aunt Roberta grabbed her, a steely voice warned Burl, "Dorotha, your daddy is just making sure the snake is dead."

Anger flashed from Mother's eyes as he dropped the snake. "Burl Sargeant, there has been just about enough misery today. Stop your foolishness. These children are tired, hungry, and scared half to death. They don't need to see grown men act like jackasses. I'm just about ashamed I know you," mother snapped as she turned to leave. Aunt Roberta held Dorotha and guided her back across the road.

"I'm telling you, Roberta. He makes my stomach churn. He is such a coward. He can't accept his own fear or the love of his own precious child. He leaves me in a raging fury. I cannot understand how that pitiful piece of humanity and Ed could ever be friends."

"He needs Ed more than the other way, Kathleen. Ed has always kept an eye out for him, that's all. Burl is a mountain man. He don't know nothing about being easy and gentle with women and children. He was raised rough, and that's all he's ever known. But if you are in some kind of trouble, he'll be right there to help you out. He's not all bad. He's just like all the rest of us."

"You are too good, Roberta, but somebody needs to keep an eye out for Fleetie."

She didn't say anything more. She didn't have to. Everybody standing in the yard got the point. In the past, she might have seemed tender, even soft, but the word would spread that Ed's pretty wife was more than a prissy city woman. From now on, Burl would watch his step around her.

Chapter 15

CONJURE TALK

After supper, Leatha and I slipped down the hill to wait for Daddy to get back from town. We climbed up on the old foundation stones that Burl and Fleetie had set for their house. It was not far from the Mulberry tree that the Willis kids claimed as their own. The Willis house was about thirty yards from us on a straight line from the roadside tree. It was about dark, and Helen came out and sat on her front steps, lit cigarette in hand. Because of the baby and Gen, she did not dare light up in the house.

George was sitting in the shadows, leaning his straight-backed chair against the wall. "I'd say from the looks of the place across the road, it'll be only one more night before Fleetie will move Gen and the baby across the road and you can smoke anywhere."

"Can't come too soon," said Helen.

I saw Daddy's car coming way down the county road. There was still no dust. Things were getting dryer, but no road dust yet. After about three minutes, he drove over the crossing and stopped, looking for someone. He didn't see me right away because George came down the steps and hailed him down. From my vantage point, I could hear their conversation.

"Evening, Helen, George. Where's Burl?"

"He and Fred went up on the mountain. They's helping with Hobe's cows. They got out, and some has scattered up to the tree line. What happened with Dovie Rose?"

Daddy said, "Roberta had already cleaned the strike out pretty good. Doc Begley said the leg will swell some, and it'll be awful sore, but Dovie Rose is out of danger. The worst of the sickness will hit her tomorrow. He's keeping her at the clinic tonight. Susanna and Dolly managed to keep themselves from going hysterical on me on the way to town, but the scare and worrying over Dovie Rose about did them in. I took them on home. They never said a word all the way back from town." Daddy laughed. "Can you believe those two, quiet as a church on Monday?" Daddy laughed again just remembering it.

"Go on! You know better. I ain't never heard Susanny quiet. Want some supper? They's plenty left. Miz Ramsey and your sister Roberta cooked enough for Coxey's Army. It's still good. Come on in the house and rest a spell," said George.

I knew that would be the last place he would go. The stories about how hard the women worked to clean up the place would make him leery of his muddy shoes. Daddy could probably already hear Mother fussing at him if he tracked the clean floors. She could bend the best intention into the worst kind of bad manners. Sometimes, Daddy couldn't please her no matter how good he was trying to be to the neighbors or kin.

"Thank you, George. Sounds good. Would Helen fix me a plate to take on home? I better not come in with the baby here. I've been in town, and no telling what kind of germs are on me. I'm beat too. You all about killed me today. I am a lazy man, and hard work don't agree with my creaking bones. How is the little fellow getting along?"

Helen said, "He seems good, but he's awful small. Those women won't put him down for a second. If you will wait a bit, I'll get you that plate." She opened the door and disappeared through the screen door and into the house.

George spoke up, "You might find Mrs. Ramsey sorta riled up."

"How so?"

"Burl found the second copperhead, and he was deviling Dorotha with it like he does. It set your missus off. I'm tellin' you right now, she didn't take to that at all."

"Lordy, I reckon not, George. She can't stand teasing. It sets her wild, and I'd say teasing a young'un with a copperhead is not right smart. Poor old Burl probably got his ears pinned back."

"That's it. She told him how it was. Pretty good. She's a feisty one, ain't she?"

"Feisty is not half of it. She'll fight a running buzz saw over a child, a puppy, or a kitten. You know women, George. A man oughtn't to be too wild around them."

George laughed and replied, "I'd say Burl will be tippy-toeing for a while."

Helen came out and slipped back down the steps, carrying Daddy's plate of food.

"Thank you, Helen. I'm about as hungry as I am tired. This'll be good."

"It's right tasty. You come back now. Don't be no stranger."

Daddy nodded, waved, and pulled away. I rose to catch Daddy before he drove on up the hill, and when I did, I could still hear Helen.

Helen watched the taillights disappear up the hill. "Bet that's the last time he'll be here for a spell. Don't talk to them from one year to the next, and then all at once, they's here ever' minute. Most of thems, except Fleetie's pretty snobby if you ask me."

"Things ought not be that way," George said and fell silent. George was too much away from his own kin. It was unnatural in this isolated valley. A man was expected to do right by his kin, but he had no way to get shut of Helen. I never could see any sign that he wanted too. As strange as she was, she seemed to suit George. Even with his crippled back and all the pain he had, he never said a cross word about her. But his people just never did quit yapping at her, and as far as anybody could tell, keeping peace between them was unlikely.

"Leatha, do you think Helen will ever do right by the kids and George?"

"What about George doing right? He knew she was a strange bird when he crossed that mountain and dragged her over here to have all that passel of kids. He ought to have left her alone if you ask me."

I had never thought of George as being forceful enough to drag anybody anywhere—even silly, half-crazy Helen. As I watched the two of them, I saw him shiver when a whip-poor-will started his night song. A deep, lonesome feeling began to creep up my back as I watched George. He squinted up, looking for the bird, not that it was any use. No one ever saw the whip-poor-wills. It was gloomy enough just to listen to their mournful song.

"That bird is out way too early," said George.

"It's a danger sign. Watch my word. Something is comin' we're not going to want," said Helen.

"Shut up that conjure stuff, Helen. Half the valley thinks we're plumb quare now." He stomped up the steps and into the dark house.

Helen smiled. "Just wait. The signs don't lie."

Leatha shivered, and we gave each other a long look before we slipped off the old foundation stones to make our way up the hill.

Chapter 16

CANNED PEAS

Daddy didn't wake me up this morning with his fiddle playing, ham frying, and coffee perking. His morning routine always started my day, and he loved to make fun of me because I took so long to drag myself out of the covers. This morning, I was wide awake, and with nothing stirring, I tried to turn over and go back to sleep, but the more I tried to sleep, the more awake I was. Then it struck me. There were no noises. I sat bolt upright and flew out of the covers. There was no ham frying, no doors slamming, no washer humming, and no Daddy playing his morning fiddle tunes. My imagination ran away with me as I threw my clothes on. Was everyone outside because the house was on fire? Had someone taken every one of them captive? I slammed my feet into my shoes and ran to the kitchen, where I nearly crashed into a very silent, grim Daddy.

Before I could get my mouth open to ask what was going on, Daddy pulled out his best lawyer voice and laid down the law. "Your mother is sick, really sick. You will have to get busy and take care of things."

There was something about the way his face looked that scared me. Nothing or no one on the whole earth was as important to Daddy as Mother. He could just barely put up with me. I mostly drove him crazy. It was one of those things I had to learn to live with, like my slanted eyes and crooked teeth. I didn't like it, but there was no changing it. Some things were as immovable as boulders on the mountain. Jane and Logan did a little better with him, but only Mother brought out his gentleness and care. He spoke to her with a softer voice, and what patience he had, which was pitiful little, he exerted for her benefit.

He adored her and expected me and the rest of the world for that matter to take care of her. Somehow or other, he didn't reckon that parents were the "taking care of" ones and that I was the one who was supposed to be taken care of. Not in our house. I was supposed to "take care of your Mother, hear me?" It was his mantra, and to me, it became as important as holy writ.

"Rachel, did you know she had been feeling sick since yesterday morning?"

"That's what she said last night when she asked me to give Logan his bath."

"And you didn't think that was important enough for you to tell me? You know she never complains. Is this the way you take care of your mother?"

I was determined not to cry, but I pretty well figured that Mother would be mad if I told Daddy she was sick. I clinched my teeth so no answer would have a chance of coming out of my mouth. I had learned from painful experience that anything I said would be wrong, so I just stood there, waiting.

"I am going to town and see if I can get Dr. Parks to come out before his office hours. Feed the kids, and get Jane to the bus stop. You'll have to stay home today and take care of your mother. Watch her close, and let me know everything that goes on with her. And I better not hear of you holding anything else back. Hear me?"

"Yes, sir, I hear. Do you think Dr. Parks will come this morning?"

"Probably not, but it can't hurt to ask."

He left the house at least an hour earlier than his usual time. I guessed it was because he was planning to catch the doctor on his way to his office. Daddy's office and the doctors' offices were in adjoining buildings, and he might see Dr. Parks in the shared parking lot.

I fixed breakfast without ham. Bacon, toast, cereal, and orange juice would have to do today. Jane brought her clothes to the kitchen and dressed so I could help her with her back buttons and shoestrings. I hurried her because we had to get started so she could cover the half mile across the valley to catch the public bus. Our school did not have buses. In fact, none of the schools in the whole county had buses. If you didn't walk, get a ride, or take your horse, you stayed home. Since none of us wanted to stay home, where the work was twice as hard, we walked without complaint.

Jane was only six, but she had walked it every day since school started, and there was no reason she couldn't cover the distance on her own. Logan was still in his sleepers, and I wasn't about to drag him all that way for nothing. Besides that, I needed to go to the back bedroom and see if I could help Mother. Daddy mostly stayed pretty wary of me and my motives, but Mother, on the other hand, always expected me to be her big girl. Daddy was so high and mighty, handing out orders to take care of Mother. I couldn't understand why he didn't know there was nothing in the world that I wanted to do more. I didn't need any reminder.

Jane didn't fuss about going alone, which was a surprise, and as she walked out the door with her first reader tucked in her arm, I gave her a hug, but I was careful to pull away, while she was still feeling brave. "Don't forget, Daddy will bring you home. Here is a dime, and since you get to walk to his office, you can stop at Creech Drug on the way and get ice cream."

First, she grinned at the dime, but then her bottom lip looked as though it might quiver, so I closed the door. I watched her through the window as she went down the steps one at a time. Her little fat legs gave her a steady stop on each. I almost ran after her, but I had to take care of Logan too. She would be fine, I knew, and if she was a little shaky today, it was because Mother's illness didn't sit well with any of us. Mother was so slender, you just can't help but know she had something of a light hold on solid ground anyway. On the other hand, Fleetie seemed sound and strong as if it would take more than a passing wind to move her, but not Mother. She did not seem sickly, but when she was ill, it took a long time before she was her old self again.

I brewed a cup of tea and made some broiler toast. While it was browning, I pulled down Mother's good tray from the top shelf and spread a cloth napkin in the middle. I added a glass of orange juice to the tea and toast and walked it down the hall to her room.

Her eyes were closed, but as I turned to go back to the kitchen, she whispered, "Where is Jane?"

I put the tray down beside her and pulled up a chair so I could sit near the bed. "Jane is on her way to school on the bus, and Logan is still asleep. Daddy has gone to get Dr. Parks. I am sorry you are sick."

Mother smiled, but it hurt her to talk. We were quiet as she drank the juice first and then her tea. She nibbled at the toast at first, but she pointed to her throat and shook her head. When she finished her tea, I moved the tray and left it on the chair while I straightened the covers and plumped the pillow. Before I finished, her eyes closed again, and soon, her regular breathing told me she was asleep. I pulled the cover up to her chin and felt to see if she felt hot, and she did. Someone in our family always measured how sick we were by how hot we felt, and from the heat I felt in my hand, I knew Mother was going to be sick a long time.

It was a long day of waiting. The hands on the yellow kitchen clock seemed stuck. Mother slept most of the day, and I fed Logan his lunch of noodle soup and played endless games of ninny-byes with him. He had, several months ago, called his little cars ninny-byes, and the name stuck. Both of us had tiptoed to the bedroom door almost every hour to see about Mother. I even fixed a lunch tray with more toast and tea, but she couldn't wake up long enough to eat it. Fever does that. She didn't say anything about bad dreams, but I could hear her softly moaning as if she was in pain.

The doctor didn't get to our house until almost suppertime. I was in the kitchen, making cornbread, when his jeep finally bounced up our long rutted driveway. Daddy was already on the front porch by the time I put the spoon down and got to the front door. The two of us stood there as we watched him climb the front steps, carrying his black bag. His stethoscope poked itself out of his jacket pocket, the silver earpieces ready to listen for trouble.

Doctors only came to our house when things were miserable, and they brought the black bag that had even more trouble tucked inside. In times past, I had seen things pulled out of that bag the doctor used to probe, cut, and stick. There were green bottles with liquids that tasted like poison and very well could have been as far as I knew. Standing behind Daddy seemed somehow safer than facing the doctor alone. Although I knew if the doctor said shots were needed, it wouldn't matter if I was standing behind the preacher or even God. The doctor would find me.

"Evening, Doc. Glad you could get to us. Katie's hot as fire and pale as the sheets."

"How about you let me see her, Ed? Unless you've got it all figured out yourself, and then I can just get on back to town."

I couldn't tell if he was trying to be funny or if he was irritated because Daddy tried to tell him about Mother's condition. Dr. Parks was short with most people all the time. I thought it was because he was mad at them for getting sick and making him drive out to take care of them.

Daddy held the door, and Dr. Parks stepped across the threshold and walked through the living room and the kitchen and down the long hall to the bedroom. He closed the door firmly, blocking both Daddy and me from going in with him. It was one of the few times I ever saw my Daddy bossed around by anybody. Everyone I knew acted like Daddy was some kind of king or something, and no one would ever think to tell him what to or not to do. Dr. Parks was pretty briggedy if you ask me, but of course, no one was about to ask me anything.

Daddy's good manners guaranteed that he would do exactly what Dr. Parks said to do. He might be grumpy, but when a doctor walked in your door, he carried with them the hope that his patient would get well. Whether they were cross or jolly, it didn't matter. What mattered was the magic they carried in their fingers and their scary black bag.

It was not long before he called, "Ed, I need to talk to you."

Daddy stepped into the bedroom and took two steps toward the bed.

"Don't get too close. There it is, diphtheria, and I thought I had about seen the last of this damn scourge. Where the hell did she pick this up?"

Daddy almost growled, "That cursed flood. There was no way to keep her out of that muck. She was constantly hauling food and clean clothes down there and finding ways to help. That has to be where she was exposed."

"Not likely, Ed. Nobody at the foot of the hill is down with diphtheria. They're all immune. Hardscrabble living does that. Homegrown DPT. We don't have to be concerned that Kathleen is in terrible danger. She has been vaccinated, so this should be a fairly light case, but she's thirty-three, and it won't seem light. Just to be safe, I've got to slap a quarantine sign on this house before I leave. No outside help. No one in, no one out."

"Damn it, Doc, I've got cases to try, and with this strike on, I can't be holed up here like a scared rabbit. Too much hangs in the balance for the men, and I have to get to the office. Everybody can just keep their distance if they are nervous."

"There's provision for hardship—I'll stop by the Health Department and tell Dr. Craft to put a department stamp on it tomorrow. But no one else. Rachel's almost grown, and she can pitch in. I'm going to inject the kids with a DPT booster. How old is that baby boy now?"

"He's two and talking up a storm. He's something else." You could hear the pride in Daddy's voice as he smiled the first time that day. Logan was almost three, but Daddy couldn't keep up with our ages. Logan was indeed the family's pride and joy, a boy after two girls. He was an instant hit with Mother and Daddy. Even Janey liked him at first. I guess that would change when he gets older, but for now, he was a big favorite.

The black bag slapped shut, and I shuddered as I watched Dr. Parks measure three doses of DPT into hypodermic needles. "I need to give the kids a round of this. It might be late, but it can't hurt." He winked at Daddy and raised his voice. "Rachel, I'll take you first, while your Daddy chases the other two in here. We can't have you getting sick with this stuff. You have to step in and take care of your mother and the little kids."

In spite of how much I dreaded a needle and shots, all of a sudden, I knew if I was old enough to take care of the family, I had to take my shot with my mouth shut.

To distract me, Dr. Parks started talking. "I've got to get on and see about one of the Sargeant children before dark. I'm afraid it will be another round of pneumonia. If I don't miss my guess, Burl is drinking again, trying to drown his sorrows over the flood and the strike. Fleetie and the kids are getting the worst of his blasted temper. He'll be paying for a funeral if he isn't careful."

Dr. Parks kept mumbling about Burl's mean spirit as he stood up and reached for my arm. I felt as though every cell in my body had condensed as I tried to think myself invisible. The very sound of his voice mixed with the smell of alcohol and his cigar smoke screamed danger. He plunged the needle into my arm, and somehow, I managed not to yell. It wasn't going to help if I started the two little kids crying. My brave attempt to save them didn't matter because Jane started crying just as soon as she saw the doctor, and Logan howled just in case something bad was about to happen.

A muffled rasp from beneath the piles of sick bed coverings pled our case. "Dr. Parks, don't! Logan just had his DPT three months ago."

But there was no saving us. Dr. Big Chief Medicine did not take chances on a disease that did its worst in the wicked black hours before dawn.

"Ed, see that she drinks pitchers of water. I am leaving some pills that will make her groggy for a few days. She should take them and some aspirin for the fever. Kathleen, try to eat something three times a day. Stay in the bed and out of drafts. This one can weaken adult heart muscle. Don't cheat. Rachel can take care of the the kids."

I could feel myself getting taller. It would not be long before I discovered that the rush of pride I felt at this tantalizing new responsibility was the only ego trip I would get out of this. Trouble was brewing.

With that, Dr. Parks slammed out the side door, stomped down the flagstone path, crowded into the battered jeep, and bumped down the mountain. The house felt suddenly empty as if all the light and comfort had been drained away in a heavy rain. No one was allowed to set foot in the house because of the quarantine. Our little family had to make it alone. As Dr. Parks drove down the hill, school went with him. Quarantined kids don't get to go to school, so there was no escape from what was going on at home.

Baby Logan was no longer just an artifact of family life whose needs made no impression on either of his two siblings. Now it was up to me to see that he was bathed and safe and had enough good food to eat. His care and safety sat squarely on my shoulders. The red quarantine sign hanging on the front door did more than eliminate school for Jane and me. In its place were long days of lessons in real life. I had always helped Mother. It was a requirement of being alive as far as I knew. I had chores at home, and all the kids I knew had plenty of work to do, but I was about to find out how little I actually did. The job was far larger than I had ever imagined. I yearned to run down the hill and tuck myself into the middle of the Sargeant kids. Leatha wasn't the eldest, and we had a lot more freedom down there than I could find up here on the hill.

Logan was, for the most part, still in diapers, and it took at least two changes of clothes a day to keep him presentable. So with baby things, the bed clothes, Daddy's shirts and socks, and all the other garments, the laundry was soon stacked high in the wicker basket. It had to be emptied into the Speed Queen every day. It doesn't sound all that difficult, and I have to admit, it was harder back when it had to be done on the wringer washer, but keeping clothes clean for all of us kept the washer running every day. We did not have a dryer, and all that was washed had to be piled up in the big basket and carried outside to the long wire clothesline that ran from the back corner of the house, across the side yard, and to a tough old winesap. The hanging work could not start until the wire line was wiped down. For this job, I placed a thick wet rag over the line, and squeezing hard, I walked to the end of the line and back. When I looked at my rag, there was always a black line embedded in the fibers, and if I didn't use enough pressure, the line would still leave black smudges on the clothes.

With the line clean, each garment had to be given a hard shake to remove wrinkles. The cold bit into my fingers as I snapped a garment and pinned it on the line with a wooden clothespin. I left it dangling while I bent to pick up the next cold, wet garment, snap it out, and pin it slightly overlapping the first. The proper procedure was to shake out the wet piece and pin it with two clothespins and then shake out the next piece, overlap it a bit with the first piece, and use the same clothespin with another one at the other end. The cold garments stiffened your fingers as you hurried to get them hung on the line. On bad days, the wet clothes would freeze stiff. You just had to hope they would dry enough before they froze so when you took them down, you could just roll them up for ironing.

Oh yes, let us not forget the ironing. Each garment had to have the hot iron run over every inch of it to smooth out the worst of the wrinkles. With the sick room sheets, the baby things, and the rest of the clothes, the laundry basket was never empty. It loomed there in the corner of the kitchen, constantly reminding me over and over of the work that lay just ahead. There would be no time to read a book or take a nap or go outside and sit in the swing. None of the jobs facing me were all that hard. The problem was the never-ending repetition—diapers to change, clothes to wash, sick trays to assemble, meals to prepare, and medicine to dispense. There were white pills, pink pills, and a brown noxious-smelling liquid. The relentless clock with its forever circular creep seemed to command my every move. Breakfast, lunch, dinner, bath, pills, water, clean sheets, bed tray— hurry, hurry, almost time for what comes next!

The meals were dreadful, and meal planning was nearly impossible. The only vegetable Daddy thought to carry home was canned peas. We didn't like them much anyway, which made them impossible as a staple. My biggest cooking challenge was getting each of the dishes finished at approximately the same time. Through mistakes and indigestible disasters, I learned to congeal a salad the night before and make pudding in the afternoon. At five o'clock, I knew it was time to peel potatoes, mix cornbread, flour the meat, heat the two skillets, and warm the inevitable peas. Even my hard-won organization was crowded with problems.

From her bed, Mother fretted that I would burn myself, the food, or the house. She warned me over and over to keep Logan away from the oven and, for heaven's sake, not to drop the dishrag. Awful things might follow a dropped dishrag. As far as I could see, we were just about as awful right now as I could stand. I guess I wasn't considering starvation, blindness, beggars, and the end of the world. Time after time, when Mother would call, I would leave the stove to check on her, and something in my absence would scorch if not outright burn to a crisp.

The Health Department officer refused to remove the quarantine sign for three weeks. It was blessedly ignored by a few neighbors who ventured up the hill. Fleetie and Geneva carried in a black pot of soup beans, cornbread, and applesauce. Susanna had sent over a can of sauerkraut and two cans of homemade vegetable soup. Two feasts without a pea in sight, but the company was as much a treat as the food. We had almost forgotten how good it was to see someone else. The visits were a great tonic for Mother. She always perked up for their visit and for several hours afterward.

But even our neighbors' best efforts didn't put much of a dent in the hardship. The days moved by slowly, covered in a blur of work. The corners of each room seemed draped in gray shadows. All laughter receded far away. It seemed to slip out the windows and down the mountain. Little sister and baby were good beyond reason, but play for them was much too quiet, and for me, there was no time for play with them.

For all the trouble packed behind that red quarantine sign, nothing matched the black hole of misery caused by the separation from Leatha and her family. I felt as if laughter had been scraped off like dead skin, and there were few places on me that did not ache. My feet hurt, my lips were chapped, and I was hungry most of the time.

The Sargeants had no phone, and both Leatha and I were too scared to sneak off up the mountain to one of our hiding places. I was scared the baby would swallow some deadly poison or Jane would set the house on fire. Leatha was scared she would die of diphtheria. There was small chance of that, as full of DPT serum as we both were. We stayed apart, even though we were actually close enough so that a good, strong rock throw could have alerted either one of us.

March always had a surprise or two tucked into its long stay. On one of those special days, the sun found itself in a blue sky. Soft breezes and cotton-candy clouds crowded around to enjoy the winter break.

That glorious morning, Mother called me to her room. "Rachel, I want to put on my clothes and get out of this bed. It is time for me to be well."

"Mother, you have to be careful. Dr. Parks said you could hurt your heart."

"My heart is fine. The very best medicine I could have is to stand in my kitchen and see about things. My legs are bound to wobble at first. That's why I need you to help. Will you be my big girl and help me get dressed so I can surprise everyone?"

"Why don't you put on your robe first? I'll help you get in the tub after breakfast, and then you can get dressed. Will that feel good?"

"It will be delicious. Just don't let me fall flat on my bottom. The last thing we need around here is for me to get my bad ankle bummed up."

She walked alone with me close behind her as we surprised Daddy in the kitchen. He was struggling with the blackened coffee pot and about jumped out of his socks when she spoke. "I'm up, and I am not going back to bed."

"Lord have mercy, Katie Bell. You scared the fool out of me. Look at you. You're skinny as a stick! That robe wraps twice around your middle."

He didn't see that her slender feet could not control the floppy slippers. She kept walking right out of them. Dark circles made her eyes look huge behind the wisps of her hair that escaped the ribbon. Daddy wrapped his arms around her and held her as if she had been away for weeks. He helped her sit down at the kitchen table.

"Rach, fix your mother a cup of tea. See her pretty hands back on the table? It won't be long now before she'll be good as new. Are you sure you're ready? Parks said diphtheria could damage your heart. We can manage for a while longer. I'll stop by and see if Roberta won't come back now. She will love to give you a hand."

"I am sure. I haven't had any fever for several days, but I'd love to have Roberta just for the company if nothing else. Do you think she'll come?"

The long illness had been hard on all of us, and for Mother, being separated from Aunt Roberta might have been the hardest. She was such a part of our lives, an irreplaceable relative who cemented the relationship with her common sense and good humor. Almost without warning, the entire family had fallen into her territory, and she didn't plan to let us escape—nor did we want to.

Two years back, Aunt Roberta accompanied her son James to Daddy's office to attend to a property dispute. The process proved to be long and costly. To save James's dignity, Daddy asked if either of them would be interested in lending the family a hand on our hillside farm. James said yes, but Aunt Roberta was silent. Daddy told us later that he knew she wasn't sure how two women in the same house fussing over the same children would work. He started working his people magic.

"Sister, my girls need someone to help teach them to be ladies. Would you consider sharing your time with them?"

He told Mother that Aunt Roberta, rising to every cubit of her considerable height, answered, "I suppose I can give the children some attention for a spell."

That was the contract, and for all the years that Aunt Roberta lent her considerable talents to our household, there was never any definition of the word *spell*. No one in their right mind would have ever considered her anything but Aunt Roberta—Burba to Logan—and she was as integral a part of the composition of the family as the other five of us. If Aunt Roberta said it in the household, it was truth. If she requested it, it was accomplished. If she was happy, things glowed. If she was irritated, we drooped.

There would never be a time in Mother's life after Aunt Roberta agreed to "help out" that she didn't cherish her friendship. The two women, far from being as different as a mountain-born and a city-born might suggest, were cut from the same cloth—regal, sensitive, intuitive women who dominated their families' lives.

It would be good to have her back with us, and no one in the family would appreciate her more than I would. I had found out that caring for a family was hard, never-ending work, and I was not yet old enough to appreciate the finer aspects of the craft. It was all just hard. Praise be for Aunt Roberta.

Chapter 17

Buses and Trains

I finally went back to school. While Daddy was adamant about living in the country, he was equally determined that his children go to school in town. The rural schools were poorly funded in the large coal-mining county, and the city school was not much better, but at least indoor bathrooms were standard. Equalized funding was as yet nonexistent.

Daddy reasoned that the children from the homes of merchants and professionals might ensure more classroom stimulation for us. None of this reasoning occurred to me at the time. I would have much preferred getting to walk to school with Leatha, her sisters, and the other kids from the valley. The two-room schoolhouse, with its outdoor privy and hand-dug well, was much more fun. The recesses were longer, we ate lunch under the trees, and if you asked first, you got to go to the well and bring in a bucket of water. I only got to do that once, but I remember how deliciously cold the water was out of the metal dipper right after I pulled it up. The only times I got to go with Leatha was when the city school had a teacher day, and they were held in the early fall or spring. The weather was perfect, and no one expected me to answer questions or read aloud or do math problems on the board. I hated math, and at the Ross's Point school, I was allowed to completely ignore it.

Daddy's struggle to escape the coal camp left him branded with a fanatical appreciation of education. No sacrifice of transportation, time, or money was too great if there was even the slightest chance it would ensure a better education.

There were days when the trip to the gritty county seat for school and work was an adventure. Before Daddy bought the old car, we had a long trek across the valley to catch the VTC, a bus line proudly named for its owner, Vester Transportation Company. The shortest distance to the state road was down the steep road to the railroad crossing across the county road, a short walk through Burl and Fleetie's yard, past the grapevines, through the back gate and garden, and to the river path. That path led to Burl's little fishing boat, which had to be poled across the river. Then the traveler had to climb up the steep bank on the far side of the river and walk along the Hensley cornfield, through Hiram Wilson's back gate, and up their steep driveway to the road.

It never occurred to me that there might be an easier way to get to school or the office. Being on the trip with Daddy legitimized it. Something about the morning trip always put Daddy in high spirits. He used the time for delicious stories about when he was a little boy. Sometimes, the stories were about us when we were babies, and these were Jane's favorite.

Only after I was a grown woman would I realize that Daddy's high spirits and invented fun was a cover. He hated for his family to have to traipse across the valley like wandering gypsies. He was silently angry at forces that prevented him from providing better transportation. I never knew if Daddy ever understood how much I cherished the gift of those early mountain mornings or if he always just felt ashamed at not having the car he felt we needed.

But the car did not save me from the afternoon trip home. I was forbidden to use the boat without Daddy. That meant I left the bus two miles further up the road, at the river bend. There, it curved enough for walkers to cross on dry land to the railroad. Rain, snow, blistering heat—the school children plowed through it all. While the morning journey was fun because Daddy was there, the afternoon walk home

129

was nothing but a tiresome trudge. It took all my ingenuity to kill the boredom of the two-mile hike. I walked the rail, stretching the time. I stayed on until no balance-beam gymnast could have beaten me. I threw rocks toward the river, scaring up flutters of birds. I practiced taking longer steps by skipping a crosstie. On the rare occasions when the valley kids were walking at the same time I was, we raced one another, dug lead out of the railbed gravel, and laid doomed pennies on the tracks.

Once in a while, I walked the county road that nearly paralleled the tracks, even though that too was forbidden because of the rare car or truck that might pass by. The road seemed shorter because walking the crossties forced me to shorten my steps.

But none of the tricks I devised rivaled the delicious thrill of grabbing the iron handholds on the side of a slow-moving freight and riding all the way to the crossing. The noise of the train gave clear warning of the danger I was courting. I remembered too well Tuck, Daddy's beloved English setter, left in two pieces beside the track. The horror should have warned me of the danger, but I reasoned I could hold on to the moving train and poor old Tuck couldn't.

What actually saved me was the scarcity of slow-moving trains. By the time the coal trains reached Ross's Point from the railhead at Lynch, they had worked up a good head of steam and were making good time. I might ignore the danger of hitching a ride on a slow-moving freight, but I wasn't suicidal. I knew better than to try to catch a ride on a train clipping along at thirty-five to forty miles an hour.

The changing mountain scenery got no more than a passing glance from me. Scenes of the tinges of bloom skirting the mountain in spring, the wild disorder of autumn color, or stark contrasts of winter was as commonplace to me as rocks. The day would come when the very marrow in my bones would ache to see that sight again but not when it was all there for the taking. The two-mile walk always loomed as the enemy and never more than on the first day back after being quarantined.

I had basked in the unaccustomed curiosity and attention at recess. Lunchtime brought on an orgy of sandwich swapping. For once," my lunch seemed especially attractive. The teacher spent extra time piling on past assignments. The head teacher even welcomed me back. But when that day was over, I dreaded the long traipse before I would be home again.

Near the end of the railroad walk, I took a shortcut and climbed up the steep bank, using the half-buried boulders as handholds. It was an old cattle path that circled and twisted itself up to the gate that opened to our driveway. Walking between the boulders and around the trees reminded me of the Saturday cowboy movies I sometimes got to see in town. It was a dream place to play imaginary scenes of desperate pioneers, masked robbers, and hungry mountain lions. At the top, I opened the picket gate and climbed up the eight front steps. When I opened the screen door, there, standing right in the middle of the living room, was Aunt Roberta. I fell on her neck. Neither one of was able to outhug the other.

"Just look at you. You must be all of five-foot-four now."

"No, just five-three, but Mother says I will grow more and be as tall as she is pretty soon."

"Well, pretty, I say. You have Pappy's hazel eyes and Mamaw's brown hair. When did you lose all those blond curls?"

"Back a while. I keep trying to bleach it back out with lemon juice, but it looks like the brown is here to stay."

"Well, good, it goes with those sun-tanned cheeks and freckles."

"I hate freckles, and buttermilk doesn't do a thing but make me smell like cornbread."

Aunt Roberta laughed her deep, down-to-the-bottom-of-the-belly laugh, "Cornbread or lemon juice, you are a pretty sight for these eyes."

On that bright March day, I knew that the tall blond woman standing in our front room made the house different. It was beyond the scope of my experience to know just exactly how different, but I knew that home was finally in one piece again.

Chapter 18

DECORATION DAY

It had been a month since the flood, and the earth was busy healing itself. Leaves surrounded the tattered debris left hanging from tree limbs. Wild grasses and plants pushed up to cover eroded banks. Each flooded house had been made livable again, with yards swept clean and white laundry flapping on rebuilt clotheslines. The early flood opened spring's gates. Mules and plows turned the earth from morning till dark. Lloyd Willis, with his two mules, worked the wide twenty-acre fields just across the river from our house and the Sargeants' until the wide brown swath of land lay deep and fertile and ready for seeding.

Sarvis dotted the mountains with their tiny white blooms, soon to be followed by the blossoming white dogwoods and wild crab apples. This explosion of white ran together until you might swear you were looking at a late snow. Added to that display, clusters of violets along with the pale yellow daffodils began to push out of the ground. First one and then another seemed determined to win the spring race. At every house, there was a field, a garden, or a vegetable patch, and the valley from a distance might have resembled the inside of a beehive. There were people everywhere you looked working at small flower gardens, big vegetable gardens, cornfields, and fence lines. The long bitter winter, the coal miners' continuing strike, and the flood left every family ready for gardens and fields.

Decoration Day almost slipped up on Poor Fork. The miners' strike, the flood, and the hard work in fields and gardens had just about squelched any thought of a day off. But Decoration, for all its somber origin, was an annual highlight for all of us. As busy as the valley was with planting, spare moments had been stolen for crafting bushels of crepe paper flowers for each family to carry to their small cemeteries. Few of the men spared any time for the actual care of the graves, but they could usually manage to find time to target shoot, drink beer, and gather around for man talk. They probably nursed the same family memories the women clung to in the cemetery gatherings on the mountains, but the men had to protect their manliness, and so they were forced to use bluster and beer to celebrate their past.

I loved Decoration, but as sure as it came, Mother had a contrary opinion, and this year was no different. I had spent the last three nights down at Leatha's covering the wires with green crepe paper to serve as a base for the blooms that the older women would fashion. I loved to watch their fingers mold and crease each petal. There was almost a magic to it. But Mother clucked her disapproval of crepe paper flowers. I dreaded to hear her start fussing about them year after year. Poor Daddy got the brunt of the complaint. It hardly seemed fair since I was the one slipping off to help make the flowers. He wouldn't know the top from the stem of any of them.

I heard her ask Daddy, "Ed, why on earth do they spend all those hours spinning out paper flowers when the mountains are alive with real beauty—growing free for the taking?"

"That's the point, Katie. What kind of gift is it for their dead if the flowers are free for the picking?"

"So real beauty doesn't count? Is that it?"

Daddy gave up on the argument early, grabbed his brief case, and took off to the back of the house.

I was still sitting at the dinner table and grabbed my chance to ask her once again to go with us. "Mother, if you look close, you'll see there's a real art to it," I said. "You can't imagine how much hard work it takes to make them. You have to really pay attention to learn how to fold, bend, and twist so the flowers turn out pretty."

"Well, who would want to? It is just cheap, garish paper that will bleed and fade in the first rain."

"Paper flowers are just part of it. A lot of the fun is that everyone works together. We grub out weeds, scrub the stones, right the ones that have fallen, trim tree branches, and make the cemeteries straight and clean again."

"Sounds to me like you are doing a lot of hard work that I could use around here to keep this place running."

"But, Mother, doing the work is the way to honor the kinfolks that have gone on. If you go with us once, you'll see for yourself."

"Don't think you're fooling me. I know you have been down there messing with that stuff for days. You and Jane can go, but I can just see me piling that stuff on graves of people I never even knew. I need to go to Richmond so I can place real flowers on my family graves. But Richmond might as well be on the moon."

"Mother, the train stops in town every day. You can get on it and ride to Richmond. I promise I'll work hard and help Daddy take care of the kids. We'll get along."

"You might get along, but the two little ones would starve or turn green from eating peas, which is the only thing your Daddy can think to buy from the grocery. I can't go, and I'm not going up on that godforsaken hill either."

She stormed out of the room. We had this argument every year, and I had just lost it again. Daddy was going to be taking depositions in Hyden, so he wouldn't be going either—not that he ever went anyway. The men were good about taking care of the funerals with all the digging, making the temporary cross, and carrying the casket, but after that, they mostly stayed away from the cemeteries. It didn't occur to me to pout about it. That was just the way it was, and as far as I can tell, it was not likely to change, but I loved Decoration anyway. The flowers might be paper, but the day was pure gold.

As I sat there at the table alone, I let my mind wander over the fun that was coming at Decoration. Early in the morning, just as soon as we would set our feet and eyes up the mountain to the first of the three graveyards, the stories would begin. Each of the women in turn would tell about mothers, sisters, aunts, uncles, brothers, great-grands, and great-great-grands as far back as memory ran. Before the day was over, everyone would be drawn in and would cry, tease, laugh, and relive the past. Even if we were silent for a few minutes, which was rare, the silences served to give homage to the bonds of life to earth and earth to death.

Decoration Day honored our dead right here in the midst of life. This annual trek up the mountain taught me about life's respect for death and our relatives now gone. It was paper flowers because creating paper flowers was a gift. It was about taking food baskets because the living were required to go on living and about remembering and caring.

Mother had not come back into the kitchen, so I began clearing the table, but my mind went right back to the fun just ahead. For Jane and me, Decoration was a day to spend absolutely free to revel in our daddy's culture. Mother worked hard to smother most of Daddy's early way of life from our daily existence. We rarely got to see as much of it as would be showered all around us during Decoration. Growing up with parents from two cultures, I always felt pulled between the two. If I leaned toward Mother's way of life, then I felt guilty about Daddy being left out, and besides, Leatha and all the rest of the Sargeants, even hateful old Burl, felt as much a part of my family as those of us who lived at the top of the hill. Decoration was one place where their competition seemed not as important. It was almost as good as a free jump on a Monopoly board filled with opposing hotels.

It worked better for everyone if Jane and I spent the night with the Sargeants so we would be handy to start off before daylight. Sleeping over was the first adventure—seven children, two beds. Each bed was a tumble of arms and legs laced together in a futile search for a bit of mattress. No one thought about comfort. The pure joy of being together with the promise of Decoration was enough for all of us.

Well before daylight, we gobbled down Fleetie's breakfast of cold biscuits, apple butter, and strong coffee. It was doubly delicious to Jane and me because no such menu ever appeared on our table. Coffee was forbidden, and cold biscuits were broken up for chickens. Nessa had braided all six heads so tightly, our eyes slanted. She was the eldest and the only one whose hair was allowed to flow loose. Even Fleetie's curly hair was pulled into a stern knot, a total waste. In an hour or two, all her auburn ringlets would work out of the pins and, to her way of thinking, leave her looking disrespectful to the dead. The truth was that when her hair turned curly like that, she looked younger and sweeter. Her dead relatives probably liked seeing her look like she did when she was a little girl.

As we left the yard, all of us picked up something: a picnic basket, baskets of paper flowers, buckets for water, rags, heavy brushes, and tools, especially the grubbing hoe. It had been a year since anyone had been to the grave sites to work, and the year's growth would be heavy. During the first mile of our walk, we were joined by other relatives from both sides, and they also carried the same loads we did. Death was never the focus during the trek up the railroad bed. There were no long faces on Decoration, and each new person melted into the group, laughing and teasing.

We left the railroad track and began the long climb up a narrow mountain path, steep enough to have been carved by mountain goats. It wound itself around the hill and then turned back on itself so that the front of the group would pass the back half, each going a different direction.

The boys used the pass to start on one another. "Anybody can be slow. What's the weather like up there? We've got the food. I've got the grubbin' hoe. You'll have to dig with your hands." The banter broke the group into two camps—leaders and followers.

"Remember when Dorotha was little and got so far behind, she sat down and refused to go another step?" asked Fleetie.

"I remember I had to go back and get her lazy bones and carry her the rest of the way," said Nessa.

"Don't start, Nessa, I had growing pains."

"You had growing pains between your ears. You were being plain good for nothing if you ask me."

Ahead, they could see the front of the group pass through the moss-covered rock fence at the Howard cemetery. As each of us walked through, we fell into teams. The adults gravitated toward a favorite chore, and the kids picked adults to follow. No one was too young or too old. The work of Decoration challenged every person making the trip. Without the hard work, there was no reason for the hours of crafting flowers, the long walk, and the anticipation. Proper respect was paid only if we poured enough sweat over it.

I stayed close to Fleetie and her kids most of the morning. She was the stone cleaner, and we had to make trip after trip down the nearby ravine to carry water. With scraping and hard brushing, she slowly removed the gathered moss, droppings, and traces of ivy tendrils. When they were cleaned, she poured a whole bucket over each stone.

Leatha teased Fleetie, "Mommy, you trying to baptize them all over again?" She dodged a swat from her mother's stiff long-handled brush.

By midmorning, Dorotha took pity on us and helped carry the heavy water buckets, while Susanna found a shady spot to rest. Dolly and Susanna had already helped the others attack the heavy growth of weeds and scrubby bushes. They pulled out every root and snag.

Fleetie wiped her face and leaned back against a big oak tree. "Whooee, I'm about wore out. You kids decorate, while we catch our breath." There were no sweeter words. Now the fun began.

We moved the baskets nearer the graves and began to select the brilliant-colored flowers. There were roses, daisies, daffodils, carnations, dahlias, lilies, and even the very-hard-to-make hydrangea. We arranged the flowers on the cleared graves under the shadow of each clean stone. We fell into an easy pattern of movement. First, we placed one color, perhaps yellow then red, followed by pink, green, and orange. Each grave received a bouquet nestled close to the stone with sprays of paper leaves trailing across the length of the mounded earth. Each family had its own distinctive decorating style. The Hensleys across the valley covered their graves completely. The Clems encircled the graves. The Howards used only green and yellow flowers. Some had even made arrangements that perched on top of the headstones.

The vivid colors made the little cemetery come alive. It looked as carefree as a day at the circus. You might think a giant piñata had spilled every hue in the rainbow across the green earth and gray stones. No trace of neglect remained in the small cemetery. The riot of color was matched by the outpouring of laughter and teasing. I wondered if down in the depths of their resting places, the ancestors and relatives were smiling too.

While we finished distributing the garlands and bouquets, the women opened the food baskets and spread a meal of cornbread, fatback, chow-chow, and slices of dried apple stack cake. Dorotha carried up one last bucket of cold spring water for drinking, and the feasting began. The phrase "remember when" began story after story about those sleeping under the flowers.

"Remember when Pappy got caught in the clothesline trying to catch a coon?"

"Remember when these poor little twins were born, and it snowed for two weeks?"

"Remember how Aunt Ethel could sing like a bird, and all Uncle Ned could do was pat his foot?"

"That was a pair if ever you saw one."

There were stories and more stories, and I relished every one of them and promised myself that I would write them down so I would never forget them. I was fascinated by the drama of years and folks gone by. None of us seemed to get tired of hearing the old tales, but there was another cemetery to clear, and the picnic had to end. Every one of us would have lingered, but both sides of the clan had to be remembered.

As our group moved across the brow of the hill, I wondered if maybe we had made the ancient Clems who were resting deep in the ground happy for a little while. Maybe they were basking in all the bright colors and the memory of the lively visit. I had never had any appetite for spook stories and cemetery ghostings. One work trip on Decoration Day was good medicine for that silliness. Those graves held real people who had left us but whose stories were important to those still living. If we were lucky, their spirits might linger, but there were no made-up sheet-wrapped ghosts.

We left the old cemetery in a line. I, along with Leatha and some of the other kids, walked behind Fleetie, but her steps slowed just at the edge of the pines that enclosed the Clement graves. Just a few dozen feet to the right of the cemetery, she pointed out a late blooming dogwood.

"Look, Rachel! I remember how Pappy loved them dogwood blooms. He told the crucifixion story to everyone that he could chase down ever' time it bloomed. I'm gonna cut some for his grave. You go on. I'll catch up in a minute," Fleetie said.

She pulled out her knife and began to trim a large blooming branch. The rest of the kids who were walking behind us headed on down the path. Leatha and I waited.

Fleetie carried her branch of bloom back to Daddy Clement's grave. Just as she bent over, I saw her shiver as if she'd felt an uneasy chill. I followed her eyes as she looked across the stone. She stepped back and then went still as a statue. Her keen eyes searched the dark shadows along the back of the short fence.

I heard her whisper to herself, "Fleet, don't you be acting quare." She even took a step forward as though she was trying to shake it off, but in spite of herself, Daddy Clement was right there. I could feel it too, but mostly, I could see what was happening because of Fleetie's reaction.

She said, "Don't go? Why, Pap, I ain't going nowhere in this world. Rest now. We're all fine." She closed her eyes and shook her head as if to shut out something she didn't want to hear. Then I heard it myself, muffled and quiet but real.

"I say, girl, don't you do it. You need to stay near. Hear me now. Don't never go."

Fleetie turned her eyes from the stone and walked toward the cluster of pine trees, looking as if she was following someone.

Leatha was watching her and called out, "Mommy! Where you going?"

Fleetie turned away and crossed the cemetery and stood looking into the deep woods. "I'm coming. Just go on, I'll catch up," she yelled down the long stony path. She shivered and glanced back into the darkness at the woody shadows once more, but the moment must have passed because she turned and walked back to where we were waiting. Sensible, hard-working Fleetie was not given to conjure, but the rest of the day, I could see her looking off as if her mind was far away, and I could not shake off the feeling that Pap Clement had been near.

We moved across the steep path on the way up over the summit of the mountain to the Howards' burying ground. There was where Burl's people were buried, and I imagined that they too were waiting for the gaiety and release of Decoration. There was no time to linger.

Quarreling under her breath, Fleetie hurried us the rest of the way along the mountain path. "I must be getting funny in the head," she whispered aloud but not really to us.

Leatha winked at me and rolled her eyes. It was her "parents drive me crazy" look. She had not heard Pap like I had, and I didn't know for sure that I had really heard him or just thought I did. Maybe I was the one getting funny in the head.

We caught up with the rest of the group, and Fleetie began scraping the nearest moss-covered stone. "Leatha, get me a bucket of water right quick now."

Everyone was back at work again, and the comfortable ritual of Decoration continued. The Howard plot was more open, and the additional sunlight made for extra vine and weed growth. Before we could even finish the cleaning and grubbing, we could hear the gunshots and firecrackers in the valley.

"Lordy, they have started that old drinking early," said Susanna. "You'd think they could wait until the flowers was spread."

"I never knowed a man who could wait for nuthin'," said Nessa.

"I swear, Nessa! You're awful young to be so soured on men," said Dolly.

"I'm sixteen and old enough to marry one of them if I was that silly, which I'm not."

"Pretty big talk," said Dorotha, "for someone who gets all moon-eyed when ole Clifford Hensley walks in the church door."

"You're just jealous 'cause no one would ever look twice at you with your old long legs and big mouth."

The girls were heating up for a fight, and I knew it would not be long before Fleetie would pounce. She almost never let us get into good quarrels, probably because Burl created enough arguing for the whole family.

"I swear, Susanny, it's bad enough that Burl's probably already drinking. The last thing I need is for those two girls to be going at it like a couple of banty roosters." She called across the stones and mounds, "That is all I want to hear of that talk. Stop it and get to work. We've got to hurry up and get on down off this mountain."

Most of us were so busy spreading the flowers and paid little or no attention to the racket the men were making in the valley. The wonder of a day filled with a picnic, paper flowers, and the rill of laughter spilling around us was worth stretching out as far as a day could go.

The older children kept up the stories of the personal histories of relatives buried far below the headstones. Uncle Lige had a peg leg to replace the one he lost across the ocean fighting the Huns. Aunt Mary had a glass eye. Her brother poked out the real one with a sharp stick playing Indians. Sook was the meanest woman in three counties. She had shot two husbands and poisoned another one. But she loved her children and left them with a whole trunk of silver she had stolen somewhere in her younger days. Daisy died from eating green apples, and her mother purely pined away for her. They were buried in the same grave.

Each story, repeated year after year, became more or less embellished depending on the amount of sand kicked up by the original subject. Poor Uncle John, plain as an old shoe, died in his bed after seventy-five long years of hard work. He merited no more than a reading of his stone, but Black Davy's wicked ways could hold us spellbound for an hour or more. He wore a patch over one eye and had a long scar running from his cheek across the crease in his chin. Stories said he had once been a pirate. From the tales that were told about him, it was not hard to believe that he might have been a pirate or anything else bad we might think up.

In spite of the fun, the day was getting short. Shadows creeping from up in behind the mountain peaks began to draw the valley together. The women and children picked up the tools and stacked the now empty baskets. As we started down the mountain, I stopped and turned back. I scrunched up my eyes, and the whole cemetery seemed to glow. I wanted to be able to visit this place in my mind if I ever started worrying about dying and the dead and what it all meant. Today broke it down for me. We lived and made our mark. We died, and our clan took care of our passing year after year and on and on. Life and death was a circle that tied all of us together. There was nothing to worry about if we just remembered Decoration.

I hoped that this year, I could tell Mother enough about how much fun it was to work together and make the cemetery plots come alive again. She was big on story writing. I just knew she would love hearing the tales of all the long-dead relatives if she would just give in and go with us next year. But I figured she had spent the whole day grieving for Grandmother Bertha, gone now all these years.

Mother was just my age, fourteen, when she lost her mother, and it seemed to me that it hurt her as much now as it must have back then. Any chatter today about our cemetery decorating would be as unwelcome to her as a gift of the colorful paper flowers we placed on the kinfolks' graves. Fleetie seemed to understand much more than I about how lonely Mother had to be at times like these.

Just before we started down, she handed me an arrowhead. "Rachel, would you give this to Kathleen? It is a caution how much she likes to find Indian things. I picked it up last night on the riverbank and thought of her. Today has probably been right smart lonesome for her."

"She'll love it, Fleetie. Thank you so much. I know this will make her feel better."

Down below, shouts and gunshots from the men rose to meet us. Smiles dropped away, and the women's expressions changed. Suddenly, all of them seemed older, more set in the work and duty patterns of their normal lives. As we moved down the path, I saw shoulders stiffen and strides lengthen. Even the youngest child in the group knew the best part of Decoration was over.

Chapter 19

PINK JELLY

The summer after the big flood, the old-timers on the front porch of the store swore that good old Mother Nature was making it up to us by sending a patch of growing weather so fine, fruits and vegetables would fairly jump out at us. Since they mostly lied about everything else they "allowed" on that porch, it surprised me that sure enough, June apple trees, red and yellow, were bent low by early summer. Bushels of the tart fruit promised applesauce and apple jelly off every tree. Even the oldest, most gnarled snag of a tree seemed bent on getting in on the show. All up and down the valley, everyone with even one tree in their patch of ground dragged out their black pots and uncovered the fire pits that would keep applesauce bubbling.

It took hours of boiling and stirring for a bushel of apples to reach the right consistency for canning. Apple butter took even longer. Summer apples worked better for butter, and spring apples made the best sauce and jelly.

A true apple jelly was a glorious, transparent pink, the color of an early morning sunrise. To reach that prized level of color, with a delicate tart taste to match, required many more painstaking steps than making applesauce. Each cooking of apples had to be strained over and over to remove any hint of apple pulp, peeling, or seeds. The juice from the straining, added to refined sugar, was brought to a full rolling boil. After what would seem like hours of cooking and stirring, the cook checked the jelly by pouring a spoonful off a metal spoon. If the jelly slowed, collected, and then fell with one dramatic plop into the black pot, it was ready. At that moment, it had to be poured slowly into small jars and left to cool overnight while the jelly set.

A golden jelly was also possible, but the truest jelly, the test of the maker and the signature of an apple artist, was a row of jelly jars filled with a treat that was so transparent and pink, it flattered the hand that held it aloft to the light.

Mr. Ben had planted a dozen early-harvest trees on our hillside farm years before. All his life, everywhere he lived, he planted fruit trees. An abundance of pear, apple, and peach trees would bear fruit long after he had moved on. I loved our orchard for the bloom, shade, fruit, tire swings, and most of all, the climbing. An apple tree was a glorious place to hide and read a book. I could stay perched high up in the tree for hours with lots of ripe apples to eat and a good book.

One Saturday morning, with the trees full, Mother and I walked to the orchard to gather a pan of the windfalls to fry for breakfast, and as we picked up the apples, she complained about the waste lying all around her because we could not possibly can them all.

"Grab your pan, Rachel. I have an idea. Let's get back to the house."

As soon as she hit the porch, here she went with the orders. "Hurry, girls, get out all the applesauce jars in the basement and line them up. We're going to have company!"

With that, she flew into the kitchen to tell Daddy she was going down the hill to get Fleetie and any other neighbors who would like to come up and can apples. Daddy sat there, watching her dash out of the kitchen with any hope of fried apples sailing along with her.

"Hey, Rach, guess you wouldn't want to cook your old daddy a skillet of apples, would you?"

"Can't do it. I've got to get the jars out of the cellar and wash the bugs out of them before Mother gets back."

I turned to leave when a fit of conscience struck me. Daddy almost never asked me to do anything like this for him, and besides, this way, I could make Jane go after the jars. She could fight the spiders and creepers off without me.

"I'll tell you what. You make Jane get the jars, and I'll cook up the apples. How about it?"

"Someday, you'll make a good lawyer."

"Will you do it?"

"I'll do you one better. I'll take your sister to get the jars and beat the bugs off her to keep her from screaming at us. Deal?"

I was already melting the butter in the skillet as he headed out the door with Jane in tow. I loved cooking apples; the cinnamon, butter, and brown sugar mixed with the tartness of the early apples lingered in the kitchen air as sweet and as rich as lilac bloom early in the morning. The apples were just ready to pop out of the skillet, aiming to land on my hands and arms, when Daddy and Jane walked in the door, loaded with sacks of jars to be washed and scalded. That's what happens in a kitchen—four things to do and only time to do two. Feed Daddy, wash jars, boil water. Here it comes.

"Jane, run hot water in the sink, pour in some Palmolive, and put the jars in top down."

She went into a pout, but she did it anyway.

It was not long before Fleetie, Mary, Geneva, and their children filled the orchard and the yard with a buzz of fun and visiting. The children's squeals put everyone in a party mood. Daddy had long since disappeared down the hill in the Plymouth but not before dragging out the black boiling pot from the cellar. He left plenty of firewood and small logs for the fire pit. No one wanted to cook apples over a coal fire. It had to be a wood fire. While he knew Mother was as smart as a keen switch, he was careful to show her how some things were done here in the mountains. He needn't have worried over this one. Bluegrass and Eastern Mountain applesauce canning was not very different except that back home, Mother would have enjoyed the applesauce without the hard work. There were always enough helping hands around to spare the only little girl in her family most of the drudgery.

Leatha and I took the red wagon down the hill to carry back Geneva's and Fleetie's canning jars stored during the long winter. We scavenged in abandoned playhouses along the creek for jars that kids had ferreted out of the storehouse for minnows, pebbles, and grampuses. These jars also had to be washed to a sparkling shine and slipped into a boiling pot of water for scalding. Any impurity in the jars could cause the sauce to spoil during the winter. The women with the lowest number of bad jars during the long winter got bragging rights. A row of bad jars was as shameful as dingy laundry or grimy kitchen floors.

Geneva brought in her tiny newborn Freddie, swaddled in enough blankets to smother a grown man. Years before, Pappy Ramsey carved a cherry cradle for his first granddaughter—me. It usually held Jane's favorite dolls, but today, the dolls were dumped in favor of a real baby. Mother and Fleetie lifted the heavy cradle and placed it on top of the kitchen table, and Geneva snuggled the baby down on the soft pillow mattress.

"What does Dr. Begley think of this big boy, Geneva?" Mother asked as she watched Geneva fussing over him.

"I didn't go last week. The union skipped strike pay last week, and Fred won't hear to me running up a doctor bill, but Freddie's doing pretty good, don't you think?"

Mother pulled open the bunting of blankets and held Freddie's tiny feet as she cooed and whispered to him. There was little response from the baby, and the frown line in mother's forehead deepened. Her fingers moved quickly as she checked his diaper and felt his little body to see if she could see any sign that he was gaining weight.

"Geneva, does he cry much at night?"

"Law', no, Kathleen. This is a good baby. He don't hardly ever cry. The twins cry enough of all three of them, I guess."

"You don't even have to get up with him at night to feed him?"

"Sometimes, I wake up, listening for him, but mostly, he just sleeps on through. Why?"

"It is a little early for him to be giving up that feeding. I believe I'd go on and nurse him, even if he doesn't cry. Maybe he is hungry and just is too sleepy to let on. What do you think, Fleetie?"

Fleetie nodded at Geneva. "No use letting a good baby go hungry, Gen. Them twins were always yelling for more, but Freddie is a patient little thing. You might ought to nurse him a couple more times a day, even."

Geneva nodded as she hurried out the back door to the porch to check on the twins. "I'll nurse him after I round up the twins and get them settled," she said over her shoulder as she rushed off the porch and around the house, chasing the toddlers.

Fleetie sighed. "Lordy, Kathleen. I knew her hands were going to be full, but I didn't have any notion Freddie would be so poor. It's a worry."

"Fleetie, he probably needs more than breast milk. Did she get the cod liver oil Dr. Begley ordered?"

"I didn't say nothing to her about it, but I doubt it. There's not an extra penny anywhere for them to spend." Fleetie picked up the tiny baby and rocked him in her arms. "We worked so hard to get him here. It's up to us to do right by him."

"Fleetie, don't say it today. Let's get the apples put up, and you and I will slip off with him tomorrow. Ed can drive the three of us to town when he goes to the office."

Geneva came in the back door, a twin under each arm. The two had found the mud puddle at the top of the driveway, and except for their blue eyes, they now resembled baby pigs more than twin babies. Mother and Fleetie both burst into loud laughter at the sight of tiny Geneva with her two squealing "piglets" and all three of them covered with mud flying off them with every kick.

Still in peals of laughter, Mother led Geneva to the bathroom and began filling the tub with water and bubbles. She set the squealing children in the water, shoes and all, and stripped the muddy pinafores over the children's mud-splattered heads, leaving the little dresses to soak in the bath right along with their shoes and socks. The little girls grabbed at the mound of bubbles and squealed with delight at the soft puffs surrounding them. Geneva rinsed out their clothes, while I tried to wash their hair. Their slippery little bodies kept sliding out of my grip, and each time they fell back into the suds, they kicked their feet in a furious flutter that splashed water on all three of us. We fell weak with laughter.

Fleetie, hearing our commotion, opened the door and, in her sternest voice, ordered all of us out of the water. "Law' me, girls. We've got bushels of apples to can and dinner to cook. Come on out of there before we flood the whole house. I never seen the beat!"

Even though Fleetie was about half teasing, Mother and Geneva grabbed the twins and wrapped them in towels, while I wiped down the drowned bathroom. Thank goodness for Conga Wall. We couldn't keep from laughing as we dressed the wet, wiggling children from the pile of old toddler clothes that Mother resurrected from the back of our closet. The twins would look at each other and explode in another round of giggles. The twins just naturally generated as much fun as a circus.

Leatha and I were put in charge of the still-damp toddlers, and the women settled into the work at hand. For no practical reason, Mother decided to make a few jars of pink jelly, but Fleetie and Geneva stayed with the applesauce project. They set up shop on the back porch. The children had gathered or picked three bushels of the precious June apples, and Leatha and I, with the twins in tow, picked a peck of the tiny red early apples for the pink jelly. Fleetie built a fire in the fire pit several yards from the porch. The peeled apples would be boiled down in the huge black pot and then spooned into the clean jars. The rings and tops would be screwed down tight and the jars boiled in the blue granite canner, sealing them safely for months.

Everyone helped with the tedious peeling, competing to see who could take off the longest, unbroken peeling. Dorotha and Nessa made a great game of throwing the longest peels over their shoulder and checking to see which letter it formed. It was supposed to be the initial of the boy they would marry. Leatha and I looked for initials of boys who might be caught looking at us. We weren't all that clear about what their looking our way might mean, but the older girls seemed to think it was the very thing.

The huge pot was soon filled with apples and enough water to keep them from sticking. As they cooked down, the apples released loads of apple juice. It took a straining effort for Mother and Fleetie to carry it off the porch and to the fire. With one heaving swing, they placed it on the cooking grid. It would not take long before the women would be ready to begin the hot, dangerous job of stirring the apples. Applesauce popped with explosive force and burned instantly when it landed on human skin. Mother claimed that the fire and pot was hers, and that made stirring her job.

Geneva and Fleetie draped her in a raincoat and a huge black hat draped with a honeybee net. She put on a pair of Daddy's heavy work gloves and her own work boots. She did the stirring with what looked like a small oar but was really an old apple paddle carved and smoothed by Mr. Ben. He must have left it in the attic years ago when he moved across the valley to open his store. It would have been like Mr. Ben to leave his paddle to remind whoever owned the trees to take care of the apples. He hated waste. The paddle was a reminder of the many years that apples had been cooked in this yard.

While Mother sweltered and stirred the pot, Geneva and Fleetie finished peeling the devilish little red apples. They were faulty, filled with wormholes and freckles, and each imperfection had to be removed to ensure clear jelly. It was tedious and painstaking work, but like Fleetie said, "Pretty, clear jelly demands a toll on the cook."

While she set them to boil on the kitchen stove, Geneva placed a drip pan under one of the cabinet doors and carefully placed the muslin drip bag in the drip pan. In about twenty minutes, the little red apples softened into pulp, and Geneva poured the cooked apples and juice into the drip bag. Working quickly, Geneva wrapped a strong cord around the top of the bag and tied it and looped the end of the cord through the handle of the cabinet door. Using the handle and cord as a pulley, she pulled the apple mash up from the drip pan. Wrapping the cord around the handle, she tied the bag off and watched as it revolved, steadied itself, and began to drip into the pan. It would drip for hours. The clarity of the jelly depended on how well the bag filtered the juice. If one of the women became impatient and squeezed the bag, the jelly would be cloudy, or if the fabric of the bag was not dense enough or if the peeling process had been sloppy, the jelly would turn cloudy. It tasted just as good but couldn't win a ribbon at the fair.

Fleetie lined up the clean jars on the back porch swing, waiting for the pot of sauce to boil down sufficiently or for Mother to throw in the oar and yell "uncle." The pops of applesauce were peppering the air around her, and I was sure if Fleetie got close enough to help lift the pot off the rocks, she would get burned. If there had been time, Burl or Daddy could have set up the iron fire pot swinger. Without it in place, they were both apt to get some burns moving the pot off the heat.

"Fleetie," said Mother, "you better get some towels to put on your arms and over your head. It's time for the pot to come off."

Fleetie took off her long white apron and tied it around her neck and turned her sunbonnet around, completely covering her face.

"Fleet, you can't see where you are going. You'll trip and fall in this sauce and be cooked alive."

"I can see through the buttonhole slits. It works fine. The bonnet'll keep the heat off my face. Mammy Howard uses her bonnet to shield her face. That's how I got on to it." She moved quickly to the other side of the pot, and with a heavy rag protecting her hand, she grabbed hold of the bale. "Here, take hold on your side, and we'll count it off. One, two, three, heave!"

Mother took a deep breath and moved with Fleetie as the two shifted the weight from the uplift to the downswing. They moved quickly from the fire pit toward the back porch. Just as they were about to swing the heavy pot to the porch, the twins came tearing around the side of the house.

You could hear Geneva's scream all the way down the hill and across the river. The sound of her mother's scream scared Annie, and her feet tangled up in the flagstone path. She fell just beyond her mother's outstretched hand and rolled toward the black pot. The sauce was still popping, and before Fleetie and Kathleen could swing it up to the edge of the porch, Annie was peppered with hot splats of sauce on the back of her plump little legs. Mary Beth also fell to her knees, catching hot splats of sauce in her hair. Their screams reamed the ears of every adult and child on the hill. Mother grabbed Mary Beth, and Fleetie swept up Annie and ran to the pump just a few steps to the right of the porch.

I could hear Mother praying that the old pump had held its prime from earlier in the day as she began pumping with one hand and as she held the toddler with the other. I grabbed the pump handle so she could hold the baby with two hands as she begged, "Oh god. Let the water come."

There was an immediate rush of the icy water as she held the baby's legs under the cold stream. Geneva grabbed her baby from Mother as I kept pumping hard and fast. By this time, Fleetie had determined that the hot sauce had only scared Mary Beth. Her thick, curly hair had trapped the hot sauce away from her scalp, and she was not burned, but her wails continued, pain or not. Listening to Annie's screams had convinced her that she was hurt too. By this time, all the other children had raced to the backyard and were huddled in a tight knot, afraid to speak, afraid to look away, and afraid to watch all at the same time.

Mother sent Jane running into the house for the aloe plant sitting in the living room window. After a few more minutes of the cold water sluicing over Annie's pudgy little leg, Mother took hold of a thick branch of the plant and broke off several of the fat, spongy leaves. She bent them double, opening them up, and began squeezing the thick liquid over each of the angry red circles dotting the backs of Annie's legs. Geneva gently rubbed each of the spots, urging the burned skin to accept the healing juice.

While the women were working with Annie, Nessa and Dorotha began to fill the glass jars with the hot applesauce, and the other kids sank to the ground, mostly silenced by the excitement. The twins were still crying, but the shrieking was subsiding, and occasionally, Mary Beth would pause and give Annie a long look, and since Annie was still crying, Mary Beth would immediately start again. It didn't take long for the toddlers, Emma, Logan, and Rebecca, to catch on to Mary Beth's trick. They laughed each time she started crying again, and this made her cry even harder, adding to the general confusion.

"Geneva," Mother said over the roar, "the burns aren't deep. The aloe will be enough to heal them up, don't you think?"

"Lordy, Miz Hill, I don't know. They's always getting something banged or cut. They don't pay it much mind later after they get through being so mad over the hurting."

Fleetie moved to the porch to help Dorotha and Nessa finish filling the empty jars as Geneva and Mother worked to calm the frantic twins. She tried to trick Mary Beth by distracting her. She set her down on the ground right in the middle of the huddled children. It might have worked, but Annie seeing Mary Beth so far away from her own center of pain and misery sent her into a new set of howls. Separating twins was not a likely task if one of them was upset. After another few minutes, both the little girls began the snubbing phase of their great upset. Annie finally began to pull away from Geneva to get to Mary Beth and what looked like fun with the other children.

It took a little less than an hour before all the sauce was in the jars and the caps screwed hard on the tops of each of them.

"Lookie, girls," Fleetie said, "we have twenty full quarts and some left over to eat on. Dorotha, you and Leatha get four big lumps of coal on the fire. It would take all night to boil all these in the kitchen. We need to do the big pot out here too."

The girls stopped dead still. They needed the coal bucket from the fireplace in the house, but they wouldn't walk in the house, coal bucket or not. At first, I didn't understand why they were stalling, so I went ahead and picked up the bucket.

Fleetie called, "Get on now. Stop dawdling. Stir up that fire good. The coal will burn hotter than Ed's logs."

With deep sighs, Leatha and Dorotha walked to the coal pile, resigned to carrying the coal one lump at a time because neither one wanted to get that dirty. It finally dawned on me that the girls weren't allowed to walk in Mrs. Ramsey's house.

"Hey, don't worry. Here's the coal bucket. We can carry more with it and not get so dirty."

Faint hope. We got just about as dirty as we would have if we had carried it piece by piece, but the coal did do the trick for the fire. In just a few minutes, the heat drove us back, away from the pit.

Fleetie placed the black pot on the supporting rocks and grid, and Leatha and I were put to pumping water to fill it. Fleetie took the buckets of well water from us just as soon as we got a bucket filled and poured it into the pot. When it was about half full, all of us helped carry the warm jars of applesauce to the warming water. The water level rose with each jar until each jar was nearly covered.

In the house, Mother repeated the same process with the blue granite canner on the kitchen stove. With the twins finally calmed, Geneva picked up the baby to nurse him. Through all the commotion and screaming, he had not made a peep. Geneva either did not know or did not take thought about how peculiar it was for a baby to be so quiet.

In the midst of the worst trouble in your life, there can be an unconscious acceptance of things the way they are. In the years to come, when Geneva could stand to think back on it, Freddie's lack of reaction to the world around him would come back to haunt her. But on this busy morning, it seemed more a blessing than a warning.

Fleetie watched the black pot outside, and Mother timed the granite canner inside. The children had drifted to the side yard and the rope swing Daddy had hung for Jane and me. Geneva and Dorotha carried Freddie in his doll cradle around the side of the house and sat to watch them play.

A soft breeze moved through the locust trees, sprinkling the inevitable leaf fall of oval-shaped, yellowing leaves. Of all the trees planted to hold the soil in place after the hillside plateau was carved, the locust had the strongest roots and the frailest leaves. The locusts leafed out first in spring and fell first in the fall. With all the protection the locusts gave eroding soil, they gave very little for anybody who wanted a shady yard. For all the years that I would live on the hill, the locust trees would seem no more than nuisance trees, and I would yearn for the beautiful maples, poplars, and oaks that grew higher up on the encircling mountains. Locust trees were like vanilla ice cream and brown lace-up Oxfords—practical, plain, and boring.

Today, however, one of those locusts had lent an arm to the rope for a swing that took all of us far out over the road bank and delivered a stomach-tightening, heart-flipping thrill with each forward ride. Geneva smiled as she watched the children push, double-pump, ride two at a time, climb the rope, jump from the moving seat, and fall into giggling heaps in the soft dust kicked up in the scooped-out hollow below the swing.

"Look, Freddie, it won't be long before you will be swinging out there with all of them too," said Geneva, holding him up to watch.

Mother came around the side of the house to call everyone to lunch. "Let Rachel and me carry the cradle back for you, Gen. It's a heavy thing. Cherrywood is solid as lead."

"Yes'm, but it just fits Freddie. He looks like a little doll in it. Someday, when he is grown, we'll devil him good about being little enough to sleep in a doll bed!"

Chapter 20

Diagnosis

Early the next morning, Mother and Fleetie rode to town with Daddy to take Freddie to the doctor.

Geneva volunteered to stay with the other children if Fleetie would go. "I can't stand for Freddie to be that far away from me, but I'm afraid to leave the twins with anybody else. Those two will find trouble in the blink of an eye." Even having their mother close was no guarantee of their safety, but Geneva knew she was their best hope of surviving childhood.

Mother left Logan with Nessa and Dorotha, but Mother felt more confident about his safety. Logan was a naturally cautious kid, and he hated pain. Daddy called him his little old man.

Mother wanted the baby to be examined by Dr. Parks. He was the older of the two doctors, and she was counting on his experience to guide the diagnosis. In spite of Freddie's dramatic entry into the world four months ago, she knew better than to think Dr. Parks would take special interest in the tiny baby because of that midnight delivery during the flood. Dr. Parks had delivered hundreds of babies in this long career, and once safely delivered, the babies went right out of his mind. Each birth represented not so much the miracle of life but yet another body to be treated in all its various life phases. He was never known to congratulate himself on a delivery. He was far more likely to act gratified they survived to adulthood.

Daddy left the office to drive the three home after the doctor's visit. He almost never came home during the day, but Geneva would be frantic to get Freddie back home. While it seemed she had no idea how seriously ill he might be, she could not stand to have him out of her sight for even a few minutes. Mother told me that she and Fleetie had little to say on the ride home. Dr. Parks had been unusually quiet as he examined Freddie, but he did ask Fleetie if she remembered how long it took him to cry after he was born. He took blood samples, weighed him, and checked his reflexes and his chest. He watched him breathe, pinched his heel, and snapped him hard on his foot to make him cry. He listened carefully to Freddie's startled and angry cry.

After nearly thirty minutes of his inch-by-inch examination, he stepped out of the room and returned with Phil Begley, his partner. Both men then began to speak to each other in unintelligible doctor language. Mother said that with all she knew about symptoms and problems with babies, she could not follow them. She was sure they were holding back something serious. She could, however, follow closely enough to know that the baby was in trouble from the expressions and frustration of the doctors if not from understanding everything they said.

As she told it later, the two doctors finally left the room, leaving orders to dress the baby and wait until one of them returned with medicine and instructions. When Dr. Parks returned, he sat down and crossed his legs and looked out the small window in the examining room a long time before he spoke.

"Fleetie, Kathleen, remember, doctors don't know much. We are pretty good sawbones, but there is still too much we don't know about what makes us strong enough or not strong enough to keep breathing. I can't find a single thing wrong with this baby, but I can also see that he is not growing fast enough, and he is unusually still. He can move his arms and legs—he just doesn't seem motivated enough to do it. I suspect the long labor didn't help him much, but again, he just might be a little slow to catch up. I've seen babies with sluggish starts grow out of it, but it usually takes a couple of years to see any serious or lasting damage.

"Tell Geneva not to miss a feeding for any reason and keep him awake while he is nursing. He will want to eat just enough to stop the hunger reflex and go on back to sleep. I want her to give him some cereal on the tip of a small spoon at least four times a day. He won't get much of it down, but there's a chance he will get some good from it. I have written down the vitamin tonic he needs. Mrs. White out front will give you a bottle as you leave. Be sure he gets it twice a day. If Fred can't buy it, Kathleen, come back here for a refill. Do you have any questions?"

He knew full well that Mother would be busting to ask a list of questions as long as his stethoscope, but he rose and stood half in and half out of the door of the examining room and gave his best imitation of a doctor in a hurry and slipped away before she could start. As he left the room, Mother told us she promised herself she would come back and get him alone sometime soon and get more answers.

When they drove up to the gate beside Fleetie's yard, Geneva, Logan, and I were standing on the porch. Each twin was propped on a hip, and as soon as Geneva spotted the car, she put the twins down on the bare ground and ran to the car.

"Oh lordy, lordy, I thought you'd never get back. I've worried till I've got my head a-ringin'. I know he's starved half to death." She opened the car door and picked up the baby, wrapped in his yellow shower quilt.

"Now, Gen, don't take on. He's just fine. Dr. Parks went over and over him," said Fleetie. But her words were lost as Geneva raced into the house to examine him and sniff out any damage that might have been done.

Laughing at her retreating back, Fleetie turned to Daddy and Mother. "This was a whole lot of trouble. We're beholden. Won't you come in and set a spell? I know Geneva is plumb taken back. She's so grateful. She'll be real shamed if she don't get a chance to say so. Please come on in."

"We better not, Fleetie. Ed has to get back to the office, and Geneva needs to hear everything Dr. Parks said. Thank you so much for asking though. Let me know what else we can do. That baby seems like he belongs to all of us."

Daddy picked up Logan and carried him out the door and across the yard to the car. I followed and climbed into the back seat of the car.

Fleetie said, "Don't know that there's anything else anybody can do, but I can sure testify you two have done your best for him." She stepped back and waved as our old Plymouth slipped up and over the steep crossing and turned right to go up the long hill.

"Katie, don't start wringing your hands and grieving. Parks didn't find anything really wrong—he'll probably grow right out of it."

"I'm not taking on, Ed, but I can't keep from worrying. You're a man, and none of you have a notion how hard it is to keep babies breathing. You all think it's automatic."

"I expect I've seen more babies buried than you ever will. I know you. You'll take on, and before we know it, you'll get down. I don't have time for a deep discussion of how much I have failed the babies in this valley. I've got to get back to the office."

"Ed, stop yelling. I'm just so worried about him. I want to run right up that mountain and cry like a crazy woman."

"Who's a crazy women, Momma?" said Logan. He caught the tone of the voices and was hanging on to O'Malley, his stuffed toy, with a choke hold.

Daddy stopped the car, got out, and lifted Logan and O'Malley out of the back seat. He carried him all the way to the front door. "Logie, I want you to tell Mr. O'Malley that your mommy is the prettiest girl in these here mountains. Will you do that for me?"

Logie grinned and started whispering in O'Malley's pretend ear. Mother couldn't hide her smile.

"I'll be back around six." He had done it again. If charm wins the day, Daddy will always wind up on top of the pile.

Chapter 21

BEAN DAY

The morning sunlight rolled down the mountain, bounced through the window, and propelled me from the bed. "Bean Day!"

Bean Day was one of the best days of the summer for the Ramsey and Sargeant kids. I jumped into the shorts and shirt lying on the floor beside my bed. I didn't want to waste a minute of it. I was anxious to get down the hill and into the bean patch and start picking at the same time the other kids started. If we all worked hard, we could pick the patch clean before the heat of day. We usually picked about ten bushels. That made a mountain of beans for all of us to make, string after string, to hang up where the wind and sun could dry them brown and crisp. We would also break beans for canning, but today was only for bean stringing.

Yesterday, Fleetie promised we could use the long needles and heavy thread and race to see which one of us could fill the most strings with the fresh beans. The winner would get a nickel for ice cream with a ride in the truck to the store. On some Bean Days, Daddy had been known to stop at the store and pay for ice cream for everybody, but we all wanted to win just in case. You never knew for sure.

Garden work could be miserable. Stinging bugs, dirt, sweat, stubbed toes, and scorching thirst trapped kids like an itchy blanket, but bean stringing while sitting in the shade of the porch was more fun than work. As we finished pulling the green beans down each long string, Fleetie would hang it on the thick nails driven into the edge of the porch roof stretcher. For weeks, the beans would hang there and swing free to catch the sun and breezes until they dried hard and crisp. In a long cold winter, shuck beans tasted like summer sunshine. They were bubbled down with a piece of salt pork for hours and then filled the soup bowls to feed hungry stomachs.

We worked lickety-split, and by midmorning, we picked all twenty of the long rows and carried bushel after bushel of the beans to the front porch. The sun was beginning to burn the backs of our necks, and sweat trickled its way down our backs and foreheads. Fleetie and Geneva sat in the swing and broke off the tips of the beans and threw them into a large dishpan—snap, string, fling. With the picking over, we joined them, and our hands were never still and never hurried. The pattern repeated itself over and over hundreds of times, and as you watched, you could almost tap your foot to the steady rhythm. From Gen's shiny dishpan, I grabbed a bean, speared it, and pulled it along the string until it rested at the end. Bean after bean, I built the long green rope until it fell over my knees. Over and over, each one added beans to long green ropes that spilled over knobby knees and coiled out on the porch floor. At first, there were lots of jokes and stories and teasing, but after a couple of hours' tedium set in, Dorotha began to beg Fleetie to get out her guitar and sing for us. The rest of us picked up on it and chimed in.

Dorotha had the guitar hidden, and no one could ever get her to tell where it was. Fleetie could play ladybugs off sunflowers, but her playing threw Burl into such a rage that Fleetie almost never played anymore. That was a pure shame because tunes seemed to live in her fingers. Clear, ringing chords, almost always in a minor key, would rise like a mountain chant, free but with a purpose. Her deep throaty voice would blend the ache of a memory with today's sunshine in a mix that set our feet tapping and throats humming. Her voice smoothed over every tricky rhythm, and all of us loved it. Fleetie finally gave in, and Dorotha slipped off the porch to claim the guitar out of its hiding place.

We settled in for the fun as Fleetie tuned the guitar, and we commenced begging for our favorite. I jumped off the porch and ran up the hill to get Mother. She wasn't a mountain girl by birth, but she loved the music as much as any of us. By the time the two of us came back through the yard gate, the whole bunch was harmonizing "Down in the Valley." As Mother stepped through the gate, Fleetie quit playing.

"Oh, Fleetie, you can't stop. Please play some more. They all love it, and it helps the work go quicker. I thought I could help out a little and maybe take a mess of beans home."

We needed more beans like we needed a house fire, but Fleetie always refused to let anyone do anything for her.

"Just some screechin' going on down here, Kathleen. Come in and set here on the swing. Nessa, get Kathleen a pile of beans."

In a few minutes, song after song rolled out and across the yard. Out of the corner of my eye, I saw Johnny Nolan coming down the railroad track not even fifty yards from the porch. He hunkered down on the tracks and listened to the music for a short while before he walked through the yard gate.

Fleetie jumped when she saw him and threw her arms around the guitar and hid her face behind it. "Oh lordy, Johnny, you about scared me to death."

Johnny grinned. "Say, Fleet, that's some awful sweet music. You oughtn't stop. The kids will flog me shore if I break up a singing. Have you seen Minty this morning?"

"Mary went up to your house to visit Minty this morning. We haven't seen them since Mary passed by here early."

"I better get on up the creek and see about her. That baby is due any minute. You all go back to singin'. I can enjoy it all the way up the hill."

"Holler down about Minty," said Mother.

"Mommy, sing some more. Sing 'My Own True Love,'" said Leatha.

Fleetie let her fingers find the tune, and she hummed her way into the song. Before long, all of us were either singing or trying to as Fleetie led us into song after song. The music streamed from her fingers as if dammed too long against a freshening creek.

For the first time in a long time, there was nothing going on but pure fun. Fleetie's cheeks were flushed a rosy pink, and every foot on the porch was keeping steady time. Mother gathered up an armful of the long strings of the freshly strung beans and walked to the clothesline beside the house, and as she moved across in front of the porch and around the side, our eyes followed her, so none of us spotted the cloud of dust rising way down the county road. The dust cloud was how we always knew when someone was moving our way. Dirt roads were handy like that for letting you know when traffic and maybe company was nearing.

We were keeping steady time to "Camptown Ladies" as the cloud of dust moved onto the straight stretch leading to the little house at the crossing. Burl's truck slammed to a stop in front of the gate, catching all of us by surprise. One glance, and I could tell he was mean drunk. Somehow or other, drinking always messed up his hair. His face was flushed red, and his eyes were squinted as if the drinking made the sun too bright. Probably drinking was something people were supposed to do in dark places. A drunk looked pretty grim if you brought them out in the bright sunlight. My stomach twisted with dread at the angry look on his face. I was scared.

"By god, what do we have here?" Burl roared. Dorotha grabbed the guitar and ran toward the front door. Burl grabbed her arm, snatched the guitar from her hands, and flung her off the porch like a rag doll. She rolled into a ball, too scared to cry.

He waved the guitar, taunting us, and nearly knocked me off the porch. "Got us a opry star, I guess."

Fleetie, trying to distract him, walked to the screen door. "Come in the house, and I'll get your dinner. They's fresh beans and sausage. Save your dinner bucket for tomorrow. The kids can finish this here bean work."

"No, by god, dinner's not going to save you. Next, you'll be dancin' and runnin' the hollers like the whore you are." With every word, he swung the guitar closer to the porch post.

Fleetie reached for the guitar. "Burl, give the guitar to Dorotha. She can take it up the hill to Mary. It belongs to some of her people."

"You're a lying whore. This is your sorry daddy's guitar." He swung one last circle and slammed it against the post. He grabbed Fleetie by the neck and forced her down.

Mother had been hanging strings of beans on the side yard clothesline. She came around the corner of the porch just as Fleetie's knees hit the porch. The pieces of the guitar were scattered at Burl's feet.

"You devil!" Mother screamed. "Take your hands off her. How dare you hurt her? You sorry good-for-nothing. Have you lost your mind? Only a yellow coward comes come home drunk, beats his wife, and scares children. Leave her alone."

Burl did not know that Mother was on the place, and her shouting fanned his fury to a fever pitch. He lunged off the porch, grabbed her, and drew back his fist.

"You hit me, Burl Sargeant, and before the sun sets, Ed Ramsey will have your sorry hide locked up. Do it. Go on! It'll give Fleetie and the kids a break from you worthless piece of trash."

At first, I was scared he would kill her for standing up to him, but as much as he hated her right then, he must have been more scared of jail. He'd been locked up before for more than one drunken rampage. He pushed Mother backward, and she stumbled just before Geneva caught her. He slammed through the front door and into the house. A loud crash in the kitchen propelled Fleetie through the door behind him.

"Nessa, you run up the hill and get Johnny. Tell him to hurry," said Mother.

Geneva grabbed her three children and ran out of the yard and down the road toward home. Fleetie pushed open the screen door, a red handprint spreading its angry stain across her face.

"Fleetie, I'm taking the kids up to the house with me for a little while. They've seen too much already, and you ought to go with us."

"Kathleen, that'd be awful good of you. Burl will be all right after I get him to eat something. He don't usually lay a finger on me unless the kids are around to know it. With them gone, he'll ease off."

"Fleetie, he's dangerous. If you won't come up to the house, you could go to Geneva's. I sent Nessa after Johnny. You can't fight off a strong man half out of his mind with liquor. Let him take Burl off somewhere and sober him up. The children will be fine with me. Are you hearing me?"

Johnny walked up behind Mother. "What's the matter?"

"Is Minty in labor?" said Fleetie. That was Fleetie all over. Burl drinking, the kids scattering, her face swelling from a beating—and she asks after Minty!

"She's fine. She's settin' up there with Mary, talking up a storm."

Mother broke in. "Burl's mean drunk. He smashed Fleetie's guitar and took after her with those fists. Can you get him away from here?"

"I've got a stash of beer hidden about a half mile down the river. By the time we row there, he'll sober up some. Things is rough at the mine. It's enough to drive anybody to hard drinkin' and worse."

"Drinking is one thing. I don't care if he drinks a river dry, but he has got to stop using those fists on Fleetie and the children. He's acting like a pure heathen. I will call in the law if I have to, and won't that be a pretty sight for these kids to see?"

"Lordy, don't call no law. There's enough trouble already at the mine. I'll get him out of here, I promise. Just don't be calling no law."

I had to hand it to Mother. Fleetie might be all about turning the other cheek, but nobody crossed my mother and came away in a piece. She took no nonsense from fools or drunks, but none of the ruckus was anything new. Men used fists, straps, belts, or whatever was handy when they got riled, and you had to learn to duck or be too tough to tackle. Burl was pure spoiled by Fleetie puttin' up with his foolishness. Those chickens had sure been chased off the roost today.

I watched as Burl and Johnny left out the back door and walked to the riverbank, where Burl's rowboat lay moored to a sycamore.

"By god, Johnny," Burl said, "Pridemore's is about to beat us, and all we can do is float down the damn river."

"Nobody has beat us yet, Burl. Maybe Ed can get us an injunction to stop all this shit. Let Ed get the law on our side. You and me will just get on down this river, catch us some fish for supper, and someone else can worry over it for a spell."

Burl baled out the bottom of the boat with a rusty coffee can before he answered Johnny. "I am pure wearied out with it. I've a notion to go see Windham and see if I can get on over at his place. He has gone and bought up about fifty head of Hereford, and last I heard, he was getting tired of it already. A money man like him can't farm no how. All he's done is spend money on that place. He's probably thinking it's about time he made a little."

I watched as Burl sat down in the boat and listened to Johnny through the fog of the rotgut he had been slugging down since he left the mine. Burl grew up in a different time before the mines were running full out in the whole county. He'd had a touch with crops and animals before he had spent the best of himself gouging the earth for black diamonds. I heard him tell Daddy that he wished he could work the land pulling crops and harvest out of the stingy ground.

One day, when he was sober, I even heard him tell his kids that lumbering would have been a better way than a deep pit where all you ever saw was the glow of the next miner's lamp and the misery of the black soot sinking deeper into your hide with each passing day. Maybe that day, I felt a little sorry for him but not much, and it didn't last because he would turn right around and do some other meanness to Fleetie or the kids.

Johnny pushed the boat off the bank and let it follow its own steering. A river calm would soon be settling in and around Burl and Johnny. The soft morning sun and trailing breeze would soon mesmerize both men. I could see they had poles and lines over the side of the boat where they dangled in the water, unattended. No self-respecting fish was going to commit suicide by giving either pole a nibble. The promised beer was still a ways down the river, and it looked like Burl had settled down to wait. It would not be long before he would lose his battle with the alcohol and drift off to sleep. Fleetie and the kids would be safe again for today.

All of us kids left the yard and went over the crossing to start the long walk up the hill. Rebecca, next to the youngest, was crying her eyes out over the lost ice cream. She was like that. Seemed like she could never just move on to the next thing. She was always looking back and whining over what couldn't never be. Nessa, always the one to spoil her the most, worked to make it right.

"Come on, Rebecca. Don't cry. Remember the mulberry tree? It's right up the hill, and the mulberries is ripe and just right for pickin'. We'll get some good mulberries. They're better'n ice cream anyway. Ice cream'll give you the headache. Nobody ever got the headache from mulberries."

I looked back for Mother just as she started out of the gate with her pan of beans. She turned to Fleetie, but there were no words. The smashed guitar had disappeared, and all that lay between the two women right then was the hurt, scraped raw and stinging, the melodies now only a memory hanging soft in the hot July air. Bean Day was over.

Part 3

SONATA

Chapter 22

AND THEY PICKED UP SERPENTS

It was late July, and dog days stole over the mountain and smothered the valley. The river flow slacked off sluggish, and jar fly buzzing filled the air. Their hiss and the heat pounding on us seemed to almost stretch each day into two. Vegetable gardens were picked clean and now sat in rows of canned jars throwing gaudy color on the whitewashed shelves. Potato, rutabaga, and turnip mounds cast competing shadows deep in the root cellar, the only cool spot left, as the rest of the world hunkered low in the gut of August.

Mother receded into the shade of the screen porch, and if we kids didn't out and out bleed, we got little more attention than the cicadas yammering on the hot rocks. She had resurrected an ancient Underwood from the storage closet at Daddy's office and pounded away, writing stories I was not allowed to read. She didn't know I found her stash of *True Confessions* magazines long ago and read each one from cover to cover before returning it to the stack behind the shoeboxes. Since she wouldn't let me read her stories, I figured they must be pretty raunchy too. If she only knew some of the books I brought home from the library practically dripped with passion, desire, sex, murder, and mayhem. For that matter, the Old Testament did its share along that line too.

I whined and drooped through August, but the brilliant sunlight inspired Daddy. I guess his good mood was a throwback to his liberation from the coal mines. At dawn, he put on the coffee pot and laid a fat-rimmed ham slice on the skillet and stood on the back porch to fiddle the sun over the knife-edged mountain that climbed straight up behind our house. His violin seemed given to sadness; even his fast and funny tunes were played in a minor key that dug under the laughter to find your hollow spot.

When the coffee perked and the ham fat was rendered transparent, he repeated his violin ritual. First, he loosened the bow then checked the bridge and snapped the velvet cinch. Finally, he opened the bedraggled case and returned Uncle Bruce's handcrafted masterpiece to its faded velvet berth.

One Saturday morning, right in the middle of "John Peel," the music stopped, and he stuck his head in my bedroom door. "Rachel, don't let the kids go near the store today. Not one step. Hear me?"

I pulled the pillow over my head, but his warning coiled its way through my Saturday sleep. I waged a hopeless battle to shut out the morning sun, the fiddle playing, and his warning, but sleep was all but gone. I shook off the rest of it and pushed back the wrinkled sheet and sat up on the side of the bed. Something must be going on at the store, and I knew in this news-starved holler, I wasn't about to miss any small tidbit of excitement. What that bunch of tobacco spitters on the store porch could have come up with just might be worth checking out.

I grabbed yesterday's clothes that lay puddled on the floor by my bed as I listened to see if Daddy had left the house or if Mother was stirring. The house was silent. I picked up a wet dishrag draped on the sink and dropped it over the screen door spring to muffle the metal screech. No use waking the whole house. If the kids got up, they would demand a dozen things, and before I could escape, Mother would be up too. I slipped out the door and held on to the screen handle until I could settle the door back against it frame. Screen doors made a smacking racket when they shut, and that sound was loud enough to wake the dead, but not this morning. I was real careful to protect my escape.

The dirt path down the mountain still held heat from yesterday's sun, and dust swirls puffed beneath my feet. I stopped and backed downhill and made perfect footprints in the warm red powder. No use lettin' a panther track me easy. I hadn't ever, even one time, seen a panther, but the hold over habit held sway this morning. I eased off the warm dust onto sunburned grass that crunched like Cracker Jacks and moved on down the hill. Leatha and I were each other's lifeline on this mountain. The need to share and explore life filled our days whenever and wherever we could manage it.

As I rounded a stand of giant poplars, I could see the Sargeants' house—part log, part clapboard—perched on the bank, overlooking the Poor Fork branch of the Cumberland River. Tuck and Blue Boy, Burl's bird dogs, were sprawled in the dust, their bony bodies hidden under the porch. In April, they would have jumped all over me, legs, noses, and tongues leaving friendly marks, but in August, sun-stunned, they barely bothered to wag a tail.

Leatha's sun-browned legs dangled off the porch swing as she minded the latest Sargeant baby. With a string of siblings, six strong, babysitting was as natural to Leatha as breathing. We Ramseys had only three kids, and we were the smallest family in the valley. How pitiful can you get?

I crossed the dirt road and pushed open the yard gate. Leatha and I were bound hand to hand, head to head, heart to heart. I suppose I ought to wonder how we came to such a place, bound as we were to each other. I didn't. She was here, and to me, that was as natural as the river rocks and steep cliffs we both loved to scale.

"Well, look who's up before eight o'clock," said Leatha. "I thought Ms. Princess slept till noon on Saturday."

"Come on, Leatha, I drug myself down here before sunshine hit the roof. Daddy woke me, yelling for us to stay away from the store. What's going on that got him riled enough to forget I get to sleep late on Saturday?"

"Nothing now, but last night, Coburn and Daddy sat out here on the porch and talked half the night. Coburn told us the whole story about the snake handling that's coming."

The hairs on my arms stood straight up, and air rushed in between my teeth. A snake handling caused as much commotion as a flash flood.

"What did Coburn say?"

"He talked about all night. It's a pretty long story. Most of what he said was about his notion of how to make some money. He told Pap that traffic at his store is down to a trickle. Money to spend is gone, and credit from most of the wholesale houses is in a sorry shape. Coburn is having trouble paying his bills for the fresh seed, milk, and bread. He needs some new traffic soon, or he will have to close the store. The way he told it was that early one morning, right after planting, when he was walking to the store, he kicked at a fallen limb and jumped nearly two feet straight up. It was a big ole black snake."

"Poor Coburn. I would have screamed bloody murder, wouldn't you? Can't you just see its long black snake tail whipping around and begin slithering away with every muscle working in that slimy way they move? Just saying 'snake' makes me shudder," I said.

"Rach, dummy, a black snake can't ever hurt you, but since his ole lazy bones are wrapped in all that snake body, it can startle you some. I hear tell that black snakes keep down mice and rats. Most people in the valley just let them be, but not Coburn. He never saw a snake he didn't try to kill. He ran to the store porch, grabbed a hoe, and chopped off the snake's head. Can't you just hear him? 'Snakes are the most useless, dangerous creatures God ever made. Snakes don't do nobody no good.' That's probably what he said."

"What else? Why does this have anything to do with a snake handling?"

"Well, Daddy told us he pushed open the storeroom door, but he was still feeling skittish, so he looked around hard and long before he stepped inside. Then he remembered—snake handling. The memory of snakes wrapped around the necks and arms of the handlers tore him up. He told Daddy that back a few years ago, a gaggle of handlers came traipsing through recruiting lost souls with their terrifying preachin'. They borrowed Mr. Ben's large storehouse just across the road from Coburn, and before he knew it, they started a revival.

Hordes of people streamed from the hollers and branches from as far as twenty miles away. The crowds grew for weeks.

"More like a carnival than any preachin' he ever saw. He couldn't close the store at night for selling pop, candy, and about every other thing he stocked. Most of the crowd was there just to gape and jaw, and there was a profit to be made while it lasted in spite of how much it made his skin crawl. After about three weeks of excitement, word got around that the law had been tipped off, and the handlers packed up their rattlers, copperheads, and water moccasins and left the valley. Most everybody thought Coburn tipped off the law, and he refused to talk about it. But today, he told Dad, in spite of himself, a snake idea tickled his brain, and he was about to go back on his own conscience. If there was to be a big snake handling, he could pay off McComb Supply and keep the store open."

The baby had fallen asleep, and Leatha stood up and went in the house to put her in her crib. When she came back and settled herself on the porch swing, she had remembered more about the conversation from the night before.

"The handlers, always on the move, are usually eager to find a safe place to hold a meeting. Run-ins with the law the last few years has thinned the faithful considerable. The store, being right on the road, is not the best place for them either. A gathering crowd is a dead giveaway, but it worked before, and so he tells Daddy he thinks it just might work again, long enough to save his business for him and for the valley."

"Why did Mr. Ben figure in the snake handling?" I asked.

"Everybody in the settlement knows Ben and Sarah used to handle. They were in their twenties not long after their newborn twins died of diphtheria. But since they're in their late eighties now, the fire to prove themselves has long since burned out. There are days now when Sarah can't even remember the names of the babies Ben buried in that miserable January over sixty years ago."

"If they handled snakes that far back, why did Coburn think Mr. Ben would help now?"

"Coburn told Pap that he promised himself he would go see Ben and Sarah after he locked up. He had figured that they probably still knew where some of the old group was living. He heard tell there was a new snake-handling preacher living somewhere across the mountain near Coxton."

Leatha kept on telling me the story almost like she was reading it from a book. There was nothing quite like Leatha's stories. I would swap a movie ticket any day to listen to her tales and yarns.

"As he walked up on the porch of Ben's old store, long since closed down, he tried to make some noise so as not to startle either of them. Ben heard the steps and made his way slowly to the door. As Coburn stood there, he marveled at the porch posts. Since he was a child, he had never stopped being amazed by the tall, round columns completely covered with bottle caps. Ben figured that bottle caps would keep his posts from rotting out. For about three years, he used his ball peen hammer and carefully placed each cap in a mosaic of prevention. It worked, and the posts were still standing in all their commercial glory some sixty-five years later.

"As Coburn told it, Ben's height filled the door. Even stooped at eighty-seven years old, his six-feet-eight was impressive. Coburn wondered what it might have been like for him to have stood so tall above everyone when he was young. Towering over everyone was bound to have caused considerable commotion all his life. Wherever Ben put his feet down in his long life, stories were repeated about his shenanigans. Being a foot taller than everybody else was a good place to start for a man as full of the dickens as Ben. He built the best stills, stole away, and married the prettiest Cherokee girl in the hills. He could shoot the eye out of a turkey at two hundred paces. He followed Captain Llewellyn all the way to Cuba. He traded for furs and panned gold. He planted more apple trees in Kentucky than Johnny Appleseed, and with little to no help, he built schools wherever he lived for more than just a few months.

"He taught himself and his Cherokee wife to read and write and never allowed any settlement he inhabited to be without a school and a teacher. He was a lawman, an outlaw, a friend, and a bitter enemy, all in the same six-foot-eight frame almost at the same time. In a different time and place, he could have been a leader of men. As it was, there was no one who knew him that did not admire and respect Mr. Ben.

"'How are you and Sarah gettin' along, Mr. Ben?' Coburn asked.

"'Tolerable, Coburn. Come in and set a spell. How about some beans and cornbread? Sarah and I just ate,' said Ben.

"'Thank you, no. Cora will have supper hot, and she'll preach my funeral if I don't eat after she cooked it.'

"As he told Daddy, they talked about first one thing and then another for nearly an hour before he got around to explaining how a revival with a few handlers might give the Ross's Point folks something to do besides worry about the strike.

"'Mr. Ben, do you reckon where any of the bunch that use to hold revivals around here might be?'

"'Coburn, as I recall, you never was much in the way of supportin' the meetin'. I've heard tell it was you that brought the law down on them last time. What's really eatin' at you?'

"Coburn would have known better than to lie to Mr. Ben. For all his eighty-seven years, he is as sharp as ever. You play right into his hand if you tried to fool him. Coburn wanted him to help, not stub up and back off because of a lie," said Leatha. "He said he went on to explain that they's been nothing much happening around here since the strike but worry and misery. He pointed out that the preaching and singing at a revival gets people happy. He agreed with Mr. Ben that he didn't hold with handling, but the danger adds to the meeting, and more people come. The more people that comes, the better the meeting will be. Coburn asked him straight out if he would help talk to the new preacher over at Coxton and see if they're ready to take to the road again.

"Ben fell quiet for a long minute. He looked far off, his thoughts reaching deep behind his pale blue eyes. 'Wouldn't hurt the store none either, would it, Coburn?'

"'No, Mr. Ben. Truth is, I've fell behind with my McComb's bill. I owe Chappel Dairy and the bakery too. If I don't come up with some decent payout pretty soon, I'm gonna have to close,' said Coburn.

"'Quint Helton. That's the preacher's name, Quint Helton. Get ahold of him. Tell him I told you to ask. They'll be here directly. Probably just about the time it takes to get the old store cleaned out and benches put up. Mind now, Coburn, be careful and plan good. I'm not tellin' you this for nothing. Everybody around here needs the store. If you are going to sell, be sure you have enough goods on hand. No use wasting all your good schemin'. Remember, I'm gonna be watchin'. Don't you never once think about calling the law down on them. They do what they do 'cause they believe, and by their conviction, they have to. You doin' what you're doin' 'cause you believe in keeping your store open. They's not much difference,' said Ben.

"Coburn went on to tell Daddy it could have been a lot worse. Mr. Ben seemed almost good natured about the plan. At least he was willing to help him save the store. One storekeeper to another, he guessed. Anyway, that's the way Coburn told it to us."

"Leatha, we have to go. We've never been to a snake handling."

"I was too, once't. 'Pint near scared me silly. Them snakes is not calm like you see 'em out in the garden. They's all riled and ugly," said Leatha.

"You gonna go?

"No way."

"Come on, let's go. We won't be anywhere near the snakes. We can stand on the porch and watch all the ruckus."

"What ruckus? It ain't no carnival. Just a bunch of hollerin' and rollin'," said Leatha.

"There'll be a crowd of boys struttin' around, acting all brave about how they's not scared of snakes or hellfire."

"Lordy, Rachel Grace, even if I was dying to go, Mommy would have a fit."

"Well, of course. Nobody is going to up and say they think we ought to cross the river for a snake handling. Let's just say we are going to the settlement to see Mary Rose and her new baby. We haven't seen her since her water broke when she was walking to church. We can take some of the kids and let them visit your cousins. We can slip over to the store to watch the excitement. You're kin to half the settlement. It's not like we'd be wandering in some foreign land."

"I'd be better off in a foreign land. You'll keep pushing till we get deep in hot water. I can feel it coming. You have to tell Mommy. You lie better'n I do," said Leatha.

I stuck my tongue out at her, but she was right. My "convincing" was slicker than hers.

I guess the day was so hot that Mother was not in a mood to argue about what sounded like an innocent trip to the settlement. Permission settled, we decided to take my little sister Jane and Leatha's cousin Peachy. About three o'clock, we launched Burl's leaky rowboat and began poling across the shallow stream. The August water gave us no resistance as if it, like the dogs, had gone limp under the fierce sun. The humid air launched every flying insect right at us, and even on the water, the heat seemed to bubble from the inside of our skin as much as it glinted off the brackish creek. Jane and Peachy leaned over the side and let their hands and arms trail in the water. Leatha and I splashed ourselves with the poles, but with no breeze to cool our skin, relief was short.

"The snakes will be too hot to fight, I bet," I said.

"Not likely, but the handlers don't always get in the spirit enough to 'take up serpents.' It takes one of the deacons to know when it's right. There has to be a passel of singing, praying, and preaching. Speaking in tongues has to bloom, or the spirit is not strong enough to protect the saved no matter how many times they've handled," said Leatha.

"How do they speak in tongues? What is that?"

"It's some ancient language, and nobody, even the person speaking it, don't really know what it means, I reckon."

"Lordy, Leatha, you're making gooseflesh all over me. If you don't hush, Jane and Peachy will be screaming to go home in a minute."

We shuffled up to shore and tied the leaky boat to a sycamore tree. Moving from shade tree to shade tree, we made slow progress to the settlement and the Roses' house, but she and the baby weren't home. We spent a couple of hours with Leatha's aunt Susanny and cousin Dolly, drinking Kool-Aid and hearing stories about the stir in the settlement over the "handling." After we finished our drinks, we slid off the porch and ambled out of the yard. We said nothing about where we were going, but as soon as we were out of sight, we began to make our way to the store. There were already at least twenty people milling about, goofy half-grins hiding their curiosity as the handlers filtered past them.

Acting braver than I felt, I propelled myself to the door with the other three trailing behind me. The heat inside the door flung itself over us as if the devil himself was warning us to stay out. We shot across a bench and grabbed the nearest window seats. We spoke to the women sitting on our side of the aisle, front and back. Leatha asked about the new babies and ailing relatives and told them Fleetie sent her best. Trickles of sweat slid down my back, and Jane's hair was plastered in Kewpie-doll curls all over her head. As the room filled and the crowd began to settle, quiet spread one by one across the gathered congregation.

The song leader stood up and led us as we sang hymns, moved the hot air in rhythm with our funeral home fans, and watched the crowd grow outside the window. As the music faded, Preacher Helton began a preaching chant, a rhythmic listing of the sins of man that got louder and louder until his voice was roughened and coarse and sounded something like he had swallowed road grit.

Each phrase was followed by a deep gasp for breath that punctuated his sermon until his words and breathing were so tied, you couldn't really tell which was which. Heads nodded to the rhythm of his delivery. From the back, soft humming began, and all of us began rocking first to one side and then the other as we caught the sermon beat that carried us deeper in the beat, word, and melody. Men and women around us rose and began weaving up and down the narrow aisles, waving sweaty arms, seeming to lift their very souls up for God to inspect. Two of the men exhorted the congregation from their knees in a language that, while totally new to me, somehow seemed to make sense to the other folks there.

One by one, women I had known all my life threw themselves to their knees, hypnotized by the surrounding frenzy. The "took" women were so violent, other women jumped to protect them from the agitated spirit that flung them back and forth. Sweat streamed from their faces and matted hair. Without even being aware of it, tears tumbled down my face. They were demonstrating a commitment far beyond what I had ever experienced in the neat, carved pews of my prim and proper town church.

The rumble in the converted store was deafening. At the very peak of noise and hysteria, when I was sure it was as wild as it would ever be, the door flew open, and in walked three men swinging rattling, hissing cages. The muscles in their clenched jaws quivered as they stationed themselves on the narrow platform. No one moved. The room went silent as a cave. The rattlesnakes didn't seem to care except for the rattlesnakes.

A long slow moaning rose around us—part song, part dirge— and the room filled with the din of hymn and the rhythmic slap, slap of hands crashing around us in crowning waves of sound. Brother Helton walked to the man behind each cage. He laid his hand on his head and whispered. The deacons went to their knees and placed flat hands on the top of each cage, faces turned upward, lips moving in fevered prayer. Brother Helton moved from cage to cage and turned each over, freeing three piles of tangled, coiling snakes. He bent over one pile and, with no hesitation, swept a serpent up and over his head. He began a slow turn as the snake slipped down and circled his arm just above the elbow. Helton spoke quietly, breathing deeply and letting his words ride the stream of air onto the snake's head.

Following his lead, one after another of the men and women reached down and brought up a writhing snake until there were twelve of them holding snakes. Some wrapped the serpents around arms, some around the neck, and some let them coil over two hands. Each of the twelve went into a slow spin and wove in and out as they moved down the center aisle. I forgot to breathe as snakes and handlers passed close enough to touch. Some snakes seemed placid, wrapped around an arm or neck; others darted sharp eyes in every direction and struggled to slither out of the grasp of the handler.

"Praise God, brother," voices cried out.

"Save me."

"Pray for me, brother."

"Save them."

"Praise God for the sisters."

"God be with them."

The feeling of power in that crowded room rose from the floor and seemed to float just above each head. We didn't have a dry stitch on, and the air seemed suspended just beyond our noses as every eye stayed glued on the handlers.

Brother Helton moved to each of the handlers, placed his hands on their heads, and shouted, "Deliver the faithful. Praise God for the believer."

As each received the blessing, they moved with measured steps as if in a wedding march to the cages and, as gently as one would handle a baby, placed the constantly coiling reptile inside.

As they stepped away from the cages, sounds of joy rose from the family groups, but in the midst of the pandemonium, we were jolted by a piercing shriek.

"She is bit. Oh my god. It got her on the face. Oh god, help her, save her."

The voice rang out louder and louder. Preacher Helton knelt by the woman and whispered into her ear. Her eyes rolled back in her head, and a trail of spit spilled over her chin as she captured air in choking gasps. Her face was already beginning to swell, distorting her earlier expression of rapture.

Leatha grabbed my arm. "Where's her snake? Where did she drop the snake?"

The escaping rattler, moving like blue lightning, and probably because of the window, picked our row for escape. As it moved in front of our bench, I lunged for Jane and gave her a shove out the window. All I saw were her scuffed sandals as they disappeared through the window. Leatha and Peachy followed Jane out the window, and I turned around to look for the snake just as Deacon Howard moved down the bench and swooped up the snake and dropped it into the cage sitting in the aisle.

A cluster of worshippers singing and praising the Lord followed as the victim's husband carried her out the only door. Wild to find Jane and Peachy, I jumped out the window, and just as my feet touched ground, a strong hand clamped down on my shoulder, and I was face to face with Daddy.

Thinking faster than ever before in my life, I immediately tried to swing his mood around to the astonishment at what we had seen. I needed something quick, or the punishment for this adventure could last the rest of the summer.

"Daddy, did you know? Did you know they believe so much, they are actually changed right there in that dirty old storehouse? Did you see what happened?"

"Yes, Rachel, I was standing in the back row, and, young lady, this is no place for Jane and Peachy. If you and Leatha are going to go gallivanting around, looking for excitement, you know better than to drag these kids with you as cover."

"Lordy, Daddy, if I had known what really goes on, I would never have brought them. Did you feel all that back there? What happened in there? These people are our neighbors. I've known them all my life. How could they lose themselves in a trance and pick up snakes? They had to be terrified. How could they?"

"They are terrified, and without the trance, the self-hypnosis we all fell under, they probably couldn't. These people have a deep, unshakable belief that this is right for them. Gawkers like you and the crowd outside should know better than to push in where you aren't needed. Now get in the Plymouth, all of you. It is way past to time for you to be home where you belong."

Jane and Peachy were more than willing to jump for the safety of the old Plymouth, but Leatha and I stopped. The ambulance rolled in, and we watched as Mrs. Slone was whisked away so quick, it felt more like a movie than the front yard of Mr. Ben's old storehouse.

"Do you reckon she'll die? She has kids at home, and Bert will sure be lost without her."

"They mostly don't die, I hear, but they get awful sick, and no telling how they are going to pay the hospital," said Leatha.

Daddy was about to lose patience, "Girls, get in the car. It is time I get all of you home before your mothers come after me."

The revival continued for the rest of dog days, sustained by its own momentum. The handlers controlled the delicate internal timing for tongues, song, snakes, and moving on, all a part of the mystery of the tiny sect's survival. As we walked in the orchard in what was left of the summer, we could hear the music echo across the valley and almost smell the intensity of faith and fear that led men and women to do a thing so contrary to their nature.

Chapter 23

PICKETS AND SCABS

One morning, not long after the snake handling, Daddy and I were on our way to town, and we drove past a line of pickets at the mouth of the holler about two miles on the upper side from Baxter. All over the county, union recruiters were working hard to sign up all the miners, and on the other side of that argument, the owners and operators of the mines were pushing just as hard to keep the union out. A strong union organization could demand and get better wages, safer working conditions, shorter work hours, and time off. The owners knew this would cost more money with less direct control. The result at most coal fields in Kentucky and West Virginia there was a bitter fight—union against owners.

Daddy slowed down as we passed, and I could see the miners' drawn, tired faces, and you didn't have to look hard to see the men were agitated. They were restless, and rather than the slow, measured walk, carrying their signs on their shoulders, they were walking fast with no place to go, round and round but without picket signs as if speed would help make their side stronger.

As we passed, Daddy looked up the long hill at the men and shook his head. "Rachel, walking a picket line breaks your heart. It drains a man like a leg full of leeches. The first few days, you hear brave words and feel the excitement. But it has been too long now, and the men are nigh on to desperate. They all have families to feed, and hungry children makes a man want to fight."

He pulled the car onto an overlook, and I followed him back as we walked to the mouth of the holler. Just as we turned up the mine road, a truck pulled up behind us, driven by Mike Pridemore, a second-generation operator and son of Old Man Harvey Pridemore.

Daddy yelled, "Mike, what are you doing out here? Are you behind whatever's got the men stirred up? Something is different from yesterday."

"The old man's gone and hired us a security man, and we're bringing up a crew to open the mine. This strike don't look like it's got any end. It's time to bust it up."

"Bust it up? Boy, if you bring in a load of scabs to cross the picket and a bunch of hired goons willing to shoot to kill to protect them, you're asking to start a war. Those men are desperate. They've spent the winter and now the summer waiting for the union and you operators to get it straight."

Daddy's voice dropped, and I could feel a charge in the air. Daddy had a trick voice that made him boom out like a loudspeaker, and when he started in that tone, all those around knew they had gone too far. Once, my little brother Logan stumbled into a nest of copperheads as he was chasing my sister Jane with a spider. I remember hearing that booming tone of Daddy's right before he grabbed the hoe, leaned up against an apple tree, swung it high in the air, and brought it down with enough force to kill the first copperhead. Another swing and a bellow to match, and the copperhead mate lost her head too. If copperheads were not so vicious, I might be tempted to say that the tone of his voice could have stopped them midslither, but you have to cut off the head to kill one. I only had one spanking when he was in full voice, and I learned quick never to mess with that much anger ever again.

Daddy took a step toward the truck, and Mike jerked his arm back inside. The smirk on his face was long gone.

"Mike, I'm not going to say it again, but you remember this. These men are sick of watching their women and children go without.

You bring in a truck full of scabs, and you might as well put a match to gasoline. It will explode this fight like nothing we have seen here yet. You get on back to town and stop this. I'm telling you, this will put blood on it, and then how you gonna get past that?"

Mike opened the truck door and stepped down. "Ed, you sound like the rest of the union bastards who are trying to steal our coal mines. Coal belongs to the mountains and to mountain people. Union is not us."

"Mike, this is not the place or time to settle this. Stop what you are doing and think. We are not talking Mingo County in West Virginia and their mine battles on Little Cabin Creek. I am warning you, this is more trouble than you want. You would be smart to pay attention."

Mike swung back up into the truck and jammed it in reverse. "Ed, what's right is right. The coal under that mountain belongs to us Pridemores, and by god, we mean to have it." He backed the truck around and tore down the road, throwing up a cloud of dust as if to underline the threat.

Daddy stood for a short while as the dust of the red dog slag settled. He turned to see the picketing miners standing as if they were on military alert with every pair of eyes focused on him. As he walked toward them up the steep grade, I wondered whether or not he knew what he was going to say to them. I was sure the hair on his neck had to be standing straight out and his stomach tied in a hundred knots. The situation had moved past talking, and no matter what words spilled out, it looked like he could not stop what was coming.

The first man Daddy approached in that crowd of desperate men was Johnny Howard. Johnny had already given Uncle Sam one lung when he took a bullet in Germany. Now here he was, filling the other one with Pridemore dust.

"Johnny, I've just come from the settlement. Your mom has taken a fall. You need to get on home."

Daddy wasn't apt to lie, but this was different. He and Johnny had run the hills as kids. You could always hear the sadness in Daddy's voice when he talked about him. "Rachel," he would say, "he had a keen mind and big dreams, but they've been ripped to shreds by too much trouble and too little peace settling into his life."

Burl turned to Johnny. "Get your dinner bucket and get on home. You can walk it in half an hour. Mary needs you more than we do. Go on, boy. Do what I say."

Burl stood beside Daddy, while Johnny walked down the hill.

"Burl, a man oughta figure some way to get more of them out of here. It don't look good. Look around you. Which one of them do we want to see dead over a few dollars that won't make a damn bit of difference at the store anyway?"

"It's gone past money, Ed. There's no moving now. The union says stand, and the union's all we've got left."

"Hell, Burl. Where's the union going to be when you have to bury some of these boys? How you going to give up John N. or Guy or Henry? Just as soon as the shooting's over, the union will pack up and go right over the mountain to make trouble for some other poor devils. Man, think. We can't just let them stand here and be shot down like they don't matter."

It was strange to see Daddy and Burl argue, and I couldn't help but wonder what was the right side. The owners spent lots of money opening mines, and the miners spent their muscle and bone pulling the coal out. Both sides gave coal all they had, and where was the right and wrong in the fight? I was with Daddy no matter what, but Burl had Fleetie and the kids to take care of. No matter what happened, the last thing I wanted was for them to be hurt in all this, and yes, even Burl. Even though he was so mean to his kids that I mostly didn't care about him one way or the other, I had sense enough to know his family needed him.

"Better get on down the road, Ed. When the scabs get here, there'll be a hell of a fight. It won't look good for you to be here. We'll be needin' you to get those of us who live through it out of jail. The sheriff will find some way to make it look like we started it."

Daddy held Burl with his stare, and I would bet that for the first time in their lives, Burl held his stare right back. At that moment, the separate paths they walked veered even farther apart. Daddy held to the rule of law, and Burl's independent spirit drove him, and today, friend or not, Burl stood his ground.

Daddy turned and made his way down the hill with me trailing behind. We got in the car, but instead of driving the Plymouth off the hill, he turned it around and pulled it up the path. He strong-armed the steering wheel until he had worked the car sideways, blocking the narrow mine road. He climbed out of the car and leaned against the fender, took his Camel pack out of his shirt pocket, shook a cigarette up, and reached for his matches. They were on the seat of the car. I opened the door and picked them up and gave them to him. He took the box and carefully selected one of the short wooden matches, scratched it against the rough side of the box, and lit his cigarette. He handed the box back to me, and as he stood there, he looked, for all the world, like he was just taking a rest. Burl never took his eyes off him. Neither man was giving an inch.

Off in the distance, I saw what I didn't want to see, and when I turned, I saw that Daddy had seen it too. About a mile down the dirt road, there was a rising cloud of dust kicked up by a huge truck hauling a load of men. They would be hell-bent on getting into the mine for that day's pay. We watched as the cloud grow larger. Daddy leaned against the front fender and was so deep in thought that he forgot the cigarette clenched between his fingers. As the truck turned into the mine road, the ash glow burned into his finger. He jerked and shook his hand and swore to high heaven. He wasn't much to curse as a rule, but today must have seemed a good time to break over. Still shaking his hand, he stepped away from the car and took about ten steps down the road toward the truck. I stayed a ways behind him.

Donyel Ball, the county's main hothead, was behind the wheel. I was still mad at him for punching Charley at Coburn's store. They both reached for the last cold Pepsi, and instead of settling it polite-like, Donyel hauled off and knocked Charley down with one punch. Charley roared back up and was about to take Donyel down when Coburn jumped between them. Donyel left mad, but he got the Pepsi after all. Here was a chance for me to get a little revenge for Charley. Not that Charley would thank me for it, me being a girl daring to fight his battles, but it would do me a world of good. I had the box of matches in my hand, and I slid open the box and pulled out several of the matches. Old Donyel was going to get a surprise.

I watched as he pumped the brakes and slowed the overloaded truck to a stop.

"Ed, man, get your car out of the way. These boys is hired legal, and they're going to work this mine, or by god, there's going to be some killing going on." He was strutting his stuff by yelling at Daddy.

I walked over to the back right wheel, crouched down and acting like I was looking for something I had dropped. With Donyel distracted, talking to Daddy, I jammed a match stick in the tire valve. The match stick was small enough to let the air out slowly, and with any luck, the tire would not go flat until Donyel got halfway back to town. Then Mr. Smarty Pants would be hoofing it and spewing curses all the rest of the way into town.

Daddy answered Donyel with a soft voice as if he were talking to a gentleman. "I didn't know you were working for Pridemores, Donyel. Last I knew, you were a Winfield man, and they settled last month. You just lookin' for any fight you can find?"

"Ed, move that damn junker. I'm coming through if I have to knock you and that goddamn excuse of a car over the bank."

"Hold your tongue, Donyel. Rachel doesn't need to hear your garbage. I'm not blocking the men. I'm blocking that overloaded truck. I'm going to take the men to work myself. You back your truck out of here and send the men walking up here. They're getting a private escort for free. No charge to the Pridemores. It'll save your hired goons from getting buckshot in their backsides. Move it!"

The men dropped off the truck and huddled in a clutch on the road. They watched Daddy wave Donyel back down the hill and onto the county road.

Daddy turned to the scabs and spoke in a low voice. "Boys, I know you need work as bad as anybody. You'd have to to be willing to walk past those men up there whose jobs you're stealing. As bad as this is, I don't want anybody dead. But more than that, I don't want any of them up there to do the killing. They are good men, and I can't see as how any of you is worth killing anyway. Hear me? I'm taking you in. It'll take a bullet through me to stop you. It won't be right smart for any of you to drag back. Either stay tight or leave down the hill right now."

Five of the men turned and started back down the hill. Somehow, they looked worse to me than scabs. A coward went as low as you can go. The rest of the men followed Daddy as he approached the double picket line of miners.

"Burl, John N., tell the others back there that I'm taking this bunch of no-good scabs into the mine. You'll have to shoot me to stop them. You better believe I'm not planning to go to bed tonight with any worthless scab blood on my hands. If any of you men are willing to kill me for Pridemore coal, go on and shoot. But this is how it's going down today. Tomorrow may be better, but not today."

He looked around for me. I thought maybe he had forgotten I was with him. Knowing that he was going to walk through the picket line with the scabs made my heart beat so hard, my mouth went dry.

Daddy wasn't about to let me stay in case there was shooting. Knowing he was that worried scared me almost as bad as that line of angry men.

"Rachel, after I escort these men into the mine, I am going to see Judge Harrison and get an injunction to stop this nonsense. Get on the railroad and walk on home, and tell your mother where I am. Knowing the judge, I'd say it might take me a long time to get it done."

I hated to leave Daddy alone with every single person there mad about something—and most of it directed at him—but I knew better than to start any begging that day on that mountain. Daddy had enough to think about. It was time for me to shut up and do what I was told. I started down the mine road and walked until I reached a giant sycamore halfway down to the base of the mountain. I put the tree between the men at the top and me and stood behind it where I was not seen but could watch what was going on.

Disobeying Daddy was bad, but if Mother found out that I left him up there alone, I would be in trouble with her. That's the way it was with those two. One minute, they could scream bloody murder at each other, but you just let any kind of threat come at them, and you found out really quick how the land lay. So here I was, right in the middle, but even in the confusion, I knew staying was the better choice. I was scared to go and scared to stay, but staying won out. Scared or not, this was better than any movie I had ever watched at the Margie Grand Theater in town.

Silence fell over the hill as Daddy led those sorry, good-for-nothing scabs past all those good men and to the face of the mine. Even at my distance, I could see that each miner's face reflected the bitterness at the defeat, and why not? You could just feel their high hopes of union protection and good jobs flying over the mountain. Too many of them faced powers that were eternally against them, while they and their people were trapped by a poverty so insidious that it ground their lives to shreds. Daddy was gambling that Burl could not raise his rifle against him, and if he wouldn't, neither would the men standing behind him. He trusted Burl enough, but he could not know if in the crowd of hungry miners, there was a man who had already been pushed too far.

The men crossing the picket line kept their heads down, and at the mine face, they scurried in their tight huddle to the mantrip. The last two men pushed the wheeled cart into the drift mouth. The miners, to a man, riveted their eyes on the backs of men who, from that day, would be labeled scum. To go against your own in a battle against big power and big money was to come away a traitor. There would be no forgiveness for them in that valley.

As soon as the last scab disappeared into the mine, Daddy said, "I'm going to town to see the judge. You boys give it up today. I'm going to try to get an injunction against Pridemore to stop this, but it's not safe for any of you to walk the picket line here now. Burl, you and John N. see that every one of them gets down the hill and pretty quick too. We'll fight this another day when we've got some odds on our side."

Burl stood looking past Daddy for what seemed like too long. Reaching into his bib pocket, Burl dug out his makings and rolled a cigarette with hands that betrayed him with their tremble. He pulled out his lighter and flicked open the Zippo, and a small cloud of smoke rose between them.

"Ed, This ain't over."

"No, Burl, God only knows when it will be. Go on for today. Give me a chance here to see what I can do."

For what seemed like a long time, Burl did not move, but then he turned with John N. They walked into the knot of miners, and Daddy walked back to the Plymouth. The narrow path and the awkward turn of the car kept him fighting the wheel for a few minutes, long enough for me to run back up and jump in the back seat. He didn't say a word to me. Maybe he forgot he sent me home, or maybe he didn't even know I was in the car. Daddy was a thinking man, and there was plenty to chew on right then.

Burl and John N. convinced the men to move, and our car and the miners began to make their slow way down the mountain. From the back window, I saw them start moving down the road. Their bodies told the story of yet another defeat—their heads down, shoulders slumped, and thumbs hooked in their pockets. Daddy made a right turn at the end of the mine road, and it was almost a relief not to have to see that cluster of men anymore.

Chapter 24

THE HALLS OF JUSTICE

When I figured it was safe to break the silence, I finally started with questions.

"Daddy, tell me about a junction? How long will it take? What good will it do? Can it really fix all this?"

"Lordy, Rach, my stomach is so knotted, it will take days to let up. Just give me a minute's peace. It is *injunction*, and I don't know what it is going to take to get one. Probably a miracle. No one is bleeding or dead right now, thank god. I'll think of something. Just let me have a little quiet. No more questions!"

I shut my mouth. Judge Harrison drove Daddy crazy. Not only was he the one person in the county who held the power in his hands to make life miserable for a lawyer, but he also seemed to take special pleasure in doing so. I guess Daddy made mistakes like all lawyers did, but Judge Harrison loved catching him at it as if it was a game. Daddy said lots of times that he was sure the judge was making a better lawyer out of him, but at the same time, he would appreciate a little less attention to his development.

As we made our way to town, I could see his hands shake on the wheel. He was so deep in thought, he didn't pay any attention to the deep burn on two of his fingers. I knew he would have those scars on his fingers for a long time. Mother was bound to get tears in her eyes when she changed the bandages, and she would give me that look that says I was somehow to blame. It wouldn't be so bad if I didn't think I was too, but I didn't see the burning cigarette in time either, and to make it worse, I gave him the matches. I'm not that good at noticing, but I can do something about where we are going right now.

Right after Daddy parked the car, I spoke up. "Daddy, I know you said be quiet, but I have a plan for you on how to get past Belle Eggars. Can I talk?"

"Talk, chatterbox. You will anyway. What is it?"

"You know Judge Harrison uses Ms. Belle as his own personal bodyguard 'cause she is mean enough to scare half the town?"

Daddy somehow managed to laugh in spite of the misery of a burned hand and the job he had in front of him. I was afraid that Judge Harrison stood mostly on the side of the operators anyway, and if Daddy can't even get in the door, it could be doomsday for him and Burl and the rest of the miners.

"What do you mean, you can get me past Belle? Planning to shoot her, maybe?"

We both laughed. Laughing felt a whole lot better than the yelling and cursing whirling around the Pridemore mine.

"When I was junior clerk for the circuit office this summer, I noticed that Sue Ann Howard always kept a lot of paper work stacked up for the judge. Ms. Belle wouldn't let me or anyone else touch it, and it made Sue Ann so mad, she always made Ms. Belle walk up all those stairs and get the folders herself. It was my job to deliver the message to Ms. Belle. I hated to do it because she always quarreled about having to stop and go upstairs, making out as if somehow, it was my fault. She doesn't know I haven't worked here today. I will just tell her Sue Ann has papers for her. When she goes upstairs, you are in like Flynn."

"Aren't you leaving Sue Ann in the middle?"

"She won't care. Besides, I don't think she is even here today. We are in her parking place. There's her name on the curb where one of the trusties painted it. I think he is her cousin."

"Pretty sneaky, Rach. You might be developing a criminal streak that I should discourage, but I am not going to start now. Today, I am going to take full advantage of all the sneakiness you can think up. When we get out of the car, you go up the back stairs and come down the front steps there by her office door. I'll stand in the courtroom so she won't see me waiting. Go to it, girl. We'll get this done together. How about you?"

My head began to swell with pride, but I had to hurry. Gloating about how clever I was would have to wait.

Chapter 25

THE INJUNCTION

He gave me a wink, and I jumped out of the car and up the back steps of the courthouse. When I got to the mezzanine and looked over the heavy rail, I saw Daddy standing just inside the wide swinging doors of the courtroom. My heart was about to jump out of my throat as I started down the hand-carved marble staircase. When I was halfway down, Ms. Belle walked out of her outer office door and down the hall to the restroom. I jumped down four steps at a time and waved Daddy to the office door. He shot through the outer door and picked up a stack of papers on Ms. Belle's desk. He clenched his jaw hard and pushed open the door leading to Judge Harrison's chambers. Daddy pointed me to the chair by the door

I figured Ms. Belle was bound to be back soon, so I hid behind the door instead. I could hear well enough through the hinge side of the open door. The judge's high-backed leather chair was turned toward the window opposite the door, and he did not see Daddy walk in.

He shuffled the papers and spoke softly, "Judge, here are some papers from Ms. Belle, sir." It wasn't exactly a lie—more of a convenient truth of the moment.

"Afternoon, Ed. Right kind of you to be delivering Ms. Belle's dictation notes. She'll be much obliged, I'm sure, that is if she doesn't pin your ears back first. What are you up to this afternoon besides sneaking in here while Belle isn't looking?"

"Judge, thank you for seeing me. I know this is somewhat out of order, but I need to get your advice about some trouble I stumbled onto this morning."

Daddy had an instinct about people. He knew better than to try to introduce the subject of an injunction. If there was going to be any help at all, Judge Harrison was going to have to decide pretty much on his own that an injunction was in the best interest of the court and the county.

"Judge, Pridemore's have ordered a bunch of scabs to cross the picket line at the mine up on Nolan's branch. I was at the mine face this morning, and I saw enough firepower on both sides to blow them all to kingdom come and back. That mine is struck and picketed just like all the others in the county. What do you think a man ought to do?"

"Stop it! By god, that whole thing has got to be stopped. Might know it'd be a Pridemore who'd try to push the strike to a bloody war. The only one of that clan worth a damn is old Doc, and he's pretty near past it these days. Those boys of his have gone and pulled the wool over his eyes this time."

"I'm sure you're right," said Daddy. "Doc saves what strength he has these days to see a few patients. Most of them won't or can't see anybody else, and he's about all that's keeping them on foot."

"I'm going to slap a temporary injunction on those shenanigans up there before some of the boys on both sides of this mess wind up dead. Ed, no legal action will hold them off forever. I want you to see if you can't find some way or somebody to get them talking again. I'm giving this thing sixty days."

"Thank you, judge. I'm just about stumped. I don't think anybody but John L. Lewis himself could put a stop to this one."

"If it takes John L., then we might just as well plan on wiping up the blood and doing some sad singing and slow walking. John L. is a big shot these days. It doesn't look to me he has any use for the rank and file. And these men are both ranking and filing right out of existence if you ask me."

Daddy chuckled at the judge's little word twist. Daddy could have given Judge Harrison strong arguments for the injunction all backed with relevant precedents, but today, getting in the door and asking the senior man's opinion had been argument enough.

"Thank you again, judge. Two months will put some pressure on both sides to get at it and get on past this."

"On your way out, please ask Belle to step in here with her pad and pencil. I'm going to get this thing issued today before another hothead decides to truck in more firepower."

"Yes, sir, hope she doesn't take after me for slipping in."

"Whatever she does, you deserve it. She thinks she's the queen around here, and she doesn't take it kindly when any of us forget that."

"I'll try to take it like a man. Thank you again, sir."

Daddy could usually charm his way through sticky situations, but Belle Eggars had his number. No amount of grace and good manners from my Daddy with his blond good looks and easy smiles could make a dent. Today, he got lucky.

I told Ms. Belle when she got back from the restroom that Sue Ann needed her upstairs. When he came out, her chair was still empty.

"Did you lock Belle in a closet?'

"I did better than that. I used the Sue Ann plan. We have to hurry before she comes charging us like a mad bull."

"I swear, Rachel, I'm of a mind to keep you, handy as you are."

"Hurry, Daddy! Let's duck out the back door."

Just as we turned the corner and out of sight, we heard her thick heels come clomping down the marble steps. We both grinned and hit the road. We didn't stop until we jumped in the car.

"You know this is worth a double-dipped chocolate ice cream cone. Let's just stop off at Green Miller and celebrate."

"Green Miller? You serious?"

He winked at me, "I don't joke about ice cream."

Green Miller, ice cream, Daddy, and the injunction all at once. Not a bad haul. It was almost enough to make me forget the desperate men up at the mine face but not quite. The trouble was never far from anyone's mind.

Chapter 26

Unintended Consequences

The miners in this coal-mining valley had been on strike for six months. Yesterday, Daddy, using his most persuasive lawyer skills, convinced Judge Harrison to issue an injunction to stem the violence at the picket line. In the middle of the morning, I heard the transmission grind and a muffled bump of tires as Daddy negotiated the car over the gullies and ruts of our steep road. He never came home during the day unless something was wrong. I ran to the door, but he was still sitting in the car. I pushed open the screen door and walked to the edge of the porch and watched as he stepped out of the car, but he stopped. He turned and looked past the car and down into the valley spread out in front of him and then put his hand over his eyes and cried.

I started down the porch steps but stopped midstep. For the first time in my life, I saw my daddy cry. Mother and I cried, but never Daddy. I knew my strong, proud daddy would have been embarrassed if he knew I had seen him crying, so I slipped back inside the front door and waited until he began walking up the porch steps. I pushed open the door. He had wiped away the tears. His eyes were red and his complexion gray. The lines in his face seemed etched deeper than usual. His dark blond hair showed the number of times he had run his fingers through it, and his wide shoulders were slumped.

"There's a fresh pot of coffee on the stove, strong and dark, the way you like it. Come sit at the table, and I'll pour a cup for you."

He nodded and looked at me for the first time. "That sounds good, Rachel. Why don't you have one with me? Sometimes, I forget how grown up you are these days."

"What's wrong, Daddy?"

"Give me a minute." His voice sounded as if it was forced through gravel.

He followed me up the steps and lingered on the front porch. I walked to the kitchen and poured the coffee. I set his cup on the table at his usual place, but when he came in the room, he sat in Mother's chair. He seemed too tired to walk to the head of the table. When I picked up his coffee and slid it toward him, he gripped my arm hard, and I swear I could feel his hurt through my sleeve. There was a hush in the room when I sat down beside him.

"What happened?"

The gravels in his voice were gone. It was soft and almost tender when he answered, "This morning, right after the injunction was issued, the striking miners went back to the picket line at Pridemore's. Sheriff Hershel Garber was waiting for them. You know I've known Hershel all my life. He was a man you could trust. I knew I could depend on him to take care of the trouble up at the mine."

"Is that the Mr. Hershel who brought us some doves after the last shoot?"

Daddy nodded. "Hershel told the men they were not to carry weapons, and if they did, he would confiscate them. He promised to turn the scabs back, but he demanded there be no interference from anyone. If there was, he would arrest them on the spot. Hershel knew how the miners felt and told them he would not send them down the mountain until the scabs were gone."

"You mean the picketers had to leave after all those weeks of walking that line day after day? You know that had to make them plenty mad. It's a wonder they didn't start shooting right then," I said.

"Hershel had it worked out that after the scabs hightailed it back to town, all but two of the picketers had to leave. That way, they wouldn't have to walk away with the scabs yelling all that filth at them."

"Did that help? Did they really agree to what Hershel wanted?"

"Yes, it seemed so. Hershel climbed in his car, placed his shotgun on the seat beside him, and drove down the hill. He turned his car sideways to block the road so he could stop anyone from ramming a truck all the way to the mine face."

"Anyone like Donyel? He would do anything he could to cause trouble."

Daddy nodded, but he didn't say anything for a long time. I sat there, really hesitant to move. After he had taken my arm the way he did, I had the feeling that he wanted someone near. That it was me was a surprise, but I was there, and Mother wasn't.

Finally, I broke the silence. "What did they do when he left?"

"The miners broke apart their wall of men and scattered. It had to be killing them to stand back and let the sheriff do their fighting. Each one to a man wanted to pull out a weapon and plunge into the middle of a fight to drive the scabs back down the mine road. The truck loaded with Pridemore scabs stopped on the hill in front of Hershel's car. He got out and stepped three steps to the side of the truck and spoke to the driver, a Pridemore agent.

"He said, 'You go tell your boss this fight has gone to the courts. Judge decided there would be no work in this mine for sixty days, and if he has any objection, he will have to take it up with the judge.' Then he told the driver and the scabs crowding the truck bed, 'I have to do my duty, and I'd a whole lot rather do it peaceful, but I can go the other way if you push it.'"

Daddy went on. "The driver spit out a string of goddamns and hell fires, enough to make the devil blush, but Hershel just stood there, not moving. He'd heard it all before. He wasn't about to shoot a man because of his poor grammar. The truck finally backed down the hill and onto the county road and headed toward town. Hershel was good as his word. Just as soon as the truck was out of sight, he told the men to go on home. After an hour, all the men but two had left the mountain, and Hershel decided to go back to town and send a deputy out to keep watch."

"Wasn't that the end of it then, after they all left?" I asked.

"That's what we all thought, but I guess it was way too easy. His car bounced over the deep ruts and rocks to the bottom of the steep road, and he turned toward town on the county road. About two miles from the mine, you know where the road dips real low near the water?"

"Yes, that's where Logan always hides his eyes because he thinks we are going in the water."

"Maybe Logan has second sight about that dip because Hershel must have seen a fishing boat moored near the road and slowed down to wave. A vote is a vote, and he never hesitates to let people know he is on the job.

"As he rounded the sharp curve just beyond the dip, the Pridemore's man pulled his now empty truck in front of Hershel's Chevy. Shots rang out, and Hershel was hit in the shoulder and hand. He slammed on the brakes, and the car spun out of control. It skidded and careened into a sycamore and threw him into the windshield. The pressure of his body on the steering wheel set off the horn. The car stopped, and Hershel fell off the steering wheel into the passenger seat, silencing the horn. The man in the truck gunned it forward, spinning rocks and gravel behind him as he put distance between him and the sheriff's car. The truck disappeared around the curve, and the two men on the river poled the boat to the shore. One jumped to the bank. The other picked up a can and a bundle of rags and scrambled up to the car. He opened the car door, slapped down the door locks, poured kerosene on the rags, and hurled them into the back seat of the car. He turned the sloshing can upside down onto the floorboard and made a matchbook igniter by placing the cover over all the matches but one. He placed the makeshift fuse on the kerosened floor and lit the single match. It burned down to its base and began to eat into the cardboard cover.

"In sixty seconds or less, it exploded the rest of the matches. He slammed down the last lock and kicked the door shut. They jumped the bank in one leap, pushed hard on the pole, and floated down the river. Two little kids were fishing off the bank on the other side of the river and saw most of this happen. Poor kids."

"Daddy, you don't mean that Hershel was in the burning car and they left him like that?" My stomach was rolling, and I felt cold all over.

"The heat and odor of the burning kerosene must have startled Hershel into consciousness. The lock prevented him from opening the door with the handle. I guess he must have slid his hand down the window, searching for the lock. His fingers could have wrapped around the metal lock post and pulled. The handle was just below his elbow, and it would not have taken much to shove it down. The door swung open, and the rush of fresh air would have exploded the already raging fire into an inferno. Hershel's head and shoulders fell out the door as he stretched his hand toward the ground he never reached. Black smoke belched its way above the trees, throwing up his last signal." Daddy's voice broke.

I couldn't do more than whisper, "Daddy, who were they? Who killed him? Why?"

"Both sides of this blasted strike are guilty, Rachel, but I played right into their hands. I was the one who got that damn injunction and condemned one of the best friends I or this county ever had. I should have realized he would enforce the court order regardless of the danger. I have to live with that the rest of my life."

He pounded his fist on the table, and the cups rattled in the saucers. He then stomped out and slammed the back door. I watched as he stalked across the backyard, pushed open the back gate, and started up the narrow mountain path. Right at that moment, from the bend of his back, it looked to me that he was carrying all the misery a man could lift. Tears spilled down my cheeks as I picked up his cup and poured out the cold black coffee.

Chapter 27

MORE TROUBLE

I stopped Mother on the front steps and told her what happened to Hershel. "Daddy cried. Mother, I have never seen him cry before."

"Rachel, don't start. You just take the kids and stay out of the house. He needs to be left alone. What a tragedy."

Mother had two opinions of me. First, I was capable of working like an adult, and second, I was as naive as baby Logan. She assumed I had no notion of what was going on around me. If I had an opinion, it was based on nothing of value, and any new idea I might have was a waste of her time. Today was no different. She walked past me on her way to the front door, determined to hear Daddy's version. I knew what was going on in her head. She didn't trust my telling of a story and knew that what I told her couldn't possibly be all there was to know, but Daddy must have been talked out. He stopped Mother on the porch and told us he had to go see Judge Harrison.

"Will he be mad, Daddy?"

It was a logical question because the day he got the injunction, Judge Harrison seemed determined that Daddy should get to the bottom of the trouble.

"He is a good man, Rachel, and he is going to want something done to stop the killing."

Daddy was always right in the middle of stuff. He took the cake, as Pappy would always say. All the miners liked him, operators paid him for their legal work, preachers trusted him, kids ran after him, and old ladies spoiled him. Any kind of trouble, and before long, somebody would drive up the hill, and pots of coffee would perk, and every bit of cake in the house would disappear.

Humph! In my opinion, it was well and good for the judge to sit back and expect Daddy to pull a miracle out of a hat. It would be something else if the judge had to face all his friends with Hershel lying dead. I felt so sorry for Daddy, I wanted to cry myself, not that anybody would take the slightest bit of notice if I cried a bucketful.

After he walked down the front steps and to the end of the sidewalk, he opened the car door and stood there, looking out across the valley. I started to go after him, but Mother grabbed my arm and held on hard.

"Grown men are not little babies, Rachel. You have to let him face this his own way."

Leaving him alone, just standing there, seemed mean to me. When Pappy died, everyone hugged everyone who came close. I pulled my arm away to go on in spite of the warning, but Daddy was already in the car. I watched as the car drove to the turnaround and waved at him as he passed us.

"You just will not leave it alone, will you, Rachel?"

I glared at her, but she turned away and picked up a broom leaning on the wall by the front screen. She started sweeping the front steps as if the leaves and dirt were her personal enemies. I knew her next move would be to hand me the broom, and before that could happen, I stomped across the porch and slammed the screen door hard. But I was wrong that time about what she was planning. She was restless and didn't seem to be interested in doing any of the day's work or, better yet, getting me involved in it. She came back into the kitchen, poured a cup of tea, and sat down at the table with Janey, who was playing with the dry cereal in her bowl. The kitchen was quiet, and Janey watched us with wide eyes, and why not? You could almost feel misery in the air, and Jane was wary.

"Jane," Mother said, "would you like to have a Polly Pigtails meeting?"

A few weeks earlier, Mother had gathered all the little girls in the neighborhood for an afternoon of refreshments and embroidery. She called the gathering the Polly Pigtails Club after a favorite storybook, popular with the girls. Almost all the girls in the little group wore their hair in braids, so the name stuck. The hit of the afternoon was a dress-up and makeup with "high" tea. Leatha and I were the eldest, and Mother used us to help her serve and be the guinea pigs for the makeup sessions. Mother gave everyone manners lessons, and they caused ripples of giggles with exaggerated curtsies and bows and "proper" talking. Leatha and I would give an example, and the rest would follow us.

Mother taught us how to do easy embroidery stitches on some tea towel fabric that she had in her sewing basket. At the very proper time of three o'clock in the afternoon, Mother announced it was time for tea. She brought out her Brown Betty teapot, a yellow sugar bowl, and a tiny flower-covered cream pitcher. On the tray were seven of her delicate teacups from the precious collection that had once belonged to her mother. She passed out the demitasse cups and saucers filled with milk tea. Fingers were crooked up, and sips were taken, and we ate cookies in dainty nibbles. It was just as much fun to laugh at one another as it was to play at being ladies. No one was ready for the fun to end, but when the cast of the sun warned it was time to think about evening chores, Mother promised we would have another meeting of the Polly Pigtails Club, and while it did not seem to fit, today must have been the day to call everyone together again.

"Let me take the note to the mothers, please, please?" Jane said. For the first meeting, Mother had written a note of invitation to each of the mothers, explaining that she was in charge and would take care of everyone. Mary Middleton, Helen Willis, and Fleetie would never allow their kids to come up the hill to our house without a direct invitation from Mother or Daddy. As free as we kids were, we could not go inside the yards of any neighbor without a definite purpose or invitation. The mountain was a different matter. We could and did roam every inch, every trail, rock overhang, and cliff. Yards were off-limits, but wild streams, rivers, and deep gullies were free for the taking.

Mother nodded. "And what time do we want to start the meeting?" She was already writing the notes.

"Right now," I said. "Then we can have lunch. Let's have a picnic and cook over a fire. We could call it hobo food."

Jane interrupted that notion. "We are Polly Pigtails girls, not hobos."

"When I finish the notes, Janey can deliver them. Rachel, you get the kindling together for a fire outside. We'll cook tin can potatoes, and we can add some dainty sandwiches. We don't have to be hobos to enjoy outdoor cooking. Ms. Sary Sargeant is a Cherokee, and she has cooked outdoors lots of times. No one would ever say she was a hobo."

Jane took the notes and folded them small enough to fit in the pocket of her pinafore. Then with her blond curls bouncing with every step, she began the long walk to invite the Polly Pigtails Club members for an afternoon of fun. She was in luck that day. The mothers said yes, and as Jane hurried to come back up the hill, she suddenly began to shriek and point.

I was standing at the top of the drive, watching her, when she started running. I looked back down the hill and immediately saw what had scared her. Black smoke rolled out of the back of the Clement house. Geneva and the twins were in the side garden, digging potatoes, and her view of the back of the house was blocked by the poplar trees growing between the garden and the side of the house.

Nothing in Jane's six years had given her a warning of the danger of smoke rolling out from under the eaves of a house. Later on, as far as anybody could recollect, Janey had never seen a house fire in her life. In spite of that, the sight had sent her shrieking up the hill. She screamed for Mother all the way, and by the time she got to me, she was almost past speaking.

She pointed down the road and pulled my hand. "Smoke, smoke. Black. Big. Smoke, smoke!"

When Mother got to us, she swept Janey up, and for just a few seconds, we stood and looked in astonishment at the clouds of smoke coughing out of the Clements' cabin.

Immediately, Mother ordered me back to the house to get Logan. "Girls, sit right here and watch for me. I'll come right back up here and get you. Do you understand me? Go now, Rachel, and get Logan."

I ran back toward the house as Mother tore down the hill, shrieking like a banshee. Everybody within a mile must have heard her. Geneva looked up and saw Mother tearing down the hill, but she couldn't make out what she was saying. A sudden popping sound must have caused Geneva to jerk around toward the house. I could hear her screaming.

"Oh god, my baby, my baby. Oh god, help me. Help me," she screamed over and over as she tore through the front door and plunged into the blackness beyond the doorstep.

Freddie's crib was in the bedroom, just to the right of the front door, and Geneva ran into swirls of smoke that shrouded her as she disappeared. She must have had to feel her way to his crib. We saw them as she tore out the door and into the yard. Mother and Fleetie got there just as Geneva sailed off the front step with Freddie in her arms. Helen Willis and her four children came across the tracks and began running in and out the front door, carrying out what they could grab from the ink-black darkness.

I couldn't stand it any longer and ordered Logan and Jane to stay put while I ran down the long hill. I could see that Mary Middleton and her children were pumping water from the well house in the side yard. I jumped in their bucket line and helped pass full water buckets to the back door. Since I was the tallest, I went to the front of the line. Roger, the eldest Willis boy, had pushed himself inside the back screen after he had soaked the floorboards around the door, enough to let him step inside to throw buckets of water into the fiery kitchen. The floor was burning in a circle of flame, and he tried to aim the buckets of water at the base of the ring.

Fleetie sent her girls around to our side of the house to start another line of buckets, and Nessa pushed herself inside the door with Roger. With two sets of buckets coming at them, they were able to make more headway against the fire. Huge waves of black smoke rolled out the front windows and door, and that provided enough of a wind tunnel to make it possible for Roger and Nessa to keep working in the burning kitchen.

Geneva, Fleetie, and Mother were on the ground with the baby. As he struggled for every breath, the rush of fresh air mixed with the smoke in his lungs brought on convulsive coughing and vomiting. The two women worked with him to clear his air passages, and Fleetie picked him up and began turning herself in circles, swinging the baby in a circle to force more air into his nose and mouth.

Mother looked back up the hill to see about Jane and Logan, but they were gone. They had run back to the house to ring the black dinner bell hanging in the turnaround. Mother brought the bell with her from Bluegrass country, and Daddy had done nothing but tease her about putting it up. With no crops worked by field hands or no lumberjacks bringing down trees, it had been hard to justify the digging and post mounting it took to secure the bell. But Mother would have it no other way. The bell was from her grandmother's farm in Madison County, and she said seeing it hang there made her feel safer.

Later on, we would talk about how hard it must have been for Jane to pull the rope free from the half hitch, but she did it, and with the racket she made, every person in the settlement could hear it, but they didn't understand what it meant.

Coburn Howard told us when he heard the bell, he came out on the porch of the store and looked across the valley. That's when he spotted the smoke roiling up in black clouds. With one jump, he was across the porch and into his old truck. He tore up the road to the bend in the river. Cora, his wife, saw him go, but she was way too late to catch him. It only took him five minutes to cross the high bridge and go the two miles down the county road to the cluster of houses at the foot of Burl's crossing. Jane finally stopped ringing and ran with Logan all the way down our hill to stand on the crossing. They didn't try to cross over. Instead, they sat down on the crossties and watched us.

Coburn pulled the truck off the road and was about to climb out when Fleetie and Geneva swooped down on him with the baby.

"Coburn, Coburn, the baby can't breathe. We've got to get him to the doctor."

The two women were in the truck, and Coburn had it rolling almost before the words were out of Fleetie's mouth. Mother was moving water faster than seemed possible. Susanna and Henry were the next to arrive with almost a dozen good-sized kids in the back of Henry's truck. With the extra hands, we were able to bring water up from the river as well as from the pump, and in less than thirty minutes, the worst of the fire was doused. Some charred embers still glowed red, and from that point, each bucket of water put the rest of the house out of jeopardy. The kitchen was destroyed, and the back bedroom was badly damaged, and everything in the cabin smelled of smoke and burning wood. Later on, people would say that Roger's discovery of the burning ring and his hard work, in spite of the heat, saved the house.

Henry walked around to the back steps and checked them out before he stepped inside the door of the burned-out kitchen. He called, "Roger, come around here and look at this. I want to make sure I'm seeing what I think I'm seeing."

Roger was tall for his fourteen years, but every inch of him was slumped down under the shade of the poplar trees with Nessa and me. He had drained every drop of energy out of his lanky body, but with a huge effort, he pulled himself up to answer Henry. "Whatcha see, Mr. Henry?"

"You tell me, Roj. What is in the floor there?"

"That's where the fire was the hottest. That's where Nessa and me poured the most water at first. It was burning in a big ring," said Roger.

"What did you smell?"

"I smelled fire, Mr. Henry, smoke and fire. It smelled like I smell now, and I expect Nessa smells the same as I do. It's not too pretty either. She's probably in the river a'ready trying to wash it off. She don't take to being dirty, Nessa don't."

"Well, don't be washing it off. It smells of kerosene. I just imagine the sheriff will want to take a look at this and smell it, too."

"Mr. Henry, why would Geneva pour kerosene on the floor? She ought to a-knowed it would start a fire."

"Never you mind, Roger. Just wait around until Coburn gets back. He can use his telephone over at the store to call the sheriff. He's going to ask you some questions about what you saw."

"I don't think I want to talk to the sheriff if it's just the same. He ain't too friendly."

Henry shrugged. "It don't matter what you think, Roger. The sheriff will get in on this. What I can't figure is why anybody would want to burn Fred's house, and why didn't Geneva see whoever it was?"

Mother came around the corner of the house, leading some of the children, and when she found me, she explained her plan to me and anyone else who might be listening. "I don't know when Fleetie will be back, and since I have already promised the girls a club meeting, I am taking all of them up the hill." She continued gathering up kids and was soon on her way over the crossing with all of them in tow. Logan and Jane were going to have playmates after all.

Pretty soon, when the smoke cleared, there would be work for everyone. The cabin would have to be repaired and scrubbed from top to bottom. Helen and Mary had already begun pulling together the pieces of Geneva's belongings scattered around the yard. Everything left in the house was smoke stained and layered with soot. The next morning, all the women in the neighborhood would build fires under a series of wash kettles and fill every clothesline in the yards up and down the road. But for now, the job was sorting and stacking and worrying about the baby.

Chapter 28

THE HOSPITAL

Henry pulled himself into his truck, and Dolly climbed in on the other side. He took off down the county road to the mine to find Fred and take him to town.

We watched them drive away, and Mother said, "Henry is a good man. I know Geneva is going to be beside herself. Fleetie will have her hands full for sure, but I suspect Henry is mostly going to see to it that Dr. Parks gets paid today. He saves every penny he can, and men who do that hate to be in debt to anyone."

I thought about that for a minute. "Sounds backward to me. Looks like if you are tight as Henry, you'd hold on to every penny no matter who you owe."

"That is a very good example of why you should spend your time trying to listen and learn instead of forming silly opinions."

I turned and started up the hill. I couldn't win a battle with her if my life depended on it, and right now was not a good day to try.

The next day, as expected, many helpers, both neighbors and those from the settlement, showed up to help Geneva and Fred deal with the results of the fire. Most of us were gathered in the front yard when Henry drove up and parked just outside the gate. Dolly stepped down from the truck and walked through the gate.

Fleetie took her hand, and Dolly pulled her closer and wrapped her arms around her.

Fleetie spoke almost in a whisper. "What is it, Dolly? You look like you might never smile again."

"On the way to town, Deputy Jackson waved us down. Just ahead, through black smoke, we could see a mine ambulance and a half-dozen men crowded around the base of the old sycamore in the dip of the road. Carl walked to the truck as Daddy stepped off the running board, and he asked Carl what was going on. Carl didn't say anything at first as if he was having a hard time getting the words to flow around his Adam's apple. Ay god, Henry, Hershel hit that big old sycamore, and he is pure burned up."

Dolly stopped there and took a long breath before she went on. It seemed she wanted to get the telling done but dreaded doing it too. Finally, she went on.

"Henry looked over at me and shook his head before he told Deputy Jackson about Fred Clem's fire and the baby getting too much smoke about a half hour ago. Then Carl told Daddy and me that when Coburn drove up and couldn't get by, the men on the picket line was already moving down the hill after they heard Hershel's car blow. They was all here, and some of them boys pushed the truck up the bank and down the railroad to get past Hershel's car.

"Jackson told Daddy that Fred went with them to take the baby to town. He said the baby looked awful bad. Then those two got to talking about Hershel. Pap told Carl, 'Me and Dolly is going to backtrack and cross over to the highway. I've got to get on to town. The rest of them back home will be crazy to know what's happening with that baby. It's a damn shame about Hershel. He's one that'll be missed for sure. He stood up to anybody he thought was working agin' the law. Not many'll do that nowadays.'

"I saw Carl shake his head so hard, he looked like a woodpecker before he told Pap, 'Hershel sure went up on the wrong side of somebody. They's more'n one or two he made mad 'cause he wouldn't never look the other way over nothing. They's some who expects to get away with a little bootlegging and stuff now and then without no trouble. But trouble was ole Hershel's middle name, but I'm shore gonna miss him.'"

Dolly kept on telling us, "By the time Pap and me got to town, the ambulance driver carrying Hershel had already rolled down Main Street and turned up Central to the funeral home. We drove up Mound Street to the hospital to find Fred and Fleetie. All along the streets, there were clusters of people talking—the word traveled fast about Hershel."

Dolly got her breath and continued, "You can just imagine what they were saying. Around here, death is no stranger. The mines chop up men almost as fast as they can ride the mantrip, but somehow, this is different. We all pretty well knew that Hershel was a tough man in a tough time and, as Pap said, that the county depended on that straight-arrow honesty of his."

Dolly got quiet and looked away. It was almost as if we were not right there in front of her. Then in a soft voice, she added, "It makes me shudder to think on what might happen. This strike has proved it could turn violent at any time, and now, with Hershel gone, who is going to protect our men? It surely doesn't look good."

Dolly went on. "When Pap pulled into the curb, we climbed the flight of steps leading to the front door of that old soot-stained hospital. Inside the front door, we found Fred sitting on a wooden bench, looking lost as a sheared lamb. Henry sat down beside him and waited for Fred to speak. Fleetie came out of one of the rooms and walked toward us. I don't think she even knew we were there. She looked straight at Fred.

"'Hit's bad, Fred. Geneva is asking for you to come in there with her. They got the baby in an oxygen tent, but he don't know where he is.'

"Fred stood up, and you could see he had to almost force himself to walk down the hall. You could just tell he was fighting every cell of his body to keep from running out the front door. Fred faced Japs on Iwo Jima, but today was more than a man should have to stand.

"When Fleetie sat down by the two of us without saying hello, I asked her, 'What do you think, Fleetie? Is the little'un going to make it?'

"She didn't and couldn't answer, and her silence told it all.

"'Oh lordy, Fleet. That pore little thing. He's never had a half a chance.'

"Fleetie stared at the floor. She twisted her white handkerchief, smoothed and folded it and twisted it again. 'I helped birth him, Dolly. He done so good to hang on during all that flood with Geneva not able to get him born. It took something out of that baby. He ain't really caught up yet. Now . . .' Fleetie stared at her hands, seeing the handkerchief for the first time. She rolled it up and folded it into the cuff of her sleeve.

"We sat there all night. It didn't seem right for Fleetie to have to be alone. It was as hard a time as I have ever lived. Waiting for the bad news about that baby, I tell you. It will stay with me as long as I am on this earth." Dolly fell silent as if the telling had hurt her all over again.

Silence fell on all of us standing there in a yard now filled with damaged things from the burned house. We began to move back to the work at hand. This was something we could do in a world left very empty of things that would help Geneva and Fred.

As the day wore late, Mother walked down the hill with the little kids following her. She was pulling the red wagon loaded with a laundry basket full of food, canned goods, and fresh-baked bread. I gathered up the little kids, and Leatha and I were about to walk them to their yards when Daddy drove up with Fleetie. She got out of the front seat and stood by the car and shook her head. Without a word, Mother moved to wrap her arms around Fleetie. Words were useless, but soft moans from both women floated above them and faded into the leaves screening the mourning dove perched on the branch not far above their heads.

Chapter 29

TWO FUNERALS

When I was little, a funeral seemed to me to be a time when the grown-ups were sad, all the women carried food to the hurting family, and even little kids wore black clothes. Beyond that, I didn't understand much about what was going on, but losing the baby gave me an understanding of the pain and misery of a funeral. In fact, having two funerals in one day was rare even in our rowdy county, and this was not about people from far away.

I knew both of them. Both the baby and Hershel were far too young to die, and neither deserved to have their life taken away from them. Hershel had been at my house many times, drinking coffee with Daddy and talking man talk about what was going on in the county. He teased Logan and called him Short Stuff, and when he laughed, you could hear him all the way out in the yard. I was in the room when little Freddie was born. He seemed a part of my family, more like a little brother who just happened to live down the hill with the Clems.

Both funerals were held on the same day, but there were no other similarities. Dignitaries from three counties and as far away as Frankfort followed Hershel's black hearse. Even *Time* magazine detailed the life of this fallen hero, and the funeral was attended by hundreds of people.

At Ross's Point, a few dozen relatives and friends carried Freddie's casket up the steep mountain path to the Clem family graveyard. Marion Howard, Burl's first cousin, had carved and crafted the miniature coffin from his store of aged poplar. I am sure Marion never shed a tear; instead, he let the carved pictures created by his hands say his goodbye. The casket was sprinkled with carved images of baby toys, flowers, and a winding vine that wrapped completely around the middle of the tiny coffin.

The day before, Leatha and I found the yellow baby gown and quilt Mother had taken to Geneva's shower. It hurt to remember that Mother had told Geneva it was all right to save it back if she wanted to. It was wrapped and stored in the cedar chest, so it was protected from the smoke and soot damage that ruined many of Freddie's baby clothes. Fleetie sent Dorotha and Nessa across the river in Burl's boat to deliver the quilt to Marion. Without Fleetie telling us, we knew it was to line the casket. I handed Fleetie the tiny gown so she could take it to Geneva. When Fleetie opened the screen door and stepped out on the porch, we could hear Geneva crying all the way from the porch swing.

"I never put this on him, even one time. What in God's name was I saving it for? Why was I such a fool to think I should save a gown when I couldn't even save him?"

Painful, racking sobs slapped my ears. I remembered the same sounds when Pappy died.

Fleetie didn't say a word. I ached for her, for Fred, and for all of us. But as Fleetie told us so often, there was nothing to do but suffer what came. It seemed so cruel to me that Geneva would have to work through the pain pretty much in her own time and in her own way. When I lost Pappy, I found out that grief couldn't be diluted or comforted. The only cure for that much loss was to let it die out on its own, and nothing but the passing of time would do that.

The service for the baby was to be at the graveside. At least Geneva and Fred would be spared having to endure the church preaching before the burial. As we all walked up the steep mountain to the family cemetery, you could see that Geneva and Fred were moving in a haze of pain. They carried their twin toddlers and refused when others offered to help. I guess that they didn't even feel their aching arms. The toddlers were heavy, but those two were the only babies they had left.

Preacher Marsh held a service of prayer, scripture, and careful words of comfort. Fleetie and her girls, standing a few paces from the group, sang a soft chorus of "Amazing Grace." George Willis and Henry Sargeant lowered the tiny coffin deep into the rocky ground, and each person filed by and dropped an offering of flowers, soil, or green leaves down into the shadowed grave.

As a clan, Fleetie and Burl's people never showed a whole lot of what they were feeling. Granny Sary said often, "The swings of hardship have splintered seats." They had, for generations, taught themselves to expect the pain of loss, hard work, short lives, and little promise. They laughed and sang and loved in huge gulps, but they didn't whine in public.

Mother was the only outlander on the mountain that morning, and she and I witnessed an outpouring of grief so profound, Mother said she feared for the health of several of them. I had never witnessed keening and had no idea how intense the suffering could be. I knew that for the rest of my life, the memory of those sounds would stay with me. I had heard the Bible story of Rachel weeping for her children. I wondered that day if she felt as sad as Geneva and her kin as they stood high on that mountain by Freddie's tiny grave.

As the last flower was dropped into the grave, Geneva, Fleetie, and the two grandmothers went rigid, arms up, eyes shut, and from the depths of their inner souls, rolled moans of agony and mourning. It was intense; it seemed to imprint the very boulders surrounding the small graveyard. They were tended by the second circle of women, all near relatives, crying aloud as they helped Geneva and Fleetie, protecting them from falling or other injuries. The third circle included the older female children and close neighbors. They served as a wall of privacy for the inner circles' grief in case one of the stricken women tore at her clothes.

The grieving men, heads bowed, did not even allow themselves tears, a custom that struck me as a cruelty as terrible to bear as the keening. Almost as if they had heard a clock strike, the men began to move into the inner circle and, one by one, took the hand or arm of one of the grieving women and began the walk back down the mountain.

Fred bent over and picked up the shovel. He worked alone and, shovelful after shovelful, filled the small grave. Geneva sat slumped up against her grandmother's stone in a misery as complete as a human being can suffer. Mother, Leatha, and I waited for them under the big oak tree near the path, close enough if they needed us and far away enough to keep out of their sight. Some things hurt so bad, you don't want a soul around you.

After a while, Daddy took Mother's arm, and I followed as we moved to make our way down the path. At the foot of the hill, Daddy walked over to Burl, and while I could not hear him, I could well imagine that Daddy's voice was as gentle as the cooing of a mother pigeon. In a very few minutes, he opened the door for Mother, and we drove to Baxter.

We parked at the Coal Monument in the middle of the crossroads and waited to join the end of Hershel's funeral procession on its way to the cemetery. As the procession passed, Judge Harrison spotted us, and he slowed his car and let Daddy in the line. We were only about a mile from the cemetery, but somehow, it seemed to take a very long time to get there. As we came nearer the gate, we could see the people lined up on both sides of the road. All the faces were grim. No one waved or even acknowledged seeing the cars move by.

The mass of mourners, shoulder to shoulder, filled all the open space in the hilly cemetery. Uniformed officers formed an honor guard of about a hundred men, fifty on each side. They stood from the cemetery gate up the steep hill to the Garber lot. Hershel's widow walked beside Buford, Hershel's brother. She, along with her two grown children, led the rest of the large family through the guard and up the hill. Muffled drums beat a slow cadence as Hershel's deputies lifted the flag-draped casket and carried it through the aisle of honor guards. As the men carried the heavy casket up the hill, one by one, they were replaced by uniformed men who stepped from the honor guard and shouldered the burden. At the brow of the hill, a mound of flowers had been arranged to form a bower, and the silver gray casket was lowered by slow inches to rest there.

A parade of men rose to speak of Hershel's bravery, his service to his country, his love of family, and his deep concern for the safety and well-being of the citizens of his county. The honey tones of a contralto threw out somber notes of "Wayfaring Stranger." The song seemed caught in the streams of afternoon sun as it echoed off the mountain. The notes of "Taps" choked everyone but the bugler. Precise folds, snapped to a silent beat, reduced the flag to a frozen tri-corner, never again to fly against a sunlit sky or catch a trailing breeze. Faces were frozen, breathing was shallow, and human sound was trapped under the weight of ceremony and sadness. The price we would all pay for life laid itself anew on each shoulder that day. Some deaths were that hard, while others seemed to slip by with the evening hush.

Daddy told us he knew the price the county would have to pay for this murder would be heavy. Hershel was not the saint his eulogizers made him out to be, but Daddy knew without Hershel, both he and the rest of the county would feel the void.

Hershel and Daddy had paired up long ago, each feeding a mutual need in the other. Hershel owned a small taxi service and had learned long ago that a taxi could move up and down the hollers and creeks unnoticed. Daddy, as lawyer and peace maker, and Hershel, as law enforcer, kept a finger on the pulse of the county. It was on one of their forays deep into moonshine country that Daddy convinced Hershel to run for sheriff.

Hershel was naturally shy, and it made electioneering hard for him, but Daddy, who never had a shy minute in his life, ran the campaign, and the combination of the two personalities proved to be unbeatable. Daddy had not foreseen Hershel's total dedication to the job. Enforcing the law came as natural for Hershel as reading it did for Daddy. He soon began to take every broken law as a personal affront and every law breaker as a personal enemy threatening the peace and safety of his people.

Not even a year into Hershel's first term, Daddy began to warn him to watch his back. Hershel had made himself a target and was not in the least shy about presenting it in defiance against any side of an argument that was likely to break the law. He was no less threatening to union men as he was to operators, bootleggers to 'shiners, or thieves to murders. He had decided he wanted a clean county, and there would be hell to pay if he found someone on the outside of that.

Both deaths weighed on Daddy's conscience—Hershel's, a result of his elected position, and Fred's baby, victim to a strike Daddy had not been able to defang. Standing in the second hillside cemetery, shaded against the August sun, his mood more matched the widow's weeds than the summer day.

In a time and place where sudden death is no stranger, hardship a constant visitor, and violence a near cousin, the deaths of Hershel and Freddie might have seemed unfortunate but not that remarkable. And that was true, except for the unexpected glare of publicity focusing on the county. No one outside the mountain community had paid any attention to the strike until someone killed Hershel. Suddenly, reporters flooded the county, and newspapers and radios began to tell the story of the brave sheriff and his martyr's death.

The truth of the story evaporated with the need to get copywritten and distributed on a deadline. Accusations flew as free as locust leaves in August. The union leaders and the operators pushed the other to a quick settlement. Enough blood had been spilled to scare both sides into temporary sanity. Months of stalemate were swept away as quickly as a mountain tide falls back into its banks.

With the shaky agreements signed, an uneasy peace settled into the valley. Hershel's brother Buford was appointed sheriff until the next election. Sweetheart deal was whispered. Collusion was hinted in the barber shops and the commissary, but no one was of a mind to go stirring the pot. The mines were going to be running, and most of the valley figured that ought to be enough. It might have been enough too, except for ancient traditions that had settled in the vein and sinew of the people who trusted clan more than law and who were bound to exact a price in their own way and in their own time.

Chapter 30

BOATS ON THE RIVER

Ever since the flood, none of us had seen much of Hobe. He walked the picket line with the others, but he stayed away from Coburn's store, and he stopped leaning on Burl's gate with his fishing pole in hand, dropping a broad hint to use Burl's boat.

On the first Sunday morning after the baby was buried, the small group of adults and kids from our side of the river gathered for the two-mile walk up the railroad to Sunday school and church at Poor Fork Church of Christ, Noninstrumental. While we waited for everyone to gather before we started, Hobe walked down the steep path in front of his wife Mary and her sister Ginny as they corralled their houseful of children. As soon as they reached the group, he left the railroad track and made his way down to the riverbank. When Dorotha saw him, she turned her back and stood behind Nessa and Leatha. She had not returned to Hobe's since the night of the flood, and she had never said a word about what had driven her across the hill in the driving rain the night of the flood. If anybody else had been paying attention to her, they would have seen the deep frown and frightened look flash across her face same as I did.

Mary and Ginny were the last to join us, and I had stood around about as long as I could stand it, so I hurried the kids along, and soon, we were way out ahead of the women. Fleetie and Geneva did not go that morning. As we made our way through the valley, other women and children joined us. Sunday school was promised for this particular Sunday, and since we did not always have that treat, the kids were more excited than usual. It was a lot more fun for the kids when there were papers to color, a craft to make, and a Bible story. Preacher Marsh had a circuit. If his schedule placed him at Ross's Station early on Sunday morning, there was only time for preaching, but if he was going to be delayed, then Sunday school was planned to fill the time until he arrived. The winter circuit was less dependable, with services held only once a month at best. Snow and ice could close the doors for weeks on end.

Summer was the best time for the congregation to gather, and Sunday school was one of the favorite highlights. A baptizing service in the river came in late August following the seven-night preaching revival. Some of the families brought picnic baskets and stayed after the baptizing, and the end of the summer meant it was time for the all-day meeting with dinner on the ground. Today, some of the women were meeting during Sunday school to plan the meal and recreation for the all-day event. It was the best attended service of the year. Few men attended church service with any regularity, but hold a "dinner on the ground," and you could count on every man in valley from sixteen to eighty showing up. It was also the day Preacher Marsh set aside for deacons' and elders' meetings.

All the work necessary to keep the church going fell to the women, yet only the men were allowed to make policy and delegate authority. No one seemed to mind. It had always been that way, and no one saw any reason to change it—no one besides my Mother. She totally refused to go with us, even though you couldn't beat her for Bible reading and praying.

"I will not participate in a service that considers me less important than a man," she would say and say it often. My only hope was that she would not say it out in the settlement and let the whole valley know how she felt. We were odd enough anyway already without her making every man mad and confusing the women over the difference between preaching doctrine and expounding on the Bible.

I kept my eye on Dorotha, who seemed to be watching for what or who might be us ahead of us. I moved up so I could walk beside her. We both could see that Hobe had disappeared around the river bend curve ahead of us about a quarter of a mile. At the head of the curve, we stopped for Peachy, who lived very close to the county road. She climbed the railroad bank to join us. Maggie Stewart and her two children joined the group with Peachy. While we were waiting for them, I spotted a rowboat moving downstream away from us. I nodded to Dorotha, and the two of us could see someone standing in the back of the boat, poling two men down the river.

"That's Hobe for sure," she whispered. I don't think she knew I heard her.

Dorotha turned to see if any of the women might be watching to see where Hobe went. But even Mary did not show a flicker of interest in the river. Sunday fishing was as natural as the river itself. But three men fishing in the same boat wasn't usual. The boats were small, and with poles, minnow buckets, and other gear, three made it too crowded for good fishing.

I had to say something to her. "What do you care where old Hobe is going? He hasn't got a lick of sense anyway, and he is mean as a haint. Don't worry about him."

"That's all you know, Rach. You better watch him. He is more than just mean. He will hurt you if you give him half a chance. Stay away from him."

"Did he hit you the night of the flood? Is that why you are so skittish about him now?"

"Don't say nothing to Daddy or Mommy. Just be quiet and mind what I say. He is more than mean. He is as dirty as he is mean."

Her words were more than enough to shut my mouth. Dorotha didn't scare easily, and it was written all over her that Hobe had her spooked bad. My imagination was working overtime. It was not a good time to talk about what did happen, but one of these days, when I could get her alone, maybe she would open up more. I was going to have to wait.

As we left that morning, Daddy was sitting on the front porch, dozing in the morning sun. For the last few years since he had gotten home from World War II, he seldom darkened the door of his old church in town, but he encouraged us to go to the settlement church with the neighbors. His great-grandmother had lived for a spell in town after her husband had been killed felling trees for Lawson Lumber. During that time, she had taken Daddy and his brother Walter to the big-brick Christian church across the street from the city hall on Second Street. That was where he was baptized, and so it would be a natural thing for him to would take us there.

That church was as different from the nonmusical Church of Christ as human beings could make it. The service was very formal, and when the church organ played, it seemed to throb right through the middle of you. There was a thick carpet on the floor that muffled sound, so it was never noisy. The Church of Christ service could rattle the windows when we really got wound up.

There was something almost holy about the way the stained-glass windows splintered the sunlight into brilliant shafts and cast color on the sills and pews. It didn't take much imagination to feel that in that place, you were surrounded by the majesty and power of the Almighty. Daddy always told us he did not have to try to imagine God's power. It seemed to be right there for the taking. He and Mother said several times that soon, the whole family would return to his church, but all that summer, he and Mother kept delaying making the move.

That was fine with me. I loved the Sunday journeys up the track with our friends and neighbors, and I might have been the excuse he needed to wait. But when fall came, the meetings at the Poor Fork Church of Christ would be fewer, and going to church in town would be a new adventure for Logan. He was a homebody and liked to stay close to Mother. When we went to town, she had to allow him to carry his stuffed doll O'Malley. That was his courage toy, and with it, he might have walked with Meshach and Abednego right into the fiery furnace.

Dorotha nodded at the river, and I could see that the boat was coming closer to us, and I could get a good look at the three men. It was for sure they were not laying any trot line or hanging poles over the side. The boat was laying low in the water and moving fast. It was hugging the shore, keeping the boat under the overhanging trees in what looked to me like they were trying to stay out of sight. Hobe was sitting in the middle, Billy Cantrill in front and Tom Hendley standing in the stern with the pole.

Dorotha was walking beside me and saw them the same time I did. "What are they doing, you reckon?" she asked.

Fleetie overheard her. "Whatever they are doing, it is none of our business. Don't pay it no mind."

That was what she said, but I noticed she let us walk on ahead, while she stood very still, watching the boat as it skipped in and out of her vision. A cold chill rippled down my back. Trouble had a way of hanging around. It sat in the air, on the mountains, along the river, and anywhere else your mind might want to run to, even on a pretty Sunday morning. I glanced at Dorotha. Her head hung low, and her hands were clenched into fists. Something was for sure bad wrong.

Part 4

ADAGIO

Chapter 31

Black Damp

The miners finally got back to work, and the first day at Pridemore's, things seemed reasonably normal. Daddy told me that reopening mines was complicated, expensive, and dangerous. If they left out or scrimped on any safety need, there could be trouble. Nerves were raw up and down the creeks and hollers. The giant fans were supposed to remove deadly gases, and they had been left running during the strike, but no one made the daily checks on oxygen levels. When the mines were working, the miners could be counted on to be vigilant about unusual sounds, movement, or odors. They protected one another against the threat of explosion, slate falls, black damp, and all the dangers lurking in the dark tunnels of coal mines.

There had been about as many versions of what happened at the mine on that Friday as there were people to tell it. Miners' wives had one version, the owners had an altogether different story, and the man on the street might give out a tale with little if any truth in it. Daddy had been gone with Burl all night, but when he finally came home, he sat with us at the kitchen table and told us as much of the truth as was known by then. Some of it, Burl told him, and some, he had figured out for himself.

Burl said that after the shutdown, the first few shifts back in the mine made the men jumpy. Time on top broke down some of the men's resistance to the nerves that came with black days deep in the earth. In spite of the tension, the first days moved along pretty well.

As the week rolled on toward payday, the men began to step a little lighter. Jokes were sharper and laughter easier. On Friday morning, just before dawn, the first twelve men of the early shift climbed on the mantrip. Gripping their lunchboxes, they eased their limber bodies onto the hard seats for the long ride to the face. The mantrip was low to the ground, and the riders were crowded together. The clank and rattle of the 'trip was so loud, the men did not try to talk to one another. They used the morning ride to shut down the outside and turn their minds to the job and the day ahead. They could not doze no matter how sleepy they might have felt in the early morning. The dangers ahead kept their eyes peeled. The banter and gossip stopped, and even the biggest joker in the bunch was pretty much squelched by the weight of the day ahead.

Friday morning was no different, but payday and the promise of some hard-earned cash at last lightened the mood. They were ten minutes into the ride when all the men felt something like rolling thunder off somewhere in the distance. Maybe they figured at first there was nothing to worry about, except in a coal mine, everybody worried about every odd sound. A man in the mine who didn't pay attention was a fool. Fools were rare deep in the bowels of the earth. Just ask any miner.

No one lived to tell the world exactly what happened, but Daddy explained that it probably went something like what Burl told him.

Hulan Howard shouted, "Roy, reverse the 'trip. That don't sound right."

Every man in the car strained to listen, and the first thing they heard was a soft shuffling off in the distance.

"Reverse, reverse—do it now! Rats is running for the drift mouth. Reverse!"

Roy slammed and locked the reverse gear rod into place just before he felt hundreds of rat feet running over him, as if he and the other men were no more than a stretch of sand in front of an ocean wave. The mantrip groaned to a stop, engaged its gears, and began backing the half mile to the mouth. The men screamed and fought off the blanket of rats and failed to see the rolling cloud racing to catch them.

Outside, the rumble had been felt through the heavy brogans and boots worn by the waiting miners. Complete silence fell in the early morning dark. Breathing stopped. The second group of that shift stood waiting for the mantrip to return. Every ear was tuned to the slightest whisper of sound that might come flying from the drift mouth. Another grinding rumble swept past their ears, followed by the soft shuffling of rat's feet sweeping ahead of the underground terror.

When Burl saw the racing flush of rats, he shouted, "Full mantrip in trouble! Boys, get at it. Roy and Hulan and the others is in trouble!"

As soon as the words were out of his mouth, the empty mantrip filled with twelve men bent on finding the endangered miners. John N. ran to the foreman shack for the emergency packs, and as he was throwing them into the laps of the two men in the middle of the mantrip, they heard the clack of wheels moving fast, and it did not slow as it closed in on the mine face. Every man in the mover rolled over the side just before the racing cart slammed into it. Metal crushed metal as both carriers ground into the steel bumper.

There was total silence in this barest piece of time from which no one would emerge unscathed. For the first few seconds, no one moved to the men, as if by standing where they were, they could avoid the truth of what had happened. They probably didn't realize it then, but those few seconds would be the last reprieve from the consequences of the explosion they would have for a long time. As long as they stood in place, the narrow piece of ground that separated the living from the dead protected them from all the tomorrows.

"Daddy, all of them? Not even one?"

"Yes, Rachel, every man was dead." He stood up and poured another cup of coffee. I supposed he was trying to get his thoughts together as he revealed the sad details. He sat back down and started talking again.

Their faces and bodies were contorted by their fight against suffocation. Black damp death is hard and fast. In just a few seconds more, the shriek of the alarm horn blasted the news from the top of the mountain. It broke dreaded news throughout the valley. All up and down the river, men and women and children stood and prayed that their family's time had not come. The days ahead would be filled with investigation, speculation, and blame. Twelve families with ties that reached into every corner of the county would carry this burden as long as there were survivors alive to tell it.

The first to move, Burl and John N., waved off the others. Stepping into no-man's-land, Burl lifted Hulan out of the wrecked carrier and brought him to a grassy rise far to the left of the mine road. He closed his eyes and straightened his limbs and clothes. John N. smoothed his face to soften the marks of death carved onto his features. He placed his hat, lamp, and dinner bucket just above his head. Eleven more times, John N. and Burl repeated the ritual for each man lost to all of them forever. Several other men unearthed mine tarps to cover each body before the first of the families began arriving. Burl lit a carbide lamp and placed it there beside each body, and then he turned and walked alone down the mine road. As he moved down the hill, the first of the families and the ambulance moved past him. He could hear the shouts of grief, followed by gut-tearing sobs as each one recoiled from the news they spent their life dreading. He stepped onto the railroad and began the long walk to Ross's Station. He told me that he had mined his last day.

"By the time I found Burl, he was nearly home. I pulled over and yelled up the bank to him to get in and let me take him home. From his fog of shock and grief, he showed no sign of hearing me, but he stopped, and I got out of the car and walked up the bank to him.

"'That's it, Ed. No more. Did you hear? They're gone. Twelve men, just like that. No more. I'm going to get drunk. Not one bone in me is going to know how to move. When I wake up, I'm never going back to the mines. There's bound to be somebody who'll hire me. I'm getting out while I can still feed the young'uns.'

"I guided him to the car, and all the way down the road, Burl repeated the same thing again and again. 'No more, Ed. No more. Ed, it's over. No more, no more.'

"I drove us over the mountain to Sal's, loaded the trunk with bootleg whiskey, and took off to the Overlook Café. There's not much use in wondering what happened during that long night. After, we tried to drink each other under the table, but instead, we fell asleep, slumped right over on that hard table.

"This morning, I brought Burl down the mountain. Both of us need a hot bath and hot food. When I let Burl out of the car, he waved off the kids who were watching his every move. Fleetie was standing just inside the screen door. She didn't keep the relief out of her voice, but she was good and angry at both of us. With the whole valley in deep mourning, it wasn't a good time for the two of us to be at the Overlook.

"Katie, Rachel, it probably doesn't make much sense, but if I'd left Burl to take out his misery on Fleetie and the kids, we'd have had more than guitar pieces to sweep up. Hulan and Roy were his first cousins. They ran these hills as kids, married in the same church, and went off to war together. Burl lifted every one of those men out of that mantrip himself. He wouldn't let anybody come near them until he had closed their eyes and covered them. I never saw a man in such pain, not even during the war. Whiskey was all I could think of to stop that much hurt quick."

Mother gave up the battle with one last jab. "You look awful and smell worse. Why were you drinking too? You might have been more help sober."

"Katie Bell," he said as he wrapped his arms around her, "a man oughta be willing to keep a buddy from drinking alone."

Mother couldn't keep from smiling at him. He looked like he had been dragged behind a fast horse, and the phrase "a man oughta" was the family joke about getting out of work.

"You are a disgrace. Go get in the tub before Judge Harrison gets back here and catches me lying about where you were and what you were doing."

"Hot bath coming up then boiled eggs, toast, and coffee, woman!"

"Don't you 'woman' me. Cold oatmeal is what you deserve."

Mother held him close for just a minute before she pushed him toward the bathroom for a bath. Jane was crouched outside in the backyard behind the hydrangea bushes. She was probably expecting to hear shouts and anger. When she saw Mother with her arms around Daddy, she came running out of the bushes.

"Daddy," Jane said, lifting her arms to him, "there was a bad thing. Mother cried, and Fleetie cried. We thought the mine 'splosion 'sploded you too. Did you see the 'splosion?"

"No, baby girl, I tried to take care of Burl. His two cousins were in the mine, and he is as sad as he has ever been in his life."

"Did you fix him all better, Daddy?"

"Girls, let Daddy get a bath. You can help me fix his breakfast."

Janey clapped her hands. "Scrambled eggs. Let's make scrambled eggs." She thought that of all foods, scrambled eggs was the dish of angels.

Daddy swept her up in his arms and carried her squealing down the hall.

Chapter 32

GENTLEMAN FARMER

Larry Windham's grandparents lived in Virginia, deep in the rich farmland of the Eastern coastal states. Larry's frequent visits as a child left him with an indelible impression. He was forced by circumstances and economy to run his mines, log his forest leases, and oversee his banking interests, but he had a compelling fantasy to see the day when he could be a gentleman farmer, a squire with rolling acres, wide fields, abundant cattle, and towering barns stuffed with curing tobacco.

When Larry turned fifty, he threw up his defenses against the weight of a half century of birthdays and gave his wife of nearly thirty years the divorce she wanted, whereupon he almost immediately married a blond beauty nearly half his age. Along with that good fortune, he also decided, in spite of geography or good sense, to indulge his childhood yearning and become a farmer. He built a barn, cleared and fenced forty hilly acres, and installed a small herd of Herefords. It didn't take him long to find out that a young wife demanded more time than Emma had and that a farm, even a mountain excuse for one, was a jealous mistress. With the bank, his coal interests, and logging business, something had to give.

The word had gone out some time back that Windham was looking for someone to keep the farm going by taking over the daily work and worry of the fields and herd. Larry was not a man that sat easy on Daddy's mind. The good life just seemed to fall in Larry's lap. He had a rich appetite for the best of everything, and nothing and no one was allowed to slow him down. If he wanted it, he bought it, or if it wasn't for sale, he connived it out of someone. Daddy admitted that Larry had never been accused of real crimes, but he just had an uneasy feeling that he did more and hid more than a truly honest man should.

Even with his conviction that Larry could leave a man hanging if it suited him, Daddy mentioned to Mother and me that a job on Windham's farm might be the answer for Burl. As he left his front porch that morning, he told me he had made up his mind to give Larry the chance to do something decent for a change.

I was very careful not to mention that I knew Daddy had another card to play in any dealing with Larry. The truth was there was a thing or two that Larry probably would do just as soon that Daddy didn't make public knowledge. Daddy had seen him one time in Knoxville having dinner with Cheryl. It was not general knowledge that he had started seeing Cheryl long before Emma left him. Who knows why? But he wanted everyone to think that Emma was the guilty party in the divorce. Larry didn't know that Daddy would cut off his right hand before he used that kind of intimidation on any man, but since Larry used all the dirt he could on people, he could not understand that he was safe from whatever knowledge Daddy might have.

Daddy walked into the kitchen, where and Mother and I were folding laundry. "Is there any aspirin in the house? My head feels like an axe split it."

She shook her head, and he picked up the car keys on the counter. "I need to go to town to see if I can work out something for Burl."

"For pity's sake, what more do you want to do now? Drinking your fool head off? Keeping him company? Looks to me like plenty to do. Burl is either always in trouble or causing trouble for someone else. It's about time he straightened up and acted more like his daddy," said Mother.

"What I'm about to do could make it easier for Fleet and the kids. You wouldn't want to stop that, would you?"

Mother stood looking at him for a long minute. He had touched an old argument between them about Burl's meanness, and Mother was not going to let Daddy off scot-free.

As they talked, I was hatching a plan. It occurred to me that I might get to escape the laundry and a whole list of other jobs that Mother had planned for me. I slipped out the back door and hid in the back seat of the car. It was a trick I pulled fairly often, and Daddy never seemed to mind. Mother wouldn't miss me. Leatha and I roamed the mountain as much as we stayed close to the house. So here was my opportunity to skip the quarrel over Burl and go to town as a bonus.

As I walked across the porch, I heard her laying down the law. "Since you have made your mind up to go, take Logan with you, I'm not about to let you leave this house alone. No telling who else you might run into who need to drink away their sorrow. You make good and sure you two are back here for your supper. And for lord's sake, keep yourself out of trouble."

"Lordy, Katie Bell, you sure are hard on a weak man. Where's my big boy?"

Mother turned her back on him, trying to hide the smile tormenting her jaw. Daddy always made her laugh, even when she was furious, but this time, she was determined not to let Daddy off easy. It was obvious that she was still upset about last night.

Chapter 33

TWELVE CASKETS

The deaths of twelve men in the Worsham mine touched every home in the narrow valley. Mine deaths were woven into the fragile threads of a miner's family life, but nothing could prepare the county for the impact of losing twelve men in a single day. Twelve widows and forty-six orphans were left to face a level of poverty more desperate than even the strike had brought. Death benefits, if they could be wrested out of the tight fists of owners, operators, and union officials, would barely cover the cost of the simple funerals.

More than one miner's widow knew she could see her children parceled out among scattered relatives much as one might distribute a litter of hound pups. It was even worse for those with no patch of land to farm for a bare subsistence. They had no hope of keeping their family together. More than one child from their valley had grown up in one of the orphanages scattered beyond the county borders.

Anyone driving through the valley could see sawhorses in yards at house after house. They were set to hold coffins as they were being built by stricken relatives and friends. Woodworking, carving, and even whittling was a craft most of the men and many of the women loved to have their hands on. But these skills and talents had to be set aside as the men went underground to carry out the brute-force work it took to pull carbon chunks from the earth. But today, the men from the stricken families ran their hands over cured boards and selected for the coffins their finest seasoned oak, walnut, or cherry.

They would pour their grief and frustration into the painstaking cabinet work it took to fashion a beautiful casket. Long into the night, men, women, and children would sand and polish the wood until it gleamed with a patina so rich and deep, their stricken faces would be reflected back at them. The splendid caskets, fine enough for a lord, would be lined by the women with their finest quilts laid back against a day there would be a special need. Yet each household would feel apologetic that they could not provide a store-bought coffin from Dawood Brothers, the local undertakers.

Behind the neighbors' doors, the women sorted through carefully saved yards of fabric to fashion funeral clothes for each orphaned child. No family would face the shame of dressing their little ones in shabby clothes. Strangers drawn in to gawk and to rubberneck by the sensational stories in the *Knoxville News Sentinel* would be disappointed by the lack of barefooted hillbillies parading their grief for the world to examine.

Daddy often spoke with great pride to outlanders about the strength and dignity of his people. As we drove through the valley that day, we stopped often, and Daddy would carry Logan, and I walked with him to pass a few minutes with people on their porches or front yards. As we joined each family, Daddy had little to say. What possible words were there in the face of the pain of all these families? One of the women would break the ice by taking Logan and making a fuss over his blond curls and his sprinkle of freckles. Daddy would run his hand over the rich work of the casket work being done and whisper, "Looks good, Lige, Enoch. Mighty fine work. A sin to lose them boys. They'll be missed."

Black-draped windows welcomed us that day in house after house. Each stop still weighed on our minds long after he had driven down the road. I had seen a little of this grief before when there were other mine accidents, and it is not something that I will ever forget. The widows' faces wore a death pallor with line-etched faces grown old in nothing but a blink of time. Of the women we met that day, not one of them was older than thirty, yet they would never again be considered young or pretty.

The price life had wrested from them had been paid early. The hardships the widows had facing them would take a deadly toll in the next few years. Mountain existence was just barely possible for two and so seldom survived by one that the rare woman who managed it at all was usually branded a witch by heedless children who had no ken of a woman living alone.

"Rachel, you know I have half a notion to turn this car around. I am in no mood to put up with a man who has never known a hard day in his life. Larry Windham has too much of this county under his control. I am not a bit happy about asking him to hire Burl."

"What about Fleetie and the kids? What is going to happen if Burl can't get a job?" I asked.

Daddy sighed. "I guess Larry's oversized ego doesn't really make that much difference when we think about what is going to happen to the family if Burl can't get on somewhere else."

"Well, it is for sure that Burl is not likely to care what happens to Fleetie and the kids."

"Rachel, that is just not true. Burl cares more than you know. He just has a hard time showing it. You are way too hard on him."

I was about to disagree, but Daddy stopped his car at the end of the Windhams' driveway. He stepped out and reached back for Logan, whose wide grin did not match the mood of the day, and the three of us walked up the sidewalk to the front door. Daddy's face was set into his "lawyer" mask, revealing nothing and hinting less. Those who knew him well would have seen the nervous twitch running along his hairline to his earlobe. He lifted his hand to knock on the imposing mahogany door, but it swung open before his hand reached the brass knocker.

"Come in, Mr. Ramsey," said Cheryl Windham. "I saw you drive up. Hello, Rachel." She walked over to Daddy and held out her arms. "Would you look at that precious baby? May I take him?"

Daddy nodded and handed a willing Logan to her. "I am sorry to bother you at home, Mrs. Windham, but I have a little personal business to discuss with Larry. I thought I might catch him before he got off somewhere. I promise it won't take long."

"Please call me Cheryl. I am so glad you stopped in. Let me get you a cup of coffee. Larry is out back, messing with one of his bird dogs. I'll go get him. May I take Logan with me? I bet he would like a cookie and some milk in the kitchen with me. Rachel, would you like to go with us?"

"No, ma'am. I'll stay with Daddy. But watch Logan. He loves spoiling. Don't let him talk you out of all the sugar in the house."

Daddy smiled at me as Cheryl turned and disappeared into the back of the house. Daddy took two steps with me right behind him toward the wide picture window and the sweeping vista of a wide tree-filled valley below. None of the misery down below was evident from this long view. It might even be possible standing there to imagine that the beauty of the valley was the reality and that poverty, death, and sorrow was the illusion.

Larry walked in as we were admiring the panorama spread out in front of us. "Afternoon, Ed, Rachel. How about that view? I use to hunt up here when I first came to Harlan County. The view was such a distraction. I never did get much game on this hill. I figured I'd build here and hide what a sorry hunter I am. Please, please have a seat. Can I get you and Rachel something to drink?"

"Good to see you, Larry. No, thank you. We won't be long, but thank you. Training a bird dog? Cheryl mentioned you had a dog out back."

"No, not training. I don't hunt enough anymore to make it worth my while. Takes forever to get a pointer working good. I miss it though. That's why I keep my dogs, I guess."

"How would you like to have a little more time to run those dogs again?" said Daddy.

"How's that? Something to do with this terrible business at the mine? Good men gone so quick. All those families . . ."

"One of those families is the reason I'm here, Larry. I heard your farm was doing fine, and you might be looking to put on a hand or two to keep it prospering. Did I hear right?"

"You'll have to come go with me to see the herd, Ed. Not a calf lost this spring, but I swear it's working the life out of me and my hand, Billy. With the strike over, the work will be picking up too. There's hardly time to take a breath. I'm gone from daylight to dark. Cheryl doesn't take to it well either. You think you know somebody who knows something about herding?"

"Most of the men who grew up around here were raised on farming, Larry. The mines might be sucking the life out of them, but what hours are left in the day, they spend tending their animals and raising some kind of little crop. That's how most of them keep decent food on the table. That commissary truck is a poor substitute for healthy eating, and besides, it takes too much of their pay. If it wasn't for their crops, they'd have nothing extra for their kids, and the women are as good at farming as their men."

Larry listened to Daddy, the lawyer defending a client, but Larry pressed the point. "Dirt farming doesn't mean any of them know how to take care of a herd of fine cattle."

"No, truth is they are all pretty good with animals, but Burl Sargeant is even better than most. His back is against the wall, Larry. He has six kids, a crippled arm, and more anger than is healthy. This last blast has taken something out of him. He needs to get out of the mines, and you and the rest of the operators need to get him out too. The boys follow Burl's lead, and in his frame of mind, that is bound to lead to trouble for everybody."

"Why should I hire a troublemaker, Ed? God bless! I've got my hands full. Hiring a hothead to herd the best cattle around these parts doesn't strike me as a smart move."

"He'll surprise you. Get him away from the anger gouging at him in the mines, and he is a different man. Your cattle will prosper under his hand. Give it a chance. You'll thank me. Your missus will thank me too."

At the mention of Cheryl, Larry looked off in the distance. Shaking himself back to the conversation, he answered Daddy, "I'll give him six months, Ed. If he can keep his head and get my herd through spring calving, I'll keep him on permanent."

"When do you want to talk to him?"

"After the funerals are finished, have him come to the bank. I want to take him out to the farm myself. I'm going to be keeping a close eye on him. I'm a bastard to work for, but he must be pretty good if you're willing to argue his case for him."

"I probably ought to thank you, Larry, but the truth is the only thanks you'll value will be his work out there on the farm. I'll tell Burl to stop by early next week. I'll get my young'uns and get on home before Katie sends out a posse and takes my scalp for missing the kids' dinner. You won't be sorry about Burl. If I thought you would, I'd have stayed out of it."

We walked with Larry to the back of the house and found Logan and Cheryl running Larry's antique Lionel train. Daddy thanked Cheryl and carried a reluctant Logan out the back door and around the house to the car. Looking at Daddy, I could only guess at how he had to be tickled inside.

He had forced himself to restrain his reaction to Larry's offer, but as he lifted Logan over the back of the seat and saw him settled, he stretched back, winked at me, and whispered, "Hey, Rooster! Want to go get some ice cream?"

Dinner was forgotten, and Mother was going to kill us, but right at that moment, I wasn't anything but happy. Daddy drove off, singing "John Peel" at the top of his lungs with Logan jumping up and down behind him.

Chapter 34

THE BANK

Leatha told me the next day that just as soon as Daddy told Burl to go talk with Larry Windham, he began talking all brave about how he was going to tell ole Larry just how it was, by god, and the rest of us were welcome to stand and watch. Leatha was not fooled by his blustering and big talk, but she was as hopeful as he was about the possibility of the new job.

Miners' kids hate the mines. They hate the fear that grows forever deeper in the faces of their mothers. They hate the smothering black that hides their fathers' faces at the end of the day. They hate the fatigue that chases away laughter and music and makes all fun hostage to deep tunnels in the surrounding mountains. While all of us who lived here knew and accepted mining as a part of life, we didn't have to like it. We didn't like copperheads and poison ivy either, but they were all around us and were part of where we lived. Guess you can get used to anything if you have to.

Burl had no trouble leading the men he had grown up and worked with, but Daddy told me the idea of having to face Windham left Burl scared and breathless. I could just imagine that his insides were twisting into painful knots. His nerves might be jangled, but if I knew him at all, I was sure that his courage had not left him. While I could cheerfully wring his neck most of the time, I had to admit that he could face up to whatever bad stuff came his way.

Fleetie told Leatha and me that Burl had not slept a wink for a week, and so after a sleepless week, he drove to town on Friday afternoon to see Windham. Fleetie was worried about him and made up some excuse to have to go to town. She took Leatha and me to help her by running errands while she went to the doctor's office for Gen. The two of us rode in the back of the truck, a treat absolutely forbidden by my very cautious mother. I lucked up and got permission from Daddy to go to town, and I just sort of forgot to tell him about the back of the truck. Of course, I didn't have to. He knew very well that if I was going with Leatha, the only place for us to ride was the back of the truck. Daddy never seemed to feel that he had to wring every drop of fun from life.

When we got to town, Burl parked a block away from the front door of the bank and climbed down from behind the wheel. Leatha jumped down from the bed and turned around to grab my hand, but I was already in midflight. We both broke into giggles. Fleetie clucked at us as she stepped down from the front seat. She hurried and caught up with Burl, while Leatha and I trailed far enough behind so Burl wouldn't pay any attention to us. He was probably so preoccupied with what he was going to say that the last thing on his mind was two kids. Besides that, we kept quiet and stayed far enough back that not even our shadows crossed his path.

As we drew near the front door of the bank, Fleetie stopped and told Burl she was going on up Central Street to the doctor's office. Leatha and I stayed behind and followed Burl into the bank.

The gleaming brass door handles, the click of marble floors, and the forbidding cashier cages worked to put one in awe of the place. I was just glad I wasn't the one who had to talk to Larry Windham. While he seemed nice enough when I went with Daddy to visit him, this place made Windham seem somehow much more vaunted and powerful.

Leatha said, "Rachel, I am going to go catch Mama. You going?"

"No, I want to hear what Larry says so I can tell Daddy."

Leatha pushed open the heavy door and stepped onto the sidewalk. I stood beside one of the marble columns just outside Windham's office as Burl walked in. I sat down next to his door.

"Come in, Burl." Larry rose from the massive cherry desk, and I could tell as his voice drew nearer, he had walked over to shake Burl's hand. He hovered so close to the door that I could almost hear him breathing. "Come in, Burl. Have a seat here on the couch. Did you ever see such fine leather?"

Burl must have shaken his head. "If it's just the same, Mr. Windham. I'd just as soon stand. Ed tells me you might need a man to help run your farm. I'd do you a good job. They's nothing I do better than farming, and I need the work."

And with just those few words, I knew Burl well enough to know he stood straight as a ramrod, held his hat in his hands, and looked Larry straight in the eye.

If Larry had expected Burl to bow and scrape, it was immediately obvious that Burl was not the bowing and scraping kind and that the two men would have to meet more as equals if Burl was going to be the new farm manager. In spite of the blunt request and the unspoken tone of independence, Larry sounded open to Burl's words, and perhaps goaded on by Daddy's solid recommendation, Larry did not to rest on ceremony.

"Ed tells me you're a good man. I am not easy to work for, and the pay is no better than what you are getting in the mine, but I don't have my fingers on your paycheck like the commissary does either."

With all the dignity Burl could muster, he replied, "I'll be there tonight to study what's going on, and I'll be there tomorrow at dawn."

The two men walked out of the office and stood near where I was sitting. Neither one of them paid the slightest attention to me as they shook hands on the deal.

As Burl left the bank, Larry walked over to one of the tellers and said, "I do believe I am going to have some more time to get things done. I've just hired a good man to take care of the farm."

The teller nodded and smiled. After all, what could she say to the boss? Burl did not exactly skip out of the bank, but he sort of walked with a jaunt that might make anyone watching him remark, "There goes a happy man."

Daddy and I had talked about it, and it was clear that the work on the farm would give Burl his first satisfaction in a day's work in seventeen years. He had gone into the mines the week after marrying Fleetie. Their plan was to save enough money with what he was making to buy a nice piece of land so he could go back to farming. The babies started coming, the commissary began eating his paycheck, and the savings never materialized.

He had won a few riverbank acres in a poker game before he was married, and that was all the land he had ever owned. He said often that across the road was a piece of lane he was going to buy from Daddy. Burl and his brothers had even carried load after load of foundation stones up there and started the foundation wall several years back.

Up the street in the Bays Building, Daddy glanced out his office window just as Burl walked out of the bank. I glanced up at his window and saw him watching Burl cross the street to the courthouse and on to the barbershop. As it took him closer to the Bays Building, Daddy waved, trying to catch his eye, but Burl did not glance up. Daddy must have given up because he stepped away from the window, and I lost sight of him.

I turned to go back up the street to the doctor's office to join Fleetie and Leatha when I noticed two men sitting in a black Chevy, watching every move Burl made. Daddy came out of the front door of his building and hurried to catch up with Burl. When he got closer to Burl, the car slipped its clutch and slowly rolled down the street and into the scattered traffic.

Chapter 35

OUTLANDER QUESTIONS

Mother had spent most of the day sewing school clothes for Jane and me. School would be starting soon, and Janey's school dresses from last year were much too short for her, and I had been begging for a full skirt and a flowered blouse. This was an outfit that was all the rage at school, and of course, I wanted to look like everyone else.

Mother relented, but her first answer was, "Why in the world would you want to look that tacky?"

There was a mysterious force that loosed itself in our house when Mother sewed. Every other thing in our house seemed to disintegrate around our ears. It was as if order was preserved in the house only if Mother remained vigilant. Just let her attention be focused elsewhere, and chaos resulted. Daddy hated to come home when the sewing machine was out. He wasn't a neat person and could be counted on to destroy order quicker than any of the rest of us, even Logan, but he wanted to walk in the door each evening and find perfect peace, complete with dinner bubbling on the stove.

Not tonight. As he swung open the screeching screen, piles of cloth, snippets of thread and fabric, and a shower of pins and pattern paper swirled in his draft. "Hell, Katie, I can't even walk through this maze. Let's eat!"

"'Let's eat,' he says. For pity's sake, Ed, you come home early, and the first thing you say is, 'Let's eat.' You must think I am some kind of mind reader. What are you doing home? It's only three o'clock."

"Larry Windham hired Burl. The two of us hung over a cup of coffee for the best part of the afternoon, planning his new house. He is finally going to get back to building that house on that piece of land I promised to deed him right after he married. He can finally finish the house for Fleetie and the kids and get them off that damp riverbank. His foundation is good and high, and they won't have to dread every heavy rain for fear they are going to be flooded out again."

"Does Fleetie know? How soon will he start on the house? How much land did you sell him?"

"Whoa, Nellie! To tell the truth, I didn't really sell it to him. We sort of cut for it, and I lost. That was when he went up there and dug that partial foundation and started the work that has been sitting there since before you decided to marry me."

"Is that why that wall is standing on that hill, looking abandoned and lonesome? I didn't know it was Fleetie's. The kids like to play around there, and when they do, it makes me a nervous wreck. Snakes love rock walls."

"Well, you can stop being nervous. He is going to finish the wall and build the house."

I walked out of the kitchen and onto the back porch, on my way to discuss this new turn of events with Leatha. We were going to be closer neighbors. Mother and Daddy were still in deep conversation about the new house. As I stepped off the porch and turned to go around the house to the driveway, I saw the same black car from this morning sitting in our turnaround. Two men had left the car and were going up the steps to the front door. They knocked, and Daddy opened the door. I went back inside the back door. Daddy invited them in, and they sat on the stiff Victorian settee that none of us in the family would touch. I stood around the corner of the hall, just out of sight.

One of the men showed a badge. "I am with the FBI. My partner and I need to ask you a few questions about some of your neighbors."

Daddy pulled up a straight chair and sat down. It was not unusual for there to be a parade of people who needed to see Daddy, but there was something different about these two. They had this stiff attitude as if they were really in charge and we were more or less expected to do what they asked. They had a cover of very polite, forced words that, on the surface, sounded very correct, but listening to them talk gave you the feeling that they didn't mean a word of it. The good manners and deference were a pretty transparent cover.

Mother interrupted them with an offer of coffee, and they were very gracious in accepting it. Here was my chance to get in on whatever it was that had brought them here. While Mother put the coffee to perking, I grabbed the sick tray and dropped a clean white napkin on it and stacked three cup and saucers and three spoons in the middle of the napkin. Before she could say to wait, I was out the kitchen door.

Just as I walked in the living room with the tray, I heard one of the men say, "We are here about a federal crime. Dead baby or not, no one can take revenge on a whole mine full of good men, Mr. Ramsey. If you know something, as an officer of the court, you know you are bound by law to help our investigation."

"You don't need to read the law to me, sir. If I knew anything to help you, I would. No one in this valley wants this mess cleared up more than we or any of the neighbors around here do. My wife helped deliver that baby. And that young lady handing you a cup and saucer was right there with her. Don't be sitting here in my living room about half-accusing me with your polite words. I am not holding back on you. You'll not find any of us in this valley protecting the bastard that killed Hershel and burned Fred and Geneva out. But you can't get us to talk about what we don't know. Whoever did this was pretty slick, and I wish you all the luck in the world finding them, but I would warn you to be careful whom you accuse. Nobody around here takes too kindly to being pushed around by strangers. Not even official, badge-carrying strangers."

I slipped back into the kitchen and picked up the coffee pot, but of course, Mother, the stickler, stopped me and poured the coffee into a serving carafe.

As I walked back in the room with the coffee, the second man was speaking to Daddy. "Will you assist our investigation?"

"I'll mention around that you are trying to find out who killed that baby. I can open some doors that you're going to find closed otherwise. But don't push it. If you start throwing your weight around, the information will dry up so quick, you'll think you're in a seven-year drought."

Mother was standing in the doorway, watching my every move to make sure I didn't scald the visitors. After the last drop was poured, she stepped back and returned to the kitchen.

"Who do you think we should talk to first, Mr. Ramsey?" You couldn't help but notice there was a big change in his attitude toward Daddy. I figured it must have been the coffee and that fancy carafe that set the new tone. Daddy had relaxed as well as he began to mention names of some of the men who would give what information they had.

I moved to the door and stepped across the threshold and into the kitchen to see about helping Mother clear the table of the sewing machine and scraps of material and thread so we could fix dinner. A worry line popped up and found its way to settle between her blue eyes.

"Lordy, lordy, is there never going to be any peace around here again?" she mumbled.

"What do you think those men are looking for?"

"More trouble. That's about all that bubbles up around here."

"The new house is not trouble. May I go down and talk to Leatha and see if she knows about the house?"

"I think you had better let Fleetie tell her. Maybe Burl wants to keep it a secret for a while. Just wait and let her tell you."

"May I go if I promise not to tell?"

"I guess so, after you help me put away all this sewing stuff so we can have some dinner. Daddy is home, and he thinks he has to eat as soon as he hits the door, or starvation will mow him down, even with the crickets. Take Jane with you, and get back up this hill in one hour. Absolutely no later, hear me?"

I was about to fly out the back door to grab Jane off the swing, but Mother caught me. The kitchen floor needed to be swept clean of the day's sewing mess.

Daddy walked into the kitchen just as I heard the men's car move down the driveway. "Ed, what is going on? You look like you've seen a ghost."

"The FBI men are working on the mine explosion. They think the blow was done by an expert, and there is only one around here."

"Ed, they can't think Burl has something to do with it. Oh my lord, no! He wouldn't do that, would he? That explosion released the black damp that killed his own relatives. Even in his meanest and drunkest rage, he couldn't kill his own. Tell me they don't suspect him. No, Ed!"

"Most murder is done by kin or friends. Not many people are killed by out-and-out strangers, but Burl didn't have anything to do with this. Burl is as good a demolition man as there is in these mountains. If he had wanted to blow up the mine, he wouldn't have planned on mine gas to fuel it. It's impossible to control black damp or methane once its loose, and he knows it well."

"What makes them think anybody did it? Mines have explosions all the time. Why was this one different?"

"They've got evidence it was set off, and they know their business. They also know Burl was giving the orders, and the men were doing pretty much what he told them. So that makes him the first one they suspect. It will be almost impossible to prove, and since Fred was burned out too, it weakens their case against him. But, Katie, what worries me is that it sets Burl up. Now it would be pretty easy for whoever is behind all this to dump it on his doorstep. Perjury is another possibility. I can see someone testifying against him for the right price if this thing gets into court."

"What in the world can you do, Daddy? We can't just let him be tarred and feathered with all this."

"Like I said, it will be a hard case to prove. Burl will need to keep his mouth shut and wait for this to blow over for lack of evidence. He can't start drinking and fighting and lord-knows-what-else."

"You have to make him behave himself, and how you are going to do that will be a sight to see. He's the most hardheaded man in all these hills. All of them are pretty stubborn, but he wins the prize," said Mother.

"Building that house will keep him good and busy. I'll talk to him. He won't let on, but I can put the fear of God in him at least for a while, if we're lucky, maybe long enough for the Feds to dig out the truth. What about supper? I'm starving!"

"Ed Ramsey, it is only four o'clock in the afternoon. Just because your foot is on the doorstep with the newspaper tucked under your arm doesn't mean your stomach is empty. Go get Logan, and take him for a ride or play with him on the swings or something useful."

"Maybe it's not food I'm hankering for then. I am a simple creature. Come here, Katie Bell. I bet I know what is better than pork chops and gravy for a starving man."

"Out of my kitchen. It's broad daylight. Stop your foolishness this minute."

Daddy ignored me as he laughed at his prim and predictable wife before he went out the back door, looking for Logan. I didn't know much about sex, but I knew enough to know that poor old Daddy had struck out. I giggled all the way down the hill. Leatha would get a good laugh out of this, even if I couldn't tell her about the house.

Chapter 36

THE FUNERAL WIND

Headlines in the *Knoxville News Sentinel* of the week of August 10, 1947, screamed out our settlement's tragedy to the whole world. The words jumped out at us—"Miners Killed in Blast," "Black Damp Claims Victims," "Strike Not Implicated in Mine Accident."

The various newspapers in Eastern Kentucky and Tennessee kept the story on the front page for what seemed like days but was really only a couple of editions. A bank robbery in Knoxville knocked the story off most front pages, but the human interest columns kept up a steady stream of "inside" stories of the plight of the widows and their orphaned children, along with interviews of other grieving relatives. These stories refused to fade away, and because of them, there seemed to be a reporter spying on us behind every bush. There was a rumor that even national magazines had alerted their regional bureaus to be on the lookout for information.

The blistering heat of dog days crept into every corner and crevice of the small houses in Ross's Point. It had been bone dry for weeks, but in spite of the hot wind, humidity hung heavy in the air. No one stayed inside for a minute longer than necessary. The funerals for the twelve men were to begin on Friday, and for the next three days and in spite of the heat, the entire valley would live in their best clothes with their feet crammed into stiff Sunday shoes. An ancient stoicism gripped the features of all the people in our valley.

Only widows and children allowed themselves to give in to the weight of grief at the ceremonies. There were gawkers with their cameras lining the streets and hanging in the churchyards, but nothing in our clan code would allow us to parade our grief in front of strangers.

Even at four services a day, the county resources were stretched tight as a cheap balloon. The new sheriff, Ambrose Childers, parceled out his two cars and, by tripling duty, managed to cover each ceremony. Lonnie Napier over at State Police Headquarters agreed to have his men help with traffic control at the cemeteries.

Daddy made up his mind to attend all the funerals, and Mother was to accompany him to the four funerals held at Ross's Point Church of Christ. She felt uneasy about taking us kids to any of the ceremonies and certainly not twelve of them.

Mother didn't seem to understand what she called "this strange phenomenon" that overtook mountain children in times of family trouble. When she mentioned it to Daddy, he laughed at her and said she could just figure that their pattern of behavior must have bubbled up with the water. He couldn't come up with any better explanation. The children in the valley could scream, squabble, and find mischief with the best of them, but when the stillness of grief or fear came upon the adults, the children became a mirror image—huge round eyes, grief-etched faces, rigid little bodies, and the unnatural quiet, so quiet, it seemed all sound had been sucked out of them.

Mother had some strange notion that her children were not like the "mountain" kids whom we were with every chance we could get. So she had convinced herself that we would not react well when we saw our friends with no more emotion that the stones on the mountain. Roberta calmed her down some by telling her that no one had a moment's thought for how her or anyone else's children might act. People had so much misery to deal with, they weren't about to be spending any energy on young'uns.

At the dinner table the night before, Mother had tackled the subject. "Ed, I think Roberta will stay with the children during the funerals. Don't you think we should spare them? I don't want them traumatized by all this if I can help it."

"Logan can stay here, but the other two are going. If they can sneak off to a snake-handling, they are old enough to go to simple funerals of men whose children they have known since they were babies," said Daddy.

The line between his eyes had deepened and given his face added fierceness. He had spoken. No one had ever been known to move Ed Ramsey once he declared a position. Mother knew better than to try. She backed off and gave up the battle. It was not the last time anger and frustration would rise up between them because of the gaping difference in their cultural backgrounds. Daddy oversimplified, and Mother exaggerated, and we kids just went our merry ways, soaking up as much of both sides as we could. As a result, our cultural mindset was, for the most part, unnoticed by either parent. Ironically, we were becoming the people that both our parents thought they would be when they married each other.

On Sunday, we drove to the church, and as we turned off the highway, we saw a dozen men lining the driveway and entrance, Daddy nodded at the men who were serving as pallbearers, deputies, and off-duty police. The hearse had not yet arrived, and as we pulled up, one of the men took our car keys, and Daddy, Mother, Janey, and I hurried from the car and slipped into the church. The small building was already packed, and at first, it looked like every seat was taken, but one of the men slipped out, and room was made for Mother. She held Jane on her lap and gave me about three inches of perching room beside her knee. I was too tall to stand and too big to actually sit. I twisted and fidgeted, trying to find some way to land. Mother gave me a stern look and placed her hand on my shoulder and held it there firmly until I quit wiggling. With no other option, I settled on a kind of lean. My feet were stretched under the pew in front, and I utilized my three inches as a leaning post. Splinters from the bench began to work their way through my clothes, giving me even more misery. A heavy silence draped itself over all of us in the congregation, and not even muffled whispers escaped the stifling heat and misery choking all of us.

In that long day, four caskets were carried in one at a time. Four times, grieving children and their stricken mother followed the slow progress up the aisle. Every person in the crowded church averted their eyes. It was not polite to intrude, even by sight, on the misery-racked families. Their haunted eyes, sunken deep in tear-streaked faces, were too painful to look into anyway, and we all knew it would be rude if we did. Four times, funeral eulogies berated those of us in the congregation for delaying conversion and turning from our sinful ways. Four times, the emotion of so much loss twisted the gut, slowed our breathing, and left us with a deep ache deep inside our very middles.

During the hour between the morning funerals and the afternoon services, long tables were stretched on sawhorses and filled with enough food to feed twice as many people as were there. But the heat and the emotion had drained away even the most voracious appetite, and very little of the food disappeared. As we sat under the two large trees in the churchyard, we were more interested in quenching our deep thirsts than eating. A soft rumble of thunder growled a warning from across Black Mountain. The whispers among the group assured one another that the rain would hold off until evening, maybe pass on off altogether. In the distance, we could see the third hearse approach. Even the children stood still as it pulled up in front of the stoop. Six men from the congregation stepped out and moved to the back of the long black car. The six of them stood, three on each side, and slowly slid the walnut casket down the guiding ramp. They took the seven steps in tandem and placed the casket on a short rolling carriage. Walking two in front, one on each side and two in the back, they moved the casket to the front of the church. As the men from the funeral home placed the flowers, we took our places once again inside the sweltering building. The only sound we could hear was the soft rustling, settling with a slight shuffle of feet. There had been some shifting on our pew, and now there was room for all of us to sit together. The widow, her family, and four children were the last to enter. Once again, we averted our eyes, but there was no way to shut out the cries and moans as we witnessed more pain and felt even more loss in this day that seemed to go on forever. Hours ago, I had started wishing that Mother had won the argument about us staying home.

Just before the last service, the one for Junior Sargeant, Burl's first cousin, Burl moved to Daddy's side and whispered, "Ed, could you give my pap a hand at the cemetery? It's a right smart climb, and he'd never admit it, but he's not strong enough to go up the whole way by hisself. Could you walk by him and spell him when he needs it?"

"I'd be proud to."

Mother whispered to Daddy, "Ed, if you can ride home in the truck with Burl and Fleetie, I'll drive the girls on home."

Daddy nodded as the last service finally started.

I leaned over and whispered to Mother, "I know where that cemetery is. We went up there for Decoration. Please let me go with Daddy."

She shook her head and put her hand over her mouth, indicating an end to my plea. I was so frustrated, I wanted to kick something. I couldn't believe she would not let me go with Leatha and the others to bury Junior. Mother ignored me and turned her attention to the service, leaving me to fume on my own.

The last funeral was mercifully short. The emotional impact of the previous week was beginning to exact its toll on every person in the valley. A preacher who did not use up a full hour of exhorting at a funeral was considered a poor specimen, but today, no one in the church was of a mind to check their watches. The heat pounding on our heads, the weight of the heavy loss, the sight of even more orphans, and the stark stare of one more widow had snuffed out any hidden wish to share in the communal grief. Stoic faces hid an even more determined wish to escape from one another and retreat to their porches, barns, or kitchens. Company was good, but time and room to think after all the pain and misery of today was better.

As soon as the congregation began filing out of the building, I asked again if I could go to the burying. As we walked from the church, Mother found herself surrounded by somber mourners for whom the choice to go up the steep mountain to the family cemetery was never a question.

Fleetie stepped to Mother's side and put her hand on my shoulder. "Rachel can walk with us. I'll watch her good. The kids always walk in front so they are in sight. I wore my old shoes so I could keep up with them. You and Jane can walk with Ed."

Fleetie moved away quickly before Mother could blurt out that she was not going up the mountain. Fleetie would have been baffled. It wasn't polite to skip the burial.

"Fleetie . . ."

But Fleetie had melted into the group. Mother took a firm hold on Janey's arm and steered the two of us around the side of the church and into the car just as a loud clap of thunder silenced me for the moment. The group scattered all in the direction of the mountain cemetery, Daddy with them.

I tried one more time. "Want me to go get Daddy? I'll bring him back."

She didn't even answer. Her blue eyes had turned the dangerous gray she flashed when we were in for it.

She waited until the casket bearers and the others made their way down the path leading to the steep climb up the side of the mountain. The wind was beginning to freshen, but the rain held off. High up on the mountain, lightning cracked as it hit the trees that provided protection from electric strikes down below. As the last of the mourners disappeared under the pine canopy, she pulled the car out of the small lot and turned it away from the cemetery path.

We had gone nearly two miles along the county road when all at once, lightning exploded, and streaks slashed across the road in front of us. She slammed on the brakes and maneuvered the car around to return to the church.

"Ed, what are you doing out in this? Oh, Lord, keep him safe," she shrieked as the two of us huddled in the back seat.

Jane hid her face in my lap, and I put my arm around her. As we neared the church, the car shuddered with a sudden burst of rising wind. When the noise of the thunder reverberated through the car, Jane began screaming at the top of her lungs.

"Mommy, Mommy, hold me," she cried as she flung herself over the back of the seat and grabbed Mother's neck in a death grip.

Mother slammed on the brakes in front of the church, but the lightning was so intense, she ordered us to stay in the car. That was wasted breath; neither one of us could have been dragged out by force.

She tried to comfort us. "It's all right, Janey. We'll sit right here. The car will keep us safe. Don't cry. Help Mother look for Daddy."

The car continued rocking as the wind grew stronger and threatened to roll our small Plymouth over on its side.

"Don't cry anymore, Janey. Hide your eyes, and I'll hold you close. We'll be fine, just fine. It's just a big wind. It's not even raining."

Mother was talking to me and to herself as much as she was trying to calm Janey. We stared through the window, straining to catch any glimpse of the group struggling to reach the top of the mountain.

"Where could they be, Mother? How in the world are they protecting themselves?"

The group was now near the top of the mountain where a looming rock ledge, named Rebel Rock by the valley's children, was thrust outward, far enough beyond the ledge to provide shelter for the women and children. We could just make out the men huddled together under an ancient oak where the water-slicked casket jutted halfway outside a hollowed-out trunk. With their bodies, they sheltered the coffin and one another from the ripping wind.

Lightning bolts hurled themselves over the shivering relatives, one after the other, over and over. As far as we could see beyond the ledge of rock, the trees were as bent as fish hooks on a trot line. The thunder pounded our ears with wave after wave of belly-shaking vibration. And then all of a sudden, I would have sworn I heard the sound of the locomotive rumbling down the mountain. I screamed and dropped to the floor of the car. Mother threw herself over Jane as the ghost train charged over us with a deafening roar, metal crashing into metal, howling its way from the mountainside and over our car.

Just as suddenly as it came, total silence captured every inch of the mountain. Nothing moved. It was over. Mother sat up and caught her breath as a twirling black cone swept on beyond the church and tore itself, twisting and writhing, across the valley and up Black Mountain.

"Rachel, that was a tornado! I have not seen a tornado since I left the Bluegrass, but a good thing about them is that once they go over, they don't come back."

That was a comfort for both of us, but Janey was still terrified. The path of the twister had veered away from the church and passed over us.

Mother picked her up and pointed to the sky ahead. "Look, Janey. See the big cloud marching up the mountain? It's going away. The storm is almost over. Let's wait for Daddy."

No sooner than she got the words out of her mouth before the rain sluiced down even harder. Huge raindrops fell so thick, we could see almost nothing out of the car windows.

"Mother, I heard some of the men say they saw some smoke on the mountain this morning. They were worried about a forest fire."

"Well, fire season is going to have to wait thanks to the rain. I think we have had quite enough misery for a while, don't you?"

I nodded, but I was not convinced. Lately, something bad is always just around the bend.

Chapter 37

BUILDING

Hobe watched from his porch as Burl and Daddy and a changing assortment of relatives worked on Burl's new house. Hobe's only neighborly contribution to the project was to witch the location for the new well. He had stomped around on Burl's property several nights in a row with his witching fork. One of those nights, I was sitting on the big rock near the foundation of the new house, waiting for Daddy to finish talking to Burl, and I watched Hobe.

When anyone came over the crossing and started driving or walking up the hill, he would slip into the brush surrounding the property lines and disappear. He for sure did not want anyone to see him, which didn't make a whole lot of sense. Everybody around here knew where Hobe lived. I swear he looked like he was dodging revenuers. He had his faults, but he for sure wasn't running a still. Still running is miserable hard work, and Hobe avoided as much of that as he could.

A few days later, Burl went up the hill to pull some wires for a drop cord for the front porch. When he came back down the hill, he told Fleetie he found Hobe's stick rammed deep into the hill that rose pretty steep behind the new house. There was a small square of blue fabric fluttering from the top of it so the well drillers could spot it right off. It was Hobe's way of telling Dougherty and his boy where a good water vein could be found without having to talk to him.

The next week, a gaggle of us watched as Jake Dougherty drove his rig up the hill to start the well-drilling project. But he wouldn't be going down in the earth from that awkward placement of Hobe's. Earlier that morning, Daddy had spotted the water flag, and I watched him as he grunted and then stood for a long time, looking at the flagged spot. He was deep in thought. He tugged at his ear, a sure sign of concentration. He stood as still as the poplars beside the road with his mind far away as he worked on some problem. Burl was in his smokehouse, planing trim for the kitchen, as Daddy stood looking at the awkward location of the flag and stick. He seemed to measure with his eye the contour on the hill above the flag before he turned and looked past the flag at the same contour as it fell below the flag and down the hill.

While he was deep in thought, the rest of us spotted or rather heard the drilling rig coming up over the crossing. If we had been paying attention, we might have been able to hear that conglomeration of cables, buckets, and drills coming a mile away. It seemed to me that there was nothing on that rig that didn't bang or clang, pop and crack, or make a noise that sounded something like a cross between a sigh and a moan. Daddy turned with the rest of us and watched as the truck, with all its drilling paraphernalia, backed off the narrow drive and ground to a stop. Dougherty and his boy climbed down out of the cab.

"Hello, Ed," said Jake. "Where's Burl?"

"He'll be along. He's trimming up some wood for the kitchen. Jake, look here a minute at the placement of Hobe's witching flag. He's got it placed up the hill on that bank way behind the house. That's a hell of a bad place for Burl and Fred to have to put in the plumbing, don't you think? You see any reason why it couldn't just as well be closer to the house? I was studying the contour, and it looks to me the vein would pretty much follow right down this line. What does it look like to you?"

"If they's water up that line, stands to reason they's water right here," said Jake. "Hit's the old-timer's way. They ain't careful about location. If they find water, they quit right there, mark it, and let it stand. You're right, Ed, they'll be good water right here and a sight easier for the plumbing and for Fleetie and the girls to get at too."

Hobe didn't show himself the rest of the morning, but Daddy told Mother he was uneasy about how Hobe might react to the change in the location. "You know, Katie, it doesn't take much to ruin a good well. I better see if I can make a little peace about this. No use starting off in a new place with old trouble."

So while Mother, Leatha, Logan, Jane, and I were standing there, fascinated by all the maneuverings and effort of getting the drill set, Daddy pulled away and began climbing the steep hill that separated the two neighbors. I figured I knew where he was going, and I slipped away from the group and followed several yards behind him. He stepped up on Hobe's porch and was about ready to knock when Mary swung the door wide and invited him in. I stood out of sight behind a stray pine that was just on the edge of their yard.

"Thank you, Mary. I'll just wait out here. I need to speak to Hobe a minute. I want to thank him for finding that good vein for Burl."

A shadow fell across Mary's face as she stepped back into the house. She looked over her shoulder and turned back to Daddy with the lie written clearly on her. "Hobe ain't here, Ed. He went up the mountain to check his traps this morning. I'll shore tell him what you said."

"Be sure and tell him I followed the vein and moved his stick closer to the house. I knew he would want the plumbing to go in easier. It'll be easier for the women to have the outdoor spigot close too. We sure appreciate his finding it for us. You be sure and come see us soon." Daddy tipped his old work hat and stepped back off the porch. There didn't seem to be much reason for me to stay hidden, so I let him catch up to me, and we walked back to watch the well-drilling excitement together.

The rig was in full swing when we got back down the hill. Burl came up the road, carrying a load of planed lumber. He put down the lumber and waved his arm and shouted, but Daddy could not hear him over the din of the drilling.

Burl yelled as he drew closer, "They're digging in the wrong place, Ed. Hobe marked it up the hill over there."

"That vein'll run down here. Wait and see. Hobe tried to make it harder to plumb after he witched it out," said Daddy. "He knows that vein runs this way down here. He is sour on everybody on this hill for some reason."

Burl stood looking up the hill for a long time, then he turned. "He ain't been right ever since his boy got killed trying to climb Rebel Rock. It done took something plumb out of him. He's been trying to take it out on everybody he knows since."

The two men lifted the lumber and walked it into the house to begin trimming out the kitchen sink and cabinets. As they worked through the morning, the rig kept a steady pounding as it dug to bring fresh water to the surface. The noise of the rig drowned out the rumble of the passing train and the rare car on the county road as they passed below them. It didn't take us long before our ears began to ring, and Leatha went on down the road to her house, and Mother, Jane, and I walked the other way.

Just before the drillers were about to break for lunch, Mother, Jane, and I walked down the road, carrying a basket of food for any of the men who might be hungry. Logan trailed after us. He wanted to get as close to the roaring rig as he could. Jane and I had trailed along, hoping we would be able to stretch the walk into some visiting time with the Sargeant kids. Fall was getting ready to settle into the valley, and school started for all of us in two days. The end of summer meant long separations from one another as Leatha went to the county school and Jane and I went with Daddy to the city school. This year, as with every fall, we dreaded the long stretches between visits. Though I truly loved school, I could not deny the pull of the creeks, hills, and sunshine. But the separation of school was only a small part of what was in store for us. It was a blessing that we did not know what other miseries fall would bring.

Chapter 38

Moving Day

The fall harvest season passed without incident. The FBI men slipped out of the county, and an uneasy peace settled over the valley. Burl was working at Windham's, and Leatha told me that when he got home, he was too tired to go out drinking with his old bunch. None of the kids had been hit up the side of the head, and he didn't even rant and rail at Fleetie like he used to do.

There was big excitement across the railroad when moving day came. It was about a month before Halloween, and you wouldn't have believed it if you heard tell of all the commotion going on. Every one of Fleetie's and Burl's kin showed up for what was going to stand in for a shivaree. This time, the shivaree tomfoolery was turned on its head, and instead of bad tricks, every person who could lift, push, carry, or pull a wagon dove in and moved all the furniture, rugs, dishes, and the rest of the household goods up the hill to the new house.

Mother volunteered to stay in the new house and direct the placement of the furniture, dishes, and bed coverings. So while the rest of us carried the things that Fleetie pointed out to us, Mother showed us where to set them down. There were about a million little kids running underfoot, and since Mother had an inside job, she wasn't handy to take charge of them. So they ran wild until Burl finally lost his temper and threatened to get a keen switch and cut the blood out of every one of them. This vile threat calmed them down for about five minutes. But they soon lost interest in the moving project and headed down the hill to the creek. It was a chilly day, but they ignored the cold and played on the bank and in the creek, turning over the smooth stones, looking for grampuses and mussels.

Leatha and I carried up load after load and then worked in the girls' room, making things neat and pretty. We were taking a break and sitting on the front porch for a minute. The house below was completely empty. Fleetie started up the hill. When she got to the crossing, she stopped, turned around to her old place, and stood for what seemed like a long time. Geneva was hurrying up the road with the twins, and Fleetie waited for them. Geneva took Fleetie's hand, and the two of them stood and looked one more time at the old house. To me, it was already beginning to look deserted.

"Mommy is about to cry, but Gen won't let her," said Leatha.

"Lots of memories and good times down there. I guess it is hard to leave them behind," I said.

"More bad than good, if you ask me. No telling how many times I got a whipping for a little of nothing in that house. I'm glad it's behind us."

"Do you think Fleetie feels the same way because of the way Burl treated her too?"

"No, you can't ever get her to say one bad thing about Daddy no matter how mean he is to her. It sure beats me, but she don't."

"Daddy always takes up for him too. He says he's not all bad, and I guess he did build this house for you all. He left the mines and got a good job when almost nobody can find anything but mine work. None of that was easy."

"Lordy, just listen to Ms. Sweet-as-Sugar-Pie Rachel. You can't usually say one good word about him. You'll be cussing him out tomorrow, I bet."

"Probably. Looking at the old house is making me soft hearted too."

Mother left the porch and walked to the back of the house to check the work we had done in the bedroom. The rest of the kin began to gather on the driveway, readying to get off toward home.

"Girls, you did a good job. Rachel, are you about ready to tear yourself away and go up the hill with me?"

I gave Leatha a hug and left her sitting on the top step. Mother and I slipped away, while the rest of the folks said their goodbyes.

For the next few weeks, Fleetie stayed busy putting the finishing touches on the house. Every window sported new white curtains. Fresh quilts, long saved back, covered every bed. The wood floors gleamed, and the new linoleum, cool and smooth, was so shiny, it caught light even in the near dark. Fleetie let Leatha and me help her braid long tubes of fabric that she curved into throw rugs for every room. She papered or painted every wall in the house. Piles of bright pillows filled the shaker chairs and porch swing. She told Mother she was as happy as she had been when she and Burl first got married.

Chapter 39

Box Supper

Every year, about this time, there was a box supper at Ross's Point School, and it was coming up that next Saturday. It was the school's big chance to make money for materials and books for all the kids, and the event always drew a huge crowd. Parents dreaded the winter coming up with its long days of being closed in, and this was about the last chance for getting together before they were trapped. The teachers had cancelled the party last year because of the strike, but this fall, spirits were high, and plans for dinners and fancy boxes rippled up and down the valley.

The Sargeant kids told me that the teachers and kids at school were in a fever of excitement. The kids made crepe paper streamers and, with the teachers' urging, scrubbed their classrooms until even the old wooden desks were shining. Marion Stewart, the school trustee, spread fresh floor oil that tickled the children's noses and kept the dust down. Mother said she remembered smelling the very same floor oil. It only took one whiff to trigger a book full of school memories for not just Mother but every person in the valley.

On the big night, Fleetie, Geneva, and Mary packed their dinners in their favorite baskets. Their husbands or other relatives would recognize the cook by their basket. However, the young unmarried women fixed up boxes with fancy decorations. They used ribbons and bows and curlicues to cover every inch of the surface. The color themes were a lot like the colors each family used for their decoration flowers. This scheme made it easier for the young men to spot which girl's box he hoped to buy.

All of us started the long walk to the school. Burl wasn't home from Windham's yet, and he and Fred would catch up with us later.

Hobe's oldest daughter, Virginia, and Nessa were sixteen and old enough to put a box in the auction for the young men to bid on. The reward for purchasing a pretty girl's dinner was not only the delicious food, but also, more than likely, he would get the chance to walk her home. Nessa's brown, curly hair fell in soft waves around her shoulders, and she was dressed in her blue Sunday dress. Clifford, her new sweetheart, would be waiting for her at the school.

She wore a pair of black patent shoes she purchased on layaway with money she made working at Newberry's. Before leaving home, she had pulled an old pair of brown socks over her shoes to keep them from getting scuffed on the rough track. When Fleetie wasn't looking, she powdered her face and slipped a Tangee lipstick into her pocket for later.

She and Virginia walked far behind the others. Leatha and I made a big show of ignoring them. Dorotha, Nessa, and Virginia were almost marrying age, and they didn't fit in with us anymore. We closed our circle without them, but none of them seemed to care. After a brisk thirty-minute walk, we stepped off the track and climbed up the steep hill leading to the school yard. We stepped into the crowded building and gravitated toward our friends and relatives in the front of the room. Ben Sargeant, with his fiddle, and Marion Stewart on his guitar were playing, "Camptown Ladies," and the first few rows of people were clapping and patting their feet. The smaller children at the front captured the space just below the platform and were spinning and stomping in their miniature version of a hoedown.

The tables along the front wall were full of a near-Christmas assortment of boxes, ribbons, and expectations. Henry Sargeant, the appointed auctioneer of the evening, walked to the front of the room and whispered to the musicians, and in turn, we received a string-strummed fanfare to settle the crowd. Susanna, his wife, was his assistant, and playing favorites, she selected her niece Nessa's box first. It was wrapped with brown paper and sprinkled with red sumac leaves and crepe paper streamers. Henry held the box high as he began his chant to urge the bidding. Clifford jumped halfway down the middle aisle and threw up his hand to make the first bid.

"Fifty cents," he stuttered, causing cheers and guffaws from the boisterous crowd.

"Can't let him have this here work of art that cheap!" said Henry.

Lige Turner's boy Ravenell and Roger Ellis threw in bids against Clifford, daring him to go higher as the sweat popped out on his forehead. Clifford turned a sickly green as he heard the bidding crawling higher and higher—one dollar, a dollar and a half, a dollar seventy-five.

Roger had been sweet on Nessa as long as he could remember. Everybody in the valley had pegged them as a match, but in the last few months, her kin had watched as Clifford, with his city airs, turned her head. Roger was fighting a rising tide as he threw in his last try.

"Four dollars!" he shouted.

The whole room could hear the tremor in his voice. It was every penny he had, and the crowd sensed it. A sudden hush then loud whispers swamped the room, followed by the low hum of rapt attention. With just a little more, four dollars would buy a baby calf or two good used tires. Clifford's face flushed scarlet as he thrust his hands deep in his pockets and shot his eyes into Roger, who taunted him with a broad grin. Nessa threw her hands in front of her face and refused to look up. She was going to be the subject of porch gossip for months after this, and she probably could feel fingers of shame creeping up her spine.

Clifford's eyes swept the entire room as he raised his hand, and with no sign of hesitation, he called out in slow, clear tones, "I bid five dollars. She's the prettiest girl in this room, and I'm bound to eat that dinner."

The crowd roared, and Roger dropped into his seat. Susanna carried the box to a shaking Nessa, while Clifford strode behind her as proud as a lord.

The crowd remained in a buzz, and Henry hurried to latch on to the momentum. He chanted off the next offering and was rewarded with more excited bidding. Box after box was bid up and out, but none of the others reached Clifford's price.

Nessa and Clifford edged their way to the door just as Susanna selected Virginia's box. Henry started his spiel, but the box was an easy sell. As young as she was, everyone in the room knew that Virginia's food was the finest in the valley and up the hollers as well. Her fried chicken was as light and as crispy as the cloud-soft biscuits, the deviled eggs would be better named after angels, and her chocolate cake lingered in the memory like a first kiss. Two years ago, the bidding on her basket was rowdy and fetched a big price but not as big as the unbelievable five dollars.

Henry accepted the first bid—one dollar, a high start. Most bidding started at twenty-five or fifty cents. Other bids, scattered across the crowded building, were shouted in, but Billy Nolan and Jeremiah Howard soon left the others behind. Billy's last bid at three dollars would take every penny in his pocket, but Jeremiah strutted down the aisle, shouting, "Three dollars and fifty cents, and she's mine, by god."

At that moment, Billy reached the full limit of his tolerance. He was not about to be outbid in front of the whole valley. In total frustration, he flung his right arm around the neck of his competition. With his heavy-muscled arms, Billy broke Jeremiah's stranglehold, and the two overgrown boys rolled, kicking and cursing on the floor right in front of Henry. He gave Susanna a nod and grabbed Billy. As if she had practiced the move, she pulled Jeremiah up by his belt.

"Out of here with that foolishness," Henry shouted.

Both the boys were just about pitched out the door. They rolled down the schoolhouse steps and continued the fight all the way into the school yard. The boys and men in the yard took sides and began baiting them even further. Finally, Marion Stewart, standing just outside the door, could see that the fight had all but stopped the big fundraising for his beloved school. He nodded at two of the men closest by, and the three of them pulled the two kicking, screaming boys apart.

"You can have the damn supper," shouted Billy. "The food might be good, but you have to eat it with that scab Hobe's brat. That ought to make it stick in your craw for a week."

Total silence fell in the schoolhouse and in the yard. And then as if on cue, it was as if every other person there started yelling accusations. Virginia grabbed her basket and flew out the door. More fights broke out, and screams and shrieks from the women and children rattled through the crowd. Marion Stewart pushed his way back into the school and took the shotgun down from the wall where it rested for protection against poisonous snakes. He shoved in two shells, slammed the rifle shut, walked to the door, pointed the gun straight up in the air, and pulled both triggers.

The roar of a shotgun will stop a grown bear on a rampage, and the effect on every one of us in the crowd was immediate. Dorotha loved Virginia as much as any person in the world, and she must have seen the shock and humiliation on her face.

Whatever triggered it, Dorotha yelled over everyone, "Hobe ain't no scab." Dorotha had a strong voice, and the anger and desperation made her voice even louder and shriller.

The room was silent, and Henry walked across the room to her side. "Girl, what is that you're telling?"

"I was hiding in his smokehouse during the flood, and they was three men came up on his porch. I heard them tell Hobe they was union and they was going to organize or they would burn down all of Ross's Point. They told him they had brought him good money to set fires all up and down the valley until everybody got so sick of it, they would settle the strike. With the operators backed down that way, the union would be right where it should be. They paid him. I saw them counting it out." She was trembling from top to toe, but she was determined to get it all told.

Fleetie pushed her way through the crowd, trying to get to Dorotha. "Dork, hush that. You don't know what you're saying. Hush now. I mean it, child. No more." Fleetie turned to the angry crowd. "She don't know what she's saying. I can't never put anything past her. When she gets shaky like this, she just rattles on. Don't you all pay her no mind."

Dorotha, flapping her arms with tears cascading down her cheeks, screamed, "I do too know. Hobe said he'd kill all of us if I told what I heard. I hain't told a soul. But you can't be callin' Virginia no scab child. Hobe ain't no scab. He's pure union. Tell 'um Hobe."

Fleetie grabbed Dorotha and, dragging and carrying, shoved her beyond the school yard and down the bank to the railroad track. Dorotha's outburst, so typical of her unsettled nature, jolted the crowd into stony silence. She was trying so hard to comfort and protect Virginia, but she blurted out a charge against Hobe far more damning than "scab." It was as if the fires that killed Freddie and Hershel and broke the back of the strike were raging again with the discovery of this new treachery. Hobe stepped back into the shadows on the far side of the school house and slipped up the mountain rising behind them.

Geneva and Fred gathered all us kids and began moving us away from the school and onto the tracks for the walk home.

"Fred, I can't find Nessa," said Geneva. "Go back and tell Susanna to take her home with her. Nessa can cross the river for home in the morning."

As Fred walked back across the school yard, he could feel dozens of eyes on him as his neighbors tried to ferret out how he was taking the news of Hobe's guilty role in the death of his baby. Some of the younger boys commenced to prattling at one another, calling names and throwing rocks. Henry and Marion stomped into the middle of them and, by collaring one or two of the taller boys, managed to scatter them and stop the commotion but not before taunts were thrown right at Dorotha. She ran down the track, tears streaming down her face, as the rest of us followed.

The women in the crowd took controls and one by ones each family moved to their trucks or took out on foot. Most of the boxes had been sold, but the dancing, games, and music died right there at our feet. The weight of Dorotha's secret stole away all appetite for fun.

At Ross's Point, ties of kinship went back generations, and the idea that blood could be guilty of such treachery left the adults soul sick and the rest of us bewildered. I had forgotten my red jacket and had to run back to the schoolhouse to get it. Mother would skin me alive if I lost one more piece of clothing. I scattered my stuff wherever Leatha and I roamed, but tonight, even in the middle of all the trouble, I somehow remembered it.

With the group fading into the dark, I saw Marion before he turned to lock the schoolhouse. He checked the back door and looked up. I followed his eyes and saw the outline of a man making his way along the mountain ridge that paralleled the tracks leading south above the county road.

"Hobe," he whispered. "Man, I hope that little gal ain't got that straight. If not, you'll not live soft in your skin another day after this. Lord, lord, sometimes trouble's all there is."

He turned out the overhead lights, and I grabbed my jacket off the hook by the door and stepped over the threshold just before he closed the heavy door and snapped the heavy lock. His slight frame folded itself into the surrounding dark as he felt his way down the bank and into his battered truck.

Chapter 40

WHERE'S NESSA

Fleetie and Geneva herded us onto the railroad track for the long walk home. Dorotha could not stop crying, and she and Virginia fell farther behind. For once, Leatha and I were not the guilty ones. No one was paying us the least amount of attention. Burl and Fred, who had gotten to the schoolhouse just as the trouble began, took the truck and headed across the valley to look for Nessa. Just as they pulled away, the deputy sheriff's car drove past our group and headed toward the schoolhouse. The car rolled by us and slipped into the dark. The brake lights slashed red streaks in the fog, leaving a trail a blind possum could follow.

Dorotha saw the deputy's car and cried even harder. "Mommy, Mommy, he's coming to get me."

Virginia grabbed her hand and pulled her off the track where the two of them crouched down on the rail bank. "Shhh, Dork. They can't see you. It's too dark. Don't yell and let them know we're here."

Fleetie lost all patience. It was not enough that Dorotha had been shamed in front of the neighbors. Now here she was, cowering in the dark like some criminal. "Get up on the track and hurry up about it. No one is looking for you, but I'm gonna whoop both of you if you don't get to moving."

For all the fierceness of her words, Fleetie had no force behind her threat. She took Dorotha and Virginia by the hand and helped them stand and find their footing in the dense dark. Dorotha kept snuffling and snubbing all the long way home.

Mother, as a rule, let us traipse about the valley with the Sargeant children without worry. But tonight, she had one of those feelings of hers and nagged Daddy into going to look to make sure we were safe. Daddy told me he knew better than to argue with her. She was more often right about her "feelings" than she was wrong. Even if he could not figure out right at that moment what was causing her skin to crawl, in the days ahead, he would discover she was right. He met us just as we were coming up the crossing at the foot of the hill. Fleetie, distracted and jumpy as I ever saw her, walked nearer the car.

"What's the trouble, Fleet? You all don't look like you've been to a party. Hey, Dorotha, you been crying? Lost your feller, did you?"

Daddy's teasing, which always brought gales of laughter from Fleet's kids, was met tonight with silence.

"Don't pay them no mind, Ed. They was a fight, and Nessa and Clifford got themselves off somewheres. We couldn't find them before we left. Burl and Fred is over at the settlement looking for them. Won't you come on in for a spell?"

"No, thank you. I'll take my girls on up the hill. Katie is pacing the floor. Are you sure Nessa is at the settlement?"

"Lord, I don't know. Young'uns'll drive you crazy, wear you out when they are little, and worry you to death when they are grown. We sure pay for our raisin'."

"Want me to drive over and see if I can find them?"

"Lord a'mercy, no, Ed. Burl will find them. No use gettin' the whole valley in a uproar, but I sure thank you anyway."

"Girls, get in the car. Your mom is frettin' over you both. Send one of the kids to get me if she don't show up, Fleet. I'll come down, and Burl and me will go scoutin'. Don't worry, kids usually land on their feet." Daddy pulled away, turned the car around, and drove up the hill.

We had barely walked in the house before Burl drove up to use the telephone. He reported that Nessa was nowhere to be found in the settlement. Burl had driven back to the schoolhouse and searched the grounds and did not find the pair. It was beginning to look as if they had run off, and Burl's temper was about to get the best of him.

"Ay god, Ed, when I get my hands on that boy, I'll not leave a spot that's not black and blue. Nessa's just a baby. I swear a man ought to drown kids as soon as they're born. They're nothing but trouble the rest of your life," said Burl.

"Slow down, Burl. I'll call the sheriff. You can't find nobody if you're shouting and stomping like a crazy man. Come on, we'll go to town together. The sheriff will most likely already know something. Kids running off to Jellico leave a pretty clear trail."

Daddy called the sheriff's office and told the dispatcher they were coming in to see the sheriff. The two of them walked down the front steps and climbed in Burl's truck. I walked right behind the truck, grabbed the tailgate, and swung myself up. I wasn't ready to let all the ruckus of tonight end. The Margie Grand didn't show movies this exciting—it was too good to miss.

Burl pulled the truck beside the gate, and I jumped off the back. Dorotha was standing behind Fleetie. All she had heard was that Burl and Ed were going to find the sheriff. No one was paying any attention to Dorotha and didn't see the pure terror cross her face. The mention of the sheriff sent her flying into the kitchen and onto the back porch, where Leatha and I found her crouched beside the washing machine.

"Dork, you better get on to bed," said Leatha.

She was crying so hard, she wailed more than spoke. "I can't! Daddy and Ed has gone to get the sheriff. He's gonna take me to jail."

"Stay there, then. You are pure dumb, Dork. The sheriff has bigger stuff to mess with than you," said Leatha.

"You don't know nuthin'. You are so prissy, you can't tell morning from night. Leave me alone. I'm not coming in. I'm staying right here where I can run if the sheriff comes to get me," she said.

Leatha slammed the back screen door, and we went inside and turned off the kitchen light so we could tell where she went in the dark. She took out across the backyard and turned up the mountain. We lost sight of her, so we moved to the back of the house to watch her out the bedroom window. She looked to be heading for the deep woods high on the sheltering mountain above us. To the far left, we spotted her as she kept climbing the steep hill and passed Hobe's back porch. In her frantic dash to get away from the sheriff and jail, she must have not noticed the red glow of a cigarette on Hobe's porch, marking the place where someone stood watching her. As she ran by the house, I could see a red glow cut through the blackness as it flew in a high arc and fell away just beyond the porch. A black shadow moved down the two worn steps and onto Dorotha's path as she kept moving fast on her way up the side of the mountain.

Chapter 41

THE STILL

Leatha and I climbed into bed, while Fleetie kept her vigil by the window in the living room. We did not mention that we had seen Dorotha leave the back porch and go up the hill. Her goofiness had a way of wearing us all down. If she chose to run up the hill, that meant extra room in the crowded bed, so we kept our mouth shut. For once, we could curl up under the covers with a flashlight and read *True Confessions* without having Dorotha threaten to tell on us. But even the delicious thrill of a forbidden magazine was not enough to keep us awake for long. Soon, Emma, Rebecca, Leatha, and I drifted off to sleep.

As the night birds gave up their low songs, and just before the first tinges of morning light nudged the day birds off their roost, a car came down the road and drove over the crossing and made its way up the hill. It stopped in front of the Sargeants' house. Leatha punched me awake. Fleetie had fallen asleep in the living room with her arms crossed on the windowsill. She jerked awake when the car door slammed. She raced to the front door and ran down the porch steps onto the path just as Nessa and Clifford were making their way up the same path to the house. Fleetie was so breathless, it was hard for her to speak. She held one hand to her chest and the other on her hip as if she was trying to hold herself upright.

"Where have you been? I have been half out of my mind. Are you trying to turn me gray overnight? I've not been to bed. Where is Burl and Ed?" Tears ran down Fleetie's face, and she could not seem to make herself stop talking. It was as if she knew that if she stayed silent, Nessa was going to tell her the news she couldn't bear to hear.

Nessa grabbed her mother and held her close, and to the surprise of both of them, she began to cry deep, exploding sobs. The two women stood weeping in the early light, while a bewildered Clifford backstepped toward the car. Daddy and Burl rolled out of the car, laughing at the sight of Clifford retreating in the face of two sets of female tears.

Daddy was still laughing. "Fleetie, you've got yourself a fine new son-in-law if you don't scare him to death first."

Fleetie shook herself loose and sat hard on the bottom step, wrapping herself into a ball, rocking slowly back and forth as the early morning dampness twisted every strand of her hair into drifts of wispy curls. Nessa sat beside her and began to tell her where they had been. Clifford stood first on one foot and then the other, not knowing whether to move forward or stay near the car. Daddy finally took pity on him and suggested to Burl that they make their way into the house for some coffee. Leatha and I jumped back in bed.

The men left the two women on the steps whispering their way through the new situation between them. The men found their way to the kitchen and began filling cups with coffee left on the stove for far too long. They bantered and complained about the coffee.

As we looked around the bedroom, getting our bearings in the half light, we first felt and then saw that Dorotha had not filled her corner of the bed. Her pillow was empty and smooth. The noise from the kitchen urged us forward as we pulled on our shirts and shorts that we had dropped beside the bed the night before. Leatha opened the door a crack, and seeing no one in the living room, she motioned to me, and we slipped out of the bedroom and closed the door behind us.

"Where's Mommy?" said Leatha as she stepped into the noisy kitchen.

Daddy smiled at her. "You've got a big surprise this morning. Clifford here is your new brother-in-law. How about that?"

"How come he's my brother-in-law? Where's Nessa? Last thing I heard, the sheriff was after them," said Leatha.

Burl said, "Nessa and Fleetie are out front. If you want to know about what happened, go ask the women. Tell 'em we're hungry and to get their selves in here and cook. I swear them women are plumb no count leavin' us men to go hungry while they moon around and beller like a barn full of orphan calves."

Leatha whipped around and tore out the front door, putting as much space between her and the men as she could. I ran right with her. At any minute, Daddy was going to realize I was not home where I belonged, and I would be on my way home before I could find out anything.

Without waiting to ask Nessa what Daddy meant about Clifford, Leatha announced, "Dork's gone. She was on the back porch last night, and now she's gone."

Fleetie flew up the steps and threw open the bedroom door and threw back the covers, exposing sleeping children, now blinking and as confused as a litter of kittens. Finding no Dorotha, she ran through the kitchen, stepping over the men's feet as she threw open the door and ran the length of the porch and down the steps. She bent over to peer into the crawl space and then ran back around to the front porch. She threw open the basement door, looking for Dorotha hiding among the rows of canned food stored in the keep. I was behind Daddy when he found Fleetie there as pale as the morning light just now beginning to swell into day.

"Fleetie, was she here last night after you all got back from the box supper?"

"She cried all the way back, Ed. You couldn't miss her. She was scared plumb out of her wits that the sheriff was going to get her for blabbing all that ugly talk about Hobe. There's no telling where she's run off to. She knows ever' rill and dip in this mountain. She could hide for days, and we'd not find her till she was too hungry to stay away anymore."

285

Daddy said, "Back in the summer, Leatha and Rachel built a new clubhouse somewhere above the flat. Send them up there to look, and the rest of us will fan out to the Kentenia line and Town rocks. She doesn't need to be out there by herself, and beside, we need to get her home to meet her new brother-in-law."

"Lord a'mercy, I purely forgot them two. Clifford can just as well go looking for her too. He better get used to what it's like to tie into this family. It's sure not nothin's as rosy as their big running-off plans last night," said Fleetie.

Fleetie and Nessa followed Leatha and me up the path to find the clubhouse, while Burl and the other men spread themselves across the brow of the hill well beyond the path we were taking. Fred drove up and followed Burl into the deep hollow, carved by a spring that ran past Hobe's and the Willises' on its way to the river.

Dorotha was not at the clubhouse, and Fleetie sent Nessa back to the house to mind the children. As Nessa left, we continued up the mountain.

Across the way, I saw Fred cut away from the group and swing far to the left and circle back above the clubhouse site. He had gotten so far above us that I lost sight of him. The three of us kept pulling ourselves up the steep mountain, but finally, when we came to a nest of small boulders resting just beyond the path, we stopped to catch our breath. None of us had eaten breakfast or slept particularly well, and the race up the mountain had pretty well drained us.

"Mommy, where was Newan and Clifford last night?"

Fleetie took a long deep breath. "They went off to Jellico. They are married, I guess."

"You mean that old Clifford is my brother-in-law, and I have to be nice to him now?"

"Yes, that is what it means. And yes, you will be nice to him, and you can stop your silliness right now. Nessa is going to need us. Being married is hard, and she don't know it yet."

"Well, it won't be hard for me. I am never going to run off with some old boy like Clifford. He's just dumb."

"That's big talk today, but wait and see. You'll come around to it one day, and when you do, you are going to need Nessa and all the rest of us to be nice to you and to him. So remember that before you go spoutin' out a bunch of words nobody wants to hear."

During their talk, I wandered over to a walnut tree to see if there were any nuts left on the ground, and on ahead, I spotted Fred coming down the mountain far to the left of where I had last seen him.

I called back down, "Fred's coming. Let's go meet him."

I waited until Leatha and Fleetie caught up with me, and by the time they got to me, Fred was about even with us to the far left. Fleetie waved her arms to get his attention, and when he saw us, he stopped, waved back, and acted like he was going to go on. Fleetie yelled at him to stop, and we hurried to get to where he was poised, looking ready to take off any minute.

Fleetie got to him first then Leatha, but I held back. Fred looked funny. I don't know funny how, just different. He didn't want to talk to Fleetie—that, I could see—but she would have none of it.

"Fred, what did you find? Where is Dorotha? Tell me, Fred. I can't take no more of this."

After a long spell of complete quiet on that mountain except for insect hum, Fred, with his hands stuffed deep in his pockets and his head tilted down nearly to his chin, finally began to talk to us.

"I pulled away from the others since I was already ahead of them in the truck, but finally, the mountain got too steep to drive any further. I walked on up to the old still site. The trees and undergrowth is so thick, you can hardly tell where the clearing is anymore. But I spotted a rabbit trail and pushed my way through the briars. What I saw, I never hope to see again as long as I live. There was old Hobe, crumpled up like some broke toy right there in front of me and right near the old fire ring. His head was split open about like a mush melon, and it was twisted so crazy on his neck that nothing looked real. His eyes was open, and they looked to be staring right past me. His fist was in a knot, and his arm stretched out like he was reaching for something. That something was little Dorotha. Bruises all over her face, and she is swoll up till you wouldn't know her. It looks like her left arm is broke and splayed awkward like from her side. Streaks of dried blood has run from her mouth and nose, and blood has splattered brown all over the front of her blouse. I stood there for a time, trying to clear my head enough to decide what to do next.

"Fleet, she is as dead as Hobe. I couldn't stand to look no more, so I backed away and went to find you all. Fleetie, I know I shoulda stayed with her, but it hurt me too bad to see her like that.

"When I got beyond the worst of the briars, I listened to see if I could hear anyone coming close that could help. When I didn't hear nobody, I pushed on and started down the mountain. I did not stop until I had cleared the brow of the hill where I could cut back through that stand of dead chestnuts. I have sweated through every stitch on my body, and there was no way I could keep from being sick. I puked so hard, it forced me down on my knees. I slumped against the trunk of one of those dead chestnuts. I wanted to stay there, but I knew you was on your way up here. Fleetie, I don't want you to go up there. It is the worst thing I have ever seen. You can't stand it."

"Fred, are you sure she is dead? What if she isn't? God almighty, she could be dying right this minute. Jesus Lord, give me strength."

Without another word, she began running up the mountain with the two of us trailing behind her.

Chapter 42

THE MOUNTAIN ANSWERS

Fleetie yelled for Leatha and me to follow close. She pointed out the faint animal trail she was following as she worked our way up the face of the mountain. As we approached the old still site, the narrow trace veered off to a sharp left. Fleetie stopped and turned slowly. I watched every move she made. I could almost feel her instinct lead her eyes over the contour and slant of land that would direct someone to a secluded place.

She was like Pappy. He had known the secrets the mountains give to those who bend their minds enough to follow the earth's signs and hints. I was beginning to learn that just living in the mountains didn't mean the land would let you be a part of it, free and clear. You had to hear the sounds, even the faintest echoes, and let your eyes see the earth, the growth rising from the ground, and the very stones tossed about centuries before. You had to let your mind be open to take in the power and sanctuary and feel it in your feet and your heart.

That mountain knew Fleetie. Ever since she was a child, her feet had traveled every slant, tilt, and stone. Years of picking greens, searching for 'sang, and trailing small game had taught her to let the mountain lead her. She listened and watched and was rewarded as she went venturing for herbs, stray dogs, and children. Fleetie knew the mountain's moods and secrets, and today, it gave her what she was desperate to know.

Fleetie moved like she had a fist in the middle of her back, and she wasn't really talking to us. It was more that she was talking to Dorotha, who was somewhere on this mountain, and Fleetie wanted her back and safe at home now.

"Dork, Dork, even if you're my worrisome girl, I still can't bear you being gone. None of my kids are lazy, but Dork, you can outwork all of them, and you're the only one of the kids who can understand and is good to your daddy. Dork, you have always been plumb skittery, but since the flood, you never seem to have a good day. Is what's eatin' at you, driven you right up this mountain? I'm coming. Wait for Mommy. We'll be there."

Fleetie pushed away the low-hanging poplar branches that covered the path into the old still site, and as she did, we heard a soft whimper, much like a hurt kitten. Right in front of us, Fleetie pointed out where someone had broken through the tangled brush cover. She stepped around a huge silver maple that blocked her view, and then she stopped.

I saw Leatha try to scream, but no sound would come out of her mouth. I could not breathe or move or think. Nothing in the grisly scene in front of me would come into focus. There was no beginning, no place in my head for seeing a dead neighbor and a broken Dorotha, who was maybe dead too.

Fleetie grabbed Leatha's arm, and Leatha grabbed me as we stood, unable to move for the first few seconds. Fleetie began a low dirge that came from somewhere deep, deep inside her. "Lord God, no, no, no. Let me help her. Don't take her, Lord. No, no, no."

Over and over, she repeated the same words. She pulled away and took the first slow steps to Dorotha. My insides shook, and it hurt to look, yet I couldn't bear to look away. If Dorotha was alive, only the barest thread was holding her on this side of death. Fleetie backed into the maple tree and slammed her open palms again the rough bark and rubbed them hard up and down. She created enough pain to startle her mind and body back so she could think again. She shook her head viciously, and then we could see her eyes clear away the last of the shadows hiding the truth from her.

A dead Hobe was of no concern to Fleetie. She did not even look in his direction. A living Dorotha, injured and bleeding, was all she had room for at the moment. She stepped over Hobe and knelt beside Dorotha. I couldn't bring myself to step over him, and Leatha and I walked around the outside of the fire ring and came up on the other side of Dorotha, lying there as still as I had ever seen her.

"Can you hear me, Dork? It's Mommy. You've done gone and broke your arm. I got to wrap a limb to it so I can get you down off'en this mountain. It'll hurt bad when I move it. You hearin' me, Dork?"

There was no movement or sound from her, and Fleetie looked around. "Leatha, Rachel, see that rotten barrel on its side? You two pull me some staves from that ring. Maybe they're not all too rotted. I need something to use as a splint to move this here broken arm."

As we jumped to grab the staves, Fleetie sat down and braced her feet against Hobe's side and rolled him over. She jerked his shirt up from the belt and grabbed the side seam and ripped out the back of his shirt and tore it into strips. She slipped her fingers under the broken arm and lifted it just enough to push the stave under it. As she wrapped the shirt strips to secure the arm, Dorotha began to moan soft, mewing sounds just loud enough to hear. Her weak response frightened us even more, and Leatha and I sat on the ground beside Dorotha and began rubbing her feet and legs. Leatha had tears streaming down her face. Dorotha must have been feeling tremendous pain with the wrapping and securing work that Fleetie was doing, but she seemed barely aware of it.

"Oh, Lord, Lord. She's near gone. Help me, oh, Lord, help me hold on to her. Dorotha, Dorotha, listen to me. Open them eyes now, girl. You hear me? Open them eyes. Talk to me, Dorotha, or I swear I'll whoop you clear to Sunday. Dorotha . . ."

Fleetie's cries echoed down the mountain. Fred was circling back to the old still, and he hurled himself through the underbrush and raced around the giant maple.

"Oh my god, Fleetie. She's alive?"

"Fred, where'd you come from? Hobe is long gone. Dorotha has been beat near to death. We've got to pack her down the mountain."

K. Bruce Florence

"Burl and them others is trailing up Gaton Creek. I'll cut across up here and get 'em to help us. We need something to lift her on so we can carry her flat down to my truck. Here's my knife. While I'm gone, cut some of them saplings. We can tie them together with some vines when I get back."

He handed her his bowie knife, and without looking at Hobe's body, he made his way around the maple and began to cross the ridge just above the still site.

Fleetie moved to the edge of the clearing and bent a slender birch to the ground. Leatha and I held it, while she slashed it across the middle of the bend. She cut five more of them, and each one snapped apart with a loud crack. Cutting and pulling, we trimmed each sapling of its branches. Fleetie spotted a dead maple limb low enough for her to cut off the tree and stout enough to hold some weight.

She laid the branch over a rock jutting out of the ground, and using the rock as a fulcrum, we held down one end, and she stepped on the other. It broke cleanly, and we gathered all the trimmed wood and took it back to the fire ring to lay out a small litter next to Dorotha's still form. Fleetie took what was left of Hobe's shirt and tore it into strips and lashed each of the saplings to the two pieces of maple, weaving a makeshift stretcher together. When she finished, she placed it beside Dorotha just as we heard voices filtering through the trees.

Burl was in front of the group and pushed his way past the underbrush and low-hanging branches. He stepped from behind the huge maple and stopped dead still. He seemed as shocked at the sight in front of him as we had been.

"Ay god! We got us a real crazy roaming this here mountain. Why'd he try to kill Dork? Hobe's been needin' killing, but looks like we got us a baby killer too."

"We got to get her down to the house, Burl. She's real bad off. She hain't hardly breathing. Send one of them boys running ahead to Ed's so some of them can call Dr. Parks. Her head is bad hurt, and she's hardly stirred since I found her," said Fleetie.

Roger Willis, standing just inside the clearing, said, "I'll go to Ed's, Fleetie. I'm gone." He disappeared into the overgrowth. We could hear his feet bounding down the rocky hillside as he zigzagged his way past trees, brush, and boulders.

Fred and Burl went to their knees and slipped their hands under Dorotha's limp body and lifted her enough to allow Fleetie to slide the makeshift stretcher under her. Speaking more to himself than any of us, he said, "I'm telling you, Fred. Someone's going to pay hell for this one. Ain't nobody safe when somebody takes after them that's no more than babies. God, what a mess."

Fred and Roger took one end of the makeshift stretcher and Burl and Fleetie the other. Leatha and I followed. It's not often that you go down a mountain as slowly as you climb up, but today, progress down was as slow and as careful as the carriers could make it. But no matter how easy they tried to make their way, Dorotha never once stopped her soft moaning. In a way, it was comfort to hear her because we knew she was still alive as we made slow progress down the side of that mountain.

Fleetie wouldn't let Dr. Parks take Dorotha to the hospital. Everybody around the valley was suspicious of the hospital. Coal operators financed it, and miners were seldom admitted, but Mother listened to every word Dr. Parks said and carried out his orders. In spite of all the careful nursing, Dorotha was unconscious for two weeks. Her face and head were so swollen, she was almost unrecognizable. Fleetie, Geneva, and Mother took turns sitting at her bedside, and except for an occasional soft moan, there was almost no response from her. I would relieve Mother so she could go home for a while to see about Jane and Logan. Leatha and I would sit there, watching Dorotha and listening to the talk in the living room.

For the next two days, several groups of serious-faced men up traveled and down the same steep path, searching for clues that would identify the man who had attacked Hobe and Dorotha. Hobe's body was wrapped in an old mine tarp and carried down the mountain on the back of one of his mules.

Currents of suspicion and blame swirled up and down the valley. Rumors and downright lies grew as thick as wild onions. Tale after tale was told by people who did not know what they were talking about, and the sheriff seemed like he was haunting the place. I kept my mouth shut, which was amazing. It was the biggest story I had ever lived through, but Dorotha's injuries squelched any desire to draw attention my way.

It was a long two weeks, and all the strangeness was beginning to feel almost normal. The sheriff's car made countless trips up and down the county road as he questioned, examined, and, for long periods of time, just parked below the point, where he could get a full view of the river. No one could figure out what he was doing there, but no one was about to ask either.

On the fourteenth morning after we found Dorotha, Geneva was asleep in the high-backed rocker where she spent the long night keeping watch. As she told us later, daylight fell across the room from the small window above the bed, and Dorotha opened her eyes and pulled up on her elbow.

She gave Geneva a long puzzled look. "Gen, whatcha doing here?"

At first, Geneva did not answer. Her hands moved down the arms of the rocker as she struggled to shake off the deep sleep.

"Gen, what's wrong? Whatcha doin' here? Where's Fred and them twins?"

Then she caught a glimpse of her battered arm and pulled up the sleeve of her gown and then stared at the heavy cast holding the other.

Shaking off the end of sleep, Geneva jumped up. "Fleetie, come quick. Oh lordy, Fleetie. She's awake. She's plumb awake."

Chapter 43

FRED'S VISIT

About a week later at dinner, Mother complained to Daddy about the sheriff's badgering Dorotha day after day. She got on a good head of steam and was preaching a strong sermon to Daddy about how ridiculous it was for a grown man to keep bothering that child. Right in the middle of her argument, Fred and Burl walked up on the back porch.

As far as I could remember, Fred had never been to our house. A worry line nudged its way across Mother's forehead. Daddy walked out on the porch, and after a few words, the three men walked across the backyard and turned to the small orchard at the side of the house.

I got up from the table, ignoring Mother, who mumbled something about aching to be excused, and went to my room. I wasn't about to miss out on what in the world brought Fred over the crossing and all the way up the hill to our house. My bedroom was on the orchard side of the house, and as soon as they passed my window, I pushed it open. There, hidden behind the white organdy curtain, I could hear them as clear as a rain crow.

"Ed, buddy, Coburn come to the house tonight and said he's heard tell at the store that the sheriff is about to arrest Burl for Hobe's killing. You know Burl ain't never killed nobody, but according to Coburn, they found evidence up there that makes it look like Burl was there. They tell they found his hat and that old brown jacket he used to wear huntin'."

"Hell, Fred, if that's all they've got, you got nothing to worry about," said Daddy. "Everybody around here knows that Dorotha wore that stuff ever' chance she got. What else are they basing this on? Or do you know?"

"Some of them union boys is telling that Hobe was working for the operators," said Fred, "trying to break the strike. The story they tell is that Burl found out and killed Hobe for going agin' his own in the strike."

"That's not going to stand up either, Fred. Every union man in the county would have the same motive. If this is all they've got, we can give them a good run for their money," said Daddy.

"They's more," said Burl. "We know who killed him, and before the law gets wind of it, it's just as well they think it was me. You said they didn't have enough anyhow. Shouldn't be much of a trick for you to get me cleared. By that time, they'll be something else holdin' their interest."

"Whoa, buddy, listen to me. If you really do know who did this, you can't tell me. I'm a sworn officer of the court. I could lose my license to practice law if I obstruct justice by letting them try an innocent man. Besides that, damn it, you are taking a terrible chance with this. Trials can be unpredictable. Just because a man is innocent doesn't always mean the jury will see it that way. With this one, the jury could be packed against you. The operators are a powerful bunch, and money talks big. Juries have been bought before, and you could be hauled off to Eddyville for life. Think, man, what would happen to Fleetie and the kids? You've seen how pitiful the miners' widows are. It'd kill you to see them suffering for something this empty."

"I have to fight it out, Ed," said Burl. "There ain't nothing else for it. For what Hobe done, dying was too good for him. They's more tales bein' told about what happened up on that mountain than a conjure woman could ravel out. But I'm here to tell you Hobe beat Dork near to death. She don't know what happened, but by god, I know she'd be dead if somebody had not went at him like they did. Let 'em all think what they want to think. People is going to get hurt a sight more than me and Fleet if this comes down agin' 'em. 'Sides, Ed, I never seen nothing you couldn't wrestle to suit you when you got your back up. It's bad, but that's the way of it."

Daddy didn't say anything for the longest time. I looked out the window, thinking they had walked away, when Daddy said, "Fred?"

"Leave him be, Ed. He don't know nothin'. If you push him, he'll just lie. Fred don't have a honest bone in his body. Just let it lay right here."

Fred dropped his head and never looked up, even when Daddy was talking to him.

"The operators are afraid of you, Burl. They know every miner in these parts would walk into black damp if you asked them to. The operators to a man all think that job at Windham's is just a cover for what you are really doing. Whoever heard of a man making a living farming in coal country? They are afraid of what you can do, and if they want to get rid of you bad enough, I might be able to make a deal with them to put the pressure on the commonwealth attorney to drop the case. But they won't do it cheap. It'll mean they'll force you to pack out of here for good. This is home, Burl, and you've never been far away from your kin. During the war, I wanted to be back here a whole lot worse than I wanted to kill Germans. I'm telling you it's a heavy price."

"They ain't nothin' here, Ed. The mines is a mess. If they don't kill you right out, you die a slow death by just breathing all that dust and watching your young'uns grow up with nothing. If I have to go, I can probably stay about half drunk enough not to miss my people and ground that don't go straight up. They's nothing else for it. Make your deal if you can. Fleetie and I will just have to strap it on. This trouble ain't gonna get no better," said Burl.

"Ah lordy, boys. I'll be going to town in the morning, but I tell you now, we've come to a place a man would hope never to be. Hobe is dead, and there's no way this is going to end good. I'll see some people, but somehow, it has to be squared out, and we're all going to feel it sure as we're standing here."

The three men fell silent in the orchard, and all I could hear was the soft hum of bees working the fallen apples. Fred and Burl turned and walked through the orchard to the road just as a whip-poor-will started his song. Daddy didn't move.

"I've heard you singing on this mountain all my life, but I've never seen you yet. I think you're nothing but a ghost bird," Daddy said to no one, unless you count the shadowy bird. He stooped down and picked up a speckled winesap apple and rubbed it hard against his thigh. He stared at it for a long time and finally dropped it in his pocket and turned to walk back to the house.

Chapter 44

GONE FISHING

A week after Fred and Burl's visit, Leatha and I were seining for minnows by the riverbank when Daddy and Burl walked down the bank to push off Burl's rowboat. Daddy waved at us, and with his rod and reel proper on his shoulder, he stepped over the bow.

"Going fishing, Daddy?" Of course, it didn't look like he was about to drive off to work, but sometimes, you have to ask a dumb question before you can jump right in and ask an even dumber one. Since Leatha and I had enough minnows to bait our cane poles, all we needed was permission to take Burl's new skiff out. We were forbidden to go fishing unless we asked an adult.

"Do you reckon Leatha and I can fish out of the skiff if we stay in eyeshot, while you and Burl are fishing?" I knew the answer would be no, but sometimes, you have to ask anyway, just in case.

"I 'spect you can. But mind to stay close to the bank. Don't go near that good trout rock. There's no catfish over there anyway. Don't be making a commotion squealing and giggling. Burl and I have business to discuss. Hear me?"

Leatha punched me. Neither one of us could believe our luck.

"Answer him before he changes his mind," said Leatha.

"We are looking for sunk logs. We couldn't hook a trout if we wanted to, which we don't."

The men pushed off, and Leatha and I put the minnow bucket and the poles in the skiff. She climbed in, and I gave the little boat a hard push and jumped hard to land in the boat and not the water. It set up a rocking motion because of my not-so-graceful leap, and Leatha had to catch the minnow bucket, or we would have had minnows flopping all over the bottom of the skiff.

There was enough current to move us along slow enough to let us troll the bank for hidden catfish. In about an hour, we had caught two nice fish, enough for one family. If we didn't catch any more, we would draw straws, but since the fish were biting pretty good, we weren't worried about straws. Since we had to stay where the men could see us, we could hear most of what they said. Water carries sound, real especially in our creek with the overhanging trees spreading so wide, they almost make a tunnel over the water.

After a while, Burl skewered a minnow and flipped his line near some reeds. Daddy watched the float on the water, waiting for an early strike.

"A man oughta fish early," he said. "It catches 'em off guard."

Burl pulled out his sack of makings and curled a tobacco paper around his finger and sprinkled in some shreds. "They's watching steady," said Burl. "Don't pay to get too sure."

I could see Daddy nod and stretch his legs past the minnow bucket. "Some say you can outsmart yourself," he said. "A man outa think what the fish thinks."

"Hell, Ed. The fish don't think. No matter what a man oughta, some fish will up-stream you no matter what you're figuring."

"Lot of thinkin' going on these days, fish or not," Daddy answered. "Courthouse is hot with it, and a man oughta pay it some mind."

"Got to think about having a little money ahead before he can get upstream, just like that fish gotta spend his energy pushing agin' the current," Burl answered.

Daddy reached out into the water to unsnag his line. "I've been thinking on getting a piece of rental property," he said. "Lawyering has some lean days, and rent dollars coming in is good tiding over money."

Burl's fishing rod nearly jumped out of his hands, and I could see him pull hard to set the hook. "By damn, it's that big old trout. Look at that thing fly," Burl yelled.

"Hang on to him. It'll make a fine supper. Fleetie's not going to take it too easy about that fine house, but you can tell her I'll hold on to it. It'll always be there when she wants to come back."

"Don't worry none, Ed. Fleet don't take on too long. The kids will sulk and beller over it longer. They don't know from nothing about all this yet."

I watched the men as Burl wrestled with the fish. The way it fought way longer than usual, it was bound to be a great big catch. Burl was a good hand with his fishing gear, and he handled that big old boy slick as a two-penny gambler.

Burl let Daddy swoop him up and into the boat. "Wish all our troubles could be handled with some hard work like this trout," said Daddy.

"Don't worry none, Ed. We've wrestled over this as long as we can. Time I made the last move."

I looked over at Leatha to see if she had heard what Burl just said, but she was set on getting the minnow bucket top back on it hinges and wasn't paying her daddy any mind right then. It was a good thing. My brain was in a whirl. What was Fleetie going to take on about, and what were the kids going to start crying about? I picked up the paddle to see if I could get us closer, but Daddy started to reel in his line.

He looked over at Burl. "I'd better be gettin' on home since you've had all the luck today. Supper will be ready, and I've not no fish to bribe my way in."

"It'll be soon, Ed. No use waitin' around for that bunch to put in a trot line to snag us on our way out."

Daddy stood up in the boat. He was silent as he attached his sinker and empty hook to the rod before he took a long, almost jumping step from the boat to the bank. "Soon is good. Quick'll be safer, but the women and kids will—"

"Follow where they have to. Ain't no remedy for it."

Daddy and I walked up the grade and over the crossing and began the climb up our long hill. He paused about ten seconds in front of the Sargeants' new house. The dread of what I had only half-heard on the river was beginning to grow in my chest. I kept quiet too afraid to ask any questions because of what the answers might be.

For days, I had heard Daddy telling Mother that he had not come up with any solutions that would really settle things in Burl's favor. The miners, the operators, the murder, the fires—all of it had piled up deep trouble, and try as he would, he couldn't seem to dig deep enough to get under it all.

Hobe's burial had been six weeks ago, and he was mourned over by so few; only the barest handful attended his funeral. Dorotha's scrapes and cuts had scabbed over, but Mother told Aunt Roberta that more than likely, those scabs only trapped a fear sunk so deep, she might never be truly free of it again. Burl's best intentions of staying out of the mines forever had helped bring him to a place even more bitter than those long years spent working underground.

I thought of Pappy and what these mountains had meant to him. It left a heavy place way down inside of me to realize what was facing the Sargeants. It was beginning to look like Burl and all his family might be forever shut away from our valley. This was their place of safety, their home, the one place above all places that stuck down somewhere deep in their gut, so strong that nothing can ever grub it out.

I grabbed on to a frail hope that Daddy would find a way to save them. Fleetie losing her home and me losing Leatha would be as hard a thing as losing Pappy. Daddy took my string of cat fish. I had managed to get several fish as well as a bellyful of knots and lurches. We walked up the hill in silence.

Chapter 45

THE CROSSING

For near on to a month, it seemed that the dire warnings that had been churning inside me about the possibility of Leatha and her family leaving George's County were false alarms. There was no talk at the dinner table about Burl or Hobe or even Dorotha. School for Leatha and me was both exciting and dull at the same time. We spent lots of afternoons doing homework and talking about boys. The little kids took advantage of the early fall days and played nonstop. The rope swing was about worn through, but it still held and probably would until a couple of freezes finished it off.

Last Friday afternoon, I was trying to hurry my homework so Leatha and I would have the whole weekend for fun. After work, Daddy stepped out of the car and walked to the house using the sidewalk from the turnaround. I knew from the slump of his shoulders and the expression on his face that something bad was coming. I held the screen door open for him, and he handed me the *Courier*, an automatic response. I took his briefcase too, but he seemed not to notice it was gone.

When he stepped across the threshold into the kitchen, he whispered, "Burl has a week to leave."

"Oh no, Daddy. Not gone, not all of them gone."

"If he doesn't go, he will be arrested and eventually tried for Hobe's murder. There's not much evidence there, and it's shaky enough for the commonwealth attorney to look the other way for a spell and give them time to pack up and leave the state." His graveled voice betrayed the tears he was trying to choke back.

Mother came into the kitchen and took one look at him and gathered him in her arms as if he were one of us kids. They stood there, holding each other for a long minute. With all the accusations around about Hobe's death and the fires in the valley, I knew that in spite of my desperate hope, Burl was going to take his family and leave.

My first thought was that l was going to lose Leatha, Fleetie, and the girls. For all my life, I had had two lives to live—the life up here on this mountain with Mother and Daddy and the life at the base of the mountain with my other family. I had two sets of knowing, two languages, two cultures. Being free to move between both sides of me gave me strong legs, a firm will, and enduring safety. Losing Leatha and all we were together was as empty and cold as losing Pappy. The difference though was there was no place now to be the other half of who I was.

I knew there were other losses besides mine. The aunts and uncles, the cousins, the grandparents, and a whole valley of friends would lose a part of themselves. Families as tight as ours don't suffer the loss of one another easily or ever think of that loss as being a natural course of things

As I stood there in the kitchen with Daddy now leaning on Mother's strength instead of the other way around, I could feel that he was as hurt as I was. He and Burl had run these hills as children. They had grown strong together on their way to manhood. In the fraternity of boys to men, only the rare few see their friendship grow stronger with the years.

Now here they were with forty years of sharing their lives about over, and there was nothing either one of them could do to stop it from happening. Even the fact that Burl had to go to save himself and his family was not enough to prevent the pain. This was a loss that would remain forever in their minds and memories. Both men had this place dug so deep in their middle that only the grave would get them shut of it.

Mother spoke in a low voice to Daddy, "Neither Burl or Fleetie has ever lived out of this county."

"Katie, there is more of this going on here in this part of Kentucky than we know about. Mine work is all there is here, and it is unpredictable and dangerous. Since the war, more and more women are demanding that their men get out of the pits."

"Do you mean right here in George's County?"

"You would be surprised at how many houses in the camps are empty. Even in good times, big-machine mining is starting to cut down the number of miners that will be needed."

"How will they live? What will happen to them? Where are they going?"

Daddy paused before he answered, "Indiana. Larry Windham has kin up there who will hire Burl to work on one of their farms."

"Larry Windham? Oh my lord, Ed, what kind of promise did you have to make to get that done?"

"Don't worry about it. You're right, he'll come knocking soon enough, but I'll have to handle Larry later. This is the only chance Burl's got to stay free. All the attorneys here together can't beat the operators once they make up their minds to win. He'll never be able to set foot back here again, but it's better than what he would suffer behind bars for the rest of his life—that is, if somebody didn't kill him first."

"Have you told them yet?"

"No, I'll go down directly. Burl has been expecting it, and I'd rather cut off my right arm, but there's nothing else for it, I reckon. They are going to need as much time as we can give them to get things together and get moved."

In just the time it took Daddy to tell us that Leatha was leaving, my world stopped. The clocks were still ticking, and dinner was still bubbling on the stove, but after those words fell into the room, nothing I knew would ever be the same. Fleetie once said to Leatha and me, "Kids need to play. Once a young'un steps over that creek, the trail back to childhood disappears forever." Right here in this kitchen, right now, was the creek, and I had no choice but to step over it. Neither Leatha or I could ever go back.

"Daddy, did you try everything? Is there no hope at all?"

"No, punkin. Burl has a new job. They all have to move to Indiana in a few days."

"Why? Why can't something be done? Why can't you do something? You always know what to do."

Mother stopped me. "Rachel Ramsey. How many times have you been with your Daddy and seen with your own eyes how dangerous it is when you rile up the operators and the union? Daddy has not slept for weeks worrying about this. He has tried everything human. Don't you know how much he hates to see Burl and his family empty out that little house?"

Daddy looked down at me and watched as tears raced down my face.

"No, Daddy! They can't go away. They have the new house. Who will take care of the garden and raise the corn, pick the grapes, and can the beans? Leatha is my very best friend in this whole world. Daddy, please, why are you sending them away? You can't, you can't!"

"Rachel, the kids don't know it yet, and I'm going down after supper. I 'spect Fleetie will be getting all of them ready to move real soon. Won't you go with me?"

Daddy waited, while I tuned up. He knew that my right foot was just before stomping. My body had gone rigid. Anger and loss fueled me, and I wanted to run and scream at a pain that hurt as much as losing Pappy.

"Rachel, stop this right now. Daddy has done everything he could do to help Burl stay here, but it can't happen, and you have to be strong enough not to make it harder. We are all heartbroken to see them go, but that is the way it is. It is not going to change, and crying and stomping and throwing yourself into a temper will not make it go away."

I turned my back on her and stormed out of the kitchen and into my bedroom. I slammed the door with all the force I could put into it. I stood against it and waited for the inevitable door-slamming punishment, but it did not come. Instead, I could hear Mother putting dinner on the table—dinner that she, Daddy, and I would mostly ignore. I took a deep breath and stepped across the threshold and back into the kitchen.

The days that followed saw a constant parade of shocked relatives making their way to the Sargeant house. In that time and place, not many folks left the safety of the mountains and their kin. Several times, Daddy had shared with me his prediction that in not too many years, the underground mines would begin to close, and out-migration would be a familiar pattern. But today, there were only raw, painful tears.

Both sides, those going and those staying, made promises to visit, remember, and return. But somehow, even though those were good words to hear, they had a hollow ring like the promise of a bike for Christmas that never happened.

Early Saturday morning, Daddy woke me, and when I came to the kitchen, without a word, he poured me a once-forbidden cup of coffee. I sat at the kitchen table with him, while he counted the money he had borrowed from the bank early in the week. Larry Windham again. It seemed funny to me how Larry managed to be a part of all that happened about Burl. First, the job, and now here was the money to buy the house, borrowed from his bank. Daddy slipped the bills into the wallet I had given him for Christmas. I watched as Mother finished filling a picnic basket and covered the food with a white embroidered napkin, one of Grandmother Bertha's that she always kept back for holidays.

She handed me a guitar case to carry, and even though I wondered, I didn't ask about it. Talking was hard. Silence was safer. Daddy led the way, and we went out the back door, stepped off the porch, and walked down the side path. There was an early morning fog enclosing us as we cut across the yard. I remembered the morning we found

Dorotha out here. It seemed such a short time ago, but so much had happened since then.

We made our way through the early morning dark and down the road to the Sargeant house. Burl was tying the last of Fleetie's things onto the truck. The children were huddled on the front steps, nearly hidden by the morning shadows and fog. I could see Fleetie through the screen door, cleaning her kitchen window. She was leaving no smeared glass to shame her. Clifford and Nessa would stay in the house and bring the rest of their belongings just as soon as Clifford finished out the month at work.

Leatha walked up the hill toward me with just as many tears running down her face as were on mine. We stood together and watched as the children began to move as silent as the stones on the mountain behind them into their places in the back of the truck. Mother took the guitar case from me, and I put my arms around Leatha. We were crying too hard to talk, and anyway, there weren't any words that could make this better.

Without a word, Daddy handed Burl the wallet and raised his fist in the air, and then he turned and walked up the hill.

Mother slipped her arms around Fleetie's strong body and held her long enough to clear her eyes of the tears she had promised not to shed. "There's some sandwiches, fried pies, and pears in the basket. They'll be better than the cardboard stuff they sell along the road."

"Law' me, Kathleen. All that trouble. Here I am, leavin' beholden to you again. Can't never seem to get even."

Mother reached down and picked up the black case and placed it in Fleetie's arms. Choking back the pain I knew was tearing at her throat, Mother whispered, "Ed found a luthier over on Pine Mountain who put it back together, good as new."

Fleetie opened the case and stroked her hand down the strings of the rosewood guitar, listening to their soft hum. Fleetie did not raise her head at first. She just stood there with her hand on the strings. There were no notes, just silence.

"Oh, Fleetie, how I wish you did not have to leave us."

"Well, Kathleen, it's best. It's been a right wearying spell around here. This'll be better for Burl."

"I want it better for you too. Promise to take care of yourself and write me?"

Fleetie nodded. She probably didn't trust herself to speak again.

I walked with Leatha to the back of the truck and helped her up. She put her hands on the side of the truck bed and I put mine on top of them. I didn't really understand what might happen to Burl if they stayed. I only knew that when the truck rolled down the hill, the best of my childhood would roll with them.

Fleetie closed the guitar case, walked around to the back of the truck, put it beside Dorotha, and then climbed back into the front seat. Dorotha wrapped her arms around the case as Burl released the brake. I felt Leatha's hands slip away as the tires moved a little faster, and the truck rolled beyond me.

The porch light was on at Hobe's, and I could see Mary standing on the front porch as the truck rolled past. Her arms were crossed, and her white apron was wrapped around them. As the truck made the turn at the foot of the hill, the Willises were there in the headlights. They stood very still on their steps. Helen waved, but the children were motionless.

When the truck faded into the dark morning, I heard the bump of tires as it hit the steel rails and, for the last time, rolled over the crossing. The porch light went dark, and Mother turned and disappeared into the mist at the top of the hill. She mourned like the biblical Rachel keening for the children of Israel until way up in the morning.